A PAPER SON

JASON BUCHHOLZ

TYRUS
BOOKS

Published by
TYRUS BOOKS
an imprint of F+W Media, Inc.
10151 Carver Road, Suite 200
Blue Ash, OH 45242. U.S.A.
www.tyrusbooks.com

Hardcover ISBN 10: 1-4405-9161-X
Hardcover ISBN 13: 978-1-4405-9161-7
Paperback ISBN 10: 1-4405-9162-8
Paperback ISBN 13: 978-1-4405-9162-4
eISBN 10: 1-4405-9163-6
eISBN 13: 978-1-4405-9163-1

Printed in the United States of America.

10   9   8   7   6   5   4   3   2   1

Library of Congress Cataloging-in-Publication Data
Buchholz, Jason.
   A paper son / Jason Buchholz.
      pages cm
   ISBN 978-1-4405-9161-7 (hc) -- ISBN 1-4405-9161-X (hc) -- ISBN 978-1-4405-9162-4 (pb) --
ISBN 1-4405-9162-8 (pb) -- ISBN 978-1-4405-9163-1 (ebook) -- ISBN 1-4405-9163-6 (ebook)
   1. Novelists--Fiction. 2. Characters and characteristics--Fiction. 3. Missing children--Fiction. I.
Title.
   PS3602.U2537P36 2016
   813'.6--dc23
                          2015025804

Cover design by Frank Rivera.
Cover images © iStockphoto.com/Jasmina007/RonTech2000.

This book is available at quantity discounts for bulk purchases.
For information, please call 1-800-289-0963.

Dedicated to Rose Lee, Alyce Hanly, and Harry Hong.

ONE

First I saw him in a teacup.

***

It was the day before the storm hit, the storm we'd been watching on newscast Doppler as it approached from Alaska, devouring the coast like a carnivorous planet made of teeth and ice and smoke. The weatherpersons pointed to it, their expressions mixes of glee and trepidation, their predictions heavy with superlatives, italics, underlining. The storm had formed in the Arctic over Siberia and had lurched eastward, devastating docks, leveling marinas, sending grapefruit-sized hailstones through windshields. Bering Sea waves had knocked some of the lesser islands in the Aleutian archipelago from their moorings and sent them tumbling southeast through sea foam, piling their igneous ruins on the British Columbian coast along with uprooted trees, demolished fishing boats, polar bear carcasses. This same fury would soon be upon us—blotting out the sun, stealing whole chunks of the peninsula out from under us—but not yet. That day, the first day back in school after the winter break, it was still clear. An unbroken blue stretch of sky filled my classroom windows; the only indications of the coming maelstrom were the taut, horizontal flags over the skyscrapers downtown.

My third graders were hard at work, their pencils scratching unevenly across their papers. They were writing about all the things they hadn't done during their vacations. I'd introduced the assignment the previous year, after nine years of reading the same excruciating paragraphs about Santa preparations and skiing in Tahoe and trips to Disneyland. Today I had received the usual panel of puzzled stares when I'd written the topic on the whiteboard.

"Can you provide an example?" Eliza Low asked, looking bemused.

"Did you get eaten by a lion over the break?" I asked her.

Eliza was destined for a station in life where she would have people twice as smart as I am working so far under her she'd never even know their names, and from the look she gave me then I could tell she was a little impatient for that day to arrive. "Actually I did," she said. "We kids heal up fast."

"Well, then you'll have to write about something else," I said.

Kevin Hammerschmidt raised his hand. "*I* didn't get eaten by a lion, Mr. Long," he said, and flashed me a grin short on teeth.

"You could have written about that, then," I said, "but now you have to come up with something else, because that was my idea. Fifteen minutes. Go."

This was not the first time I'd augmented the common core curriculum. I teach my kids cooking and bicycle repair. In P.E. they like to play dodge ball, but every now and then I make them do *tai chi*. I tell them it will make them better ball dodgers. In my English lessons I charge them with the guardianship of the language. I have them identify and revise poor writing from the adult world. Despite the school's ban on handing out refined sugars, I distribute Hershey's Kisses to anybody who brings in a newspaper or magazine article with grammatical errors. I teach them words they'll appreciate, like "brachiate." They love the monkey bars, after all. "To brachiate," I tell my class each year, "means to propel oneself by swinging from arm to arm, like a monkey." Shortly after this year's lesson I heard Amanda Martin say, "Nice brachiating!" to her friend Savannah Steward as Savannah dismounted, and I was again reminded why I love my job. I also teach them to be better storytellers. Problems are the main ingredient, I tell them. At the beginning of each term I tell them to create a character, and then give him five problems in one page.

Just before the first recess bell rang I collected their papers and encouraged them to go outside and play at triple their normal intensity. "When this storm hits," I told them, "it's going to be the end of everything we know and love." This was a game we played. I'd make a dubious proclamation and their job was to show some skepticism. To investigate. To question adults, especially their teachers. We all glanced out the window, as if the sky might tell us how much time we had left. Several gulls wheeled over the playground, anticipating the spillage of raisins and graham crackers.

"My birthday party?" someone asked, after a time, without turning from the window. "Will it be the end of my birthday party?"

"Where is it?" I asked.

"Golden Gate Park."

"Ask for waterproof presents," I said.

"Barney?" Kevin asked. "Will it be the end of Barney?"

Kevin's mythical dog Barney was a frequent topic. He was an ingenious creation, standing in for actual beings when our classroom conversations had to touch upon the personal, the uncomfortable. He also garnered Kevin the laughs he felt he needed each day. But this time there wasn't much laughter, and I knew some of them were worried about actual pets. "Barney will be fine," I said, "but you may want to keep him inside."

Beyond the playground lay the broad grassy field, and at its far edge stood the sports shed and the tall chain-link fence that kept balls, flying backpacks, and wayward children from tumbling over the top of the high retaining wall and down the cliff. In the distance stood the skyline of downtown San Francisco, quiet and still but for the trembling of its flags. I figured by then the storm must have crossed through Vancouver and made its way into the lower forty-eight. It wouldn't be long now. And here we all sat, energetic and innocent and helpless like teenagers in a horror movie forest cabin. The bell rang and my kids scrambled for the door. "Get out there and make it count," I said.

I kept to my room through the recess break, and through lunch and the second recess as well, declining the first-day-back-after-break faculty reunion in the lounge. I tended to avoid the place on days like this—it was always too busy, too full of energy, too noisy with accounts of exotic vacations. For a bunch of public servants, my fellow teachers managed to do a lot of island hopping and helicopter skiing. Four of them—three women and Mr. Benson, who taught first grade—were married to investment bankers. I did have quite a bit of work to do in my room as well—lesson plans, and organization for the Chinese New Year/Valentine's Day phase of the teaching calendar. But my primary goal was the avoidance of all that collegial exuberance. It wears me out.

Henry made his teacup appearance just before the final bell. A single cloud had breached the frame of my windows—small and compact, with a faint dark core. *A warning shot,* I thought. I had poured myself a half-cup from my teapot and I was working at my desk when I *felt* something along the edge of my vision. When I looked up, the steam from my tea had ceased rising; it stood motionless, three or four inches of linked spirals, loops, whorls, all as still as if photographed. Without thinking (what would there be to think?), I reached for it. I was barely able to stifle a gasp when it collapsed back into the mug, sucked in with a force that made me think something huge at the bottom of the mug had taken a great sharp inhalation. I leaned over and looked inside, and there they were, the four of them, standing at a railing. I suppose I would have blinked, or rubbed my eyes, or looked around the room in a weak attempt to make sense of it. I don't remember. Somehow the room vanished from around me, the chair from beneath me. Even the sense of strangeness I should have been feeling did not quite materialize in the presence of this image, which now filled the copper disk of my tea's surface. It was actually Henry's mother that struck me most, at the time. She stood over her children, her arms around their shoulders like the eaves of a home, sheltering them from whatever loomed before them. Henry peered out from just below the top railing; his sister peered just over it. They were all looking off to the side. Only after I'd taken the three of them in did I see their father, standing just behind his wife, his hands planted on his hips and his chest out, a smile on his face. They were Chinese, like me. Like half of me, anyway. From the way they were dressed and the way their hair and clothing shifted in the wind, I thought they must have been on the deck of a steamship. I pulled the mug toward me and the vision dissipated. The tea settled but the family did not return; instead the reflection of my classroom's fluorescents made their more conventional appearance. Steam spun back out. I dipped my head, sniffed. It smelled like rain.

"Mr. Long, is there something in your cup?" whispered Eliza Low, from her seat in the front row.

"Yes," I whispered back, trying to recover. "Tea."

She wrinkled her brow and studied me before returning her attention to her math sheet. I glanced back into the cup, but the family hadn't returned. I told myself it had to have been a trick of light, a shifting projection, the reflection of a photograph I knew did not exist.

***

I scrambled down the hill for the refuge of my apartment, trying to figure out how I was going to explain my afternoon tea to myself. Just beyond my conscious thoughts a headful of difficult theories lurked, like party crashers waiting for the right moment to leap in through a window. I wouldn't be able to keep them out, I knew, but my hope was that I could get home—and into the bottle of Scotch I kept around for emergencies—before I had to confront them. To recalibrate my senses I focused on the immediate as I walked: leafless sidewalk trees trembling in their square patches of dirt; the hum of mid-afternoon traffic; exhaust; the solidity of the concrete beneath my feet. A fist-sized knot in my stomach. I reached my street and trotted across it. As always, there was a puddle in the gutter in front of Ike's corner store, the remnant of his afternoon sidewalk hosing. I stepped over it and onto the curb, and again there was that sense on the edge of my vision that colors and shapes were not in their right places. I turned and leaned over the puddle. My reflection looked up at me. It was wearing a hat. My hands shot up and felt my bare head. I whirled and checked my reflection in the store's windows. No hat. I held my breath and looked into the puddle again. It was unmistakable: a short-brimmed, dark blue hat, pulled down to just above my ears. Everything else on the puddle's surface looked normal—the bare branches of a nearby tree and the tops of buildings reached down to an underlying sky. A woman in a long coat approached. She slowed, looked down into the puddle, looked at me, continued on her way. A gust of wind blew a paper cup into the water and the image splashed apart.

I took the stairs two at a time, threw my bag onto my couch, pulled down the Scotch, and poured two fingers. I took a bracing slug and headed to my desk, where sometimes I could think. Figure this out, I told myself. In a college psychology class I'd learned that schizophrenia usually started with auditory hallucinations and showed up during the teen years, which I'd been clear of for fifteen years. It was reassuring, I supposed, that my new visitors hadn't called me Jesus. But I couldn't rule that theory out. I moved on to my genetic heritage. My mom was above suspicion. The example she set for us—utterly practical, unfailingly even-keeled—was so strong that I still had trouble accepting the relative flightiness of the rest of humanity. My father, however, had been a bona fide eccentric, of the reclusive software genius variety. He might have been completely insane, for all we knew. He never interacted with anything organic long enough for anyone to get a good read on him. My sister Lucy was three years older than I was. She lacked what some people might call direction, but I understood her in a different way. She did what she wanted from year to year, and things seemed to work out for her. From what I could tell she didn't give a shit what anybody thought. She orbited in and out of California every so often. Right now she was out—in New York City. She was brash, but probably more sane than the rest of us.

I swallowed another slug and continued to further theories as the Scotch emanated its heat and calm. There had been no blunt force traumas to the head, no volunteering for any weird government experiments. I had only dropped acid twice, and not since I was an undergrad. No inexplicable memory losses, no alien abductions. I finished the glass, stood and made for the kitchen for more, and then I remembered the doves. I had been seven, one of twenty-some second-grade students assigned to the young but embittered Ms. Ferguson, whose failing vision had cut short her bid at a career in ornithology. At least once a week she made it clear to us that she would have much preferred to be out bird watching than stuck inside with us. Even my name—Peregrine— earned me no favor. Sometimes it even seemed to work against me, as if it disgusted her that something as graceless and earth-bound as a seven-year-old boy would dare share a name with one of her beloved.

The disdain was mutual. Though we were early in our school careers we all knew the difference between adults who liked kids and adults who were forced, for one reason or another, to toler-ate them. At recess we often discussed the many careers we felt Ms. Ferguson was better suited for—dog-catcher, garbage collec-tor, bridge toll-taker. The two-way antagonism abated for a few minutes each day, however, when she talked to us about birds. In the final minutes before lunchtime she would introduce us to the Bird of the Day (the "Daily Aves," she called them), and for that short time we struck an unofficial truce—she forgot she was our teacher, and we forgot we were Plan B. Her voice would soften as she described the traits and range of a cedar waxwing, a condor, an emu. Her gestures would become graceful and her eyes would shine behind her thick glasses. She would almost become pretty.

Once the Bird of the Day had been the mourning dove. My upper-middle-class classmates lived lives of blithe contentment, and even I was still a few years from learning what it meant to mourn, so we all assumed that this dove had been so named because of its preference for conducting business before lunchtime. In the way of playground rumors this one captured our attention and grew until it was widely held that all mourning doves had to vanish at noon—where they went, or what would happen to them if they stayed around, were the subjects of wide speculation. They slept in trees because they awoke early, and grew tired; they hid in underground burrows because the sun got too hot for them. A couple of days later I was sitting alone in my backyard after school, watching the trees move in the breeze, when a mourning dove landed on the fence. I recognized it immediately from the whistle its wings made as it landed, which Ms. Ferguson had imitated perfectly for us. It looked right at me for several seconds before it took flight, accompanied again by those staccato whistles. For a long time I wondered whether I'd seen something I wasn't supposed to see, or if I'd been singled out by the birds to receive the message of their true and secretive nature. Either way, I didn't know what to do. I didn't tell anybody.

Back in the kitchen I capped the bottle of Scotch and brewed a cup of tea. I set it on my desk, angling myself so that I could see the reflection of my overhead light fixture in its surface, and I stared into it. Shades of meaning flipped back and forth in my head—what separated a hallucination from a vision? A schizophrenic from a seer? My tea revealed nothing. No steamship appeared. The steam rose and spread.

That night as I lay in bed I thought about the woman at the railing, her husband and children, the looks on their faces. I tried to see into their futures. I tried to see where the ship was going, but there was only mist.

***

The next morning it was still not raining. After a night of sound, Scotch-assisted sleep, a square breakfast, and two cups of coffee which remained only coffee, I nearly managed to convince myself that nothing amiss had happened the day before. Ike's daily puddle had yet to collect, but when I reached the corner I felt my head anyway. No hat. In my classroom I inspected my tea-making paraphernalia—electric kettle, pot, mug, tin of leaves—as though seeing them for the first time. I turned on the faucet and filled my kettle. Yesterday it had been water but now it was a confluence of molecules, the simultaneous arrival of billions of atoms, each of which had traced its own pathways around and over the planet, through rivers and rains, glaciers and clouds, down throats and through cell walls, each through countless years. When I thought of it this way, all those long journeys collecting in my teacup, it seemed strange that there would only be one ship in there. I poured the water over a tea bag and sat down at my desk, feeling a little trepidation. The water settled, and there it was. Now I could see beyond the ship's prow. I could see what the family was seeing. It was a vast, dark city, with columns of smoke rising into a late afternoon sky.

"My mom says some people can tell fortunes from tea leaves," a voice said. It was Eliza Low, her toes parked exactly at my door's threshold, in accordance with my pre-bell rules. "Are you one of those people?"

"Not that I know of," I said. I looked back at the family and the dark city before them. "Do you want to see them?" I asked. Eliza nodded and I beckoned her in. She approached my desk and stood just opposite me. The ship remained where it was, bearing toward the city's port. I didn't know if I wanted her to see it or not. Eliza leaned over and peered into the cup. The steam rose as if from the ship itself and parted around the contours of her forehead.

"She says fortune-tellers look at the way the leaves land on the bottom of the cup, and the pattern tells the future. But I think that's ridiculous."

"People certainly have a wide variety of beliefs," I said.

She didn't bother to suppress a flash of annoyance. "Yes," she said. She stared back into the water. "I only see little wet leaves," she said.

I lifted my cup, shaking the image free, wondering how I was going to get through my teaching day with phantoms floating through my beverages. I took a sip and imagined the smells of cooking fires, of fish and oceans, hiding within the layers of my jasmine green. "There are people who tell us the future, actually," I said to her, working to keep my voice steady. "The weathermen. And they say this is your last chance to play tetherball." I pointed at the clock. "So I'll see you back here in seven minutes."

Throughout the morning the sky continued to darken and the rattling of the tree branches grew more feverish, but by lunchtime the rain still had not arrived. I headed for the faculty lounge and found it to be as quiet as I'd hoped. With the specter of the long-ago travelers steaming through my thoughts, I was even less prepared to make small talk than usual. Among the few gathered in the lounge was Franklin Nash, our principal, a massive black man with a gray beard and a gray suit, who made the furniture in his vicinity look as though it had been collected from dollhouses. He noticed me and approached, navigating with effort through the maze of tables and chairs. Whenever I saw him like this, moving in tight quarters, I had the impression that he would have preferred to simply kick things out of his way. Despite the imposing bulk, the kids loved him for his smiles and warmth and for his tie collection. Today's selection featured ice-cream cones.

"Peregrine!" he said, enveloping my hand in one of his. He handed me a yellow sheet. "I found this and thought of you."

It was a flier announcing the launch of a new literary journal, to be called *The Barbary Quarterly.* Now accepting submissions of fiction, non-fiction, and poetry, it said. A Grant Street address was listed. I had all but abandoned my attempt to assemble a collection of short stories. A few years earlier, I'd managed to finish and send out what I thought were two decent stories: one about a vengeful architect and the other about a deaf poker player. The latter had been picked up by the in-flight magazine of a regional airline based in Indiana, which had since gone out of business. In the heady days following my receipt of the acceptance letter, I'd formulated a plan to put together a batch of fifteen stories or so and submit them for wider publication. If they were good enough for Midwestern puddle jumpers, I figured, they'd be good enough for anyone. I wrote one more, about a vagabond minister, and then I ran out of ideas. I forced myself to finish a story about a haunted mobile home but it was as terrible as it sounds. Since then I hadn't written much beyond grocery lists and lesson plans.

"Thanks, I'll check it out," I said, forming no plans to check it out.

He drifted toward another of the seated groups. "Let me know how that goes," he said, as he went. "I'm still hoping to read something of yours someday."

I slid a bowl of leftover lasagna into the ancient microwave and punched in several minutes, which usually wasn't enough. I had watched it make a half-dozen revolutions on the carousel when a voice asked, "Interesting show?"

Annabel Nightingale appeared at my side. Her straight black hair fell down on either side of her face and curled in slightly just beneath her chin. Her eyes were wide and as dark as her hair. Her skin was pearlescent; a small jade circle hung from her neck on a silver chain. Faint crescents of pink on her cheek were the only indications of an interior made of blood and tissue, and not snow or cream. She held a red plate, upon which a pair of shish kebabs flanked a mound of yellow rice.

I tapped the microwave door. "Lasagna," I said. "It's a rerun." Actually, it was to be the fourth consecutive meal (not counting breakfasts) that I would have mined from the pan I'd made a couple of nights earlier. Not wanting to sound like too hopeless of a bachelor, I kept this information to myself.

Annabel had just joined us the previous fall, and as her "buddy" teacher I'd been unofficially tasked with welcoming her to Russian Hill Elementary School. Every year, each third-grade class was paired with a kindergarten class, and each third grader was assigned a kindergarten buddy. A few times a month we'd get our classes together and give the partners a project to complete. In the process my third graders shared their wisdom and experience with the kindergarteners, earning in return their little partners' admiration and a sense of maturity that lasted until the moment our classes parted ways. Our first semester had produced among other things some amusing art projects, a treasure hunt, and an afternoon of comical skits, but hadn't revealed much about the newest addition to our faculty.

Annabel pulled a fork from a drawer, yanked a skewer from its queue of steak and vegetables, and flipped it toward the trash can. A burst of light caught it in midair; the murmuring groups behind us fell silent. There was a lone gasp, and then the scraping of a chair against the floor. We waited, breaths held, the microwave's fan the only sound in the room, and then the crack of thunder slammed into the building. The tables emptied immediately, leaving me alone with Annabel. The microwave beeped, and I retrieved my lunch.

"You're not worried about your kids becoming lightning rods?" Annabel asked, yanking the second skewer from its contents.

"We're doing the old key-on-the-kite-string experiment this afternoon," I said. "It's good practice for them." I usually managed to be slightly more witty than normal when I was around Annabel—or maybe she just felt she had to humor me until she got settled in. "What about you?" I said.

"I teach kindergarten, remember?" she said. "My kids are sitting on their mommies' laps with cocoa and cookies right now." She took my place in front of the microwave and slid her food into the hot lasagna-scented interior. "When yours get out of the burn ward later this week, you should come over," she said. "We'll have a New Year's thing."

"Sounds good," I said. "Friday?"

"It's a date," she said. She looked over my head toward the window and the blackening sky beyond. "I should put my schefflera outside," she said. "It loves rainwater."

***

It didn't rain, though, not yet. Lightning continued to fracture the sky and thunder buffeted the hill but the ground was still dry by the time I closed up my room. As I walked back home, the air was as heavy as a pendulum. I stopped at the edge of Ike's puddle and looked down. The phantom hat was back on my head, but I only had a second to consider my reflection before a great fat drop of water crashed into the surface and scattered the image. Another fell, and then another. Within seconds, the puddle was roiling. I continued home without hurrying.

My one-bedroom apartment was on the top floor of a five-story building near the bottom of the hill. I'd lucked into it nearly ten years ago, and I had never wanted to live anywhere else. It was a beautiful building—a lobby with forest green walls, dark wood and brass trim, double-decker rows of bronze mailboxes. The elevator smelled like wood polish. Even the stairwell was carpeted. The color of my walls were cream at midday, and took on the color of sand on sunny late afternoons, so I didn't mess them up by hanging art. The floor plan was simple: a living room ran through the middle to a sliding glass door and a small balcony. On one side of the room a wide arched doorway led to the kitchen, which was full of windows that looked back up the hill. On the other side a short hallway led to the bedroom, bathroom, and a big closet I would never fill. I had a bed and a pair of nightstands (one of which I used and the other of which I didn't), and a dresser with a small TV on it. In the living room was a couch and a bookcase that held a slightly larger TV, novels and biographies, a few old college textbooks, and some framed pictures: my sister and me in the snow; my mom and the two of us in the wooded mountains near her place; an old one of all four of us when Lucy and I were still kids. By the balcony door sat a small round table with wooden grinders for pepper and rock salt. My desk was in the corner.

My last girlfriend, a student at the San Francisco Art Institute, told me that my apartment reminded her of a fancy hotel suite. "Like for a banker," she had said. Her name was Joy, which even she found ironic.

"That doesn't sound so bad," I said.

"It's the worst thing possible," she said.

"This is how I like it," I said.

"No," she said.

A few days later she brought me a half-dozen paintings and prints, of various sizes and subjects.

"I'll put them up for you," she said.

"I'll do it later," I said. After a week or two I hung them all above my headboard, so I wouldn't have to see them while I was lying there. Joy saw them, looked around at all the other empty walls, and put her hand over her mouth. She dumped me a few days later. We had the big talk at her loft, after a tense lunch of pho and spring rolls. Collage was her medium—she built reproductions of corporate logos out of combat photographs. A Chevron logo made of mass gravesites loomed on the wall above us as we sat on her couch; across the room, the golden arches comprised assault rifles. It was the standard break-up conversation until she told me that she really liked the concept of me, but she had misgivings about the execution. At that point I knew it wouldn't be too hard to get over her. She collected the paintings and prints and I puttied and painted over the holes they'd left in my wall, and went back to being content.

Now in my banker's suite I tossed Franklin's flier onto my desk beside my laptop, and prepared a cup of tea. Outside the storm attacked with the frantic energy of a novice fighter in the first round. I felt strangely calm now, and ready for the family at the railing. I had an idea now of why they were there, and what I was going to do with them. The water settled and there they were again, with the twilit city spread out in front of them. The woman's name was Li-Yu, I decided. Her children would be Rose and Henry. Her husband would be called Bing. The city wasn't San Francisco—it was too dark, too far away. I decided on Canton, the origin of uncertain journeys somewhere in my own family's distant past. The year would be 1925. I opened my laptop. *From the deck of the steamer,* I wrote, *they can see what must be nearly all of Canton.*

From the deck of the steamer they can see what must be nearly all of Canton. In the day's last light the city's buildings look secretive and dangerous as they crouch inside a smoky haze, their haunches illuminated by diffuse, flame-colored lights from unseen sources. The wharf uncoils and reaches toward the ship like a dirty claw. The air is cold, and smells of fish and garbage. So this is it, Li-Yu thinks. The fabled heart of China.

It has been hours since they steamed past that outer armada of islands, past Hong Kong, and were swallowed by the hills and plains of Guangdong. The Pearl River, Bing said, looking inland, northward, his excitement clear. Li-Yu had spent weeks at sea, and weeks before that, trying to absorb some of this excitement, but none of it had settled in her. Even now, with the end of their journey so close, and the oppression of the ship's steerage compartments nearly behind them, she couldn't shake the feeling that she was offering herself and her children to the throat of a hungry dragon. She watched the hills and rice paddies glide past, wondering what sort of river could so easily consume a ship like this.

She knew well a version of this country, one she had pieced together from thousands of miles away, from her parents' stories and from clues like the smell and feel of the clothes and the few things that had survived their trip across the Pacific, the year before Li-Yu was born. In her mind the countryside was dotted with mist-shrouded mountains and temples with roofs curling like phoenix wings, its halves divided by that stupendous wall. The government consisted of soldiers, their columns bristling with rifles, marching through the grainy landscapes of news clips and magazine photographs, and of the boy Puyi in his embroidered silk robes, with his hat and his haughty stare, an emperor without an empire, and now nothing more than a commoner. Before seeing this view of Canton she felt she might have known something about its cities, having been raised in the Chinatowns of Stockton and Oakland and San Francisco, where her sisters now live, far behind her. She knows the sound of twenty men speaking Cantonese all to each other at once, and she knows the smells of roasted duck and dumplings and the steam of rice. She knows the shops and their wares, and the textures of jade and ivory and bamboo and silk. But there is nothing familiar about this city that now reaches for them with its claw of a wharf and pulls them into its shroud of twilight and smoke. The quays teem with cargo and equipment, and the sounds of hundreds of shouting voices rise up over the growl of the ship's engines. The mouths of streets appear, revealing narrow corridors that twist from the docks into the city's interior.

Li-Yu tightens her grip on Rose and Henry. Bing turns from the railing, where he has been smiling and breathing in great draughts of the smelly air. He squats down next to the children. "This is China, our home," he says, steadying himself with a loose hug around their legs. "What do you think?" Neither of them speaks. He looks back and forth at their blank faces. "You'll love it," he says. "Ask your mother." He looks up at Li-Yu. "Tell them," he says.

Neither of her children looks to her, and Li-Yu offers nothing. Bing stands and leans toward her ear. "I thought we were supposed to be together," he says.

"We are," she says.

"I thought you were going to talk to them," he says.

"What can I tell them?" she says, looking out across the dark city. "What do I know?"

But Bing has already stopped listening; he's gazing down at the wharf, which is now just beneath them, and crawling with people. The ship docks with a bump and a heightened groan as the engines work to check the rest of its momentum. The deck rings with footfalls as the passengers clamor for the stairs. Li-Yu gives each of her children a small canvas bag to carry, tells them to hang on to the back of her coat, and hoists her bags. Bing takes his own suitcases and plunges into the crowd. Li-Yu chases after him, and though she can feel the tug of both children's hands, she imagines how easy it would be for them to be pulled away into the crowd, like fruit plucked from a tree. They make it onto the dock without getting separated, but Henry is fighting tears, and Rose's jaw is hard and set. The wharf is nothing like Li-Yu imagined. The signs are in Chinese, but the faces are from all over the world. She hears a dozen different languages before they have gone a hundred steps. Bing is jubilant. He is congratulating strangers, laughing, turning and calling things out to Li-Yu and the kids, his words garbled like he's been drinking. At one point she loses sight of him completely. She stops, gathers her children against her sides, and searches the crowd before her. Just when she is about to panic he comes bounding in from the side.

"Over here," he says, smiling, pulling them toward the edge of the crowd. There is an open-air restaurant, little more than a cart with a few upturned wooden crates around it. Bing gestures at them to squat and after a quick exchange with the cook he returns with bowls of rice porridge, slices of grilled pork, boiled peanuts, a dish of lotus root and tree fungus in a rich brown sauce.

"Eat, eat," he says, spreading the dishes on the crates, beaming as if he has just cooked them himself. He tousles Henry's hair. "Real food!" he says. "Eat up, we only have half an hour."

"Until what?" Li-Yu says, picking up her chopsticks.

"Until the boat to Xinhui!" he says. "We'll be there before the sun sets tomorrow!"

Li-Yu shakes her head.

He points somewhere, vaguely inland. "Nearly there now!" he says.

"Not tonight," she says. "The children need to rest. I need to rest. Even you need to rest."

"We'll rest! What could be more relaxing than a quiet boat ride? We'll look at the stars, and the river will rock the children to sleep."

"I've been on a quiet boat ride for weeks," she says. "We're staying here."

He jabs at the crowd streaming past them with his chopsticks, sauce dribbling from the corner of his mouth. "This is rest?" he says. "Nobody sleeps here. You'll see."

"Henry is nearly asleep in his *jook*," she says. "We stay."

Bing curses through a mouthful of mushrooms, drops his chopsticks on the crate, and storms away. One of the chopsticks clatters to the ground. Henry picks it up, places it neatly alongside its mate, and attempts a smile at her.

"Where is Dad going?" he says.

"He'll be back," she says.

He returns minutes later and points up one of the narrow serpentine roads that fan out from the wharf. "Let's go," he says.

Once in their bed the children fall asleep instantly. Bing seems to forget about the delay. He holds Li-Yu and talks on and on about all the things she and the children will love in Xinhui. His voice grows quiet, his words soft and far apart as he tires and fades. Li-Yu stays awake until very late, listening to the breathing of her children and her husband, and to the sounds of voices outside, and wooden wheels rolling on stone.

***

While I'd been writing, the storm had continued its siege on the city. A wind had risen and now my windows hummed and rattled. My teacup sat where I'd left it, untouched, its heat gone and its mysteries inert. My computer's desktop was littered with a dozen open browser windows: maps and images of China, articles on its history and geography, articles on steamships and Pacific crossings. I closed them all and centered my document on the screen again. I checked the clock. I knew I was supposed to be hungry by now, but when I thought about looking in the refrigerator or in the cupboard all I could see was Li-Yu, lying awake in that room, listening.

***

The next morning Bing awakens them early. After a breakfast of steamed pork buns from a street vendor they return to the waterfront, where they wait in a thick dark fog for the water taxi. By the time it is fully light they are underway. The city seems as though it will never end but finally it shrinks and clears, and soon the little boat is plying up a wide avenue of water that runs through an endless patchwork of fallow rice paddies, which are empty but for puddles of rainwater and small piles of rotting stalks left from the fall harvest.

Rose and Henry say almost nothing, except when they lean in to whisper to Li-Yu that they have to use the bathroom. The other children on board stare at the scenery for a time, but then they scatter to find other diversions. Hills emerge from the fog, ghostlike, and then disappear back into it. The air grows colder. A breeze pushes against them. Li-Yu gathers her children and squeezes them against her sides.

"We're almost there," Bing says, smiling broadly. "Just one more night." He drops to a knee in front of his children and points to the empty rice paddies all around them. "You wouldn't know it this time of year, but the fields of Guangdong are where the best rice in China grows. And since the best rice in the world grows in China, what do you think we'll find growing here next summer?"

The children nod but do not answer. Li-Yu looks upriver, peering through the fog for the land Bing has described, for the memories of her parents. She sees nothing but endless paddies, and looks to Bing for an explanation. This doesn't look like the place you described, she wants to say. Where are the valleys, the mountains, the blossoms? There is only this river, the endless mud of these rice fields, and the occasional village. But Bing is staring off into the distance, perhaps seeing things in the mists that she cannot. In the months leading up to the move he had been expansive, holding on to her at night and telling her over and over again how things were going to be. He'd indulged all the kids' wishes—all they'd had to say was that they were going to miss something: cinnamon buns, ginger ale, chewing gum—and he'd be on his way to the grocery store. But then they departed and San Francisco diminished behind them. At sea he had spent more and more time, it seemed, lost in thoughts of something else. She had to ask him questions two and three times before she knew he'd heard her.

The boat drifts past a little riverside village. There are women washing clothes along the riverbanks, but they do not look up or wave. Li-Yu wonders again how she let Bing talk her into this. Her parents had been stunned when she'd first told them she was considering it. She had been in their living room. They had stared at her in silence for what seemed like several minutes. Finally her mother turned slightly, almost imperceptibly, toward her father.

"Do you know how hard it was for us to get here?" her father said, quietly. He took off his glasses and rubbed his eyes, as if this foolhardy daughter before him could be cleared away like a trick of light.

"Yes," she said.

He put his glasses back on and folded his arms across his chest. "Our grandchildren were born in America," he said.

Li-Yu shrugged.

Her mom said, "Here are a few things you wouldn't have in China: those shoes you're wearing, and those clothes. That purse, or that chair you're sitting in."

"I'm sure they have chairs in China," Li-Yu said. "They even have thrones."

"Used to."

"Don't you think it would be good for me and for the kids to see China?"

"No," her dad said.

"This room and pretty much everything in it," her mom said, looking around, "except the dirt."

"They have never met their other grandparents," Li-Yu said.

"Bing chose to come here," her father said.

"Let's go look in the kitchen," her mom said.

"I don't want to go look in the kitchen," Li-Yu said. "Bing says it's a nice big house, the largest in the village."

Her parents exchanged looks. "It's a terrible plan," her father said, "and that's that."

"If Bing wants to take you and the children to China," her mother began to say, but her father cut the sentence off with a stamp of his foot.

"Resist," he said.

The stamp echoed through the house. Her parents stared at her, their unblinking eyes steely.

"We didn't raise you to be a Chinese wife," her mother said.

"It's not like it is here," her father said.

"I'm Chinese, and I'm a wife," Li-Yu said. "Not much is going to change those things."

"You have no idea what you're saying," her father said.

"Maybe that's why I need to go," she said. "If it doesn't work out, I'll come back."

Her mother emitted a short mean laugh. Her father took his glasses off again and rubbed his eyes. "Do you know how hard it was for us to get here?" he said again.

"Yes," she said.

"No, you don't," he said.

The boat sails through the morning, navigating a complex network of rivers and tributaries. Li-Yu quickly loses track of their turns. The paddies around her might as well be endless. Around midday they begin to shrink; the ground buckles and rises, transforming into hills and ridges. They sail past the mouths of river valleys, whose curving interiors open and reveal themselves and then close. Flood plains appear and recede, each of them dotted with villages. That night she helps the children make beds on the deck with their clothes and bags. She and Bing watch the stars, and then she falls asleep, sitting up, leaning against him.

In the middle of the next morning the ship enters what looks like just another wide floodplain, but when Bing studies the surrounding hills he jumps as though pricked by a thorn. "This is it!" he cries, pointing upriver. Li-Yu and the children lean over the railing but see nothing. He addresses the children. "Are you ready to meet your *yeh* and *mah*?" he says. Rose and Henry nod, all the while scanning the landscape.

At the far end of the floodplain the boat follows a final curve in the river and a small wharf appears. The boat jostles into position along the pier and once it moors the family disembarks, along with a handful of other passengers. There are men to help them with their luggage. Together the little group heads up the road, Bing talking happily with the porters. He recognizes one of the other passengers, and the men embrace. Bing fires off a string of rapid questions, but is almost too excited to listen to the answers. Now Li-Yu has to smile. For years, the image she has held in her mind of her husband has had him behind the counter of his little shop on Channel Street in Stockton, talking noisily with his customers. But far more of his life has transpired here at the base of these hills, alongside this river. She reminds herself that even though they have been married ten years and have had two children together, there are parts of him—whole countries—she doesn't know. Henry and Rose are watching him, too, and for the first time in weeks she sees an end to their fatigue and boredom.

The road runs along the hills' feet, a dirt line that divides the slopes from the rice paddies. Buildings soon arise, made of bricks the same color as the earth, and crossroads appear and branch through the growing village, carrying men in dark clothing who walk with purpose, their farming tools swinging and catching the sunlight on their blades. There is an old woman in dark robes near the side of the road. She lifts a wrinkled hand and lets out a happy cry. Bing all but leaps. He drops his bags and runs to her, and the two of them embrace. A smile illuminates her face—Bing's smile. Bing turns and beckons Henry to come to him.

"This is your *mah*," he says. "Her name is Jiao. Say hello!"

"*Nihau*," says Jiao, squatting down and wrapping her arms around Henry. Henry stiffens but brings his arms up and returns the woman's hug. She holds him with a look of such joy on her face that Li-Yu feels herself warming all over, her misgivings breaking apart. Finally Jiao releases Henry and stands. Rose steps forward, a smile on her face, her arms outstretched. But Jiao does not reach for her—instead she tilts her head and looks her over, as if uncertain what she's seeing. Li-Yu looks to Bing but he has already gone; she sees him hurrying up a pathway among some houses, pointing to things and talking again to the porters, who are scrambling to keep up with him. Li-Yu cannot hear what he is saying. The women stand for a moment longer, considering one another, and then Jiao takes Henry's arm and darts after Bing. Li-Yu and Rose join the pursuit.

The caravan weaves quickly through the village, up and down through a sloping network of serpentine dirt paths. As Li-Yu follows she searches for explanations. Jiao had not heard, or she had misunderstood. Perhaps she had mistaken them for someone else? Who? She sees Henry struggling to keep pace with Jiao, who still has him by the arm, and who moves with surprising ease for her age. He glances over his shoulder and gives Li-Yu a look that stabs at her heart. You don't have to pull him like that, she wants to cry out. Now she can hear Jiao calling something out to Bing, but he will not slow down or turn around. They reach the far edge of the village where there is a clearing, and then a doorway, and without having registered a single impression of the house's exterior, Li-Yu finds herself standing inside, along with the rest of the heavily breathing procession. The floor of the front room is made of wooden planks, and there is a faded carpet covering much of it. Vertical wooden posts support heavy roof beams. Across from them, on an ornate wooden couch covered with blankets, there sits a woman with an imperious look on her face. Her hair is drawn up into a tight bun, her body hidden beneath layers of robes. She does not rise or speak or smile. Bing takes Henry by the hand and pushes him into the center of the room, as though he is some sort of offering. She looks him up and down, not smiling, and then her eyes flash across the rest of the faces in the room. When they reach Li-Yu's, they narrow, and drill into her.

Jiao appears at Li-Yu's side. She looks her in the face, and then gestures toward the woman on the couch. "Wife number one," she says, a tiny smile touching the corners of her mouth. She places a hand on Li-Yu's shoulder. "Wife number two," she says.

The room goes gray, along with everything in it. Li-Yu gropes for her children, to pull them in to her, but Henry is too far away, and she does not find Rose.

* * *

I looked up from my laptop, and the wooden room in long-ago China became my living room. Its couch morphed into mine; its occupants became my bookshelves and television. It was nearly ten o'clock. I had been at my computer for five hours straight, and my eyes felt as though I hadn't blinked once. I clamped them shut. Orange lights wheeled across the interiors of my eyelids. I read over my last few sentences, saved my document, and shut my laptop. It had been years since I'd managed a session like that. I rose and headed for the shower, shaking the feeling back into my arms. I climbed in and turned my face into the stream. Over the water I could hear strains of music rising from somewhere in the building, a strange and lilting melody that must have been turned up loud to reach me through the walls and the sounds of the shower. It died when I stepped out. I went to bed, fell asleep without effort, and dreamed I was lost, adrift on a white sea on a raft made of pages torn from a giant book.

TWO

I awoke before dawn. Great raindrops burst apart on the black windows and smeared the light from the street lamps in rolling patterns. I rose, turned on my teakettle, and sat down at my desk. The flier from *The Barbary Quarterly* still lay there, beside the computer, an e-mail address on its corner. I read through the pages I'd written the night before, looking for something I cared to rewrite, and because it seemed strange that nothing should present itself, I changed a couple of words and then changed them back. I opened a new e-mail, typed in the address, tapped out a few lines of introduction, attached my story, and sent it off.

I drank my morning coffee, ate a grapefruit and a boiled egg, and when it was time I gathered my things and headed outside.

The world was made of wind and water; my umbrella's efforts were laughable. Once in my classroom I dumped my things, spooled out several feet of scratchy, semi-absorbent paper towels, and mopped the water from my hair and clothes. I brewed a pot of tea and found the family absent from my mug. Perhaps with my story and my submission they were satisfied that they had my attention. I'd check back later. Only then did I realize I'd failed to plan anything for the day. I hoped it might be Wednesday, which would mean back-to-back trips to the music room and the computer lab that morning; that would buy me the time to pull something together. I consulted my calendar and confirmed my hope.

"Everything okay in here, Peregrine?" a deep voice called from my doorway. It was Franklin Nash. A cheerful red and blue robot on his tie squinted at me through the sights of a gigantic laser cannon.

"Everything's fine," I said. "Had you heard otherwise?"

"No, no," he said. "I was just making my rounds. But now you're making me wonder." He grinned.

"What's with your robot?" I said. "Is he a sadist or something?"

He laughed. "I tell the kids it's a telescope."

"And they buy that?"

"Not for a second." He pointed across my room, toward the windows. "This rain," he said. "I don't think you're going to get much in the way of recess today. If you need a reprieve, give me a call and I'll come spell you for a few minutes."

"Thanks," I said.

"Remember, I can only be in five places at once." He knocked twice on the doorframe, the signal he would be moving on. "Don't be the sixth to call." Annabel Nightingale immediately filled his space, as though pulled into the vacuum he'd left. She wore a raincoat that reached from her ankles to her throat. It was blood red, and covered with concentric circles and spirals in reds, yellows, and oranges. She looked like a Klimt painting.

"Did you see the kindergarten playground yet?" she asked.

I shook my head.

"Follow me," she said.

She led me through the slick hallways, which were filling with dripping children and the smell of mildew. She pushed through the doors that led to the scaled-down playground at the back of the school. The drain had clogged and now perhaps two inches of water covered the ground. The surface was a chaos of droplets, falling and leaping and diving again.

"And this is after just one night," she said.

***

The rain continued over the next few days, its assault on the city relentless. Sewers clogged and streets flooded. The power blinked on and off across the city; traffic crept and knotted in darkened intersections. The weathermen advised us all to spend the weekend inside and I was content to comply, reading and watching movies and making loose plans for the family I'd stranded in rural China. On Monday my classroom windows were buffeted by alternating waves of rain and wind and the sounds of sirens rising from the city below. My cooped-up kids did their best to contain their energy and anxiety. My tea revealed nothing.

Sometime later that week, my story appeared in *The Barbary Quarterly.* The editors hadn't contacted me at all—no acceptance letter, no corrections or suggestions, no galleys—so I was surprised to arrive home, after another long wet day at school, to open the manila envelope and find a copy of the journal, along with a handwritten note on yellowed paper that said, "Thank you. Send more please." A twenty-dollar bill fell out of the package and onto my desk. The envelope's contents were all damp, and smelled of seawater. The journal's paper felt cheap; the printing was off-center and slanted slightly. My story had top billing. At its conclusion, they'd added, "To be continued." Next was an excerpt from someone's memoir that had to do with memories of a ballet class and someone having typhoid. Also included were a pair of short stories and a handful of poems. The cover bore a striking image—a sepia-tone photograph of a Chinese girl about the age of my students, her hands clasped behind her back, looking directly into the camera with an empty expression. She was standing in the middle of a Chinatown sidewalk. She looked a lot like Rose, I thought.

My phone rang and I dropped the journal onto my desk. It was my sister Lucy. "How are you doing, you sweet soggy apple-cheeked son of a bitch?" she said. I do not have apple cheeks. My face is on the narrow side, and my complexion is a touch paler than average. "Peregrine, I have some tales for you that will make your hairs stand on end. This city is a strange and twisted place and if it sounds like I'm okay with it right now, it's only because

I've been drinking Irish coffees for the last two hours. Shit. Hang on a minute." She was muffling the phone, and then barraging somebody with profanity. I waited a minute, and then another, and then she was back. "Sorry about that. My car was about to get towed. I told the fucker I'd pepper spray him if he hooked it." She loved to pepper spray people—I had stopped keeping track of her victims somewhere around her junior year in college. "But listen, the reason I'm calling is to tell you to get ready for a houseguest." She let out a yelp. "Holy crap, Perry!" she yelled. "I gotta go. This guy is coming back from his truck with a gas mask and a crowbar and—"

And she was gone.

***

Two nights later I was stir-frying chicken when Eva Wong came through my door, with her rain-smeared mascara and her wet luggage and her bewildering accusations. She was about sixty. She wore a clear vinyl raincoat that reached her knees and a matching rain hat, and something black underneath. I expected to hear an accent, but when she spoke she sounded as American as my mom.

"You're Peregrine Long?" she asked.

"Yes."

"Do you recognize me?" she asked, without smiling.

I shook my head. "Should I?" Only then did I remember Lucy's mention of a houseguest—it had been lost somewhere between her cursing and her gas mask report.

Eva reached down, lifted a canvas suitcase, and walked past me, limping slightly, heading for the couch. She sat down with a heavy exhalation and looked around the room, taking in the empty walls, the small bookshelf, perhaps her own warped reflection in the black television screen. "My feet hurt," she said, "and I could use some tea." She dropped her bag on the floor, removed her raincoat and hat, and tossed them alongside her bag before sinking into the couch. She looked over at me. "You're letting in a draft."

I shut the door. "Sorry, I didn't quite get all the details," I said. "You're who, exactly?"

She reached down, unbuckled and removed her shoes, and sat back up, looking pained. She was out of breath. "Eva Wong," she said. It sounded like a proclamation rather than an introduction. I hoped she'd continue, but apparently I'd have to wait until her panting subsided.

"Well, welcome, Eva," I said, rounding the corner for the kitchen. I started water for tea and returned my attention to my dinner, which, I noted, would not be enough for two. I could make a big pot of rice and stretch it, though. "Are you hungry?" I called to my guest.

"Why, how kind of you," she said, her voice cheerless, perhaps even borderline sarcastic. "But the tea will be just fine."

I know you're wet and tired and out of breath, I wanted to say, but make a little effort here. I gave the wok a flick and started silently rehearsing a bit of the grief I'd have to give Lucy, not that she would care. It wasn't the first time she'd sent a vagabond my way. She'd always had an appreciation for the full spectrum of the human character, and was capable of striking up a friendship— or a rivalry—with anybody. She'd introduced me to felons, to middle-aged circus performers, to people with words tattooed on their faces. In her travels she liked to tell people this was her place, and if they were ever in San Francisco they should just come over for a night or two, no need to even bother calling ahead. I never really minded—it's not as if I had a lot of uninterruptible extra-curriculars. It even made me feel a little closer to her. I'd learned a lot of things about my sister from people I'd only just met. Eva seemed like an unlikely friend of hers, but Lucy had built a life out of unlikelihoods. I turned the burner down, put a smile on my face, and headed back into the living room.

"Funny," Eva said, her expression humorless. "What kind of name is Peregrine, anyway?"

"Long story," I said. I wasn't about to go into deep familial history before she'd even told me who she was. I didn't feel comfortable taking a seat by her on my own couch, so I opted for the desk chair instead. "So how do you know my sister?"

I thought I saw her wince. "'Sister?'" she said, shaking her head. "That's a little bizarre, don't you think?"

Ah. One of those. Lucy hadn't always been forthright about our siblinghood when she was commissioning guests for my apartment. It was a little joke she liked to play on me. They'd show up thinking I was her fiancé, her college roommate, even, once, her lawyer. Maybe some of Eva's surliness could be attributed to one of these fictions. "I'm not sure what she told you," I said, "but she's my sister. Same last names, DNA, the whole bit."

"What are you talking about?" she asked. I couldn't tell if she was angry or merely exasperated. Either way, it wasn't the reaction I usually got at that point. Eva reached into her suitcase and produced a copy of *The Barbary Quarterly*. She smacked it flat on the coffee table and looked at me. Now I could read her expression: It was contempt. "Here's the thing," she said. "I imagine a publication like this doesn't pay much more than about fifty bucks, tops. And I imagine it doesn't get you more than about that same number of readers. So what's the point?"

I was starting to feel disoriented, as in those childhood anxiety dreams when you're suddenly faced with an exam you haven't studied for. I'd missed episodes; I'd driven off the edge of the map. "You're asking me why I write?"

"I'm asking you why you steal," she said.

Heat flashed across my chest. In my anxiety dream I was now not only unprepared but naked as well. I stared at her face closely now, searching for an explanation, maybe even a punch line. Webs of wrinkles fanned across her temples. Her mouth was thin and drawn. If Lucy had put her up to this, she'd found a good actress.

"How much *did* you get paid?" she asked.

"Twenty whole dollars," I said. "Earned, not stolen. Not that it's any of your business. Who are you, exactly?"

She turned the journal around so the photo was facing me and she tapped the girl's face. "I'm her daughter," she said. "Eva Wong."

"I don't know anything about that photograph," I said. "The editors put it on there. I've never seen it before in my life."

"I don't believe that for a second, but that's not even what I'm talking about, and you know it." She sat forward and planted her elbows on her knees. "You stole my story. It isn't yours. Maybe you thought you could publish it in this fourth-rate journal and get a line on your resume, but unfortunately for you I read a lot. So cut the bullshit." Flushed, she let out a breath and glared at me. "You made me swear," she said. "Really, I hardly ever swear."

"That's crazy," I said, and as I said it I realized there was probably more truth to it than I'd meant. This was unprecedented. Lucy had never sent me a lunatic before. I wasn't sure how I was expected to proceed.

"I didn't steal anything," I said. "I made it all up. Last week, sitting right here."

"You didn't bother to change a single detail," she continued. She stood and clasped her hands behind her back, and seemed to be scanning the room for something. "What are you, a historian or something?"

"I'm a teacher."

"Of history?" She crossed the room and began studying the photos and the books on my bookshelf.

"Of third grade," I said. The kettle whistled and I hurried into the kitchen to find my chicken nearly done. Before making Eva's tea I pulled out my phone and shot Lucy a quick text: *What the hell is with this lady?*

"Can we back up?" I called. "Where exactly did you publish this?"

"I didn't publish it anywhere," she said. She appeared in the doorway, her fists half-clenched. "It's not a story. It's a life. My mom's life."

I set her mug of tea on the counter and rotated it so the handle faced her.

"Where do you live, exactly?" I asked her.

"What does that matter?" she said, reaching for the tea with a nod of her head. "I've never even seen that picture before," she said.

"That makes two of us."

I followed her back into the living room, where she sank into the couch again. "How could you have known about Channel Street? And *Xinhui*?"

"I picked them off maps," I said. "Is there somebody looking after you?" I asked her. "Do you have a husband, or a neighbor or something?"

She went very still, and looked at me for a little too long before answering. "My husband is dead, and who in the city doesn't have neighbors?"

"I thought maybe we could give someone a call. I think you might be a little bit confused."

Her face twisted and then slowly cleared, as if it were a pond into which I'd just heaved a chunk of broken concrete. "You are correct," she said. "I am confused." She sat forward and leveled a finger at my forehead. "I am confused about who you are, and how you came to know my family's history, and what you hope to gain by stealing it."

"I don't know anything about your family," I said, trying to make my voice sound calm. "I have no idea who you, or who any of them are."

"Bing?" she said, her face reddening. "Li-Yu? Rose, Henry, Mae? I think our names might be familiar to you."

"There's nobody named Mae," I said, but even as I formed the words an image rose in my mind: Bing's first wife, sitting on her wooden couch, her bound feet hidden beneath her colored robes.

Eva leaned back into the couch. She held the mug up and a cloud of steam embraced her face. Some of the tension seemed to fall out of her. "Listen," she said. "So I'm angry. You would be, too. And I figure you owe me that twenty dollars, but I'm not going to be leaving until we get this sorted out, so let's call it even. It's not about that. In fact, I don't even really care whether you believe me or not." Her voice was quiet, almost distant. "I only want to know one thing."

The smoke detector in my kitchen went off. I bolted for the stove, jerked the wok from the heat, and plunged its charred contents under a stream of water. I threw open the kitchen window and a gust of cold, wet air rushed into the room. I jumped on the counter, snatched the smoke detector from the wall, yanked out the battery, and let both fall onto the counter next to the mess-filled sink before climbing back down to the floor.

I went back into the living room. "I'm glad you weren't hungry," I said. "What were you saying?"

Eva was back on her feet, staring at the photographs of my family. "I just want to know what happened to my uncle," she said. "I want to know what became of Henry."

I was going to respond, to tell her that I hadn't quite figured him out, that of the four of them, he was the least clear, but she cut me off with a wave of her hand. That's when I noticed the slip of paper in her hand. She continued, without looking at me. "Something happens next," she said. "Something big. In your story. My story. What is it?"

I'd decided to kill Bing. It was the perfect development. I'd thought of it over the wet weekend, and I'd been kicking it around in my head for the last couple of days, preparing to write it. I was going to kill Bing and leave Li-Yu and her son and daughter stranded in Xinhui and watch them adapt. Suddenly I didn't want to say so, though. I didn't want to say so, and I didn't want to know why she was holding that slip of paper. "I don't think I want to give that away," I said. "You'll have to wait for the next issue."

She handed me the slip. "Don't open that yet," she said. It felt warm in my hand. "First tell me. Tell me what will happen."

"Bing is going to die," I said quietly.

She nodded.

I unfolded the slip. "Bing died," she had written. My phone chirped. It was my sister's response: *What lady?*

By the end of their fourth night in Xinhui, Bing is dead. He grows weak and dizzy within hours of their arrival and takes to a bed in one of the little rooms that protrudes from the side of the sprawling house. A bent man in black comes to the house with powders tied up in little cloth bundles and tinctures in small glass jars, and teaches the women of the house how to mix elixirs that will correct the flow of Bing's *xi*. He tells them to change the position of Bing's bed. Before he leaves, he instructs Bing not to speak, which almost seems unnecessary. Bing's mouth dries out until his breaths sound like sand falling against itself; dried pieces of spittle like rock salt form on his lips.

Li-Yu sits in a chair next to his bed and watches him dry out and shrivel, hour by hour. The woman on the sofa—her name is Mae, Li-Yu learns—does not come to see him. The other women of the house, Jiao, and the servants file past Li-Yu's chair with cups of hot brown mixtures that smell like wet earth, which they pour into Bing. They speak to one another and to Bing in quiet encouraging tones, and then they leave, and Li-Yu watches their potions flood out of him: black liquid vomit that spreads out over his pillow, and black liquid shit that seeps down into the stuffed pad beneath him.

The children wait in an adjacent room, where there is a bed for them, and they come in when Li-Yu will let them, but only for seconds at a time. She hopes this brevity will keep them from remembering this mute and desiccated stranger, dying in this foreign bed. This is not their father, not her husband.

When she and Bing are alone, she tears pieces from him, kills them, and tosses them away. Here is his little shop, on the night they first met: She plays it over, recasting him as a liar and a married man. Here are the lilies he brought to her the second time he took her out—another lie, another deceit. She is so relentless and merciless in her attempts that by the time he dies she has rewritten every memory she has of him, and there is nothing more to release than this small husk of a body.

At the funeral the mourners are dressed in white. Mae tries to keep Henry nearby, but he slips from her grasp and comes to Li-Yu. Rose stays at her mother's side, silent and unblinking. First there is a parade—many of the villagers, it seems, did not even know he had returned, and the atmosphere is not one of grief, but of astonishment and curiosity. They scrutinize Li-Yu and her children, and then turn their gazes on Mae, and then hold conversations they barely attempt to hush. Li-Yu catches a number of smiles. The procession arrives at the graveyard. The men lower Bing into the ground and he is gone, swallowed up by his beloved China, a motherland that could not forgive him his duplicitous sojourn.

A few days later, Li-Yu goes to Mae with her question, already knowing the answer. She finds her on her couch, speaking to one of the servants. After several minutes, Mae dismisses the servant with a wave.

"Auntie Mae," Li-Yu says, her head bowed in deference, "this is not our home. Please let us return."

Mae shrugs. "Nobody is keeping you here."

"And the children," says Li-Yu.

"Take the girl and go," says Mae, looking past her. "Catch the next boat."

"And Henry," says Li-Yu, "my son . . . ."

Mae smiles. "Our only heir? The man of the house?" She shakes her head. "That wouldn't make much sense, would it?"

"But he is my son," is all Li-Yu can say.

"I'm not sure he is," Mae says, "because no mother would want to steal an heir away from his household and his family."

Li-Yu is quiet for a moment. "There was money," she says. "Some of it is rightfully mine. If this were America . . . ."

Something beneath Mae's robes moves suddenly, and the dull thud of a foot or a knee hitting wood rises through the layers of cloth. Mae's face remains unchanged. She shakes her head again. "No, there is no money," she says. "I'm very sorry." Theirs is one of the richest homes in the village, Li-Yu knows—rooms spill out from every side of the courtyard, and the servants' building is nearly as large as the home she and Bing left behind in California. "We are just rice farmers here," Mae says, "not rich American travelers."

"But back home . . . ."

Mae raises her hand. "Ten years I've waited," she says. "Ten years, with no husband, and no son, while you lay in his bed." She drops her hand into her lap. "He doesn't belong to you. He is a son of China and a son of this house."

Li-Yu's legs begin to go numb. Her tongue feels thick and knotted, but she continues. "Please," she says, and her voice sounds far away, even to her own ears. "They have a family back home," she says. "Aunts and uncles, a *po* and *gung* who love them very much. Please . . . ."

"He will start school next week," Mae says, looking away, as if it is painful to have to explain such things. "He has much to learn, and much time has already been wasted. You and the girl may leave, or you may stay if you wish," she says. "We can always use some extra hands around the house." She cuts off any possible protest with a knife stroke of her hand. "Now bring me your papers. I need to see them."

"Papers?" Li-Yu says. Beneath her frustration and helplessness she sees the quick glint of something hard and bright and sharp, a hidden dagger.

"Your immigration papers. I need them."

"I don't know where Bing put them," she says. She waves her hand toward the main part of the house, toward the others' rooms, where she is not welcome, and has no business.

Mae grimaces. Li-Yu returns to her room, finds the papers, and hides them deep inside her clothing. That night she transfers them to her bedclothes and sleeps with them, and when she awakens she hides them in her day clothes again, just as she will do every night and every morning, for as long as she has to.

THREE

In the shower the next morning I heard again those lilting musical strains over the sound of the water. I turned the water off. The pipes shuddered and the music died. I turned the water back on and it started again, drifting in as if from a great distance, on a shifting wind. I added it to the growing list of things I couldn't understand.

Eva was asleep on the couch, one black-socked foot jutting out from beneath her blankets. I had not thought about her much since I'd retired to my room the night before to write, leaving her dozing on the couch. She'd wrapped herself in her vinyl raincoat, and when I'd turned the lights off it had gleamed like armor plating. Once I was engrossed in my story the images of Bing's bedroom had pushed her sudden and strange presence from my mind, but now in the cold morning light I had the chance to regard her with a little more lucidity. Sometime in the night she had shed the raincoat and pulled up the blankets I'd left beside her. (She'd declined the pillow.) She was deep in sleep, a wet stray cat too exhausted to remain wary. I still was not sure what to make of her prediction about Bing. Maybe she just had writerly instincts as well, a sense of drama. She did say she was an avid reader. But no matter. I'd learn who she was and where she belonged somehow. In the meantime it seemed easier to let her sleep than to awaken her and hustle her out. There wasn't much damage she could do in my apartment.

I walked up the hill through steady rain. The gutters ran wide with brown water, carrying coffee cups, food wrappers, a newspaper ad that said "less" when it meant "fewer." I had to leap across the rivers a couple of times and failed to make it to school with dry shoes. My waterlogged students arrived, dripping rain all over the floor, strewing coats and wet backpacks and umbrellas around the room and settling in to their desks. A number of them were missing. The heat was on and within minutes the windows were fogged completely.

"Hey Mr. Long," Kevin said. "There's a pond in my backyard and the roof in my sister's room is leaking and my dad put a bucket under it but the sound of dripping kept her up so she had to sleep on the couch. And this morning Barney was swimming around in the puddle. He likes to doggie-paddle." He grinned his toothless grin.

"That must have been some puddle," I said.

"He could have used an old shirt or a towel," Eliza Low said.

"Barney?" Kevin asked.

"Your dad," she said. "In the bucket. Sticking up. So it would muffle the sound. That's what we did."

Kevin grinned. "Hey, that's a good idea," he said. "I'll tell him that."

The bell rang. When the class settled I said, "This morning I saw a cell phone advertisement that said, 'More minutes, less dollars.' Can anyone tell me what's wrong with that?"

No one could, so I explained it. When I thought they had it down I quizzed them. "So, of what could you have 'less?'" I said.

"Chocolate milk," someone said.

"Right," I said. "How about 'fewer?'"

"Chocolate bars," someone else said.

"Right," I said. "And we're going to always remember that because why?"

"Because we're guardians of the language," Eliza said.

"Right," I said.

A light but rapid knock sounded on the door. "Take out your homework from last night," I told the class, striding toward the door.

"We didn't have homework last night," someone said.

Annabel was damp but she still managed to look elegant. "Do you have space for some refugees?" she asked. A silver bird on a chain at her throat fluttered with her words. Lined up in the hallway behind her, in two quiet rows, were the members of her class. Each of them had wide eyes and a tiny blue plastic chair. "Our room is flooded," she said.

My students, thrilled by the double excitement of the flood and their little buddies' unexpected arrival, arose to receive our visitors. The room grew loud as twenty-five different accounts of the displacement commenced. Annabel explained to me that they shouldn't need to stay long. The custodians were setting up makeshift accommodations in the cafeteria for all three kindergarten classes.

"Stay as long as you need to," I said. "Maybe they should share desks with their big buddies?"

"Thanks," she said. "First, though, could we treat you to a little performance? It will only take a minute."

"Of course," I said.

She turned and clapped twice, and her students dropped their conversations and lined up along the front of the room, still holding their chairs. Annabel issued a command I didn't quite catch and in unison, each of her kids set his chair on the floor in front of him, and then climbed upon it.

"Un, deux, trois," she said, and twenty-five little mouths opened and began singing in French. It was lovely.

Later, at lunch, Annabel explained. "It's foreign-language Friday," she said. We were sitting in the teacher's lounge, munching on salads and droopy pizza from the school's kitchen. Her class hadn't had to stay long. My kids were in the midst of applauding the song when Albert, one of the school's custodians, opened my door. He waited for the clapping to die down, and then ushered Annabel's class to the cafeteria.

"Foreign-language Friday?" I said. "How often do you have that?"

"Once a week," she said, "usually just after Thursday." She smiled and crunched down on a crouton.

"Thanks," I said. "Is it always French?"

"Oh, no," she said. "Then it would be called French Friday. I mix it up."

"So how many languages do you know?"

"I'm not sure."

"How can you not know?" She shrugged and took a bite of pizza. I watched her, waiting for her to smile. She didn't. "You're fucking with me," I said.

She shook her head emphatically. "*Nein*," she said. "*Nyet*."

"Okay," I said, "what was last week?"

"German."

"How do you know German?"

"My dad was stationed there for a time."

"Next week?"

"Spanish."

"Everybody speaks Spanish. What else?"

"Norwegian."

"How the hell do you know Norwegian?"

"An au pair."

"Okay. Italian?"

"Once you know Spanish and French, you basically know Italian. And Portuguese."

"Japanese?"

"Next time we'll sing *Atama kata hiza ashi*."

"Chinese?"

"Cantonese, yes. A tiny bit of Mandarin."

"How . . . ?"

"Peace Corps."

My food sat in front of me, forgotten. Annabel picked up her slice of pizza and bit off the point. She wore the faintest trace of a

---

---

smile. A trickle of grease dripped from the corner of her mouth. She wiped it away with the back of her hand.

"Would you want to have dinner with me tonight?" I said. It was an unplanned question. Suddenly it had just seemed like the thing to say, and I'd said it before I could change my mind.

She finished chewing and swallowed. "That's sweet of you," she said, glancing at the window as if checking on the storm, "but I can't. I have a very busy night ahead of me." She carved off a corner of her iceberg wedge. "Don't let that deter you too much, though."

***

I left school and found myself half-soaked within two blocks, so I turned and headed for the pool at the local Y to complete the drenching. Few considered this swimming weather, but for some of us it was our preferred mode of exercise, year-round. The other winter swimmers at the Y tended to school in masters' classes, gathering before dawn and in the evenings, paddling easily and all the while communicating underwater with clicks and whistles and songs, vocabularies they'd somehow remembered. I was not one of these aquatic creatures, not an obvious descendant of the oceans. I was a landlubber. I just swam because I couldn't do much of anything else.

Determined not to end up like my dad—overweight, perpetually out of breath, plagued always with the faint sour smell of inaction—I had searched extensively for a workout regimen I wouldn't hate. Lifting weights made me feel like a high-school football player and I was always aware that the guy next to me was lifting twice as much. I tried cycling, but after two perplexing bike burglaries from my fifth-floor balcony I gave up on that. I didn't mind running sometimes, but this city was brutal on the knees. I tried swimming and found no reason to leave it behind. It was private, less subject to theft, and there were no hills involved. I had even come to embrace the benefits of my dismally inefficient technique. I could burn a marathon of calories trying to stay afloat for forty-five minutes, and then I'd have the rest of my afternoon to do other things.

Beyond the exercise the water also helped me wash the clutter from my mind. Once I'm done with my laps I like to fill my lungs with as much air as I can stuff into them and then push myself with closed eyes off the wall into the deep end. I let myself turn and drift and sink until I lose my bearings, until I sense that equalization of pressure, when my organs and fluids stop straining against the inside of my skin, looking for a way out, and instead, enfolded by the density of the water, quiet down and rest.

Today as I walked home I figured the pool would be empty. The masters' societies wouldn't congregate until later, and any afternoon swim classes would have been cancelled. A swim also delayed my return home. I'd produced no explanations about Eva's appearance during my school day, and as such I was not in a hurry to go back and confront the mysteries there. Swimming might give the situation another hour or so to resolve itself.

I knew the woman working at the counter of the Y. Her name was Doris. I didn't know much about her, but she had Eastern European origins, circa wartime. She had worked that counter the entire ten years I'd been a member, and probably well before that, too.

"Looks like you've already been swimming," she said. She pointed to the door that led into the locker rooms. "No other crazy men right now, just you."

I changed into my swimsuit (which I kept in my bag for these unplanned trips to the Y) and pushed through the double doors. A blue canvas awning was all that held the storm away from me now—the sound of the rain beating into it was like static, an old television turned up too loud. The pool was empty as promised, its surface chaotic with motion, the lights below barely visible. I set my bag and my towel down beneath the awning, pulled my goggles over my head, and when I ran out into the rain the weight of the water fell upon me like a blanket. I leapt and fell through the roiling surface into the silence beneath.

I kept my eyes clamped shut until I ran out of speed, and when I opened them I saw utter emptiness, endless water in all directions. I twisted, searching, and found that the pool's walls and floor had vanished, and beneath me yawned a blue-green chasm. Vertigo flashed through me like a panic. I think I may have gasped—water choked me and I clawed toward what I hoped was the surface. I emerged spluttering and gasping. The Y had returned, but its lines were wavering, out of focus. I fought my way to the side of the pool and scrambled onto the deck. On my hands and knees I coughed and gasped, trying to clear my airways. Eventually the air came back and my heart began to settle. Above me, on the wall, was a large white sign, with large red letters: No Lifeguard on Duty. I pushed myself to a sitting position, tore my goggles off, and stared into the churning surface.

It took me several minutes to gather the courage to ease myself back into the water. I walked on shaky legs to the stairway and stepped one foot in, and then the other, my knuckles white on the railing. I descended slowly, one step at a time, until I was up to my waist. I took a deep breath, clutched the metal bar with both hands, and lowered my face through the surface.

The floor fell out from beneath me; the pole turned to vapor in my hands. I pulled my head up so quickly I pulled a muscle in my neck. The stairway reappeared. I jumped back out as if the water was boiling, changed without showering, and headed for home.

"Bye-bye, crazy man," Doris called out cheerfully as I walked past her.

***

I was so overtaken by the advent of this new mystery that I forgot about the old one, and when I came through my door and saw

Eva's pallid figure sitting on my couch with the lights off I jumped and swore. I headed for the kitchen and the bottle of Scotch, feeling her watch me as I walked past.

"You stayed up late last night," she said.

"Yes," I said.

"Writing?"

"Yes."

"Did you kill Bing off?"

"Yes."

"Can I read it?"

"Yes."

I half-filled the glass, not bothering with ice. Back in the living room I sat down at my desk. My mind was buzzing; Eva was saying something but I couldn't hear what. "Did you say something?" I said.

"You're no historian," she said. "I had plenty of time to look around today, and you're no historian."

"I could have told you that," I said.

"You did tell me that," she said. "I just wasn't sure if I should believe you or not."

"You should," I said, taking a sip. The whiskey crackled through my head and throat like electricity.

"I found a spare key, by the way," she said. "So you don't have to worry about that."

"I wasn't," I said.

"What's wrong with you?" Eva asked.

"I had kind of a long day," I said.

"But you're a teacher," she said.

"So?"

"So you get off work in the middle of the afternoon," she said. "How could you have had a long day?"

She was leaning back in the couch, her hands folded in her lap, her feet flat on the floor, watching me. I couldn't tell if she was serious.

"Can we review a couple of things?" I asked, feeling my half-formed thoughts about the Y's bottomless pool disintegrating. Its contemplation would have to wait.

"Let's," she said.

"You didn't come from New York?"

"What does New York have to do with anything?"

"And you don't know my sister Lucy?"

"How would I?"

"Long story. Where did you come from, exactly?"

"Hayes Valley."

"Hayes Valley, as in, right here in San Francisco?"

"Is there another one?" she said.

"And why is it that you need to stay here?"

"My place got flooded. I told you that last night."

"I don't think you did."

"I did. You must not have been listening."

"So how long do you need to be here?" I said.

"As long as it takes," she said.

"As long as what takes?"

"You're not much of a listener," she said.

"Remind me," I said.

She sat forward. "My uncle Henry."

I looked around my apartment. "And why do you think that information's here?"

The copy of *The Barbary Quarterly* was still on the coffee table in front of her. She reached out and tapped it with her finger. "Because here is where this came from," she said. Together we regarded the journal, the sidewalk, the girl and her gaze.

"So we're back to that again?" I said.

"That's all there is," she said. She leaned back into the couch and yawned. "That, and maybe twenty bucks."

"And how exactly did you find me?" I sent another crackle of liquid electricity down my throat. Back-to-back afternoons with

Scotch weren't my norm, but neither were teacup visions or bottomless swimming pools. If this kept up I'd have to find another coping mechanism.

"You're in the phone book," Eva said. "My place got flooded, and you owe me." She spread out her arms. "So here I am."

Those were the easy questions. When I asked the next one my voice sounded thin and feeble, a faint breeze through my skull. "How did you know Bing was going to die?" I said.

"Because that's what happened," she said. "The question is: how did *you* know he died? And, again, and more to the point: what else do you know?"

I shook my head. "That's where things stop making sense."

"Well," she said, brightly, "it would appear we're now on the same page, anyway. Oh, by the way, your mom called." She pointed to the corner of my desk, where my answering machine sat. My mom was the only reason I even had a landline—she refused to call me on my cell phone. She was concerned they caused brain tumors, and she refused to be a contributor to mine. I hit the button. "I need you to come pick something up," she said. "Call me." Suddenly, getting out of the city and seeing my mom seemed like a great idea. I checked the window. The rain was still falling, but it had lightened a bit. It wasn't rush hour quite yet. I had decent wipers. I'd drive slowly. I stood up and grabbed my keys.

"You're going now?" Eva asked.

"I am."

"I'd like to come."

"My mom doesn't really like unannounced visitors."

"So announce me."

"She doesn't really like any kind of visitors."

"I don't like finding my family's history printed up beneath someone else's name," she said, "but nonetheless, it happened."

My mom lived by herself in a little nook in the Santa Cruz Mountains, outside the town of La Honda. On those rare days when there was no traffic and the road was dry, it took about an hour to get there. I crept out of the city amid the red splatter of taillights and rain. Eva fell quiet, and all the confusion of the last couple of days descended on me again. My faith in the stability of the materials and liquids that made up my surroundings had been shaken; at any moment the road could turn to ash, the steering wheel to salt. I drove on anyway, hoping things would hold themselves together somehow. I had found a way out of the pool, after all, and I had chased the family out of my teacup. If Eva was a delusion, if she was the embodiment of a voice in my head, well, she wasn't asking for much: corroboration on some plot predictions, some tea, a half-hearted request for a twenty. If her demands got more elaborate I'd re-evaluate.

I called my mom to let her know I was on my way. "I'm bringing someone with me," I said.

"What the hell, Peregrine?" she said. "That's unacceptable."

"Sorry, but I didn't have much of a choice."

"He has a gun to your head?"

"She."

"She? A girlfriend?"

"No, a woman. She's staying with me for a few days."

"A girlfriend?"

"No." I could not say: an old Chinese lady who appeared at my door and accused me of stealing her family's history, and then correctly predicted my next major plot development. "She's helping me with some research," I said instead.

"Well, you're not coming in, then," she said. "I'll bring your things out."

"It's pouring down rain, Mom. We're going to need the pit stop. Besides, I'm positive she will be totally uninterested. She's probably your age. She's Chinese."

"What does that have to do with anything?" Eva asked.

"Does she smoke pot?" my mom said.

"No," I said.

"You asked her?"

"No," I said.

"Ask her."

"I'm not asking her that. Her interests lie elsewhere, I guarantee it."

"I don't like it, Peregrine." She hung up.

My mom grew marijuana and sold it to medical cannabis clubs. She made a decent living, but she worked hard. The entire house but for her bedroom, one bathroom, and part of the living room had been given over to her operation. The other bedrooms housed hydroponic planting beds and tables where she crossbred and cloned plants. Clotheslines ran the length of the hallways, where whole plants hung upside-down at harvest time, drying. In the kitchen she made box after box of cellophane-wrapped cookies, brownies, scones, cinnamon rolls, loaves of banana nut bread, and apple turnovers, all of them tinged a slight shade of green. Constant maintenance chores presented themselves: fans ran too slowly, light bulbs burned out, the filters in the air conditioning and exhaust system needed replacing, temperatures and pH levels fluctuated. The house hummed and pulsated constantly with the automatic comings and goings of servo motors and thermostats, which pulled lights on tracks across the ceilings, regulated temperatures, and flushed and refilled the water in the hydroponic beds. During the harvest season she would develop problems with her fingers, her neck, and her eyes. The air was hot and close and reeked, all the time.

I worried about her. The state of California left her alone, but the Feds were a threat, as was theft. Her outdoor beds, which were scattered throughout the hills, relied on concealment and poison oak barriers to carry them to maturity. And even though her house was tucked into a notch in the hills, a warm day with a breeze could carry the smell hundreds of yards, and anybody with a nose for it who happened to be wandering within a half-mile of her property might catch a whiff and decide to do some snooping. She had motion detectors and automatic lights, but they were primitive, and half the time they didn't function at all. And it was lonely work. She rarely went into town. The only things that kept her from becoming a complete hermit were some aging Santa Cruz hippies in the same business who appeared from time to time to help her out with things, and her delivery routes. These were not without their stresses, either. She had clients from Santa Rosa to Santa Cruz and the circuit took her hours. I was sure that someday her car was going to go out on her, and leave her stranded by the roadside with thousands of dollars of produce in her trunk. At least she kept a low profile—nobody paid much attention to a graying middle-aged Chinese woman in the slow lane in an outdated Prius.

I could never quite understand why she'd chosen this life. After my dad had died and my sister and I had left the house, she could have done anything, anywhere. "You don't even need to work," I had said to her, on more than one occasion. "Why don't you just volunteer somewhere so you can meet people, and then you can come back home and grow orchids or tomatoes or something."

"Everybody has to work," she'd say. "I don't want to meet people. And I can't sell orchids or tomatoes for hundreds of dollars an ounce."

We exited at Highway 84 and began our climb into the mountains. The woods closed around us and blocked out what little glow remained of the peninsula's electricity. Occasional homes crouched among the trees; light struggled through their windows and lost itself in the rain.

"I can't remember the last time I got out of the city," Eva said quietly at one point, more to herself than to me. She reached up and touched her window as if she could feel the wet trees through the glass.

The road climbed out of the wooded valley and onto the ridge. Occasionally we caught glimpses of other faraway cars, our counterparts on adjacent hills on their own two-lane roads, head-lights held out feebly before them in a wet and immense darkness. The road continued to climb, up and to the west.

My sister Lucy and I had not been raised like this, the children of mountaintop pot farmers. We grew up closer to the bay, just off 101, in a small house with empty walls and hardwood floors and a yard made of gravel and weeds. For the first ten years of my life I remember little but my father's battles with cancer. It was an endless series of remissions and resurgences, treatments and medications, clinics and operations and specialists. He had been a software engineer, part of that first wave of scientists and visionaries who helped lay the foundation for home computing and the emergence of Silicon Valley. We had a spare room completely given over to a mainframe the size of a refrigerator. Our dad spent all his time there, sometimes staying up for two and three nights in a row, sweating, gazing through the monitor into the capabilities and future of his machines. My mom tried to get him to take walks, to get fresh air, to eat healthy foods. She made appointments for him with acupuncturists and herbalists. He ignored all her efforts.

"This is a fight," she would say to him, carrying away a plate of uneaten broccoli. "You need to think like a fighter."

"It's not a fight, Pam," he'd say, rising from the table to return to his work. "It's a race." It wasn't until later that I understood what he meant.

Our mom worked the community college circuit, teaching biology, botany, natural history, and any other subject in which she could pose as an expert for long enough to get past a hiring committee. She never complained, but I don't think she liked it much. Her schedule changed every semester. We never knew when to expect her. At home her usual spot was the dining room table, with her books and papers spread around her.

Lucy and I constructed our childhood at the feet of these two monoliths, drawing on the backs of the endless strips of serrated paper the computer's printer spit out, or reading beneath the table as our mom worked, listening to the scratches of her pen above us. There was no television, no stereo in the house. "Other families stare at TVs," she would say. "We converse." And then she'd tell us not to talk to her because she had papers to correct. The walls were bare but for a few yellowing drawings that Lucy or I had done, tacked beside doorways. We rarely used the yard, and when we did, we didn't know what to do. There were no balls, no shovels. We collected pebbles and threw them at the fence.

Our dad died, at home and sleeping, when I was ten and Lucy was almost fourteen. It was a bright clear day, and though it was January it wasn't cold. Mom came into our rooms that morning—first Lucy's, then mine. "Your father died last night," she said, giving me a short but tight hug, "so come and say goodbye to him."

I wondered if he'd won his race. At the funeral I asked my mom, but she said she didn't know. A few days later two of the men he worked with came to us and said that they had made a deal with our father—upon his death, everything in his office was to be sold to them for five hundred thousand dollars, payable right then. One of the men opened his briefcase and wrote my mom a check. She thanked him. The man said that it was they who should be thanking her. The company owed its life to our dad, he said. He looked over to where Lucy and I were watching, half-hidden in a doorway. He had kids, too, he said, and our dad's work fed and clothed them, too. He said he was sorry. They went into Dad's office and boxed up all his things. A team of men came in a van and took the mainframe away on a metal dolly. The man who'd written the check went on to explain that in addition to the money, my mom now owned twenty percent of the company, and that we'd receive payments every quarter based on the company's income. The lawyers would arrange it. They said some more nice things about my dad, emptied his room, and left. My sister and I emerged to see what a half-million dollars looked like. It seemed like a prize, so I figured he must have won his race. My mom folded the check and put it in her purse. "Go finish your homework," she told us, "and then we'll go get some pizza."

By the time Eva and I reached my mom's gate we were miles from the nearest streetlight. Using my headlights as illumination, I wheeled through the numbers on the combination padlock and then swung the gate open. I locked it behind us and we drove up the long driveway to the house.

Mom answered the door in her red-and-white striped apron, which was dusted with flour. She looked quickly at Eva, and then back to me. "Hello Peregrine," she said, and gave me a quick hug. "Did you lock the gate?" I nodded. She extended a hand to Eva. "I'm Pamela," she said, without smiling.

"Eva," said Eva, taking her hand, also not smiling. My mom bolted the door behind us.

I hadn't been there in a few months, and things had changed. The front of the house, which consisted of a living room and the open kitchen, had been consumed by her crops. Rows of waist-high plants had replaced the couch, the coffee table, the easy chairs, and the television. Piled in one corner of the room were her bed, a dresser with a few books on it, and a lamp. I could only imagine what had become of her bedroom. The kitchen counter had been completely taken over by low planters, out of which baby plants sprouted. A cheap card table with folding legs now stood in the middle of the kitchen floor, creating a path just wide enough to move around the room. It held her mixing bowl, bags of flour and sugar, chocolate chips.

"You've made some changes," I said.

"Yes," she said. "Market pressures. Have a seat." There were a few stools hidden beneath the kitchen counter's lip. We pulled them out and found spots for them in her narrow walkways.

"What did you do with all the furniture?" I said.

"Sold it," she said.

"This doesn't look healthy," I said.

"What do you mean? It's an oxygen-rich environment."

"These are lovely," Eva said politely, eyeing the plants. "What are they?" She reached out and touched a leaf.

My mom had gone back to work, and was now dragging a long wooden spoon through some thick chocolate batter. "Cannabis," my mom said.

"Never heard of them," Eva said.

The slightest smile touched my mom's lips. "Give me one minute and I'll make some chamomile," she said. Her voice sounded a little friendlier. She poured the batter out into a couple of cake pans and slid them into the oven, then turned the flame on beneath a teapot. She leaned a hip against the counter and we considered each other. She looked tired. At some recent point the gray in her hair had come to exceed the black.

"So," she said, "two things. I need you to haul a couple of boxes of your stuff out of here. I found them in the back of the hall closet, and I need the space in there." She glanced at Eva, and then back at me. "So what are you researching?" she asked. "Aren't you still a teacher?"

"Sure," I said. "But I've also been working on a story. I'm publishing chapters of it in a journal in the city. I should have brought a copy of it to show you."

"That would have been nice," she said. The kettle began to whistle. She dumped tea bags into a few mismatched mugs, poured the hot water over them, and brought them to us.

"It takes place in China," I said.

"Well, bring it along next time, and I'll read it." She set her mug down on the counter with a clunk. "Let's go grab those boxes."

I followed her down the hallway. Plants lined one of the walls, leaving just enough room for us to slip through. She pulled open the closet door. A giant hooded lamp hung from the ceiling, awaiting more plants. Impeding the process was a large cardboard box on the floor, which I recognized right away. It contained old drawings, elementary school papers, notebooks, collections, paper planes—the unabridged works of my boyhood. I hadn't seen it since I'd helped her move in, well over a decade ago. I hauled the box into the front room and found the floor was so completely occupied that the only place for it was on the bed. I set it down and pulled a flap open, feeling the years quickly sliding backward.

Eva was watching us through her tea steam. "Is this where you grew up?" she asked.

"No, Redwood City," I said. On top of the box was a report I'd written on the gold rush while in fourth grade. Beneath it was a Thanksgiving story I'd written about a vampiric turkey that had garnered an A-. I rifled through the strata below, the geologic record of my intellectual growth. It would be fun to sit down later and spend some time digging through it. I closed the box and returned to my stool, where my tea sat, still steaming.

"You said two things," I said.

"Your sister is coming back." She glanced around the room. "Obviously, she can't stay here, so she's counting on you. She said she mentioned it to you." She fished a piece of paper out of her apron and handed it to me. I unfolded it and saw that it was the ripped page of a book.

"What's this?" I said.

"Sylvia Plath. I ran out of notepaper. Turn it over."

I did. There was a phone number printed on it.

"She had to change her number. That's her new one. And she no longer has a driver's license, by the way."

"So I'm hosting and chauffeuring?"

"I'm sure the two of you will work something out," she said.

Eva was asleep by the time we were back on 280. It was a long quiet drive back to San Francisco, with too much to think about. All around the rain fell, moving through the darkness.

三

The school is in the next village, an hour's walk away, and on Henry's first day it is raining and he is terrified. Li-Yu awakens next to him and he is already crying, quietly, his face turned toward the wall. She wraps her arms around him and instantly finds such great sobs rising in herself that she quickly lets go. After tossing the blanket aside with false decisiveness she rises to her feet. Rose remains curled up in the bed's corner, her breaths loud and oblivious.

"Time to get up, my boy," she says to Henry, briskly. She speaks only Cantonese to them now, and forbids them to speak English to one another. She tolerates neither complaints about Xinhui nor nostalgia about California. "This is where we live," she tells them often, "and it's our duty to try to live well." She can barely form the words without wincing, knowing that her children's opportunities, especially Rose's, have all but vanished. Rose is old enough to understand the desolation of her once-boundless future, and when she argues, it takes all the severity Li-Yu can muster to silence the complaints. As for her own fury and desperation, Li-Yu compresses them until they are small and hard as diamonds and then she hides them away, far from the eyes of her children and the rest of the household. She knows where to find them, though. They color her dreams and each morning when she awakens she uses them to fuel the promise to herself that she will do anything—commit any act, seize any opportunity—to return her children to their home.

Henry stirs to let her know he is awake, but he does not yet rise. She knows he is composing himself; she sees his furtive movements as he hides his tears in the folds of the blankets.

"Rose, you too," she says, giving her daughter a gentle shake.

Rose sits up, grumbling. "Why do I have to get up?" she says, in English. "I don't have to go anywhere."

"You still have your lessons," says Li-Yu. In the breaks between their duties she has been trying to educate her daughter, an endeavor that earns her the scorn and ridicule of everyone in the household. Some of the men even try to get her to stop. But she ignores them and persists, even though Rose already knows half the things she tries to teach her.

Henry stands now and attempts a brave face, but looks outside and sees the rain and cannot prevent himself from crying.

"That's enough," says Li-Yu, but she cannot look at him. She helps him into his clothing as his sobs dwindle and become sniffles. Together they walk into the main part of the house where they become the center of some unclear commotion.

The members of the household—Bing's father and mother, the uncles, some of the maids—are all gathered, exchanging smiles with missing teeth, gestures of steam rising from their teacups. Mae is in her usual position on the couch, covered in robes. When Henry comes into the room she tosses aside a blanket and unveils a new pair of pants and a jacket. She holds her hands out to Henry, but he does not go.

"Come here," she says. Still Henry does not move.

Li-Yu eyes the clothing. Both pieces are dark blue and look like cheap denim. The fabric looks stiff and uncomfortable. She knows they are unlike anything she would choose for him, or anything Henry would choose for himself, and she can see right away that neither will fit.

"Come here," says Mae again, now with impatience. Li-Yu puts a hand on his back and pushes him. He resists at first and then takes two or three steps forward. Li-Yu takes him by the hand and walks him toward the couch. Henry pulls in close to her as if he would like to vanish into her leg. She puts him in front of

Mae and then steps aside. He looks up at his mother and tries to reach for her, his face beginning to scrunch with tears again. But Li-Yu nods toward Mae and then steps back, leaving Henry alone to face her.

"New clothes," Mae says, "for you." She picks up the jacket and shakes it. It sounds stiff, almost wooden, like pieces of kindling knocking together. She hands it to Henry. "Here," she says, "put it on."

Henry forces an arm into a sleeve and begins crying again. Behind her, one of the uncles turns to another and whispers something; the men stifle laughter. The jacket is too big for him, as Li-Yu knew it would be, and the fabric is so stiff it pushes up into his neck and jaw.

"What's wrong with him?" Bing's mother asks.

Mae holds up her hand. "Have patience, Ma," she says. "He still has American manners." She smiles and shakes out the pants. "And these," she says to Henry.

Li-Yu steps forward, burning. "He'll finish changing in the bedroom," she says, controlling her voice. "Henry, what do you say?"

He issues a muffled thank-you and they return to their room, where Li-Yu helps him into the new pants. Each of his whimpers is a knot in her gut but her face shows nothing while she works. The pants are far too long—she has to roll them up three times before his feet emerge. They have a long walk to school, and she can see the fabric will chafe his ankles. Once he is dressed and in his shoes Li-Yu rises and wraps her arms around him and squeezes him quickly but tightly. It is enough. His face becomes as resolute as hers as she leads him back into the kitchen where the maids make a fuss over him. They have prepared a special breakfast of *jook* and steamed dumplings, which he eats methodically and without relish. They return to the front rooms in preparation for their departure and Mae calls to Henry again. This time he shuffles over to her, the stiff fabric of his new clothes rustling. She gives him a small cloth bundle tied with cords. He accepts it with both hands, thanks her, and because he does not recognize it as another gift, he remains standing there, unsure, rocking himself slightly.

"Don't you want to see what's inside?" Li-Yu asks him.

Henry nods. He pulls at the cords and the bundle unrolls, falling open neatly. Inside there are sewn pockets with new pencils, sheets of thin, almost translucent paper, and a small abacus. It is a beautiful and elegant gift, exactly the sort of thing Rose would love. Li-Yu does not risk a glance at her daughter, who is standing in the corner of the room, hoping to remain unnoticed. If she were to catch Rose's eye now, even for the slightest moment, it would serve as an acknowledgment of this injustice, and all the injustices that have come since their arrival in China, and all that are awaiting her. Li-Yu knows her daughter won't be able to weather a lifetime of this, the way Chinese women do. Even decades here would not wipe out her memories of the way life had been in California. For now, though, the only defense either of them has is stoicism.

Mae reties the bundle and hands it back to Henry. "Thank you," Henry says again. He returns to Li-Yu's side, and together they move toward the door.

"It's a pity," Mae calls. "This should be a happy occasion for him."

"He can walk alone," calls Bing's father, from the next room. It is the first time he has addressed Li-Yu in all the days they have been there. He rises from his chair and comes into the doorway, his hands clasped behind his back, wearing the look of someone who has never been disobeyed. "He's starting school, and it's time for him to start learning to be a man. He can walk alone."

Li-Yu takes Henry by the hand and leads him through the doorway, with Rose close behind. There is a shout from inside, but she cannot hear what is being said, or to whom. She moves her children quickly down the pathway, waiting to hear the door fly open, or to hear footsteps flying after them, but neither comes. The three of them plunge through the rainy village, and the house diminishes behind them.

FOUR

"I didn't think much of that trip to your mom's last night," Eva said to me late the next morning, when I emerged from my room. The rain had persisted overnight and was now falling heavily from a lightless sky. "I mean," she said, "I don't think it got us any closer."

"To what?" I said.

She narrowed her eyes and seemed to be studying me. "Where's your dad?" she asked, after a time.

"Dead," I said. "A long time ago."

"So what was your mom's maiden name?" she asked.

"Bloomfield."

"Seriously."

"She was adopted. She grew up in Iowa."

"So 'Long' came from your dad, who was white?"

"Correct," I said.

"But 'Long' is Chinese," she said. "It means *dragon*."

"It's English, too. It means *lengthy*." I walked to the kitchen and started the coffee. The remainder of my Saturday stretched out before me, empty but for rain and a lack of privacy.

"Regardless," Eva said. "I thought the trip might have been a little more productive."

"I got the box, and we got back in one piece," I said. "What were you hoping for?" She didn't say anything. I sat down at my desk. "What does my mom have to do with it?"

"I don't know," she said. "It's too bad she was adopted."

"Yeah," I said. "Orphans have it great." But I knew what she meant. She had latched on to my family history, and she was talking about the severance, the discontinuity. My mom had been born here in San Francisco to a single mother who'd died

67

when she was five. All she could remember from before that time was the sound of Cantonese, and in that way she knew she was a descendent of southern China, and probably from a family who had passed through Canton on the way to the States. And that was all we knew. There were no grandparents, no links, no stories.

"You were up writing last night," Eva said.

I retrieved the laptop from my room and set it down on the coffee table in front of her. "I'm going out," I said. "I'm hungry. Do you want anything?"

She shook her head and bent down until her nose was inches from the screen.

Outside there was nothing that hadn't turned gray and wet—red, blue, and green cars alike had turned gray; the trim on the painted Victorians had turned gray. Even my hands looked gray. I put them in my pockets and headed down the hill toward Polk Street. Before I could settle on a specific destination my phone twitched in my pocket. It was Leonard Shelby. Leonard and I had been roommates at Sacramento State, where he'd studied poetry. He was now a prosecutor in L.A. with a wife and two kids, whose ages astounded me every time I talked to him.

"What's wrong with this city?" he asked.

"Which city is that?" I said.

"This one. Your city. I'm here. I'm here and it sucks, and I don't want to hear that stupid Mark Twain quotation again."

"It isn't summertime, so that wouldn't even be germane."

"Good. What are you doing right this minute?"

He was staying on Post, in the middle of the theater district. We met at a shoebox café and took a table near the window where we could watch the matinee crowds struggle through the rain.

"You're a little outside your jurisdiction, aren't you?" I asked him. In the time since I'd last seen him, he'd almost come to look at home in his suit.

"I'm working too hard," he said, with a smile. "Someone thinks my jurisdiction ought to be expanded a bit."

"Not enough bad guys in L.A.?"

"Let's just say there's a good chance a couple of nice men in black will be visiting you soon to chat about me."

"Feds? Do they know you're a redheaded poet?"

"I can't really hide the hair," he said, "but I was hoping you wouldn't tell them about the poetry. It would ruin my career."

"I could be persuaded to forget about it," I said. "Breakfast on you?"

His wife—Sydney—was well, and the kids—Caleb and Patrice—were already eight and five, somehow. There was Little League baseball, soccer, gymnastics, judo. Potlucks with neighbors and their kids and trips to preposterously expensive amusement parks. The rest of the guys we'd known together were fine, doing the same sorts of things with their corresponding sets of wives and kids and neighbors. He worked his way back up to the present, and his recruitment by the Department of Justice. "I'm excited about it," he said, "but I have to admit I'm a little bit conflicted. The assholes in law enforcement are a lot more aggressive than the assholes in poetry, and now I'll be dealing with national-level assholes." He waved for more coffee. He had become the sort of guy who could do that, and know that his cup would be refilled within seconds. "In fact, I can't really stand any of the people I see regularly. The DA, the other prosecutors, the defendants and their lawyers. Judges, jurors, bailiffs, cops, you name it. And don't even get me started on the fucking stenographers."

A show had just let out somewhere nearby; the sidewalk was a mass of raincoats and umbrellas. Taxis gridlocked the street. Making his way along the sidewalk through the crowd, I noticed, was one of the actors from a nearby production. He was dressed in an old dirty soldier's costume and he wore a rifle over his shoulder. As I watched him approach, I noticed he seemed to still be in character—he looked as tired as his clothing, and walked with a limp. He seemed impervious to the rain.

"But you know what?" Leonard was saying. He skewered several pieces of fruit on the tines of his fork. "I love my job. I love practicing law, and I love beating all those other assholes at it. It's a life of extreme passion and drama, which is all I ever hoped for."

"Look at this guy," I said, pointing to the actor outside.

"Who?" Leonard said.

"The actor," I said. "Right there, the Chinese guy with the rifle."

Leonard scanned the pedestrians, shaking his head.

"There," I said, pointing, but the crowd was already swallowing him and then he was gone, his rifle hidden in a river of umbrellas.

"That's the difference between L.A. and San Francisco," he said. "In L.A., that would have been a real rifle. What about you, anyway?"

I was good. Teaching still, and living in the same place. Writing some and swimming a little.

"Jesus," he said. He tracked down his last glob of scrambled egg whites with a corner of sourdough toast. "That sounds magical. Plane rides are about as close as it gets to downtime for me these days," he said. He swallowed his last bite, threw down his napkin with finality, and wrapped a hand around his coffee cup. "I'm not complaining though. I wouldn't trade any of it for anything. But I'd be bullshitting you if I didn't admit that I felt like something's been lost. The potential for spontaneity, maybe. Like coffee in Tahoe? That sort of thing."

He took a sip from his mug and let the memory swell into the silence. In the middle of some sleepless winter night our freshman year we'd decided we wanted to have coffee with a view of something less depressing than the interior of the local Denny's, so we packed supplies into his beat-up 4x4 and drove through the snow to Tahoe City. We set up folding chairs and a camp stove on the frozen shore and drank coffee and watched the stars working to penetrate the diaphanous layer of clouds that hovered over that great black lake. We made it back to Sacramento well before dawn with several giant garbage bags of snow and left a seven-foot snowman blocking the door of our dining hall. We awoke a few hours later to the sounds of an all-out snowball fight.

He looked at me over his mug; we were both grinning. "Your idea to grab those garbage bags and that shovel on our way out of town remains the single greatest piece of inspiration I've ever witnessed," he said. "And that's what I'm talking about. Spontaneity." He shrugged and gave me a self-conscious half-smile. "Do you realize my new job comes with the license to carry a concealed firearm? I could be packing a Glock, sitting here eating eggs. That's the opposite of poetry." He set his mug down with a thump. "Fuck it," he said, standing. "I gotta go get some bad guys."

We paid, headed out to the street, and parted ways. I looked up the sidewalk, the way the soldier with the rifle had gone, as though he might have left some sort of trail through the storm.

**

Upon returning from my mom's the previous night my only plan had been to drag myself upstairs and fall straight into bed, so I'd left the box sitting in my car's back seat. When the cab dropped me off after my breakfast with Leonard I trotted across the street to retrieve it. The inside of my car was beginning to smell like a goldfish bowl. I pulled the box out, slammed the door, and hurried through the rain, trying to shield the box beneath me. Eva wasn't on the couch. After shrugging off my raincoat I cleared a spot on the coffee table for the box, sat down in front of it, and pulled the flaps open. On top of the pile was a faded red folder full of drawings. In bright crayon outlines, dinosaurs fought one another; a caveman battled a giant gorilla; spacemen with laser guns dueled with aliens.

Eva emerged from the hallway and circled around to the other end of the couch. She didn't look at me. "So I read those pages," she said.

Beneath the folder of drawings lay my collection of old greeting cards. I opened the first couple and then scooped the rest out and piled them on the floor. "So?" I said. "Do you have a reaction?" Another red folder appeared beneath the greeting cards. I opened it up to find my mazes. As a fourth-grader, I'd been able to sit for hours with my mechanical pencils and a drafting kit I'd gotten for Christmas, devising intricate and dense mazes. I would carefully ink them and then I would refuse to let anybody deface them. They had been sitting in my folder ever since, unsolved.

"No," Eva said, quietly. She was sitting very still, her hands folded in her lap. A twitch, nearly imperceptible, rippled across her mouth, and then touched the corner of her eye.

"No?" I said. "No what?" I spread a few of the mazes out on the table. I'd spent hours on each one, and they were beautiful. Nothing I'd done since had been as artful, or exhibited as much focus or determination. Maybe I'd reached the height of my artistic powers as a ten-year-old.

"No, I don't have a reaction."

"What does that mean? Of course you do."

She took a deep breath. "They were okay."

"Okay? That's it? What about the story? You don't have a new round of accusations for me? Predictions? Aren't I still stealing your story?"

Eva grimaced. She picked up one of the mazes and began to rotate it, as though searching for the top. "When do you think you're going to write some more?" she said, after a time.

"You have nothing else to offer at all? Just 'okay,' and that's it?" She continued to spin the maze on her lap. "It doesn't matter how you look at it," I said. "You go in one end and you find a way to come out the other end. It's the same problem, no matter which way you want to turn it."

"I don't think so," she said.

"Haven't you ever seen a maze before?"

She traced her finger back and forth across the lines of the maze. "So if you're not a historian, that means I have to figure something else out."

"Why won't you talk to me about those pages?"

She tossed the maze back on the table. "We need to go see the mahjong ladies," she said. She sank back into the couch and closed her eyes.

"Who?"

"The mahjong ladies," she said. "They'll know what to do."

"About what?"

She waved her hand in a way that took in not just the stack of mazes, but me, and my apartment, and everything in it.

"About what?" I said again. But she wouldn't say anything else.

四

The rain worsens as Li-Yu, Henry, and Rose join the main road and follow it away from the river, along the narrow strip of unculti-vated land that separates the large, open paddies of the valley's floor from the terraced paddies of the hills. Li-Yu can't help but marvel at the evident transformation—every bit of land everywhere, up to the steepest flanks of the hills, has been flattened, walled off, waterproofed, irrigated. It is the sort of work that can only be done over the course of generations, with a single-mindedness that passes from parents to children in a steady unbroken stream. Despite her misery in Xinhui, Li-Yu finds herself curious about the spring plant-ing, and the growth that will follow.

They make slow progress now—the roads are marred from the hoof prints of oxen and the wheels of oxcarts, and wide puddles force them to weave back and forth. There is other traffic: Boys walk in their same direction, nearly all of them, Li-Yu notes, accom-panied by their mothers. Farmers circulate among the fallow rice paddies. Oxcarts trundle past, their woodwork creaking, the oxen breathing and emitting soft grunts.

She has not left the village since their arrival, and to Li-Yu there is something secret and ominous about the terrain. When they have walked a mile or so the road splits. One lane continues around the edge of the valley floor but the other rises up the hillside, climbing toward a saddle in the ridge. They have been told that it's a fifteen-minute climb to the ridge, and then another twenty minutes into Jianghai, the nearest village large enough to have a school. The road narrows as it rises and Henry and Rose slow their pace a bit. Other children overtake them easily, catching them with quick sideways glances as they pass. Some of them carry umbrellas.

A half-hour passes before they attain the ridge, which is wrapped in clouds. The mists close in around them and the paddies below disappear. The trail levels out for a time, and just when it begins to descend they come upon a group of three men, each of them walking with the slow, lilting gait of sleepwalkers. Rifles hang from the hunched shoulders of the first two, and their heads are down. Their uniforms are mismatched and dirty. The third, an older man, trails a bit behind them. The other children pass the men quickly, without a glance, but Henry and Rose cannot help but stare as they pull even with the last man. He looks down, sees Henry, and smiles so broadly it startles Li-Yu. Nobody has smiled at any of them that way in weeks.

"You look just like my littlest grandson," the man says.

Henry smiles back. Rose is immediately warmed by this flash of friendliness, and speaks. "Where are you going?" she asks.

The man shrugs, but his smile does not wane. "That way," he says, nodding toward the road ahead of them.

"Are you going to a war?" Henry asks, looking at the rifles. It is unlike her children to be so outgoing with strangers, but Li-Yu can see why. His smile has the same shape and warmth as their grand-father's, back in California.

He thinks before answering. "There are some men doing bad things," he says. "We're on our way to ask them to stop."

"What are they doing?" Rose asks. "Where are they?"

"Lucky for you, and unlucky for us, they are far, far away," the soldier says.

"Why don't you have a gun?" Henry asks.

"We don't have enough!" he says, his smile still broad. "But that's okay. I have a different job."

"What is your job?" Rose asks.

He points to the men ahead of them. "They don't know where they're going," he whispers, with a wink. "They need someone to show them the way."

"Really?" Henry asks.

"Yes, really. Funny, isn't it! But what about you? Where are you going?"

"I'm going to school," Henry says.

"Ah, I have something for you, then," the man says. He reaches into his jacket. Henry's eyes widen.

"It can't get wet, though," the soldier says, "so when I give it to you, you need to quickly put it somewhere dry. Are you ready?"

Henry nods. He has been holding Li-Yu's hand, but now he releases it, readying himself. The soldier produces a book with a tattered red cover. He thumbs through it quickly, rips out a page, folds it in half, and hands it to Henry.

"Quickly now, inside your jacket," he says. "Poems need to be kept warm and safe."

Henry stuffs the page through one of the openings between his coat buttons and then takes his mother's hand back. He beams up at the soldier. "Do you have one for Rose, too?" he asks.

"Of course I do," says the man, studying her with a look of exaggerated thoughtfulness, "but this one is a little trickier." He thumbs through the book again, glancing back and forth from Rose to the pages, his eyes bright. Eventually he slaps a page with his palm. "Perfect," he murmurs. He rips another page free of the book and passes it to her. "Keep it dry, now," he says. "Don't let the words wash away."

His companions have stopped by the side of the road and are now hunting through their pockets as they wait for him. "It must be breakfast time," the man says. He squats down in front of Rose and Henry and looks at them earnestly. "You be good now," he says. "Make your mother proud."

They thank him and tell him goodbye and continue their descent. Soon they emerge from the mists and a new valley appears beneath them. Its floor and foothills are covered with a patchwork of rice paddies and terraces, just as in their own valley. In its center sits a village, three times the size of Xinhui. It takes them twenty minutes to make their way down the hill, through the paddies, and into the village's outskirts.

Although the houses here are also made of mud bricks, they are larger than the homes in Xinhui. Women lean from their front windows, calling out menus or the names of things for sale. Small clusters of shops and restaurants sit on the corners. Li-Yu, Rose, and Henry follow the other children into the heart of town.

The school is made of concrete blocks, its roof corrugated tin panels that sound like drums in the rain. Children file through the door, quietly and with purpose. Henry releases Li-Yu's hand and latches on to her leg. He buries his face into her side. "I don't want to go, Mommy," he says, in English, his voice muffled.

"You must," she says, in Cantonese. She pries his arms from her legs, hugs him briefly, and then hands him the cloth bundle of paper and pencils. "No more of this. Your sister and I will be here when you are finished. Now go."

He turns from Li-Yu but he does not head for the door. Instead he goes to his sister. Desperation covers his face. He takes her hand. "Come with me," he says. Li-Yu is about to step toward him, but something in Rose's expression stops her. Rose puts her hands on her brother's shoulders.

"Listen, Spider," she says, in English. It is a nickname she gave him when he was first learning to crawl, a name she called him in a different time, a different place, and the sound of the word sends a shock through Li-Yu. When the impact of it clears she finds in its place a sudden catalog of memories. She sees her two children sitting in the room they shared in their little wooden house in Stockton, playing quietly on the faded blue rug, motes of dust dancing in the sunbeams. She smells the wood baking in the heat and hears the creak of the planks as the children pad about the rooms, exchanging one toy for another, making messes. She hears Bing's voice echo through the house, recounting stories of things that happened at the store that day—a winning lottery ticket he sold, perhaps, or some neighborhood gossip. She hears the sounds of gleaming cars passing by, and sees the way the light inside the house changes as the cars' reflections dart across the walls. When she returns to the rain and the doorway of the little school, she is surprised to see that the nickname has inspired a sudden change in Henry, too. He is standing a little taller, and his shoulders are back. His face is calm. "They don't let girls go to school here," Rose is saying, "so you have to listen very carefully to everything they teach you, and remember it all, and you can tell it all to me on our walk back home. Okay? Promise me you'll do that." Henry nods. He looks down and seems to discover the cloth bundle of supplies in his hands. He pushes it into his sister's hands, turns, and runs into the building, ignoring Li-Yu's shouts.

* * *

I emerged from my room, vague thoughts of food on my mind. It had grown dark and rain assailed the windows. Eva was asleep on the couch, lying on her side, her face buried in the crease between the seat cushions and the back, her clasped hands sandwiched between her thighs. The volume was off, but the television had been left on, tuned to a newscast. A Cadillac slid sideways across a flooded intersection, its headlights sweeping uselessly across the storefront windows. I decided I wasn't that hungry.

I climbed into the shower and immediately heard the strange song of that violin again. I turned the water off and on, off and on, and the music fell away and returned, fell away and returned.

It had to be something in the pipes, I decided. I'd talk to the manager about it soon. I angled the stream out and over me so that it fell quietly against the far wall, and I crouched down, out of the water so I wouldn't hear the sound of it hitting me. I let it slant over me and I closed my eyes and listened as the music and the mist fell down around me.

***

It is late afternoon by the time they arrive back in Xinhui. Rose follows her mother and brother into the house, the prized bundle of paper and pencils hidden behind her back. She has learned how to stand behind things—other people, the pillars that support the house's joists, furniture—and so to be virtually invisible. She trails Li-Yu into the house, catches sight of Mae's face, and though she is cold and wet and tired, she stops and backpedals through the door. She pulls it shut behind her and she is alone on the stoop. Since that morning the rain has lessened, but large wet clumps of mist now drift back and forth through the village, like watchmen on patrol. She heads out into the road, looks one way, and then the other. There is nowhere for her to go in the village—everybody would notice a girl, especially her, walking alone. But she has to vanish, before the door swings open and her mother calls for her, or Mae shouts at her. She darts to the corner of the house and circles it, heading for the back reaches of the property. She runs down the length of the wall, across a small clearing, and past the servants' house. At the very back of the property, beneath the branches of two barren trees, there is a collection of sheds and small storage buildings. She ducks into the largest of the sheds and stops, her heartbeat sounding in her ears. It is dim and smells come to her before images can—first there is dirt, and then metal, and then the fainter scents of oil and rust. Her eyes adjust and the contents of the shed come into focus. There are bits of discarded furniture, too broken to mend, metal pails, stacks of wooden crates and lids. One corner has been reserved for tools. Here perhaps twenty long bamboo handles rest neatly, their top ends against the wall, their shafts lined up and parallel like the planks of a leaning section of fence. Rose hears footsteps approaching outside, through the mud, and she plunges into the triangular space between the handles and the wall. There is just enough room for her. The floor is hard-packed earth, but the roof and walls have been made well, and it is dry. Rose crawls into the corner of the room, far beneath the leaning handles, deep into the triangular fortress. She lies on the ground, trying to quiet her breath, listening. The footsteps continue past the shed without pausing at the door, but she stays there, curled up in the corner for several minutes, before sitting up.

Now she takes Henry's gift and slowly unties the knot, running her finger along a line of stitching as she lets the cords fall away. She pulls out a pencil and a piece of paper, carefully sets the bundle on the dirt floor, and glances around for something she can use as a surface. Within arm's reach is an old metal bucket, forgotten beneath the leaning bamboo handles. Rose pulls the bucket into her lap and settles the paper against it. There is already a curve to the paper, from the rolled bundle, and the sheet clings to the side of the bucket as though the two were made for each other.

It is the first time in weeks she's had a pencil in her hand, and with its tip poised over the clean white sheet, she finds herself stymied. Back home she might have casually filled the page with drawings of flowers or dolphins or practice signatures, or written a note for her mom or her brother, as she's done a thousand times before. But now paper is a rare and precious thing—there were only a few sheets in the bundle and she doesn't know when or how she'll get more. She sits there with the bucket on her lap for some time, the pencil poised, as images and ideas compete in her head. Finally she touches the tip to the very corner of the sheet and begins to write, in English, in the smallest script she can manage. There is a slight roughness to the bucket's metal, and she can feel it pulling the bits of gray from the tip of the pencil. It is a magical feeling. *It was after school one day when Dad first came home from the store and told us we were moving to China,* she writes. She continues, describing the days before the voyage, and the voyage itself, and the house where she is learning to disappear.

Just when it is getting too dark for her to write, she hears her brother's little voice, calling for her. He doesn't sound like he is far away. Leaving the paper curled against the bucket, Rose crawls back out of the fortress toward the door. Still on her knees, she pushes the door open and peeks out. Henry is peering around the corner of the main house, his brow wrinkled. He sees her right away and a wide smile breaks across his face. He runs to her and plunges into the shed.

"What are you doing in here?" he asks, looking past her, waiting for the shed's contents to take shape in the gloom.

"Down here," she says, and leads him back into the shelter of bamboo handles. He sits against the wall, his little hands on his knees, taking in the details of their new hiding place, his eyes bright and a smile growing on his face.

"I like it here," he whispers.

"Me too," Rose says.

"It smells good."

Rose nods.

"Does Mom know about it?" Henry asks.

"No."

"What about Mae?"

"I don't think so."

"The others?"

She shakes her head.

He beams. "So it's just yours?"

"Mine and yours," she says.

They are quiet for a minute. Henry spies the bucket and the sheet of paper. "What are you writing?" he asks.

"Our story," she says. "The story of how we came here."

"To the shed?"

"To China."

Henry nods. "There's more paper at school," he says. "I can get some if you need it."

Rose smiles. "Then I won't have to write so small," she says. Henry crawls over and peers at the sheet, one side of which is already covered in his sister's tiny handwriting. "Do you want me to read it to you?" she asks him.

Henry's face lights up, and Rose smiles. She remembers how much Henry loved their collection of books back in California. He would sit with them on the floor for hours. Rose pulls the sheet from the bucket and settles herself against the wall with her legs folded and her brother pressed closely to her side. It is too dark for her to make out the words now, though, so she begins to recite from memory. She tells him as much as she can remember before they hear their mother's voice calling for them. Rose retrieves the little bundle of supplies, slips the sheet back into it, and ties the cords. "We'll come back tomorrow," she whispers.

FIVE

"Hey Mr. Long," Kevin said to me, upon entering the classroom the following Monday. "Did you know it's been raining for fourteen days in a row?"

"No," I said, "but that sounds about right."

"It *is* right. I was wondering something. Where does all that water come from?"

"Duh," said Eliza. "The clouds."

"But how does it get into the clouds?"

"It evaporates from the ocean," Eliza said.

"Yeah, but what part?"

"All the parts. It doesn't matter."

"It does matter," he said. "We have all this extra water here, so that means somewhere, some fishies are missing a lot of their water."

"That's dumb," Eliza said.

"That's not how we respond to one another's ideas in this classroom," I said.

"The fishies don't think it's dumb," Kevin said, and stuck his tongue out at her.

The bell rang. I opened with a lesson on the word "myself." That morning I'd been watching the news in my apartment as I dressed, and an interviewee was talking about his flooded basement apartment. "And who lives there?" the reporter asked. "Myself and my roommate," was the answer. I cringed and vowed to bring up reflexive pronouns with my young language guardians that day. I ran through that and then during the first recess, with Franklin Nash entertaining my room-bound kids, I slipped out of my room and headed for the bathroom and the photocopier. Hanging from my shoulder was my bag, and inside it was my folder of mazes. With no possibilities for dodge ball in the local forecast, I needed all the indoor activities I could muster. The photocopier was churning out copies of my second original when Annabel appeared.

"So thanks for breaking my heart," she said. She lifted her bag onto a nearby table and patted it, as if it contained the broken pieces.

"I think it was you who turned down my dinner invitation," I said.

"That's right, I did, didn't I? Well, we're even, then." She pulled out a couple of books and laid them on the table. "I was referring to Li-Yu and her poor kids," she said. I must have looked startled, because she laughed, and then she said, "Are you that surprised to find you have readers?"

"I guess I am," I said. "I didn't know anybody read anymore. You really read that?"

"I can't believe you just dispatched Bing like that. I mean, sure, maybe he deserved it, but what a nightmare for Li-Yu and those kids. I'd ask you what happens next, but I'm sure you wouldn't tell me, and I think I'd be disappointed if you did anyway." She continued to talk about the story, but suddenly I couldn't understand what she was saying. Something was wrong; something wasn't fitting together. And then I realized—I hadn't submitted that installment yet. The first draft was still sitting in its folder on my computer. And then I thought of Eva, sitting at my desk and reading my story. On my laptop where my e-mail program resided, perpetually open and active.

Annabel had finished talking, and was now looking at me, expectantly. I think she had just asked a question.

"Sorry, what did you say?" I said.

"Autographs," she said.

"Where did you get these?"

"Franklin told me to be on the lookout for them," she said, handing a pair of journals to me. "He said you'd be too modest to mention them yourself. Everything okay?"

On one, the familiar girl with the empty face stared at me. The photograph on the other journal was a shot of a gray tombstone on an overcast day, black Chinese characters carved deep into the stone. Some flowers, drained of their colors, wilted in an attached glass vase half-full of black water. I opened it to the table of contents. There were a handful of poems, as in the first journal. There was an excerpt from someone's memoir. And there was the second chapter of my story. I flipped to it and skimmed. It was exactly as I'd written it.

"I hope you won't mind if I comment on your bio," Annabel said, "but I'm not sure if coy is your thing."

I hadn't sent them a bio. They had never asked for one. I'd never heard anything from them at all. I fanned through the journal and found a listing of contributors and their bios on the final page. Mine read: "Peregrine Long might be a San Francisco writer."

"Can I borrow this?" I said.

* * *

Immediately after the last bell rang I vacated my classroom, bypassing with mumbled apologies three or four parents who were hoping to have a word with me, and trotted home through the storm. Eva was sitting at my desk, at my computer. The lights were off and the glow from the monitor made her look ghostly.

"Not exactly the patient type, are you?" I said.

"What's that?"

I flicked on the light and crossed the room. "So this came to my attention today," I said. I tossed the second copy of *The Barbary Quarterly* onto the desk. It slid past a bowl, which contained a half-eaten baked potato, and bumped into her elbow.

She looked at it for some time, and then traced the characters on the tombstone with the tip of her finger. "I thought quarterly meant once every three months," she said.

"Good point," I said, "but that's not what I meant." I retrieved the journal and thumbed through the pages, searching for my story.

She picked up her dish with the potato and held it in a cupped hand, under her chin like a rice bowl. "What's this about patience, now?" she said.

I found my story, bent the spine back so it would stay open, and dropped it in front of her. "This," I said. "I don't get it."

"What are you talking about?" she said, prying loose a chunk of potato, rather casually I thought. "You don't get what?"

"Why you would send this in! Despite our arrangement, there are some boundaries here, you know."

"I didn't send anything anywhere," she said. She shook salt into her potato, sniffed it, gave it another dash. "Why would I do that?"

"I need to see that," I said, pointing to my computer.

"It's yours," she said. "You don't need my permission."

I pulled my laptop out from under her and took it to the couch. She'd been browsing through a page of obituaries. I hid her window, found my e-mail program, and steered the arrow toward the sent mail folder. There was nothing with the journal's address from the last couple of days. When had I written that chapter, exactly? Wednesday night? Thursday? What was today's date? I looked around for the flier, but it wasn't on my desk where I'd left it. I scrolled back through the previous week's e-mails but I didn't see anything.

"So you're accusing me of what, exactly?" Eva asked, jabbing her fork back into her potato.

I kept searching. There was my first submission—nothing besides that. This wasn't making any sense, and I said so. Eva didn't respond. She watched me, the sound of her chewing suddenly obnoxious, too noisy. Where was that flier? I looked under the desk, and then under the table. Had I put it away somewhere? I searched the coffee table, the shelves, any obvious place I might have set it in an absentminded moment. I looked through my desk drawers and found nothing; an Internet search was equally fruitless. I even called 411, something I hadn't done in years. I was a little surprised when someone answered. The operator made small talk about the weather as she searched her system. I got the feeling she hadn't spoken to anyone in a while. But she couldn't give me information on *The Barbary Quarterly*, either. I reached for my phone and scrolled to Franklin Nash's name.

Eva appeared in the kitchen doorway. "I have a theory," she said. I held up my hand, pointed at the phone. Franklin answered on the second ring.

"Peregrine!" he said. "How can I help you?"

"That flier you gave me, for *The Barbary Quarterly*. Where did you say you found it?"

"Pier 23. I'm enjoying your story, by the way. I'm sorry I haven't had the opportunity to mention it to you yet."

"Thank you," I said. "What, was it sitting on the bar or something?"

"No, not at the restaurant. Next door, just near the entrance to the warehouse. Tacked to a bulletin board."

"You were at the warehouse?" I said.

"Passing by," he said. "My eyes are always open."

I thanked him, hung up, and checked the time. It wasn't quite four o'clock. Pier 23 wasn't far—maybe a five-minute drive. It was a long shot, but it was all I had. Eva watched me don my raincoat. "You're going somewhere?" she said.

"Looking for something," I said.

Outside the rain hammered on the sidewalk, the parked cars, the mailboxes and the leafless trees. I drove through it and tried to figure out how things would end with Eva. What would she do when I failed to conjure her uncle Henry from out of my pages? Would I eventually just make something up about him? Would she believe me, and just go away? I didn't think so. She had a shitty poker face and her reaction to my last batch of pages told me she knew a lot more than she was admitting. I wasn't going to be able to just write a chapter about how he'd run away to join the circus and lived happily ever after.

I made my way to Bay Street and headed east. Wide brown rivers littered with flotsam churned through the gutters. The road dropped out of the hills and into the city's flat skirt where ponds stood in the intersections, their surfaces riotous. On the Embarcadero, rush hour traffic inched through the rain. A street car clattered down the median, its steel wheels hissing on the wet tracks. I found a parking spot a block from Pier 23 and crossed over to the wide sidewalk that ran along the boulevard's outer edge. On sunny weekends it would have been clogged by joggers, strollers, tourists on bicycle taxis, but today it was barren. The huge warehouse door at Pier 23 was open, but it was quiet inside. Spheres of yellow tungsten light shrank and dulled as they receded into the building's cavernous depths, where endless rows of loaded pallets towered two and three stories high.

The bulletin board was on the wall, on the far side of the doorway. Tacked to it was a flier identical to the one Franklin had brought me, a single pin stuck through it, yellow dye bleeding from its bottom edge and streaking down the cork board. It was barely legible, but I could just make out an address—1326 Grant Street. The flier would have turned to mush in my pocket so I committed the address to memory and then, without really planning to, I stepped into the dark warehouse. In its front corner stood a two-story structure made of modified, stacked shipping containers that looked as though they might house offices. Its door stood open and a weak light leaked out of the windows along the top level. From somewhere inside the building came the sound of chair legs scraping on a floor. I stopped and strained to listen, but no other sounds came to me. I stepped through the door, hoping I might find someone who knew about the flier. Just enough light trickled down the stairway to reveal an office that looked like any other warehouse office might—a scuffed linoleum floor, desks covered in papers, clipboards hanging from screws in the walls, shelves full of binders with printed spines, a layer of grime over all of it. With my heart rate rising and my breath held, I circled around the room, looking things over, reading labels, looking at the headings on papers.

There was one computer in the office, circles of dirt in the indentations of its keys. The clipboards held documents for shipping and receiving—signatures, dates and times, weights, quantities, origins and destinations. On the wall hung a calendar that featured women in bikinis and power tools. There was no reference to the *Quarterly* anywhere.

I headed for a stairway, where a once-red strip of carpet ran up the middle of the plywood stairs, its center blackened by traffic, its edges the color of wine. It was strangely silent—the traffic outside, the streetcars, even the rain had quieted. I began to doubt I'd heard the scraping of that chair. I climbed slowly and at the top I turned and entered a long dim hallway whose sides were lined with doorways, all closed but for the last one. I approached, straining to catch sounds, and leaned into the weak yellow light. I caught a taste of machine oil.

It was a workshop, far larger than I expected, and it looked as though it had been brought there from an earlier century. Squat low machines of greased steel filled the bulk of the room, bristling with cogs and levers and rollers and spindles. Everywhere around them stood wooden tables, holding wooden racks and boxes, all of them stained black. Against a back wall leaned wide long rolls of paper, and when I noticed the arrangements of carved metal letters laid out in the racks on the tables I realized it was a printing press—over a hundred years old, I guessed, but evidently still in use.

Only then did I see the women. There were four of them, hunched over a square table in the dark far corner of the room, studying something by the light of a small fixture on the wall above them. They brought their hands together in the middle of the table and a soft clattering sound, like rocks tumbling beneath the recession of a wave, rolled toward me. It was the mixing of mahjong tiles, a sound I'd heard in the parks and cafés in and around Chinatown.

And then the ring of my cell phone burst into their room with a clang like a fire alarm. The heads of the four women snapped up and around and centered on me. We stared at each other, all of us motionless. My phone rang again, and I slapped a hand over it, as if I might hide the sound. And then I realized what I was seeing. The women's faces—all four of them—were identical. I turned and ran back to the stairway.

***

"Eva," I shouted when I burst through the door, "the mahjong players. Who are they?"

She'd been watching television, and now she looked at me over the tops of her glasses. "What?" she said. She lifted her arm and clicked through a couple of channels.

"The mahjong ladies. You mentioned them yesterday."

"I think that was on Saturday."

"Fine. Who are they?"

"Why is your face all red?" she asked.

"I'm fine," I said. "Are they related?"

"To whom?"

"To each other."

"No. Why?"

"They aren't sisters or anything? Where do they play their games?"

"Chinatown. Where else?"

"Not at the piers?"

"Why would you play mahjong at the piers?"

"Do they run an old printing press or something?"

"Certainly not," she said. "What gave you that idea?"

"You said they'd know what to do. Or something like that. I need you to take me to them. Would you do that, please?"

"I can't," she said. "They're out of town."

"Maybe they're back," I said. "I really think we should go to see them."

"They aren't back. They're on a cruise. They're somewhere in the Caribbean right now."

"Why did you bring them up? Why did you think they could help?"

She shrugged. "They speak Chinese. That's all."

"Why do we need someone who speaks Chinese?" I said.

She lifted the remote again and clicked through another couple of channels. Canned laughter leaked through the speakers. "I thought they could come in handy at some point, that's all," she said.

I attempted a deep breath. "Okay, we'll look into these mah-jong ladies later," I said. "But for now I've got a place in Chinatown I need to visit." I checked my memory and was glad to find the *Quarterly's* address still there. "Actually, I'd appreciate it if you'd come." I wasn't entirely sure why I'd asked for her help. Maybe I needed an objective third party. A touchstone.

"No thanks," she said, pointing through the window at the storm outside and turning her attention back to the television. "This weather isn't fit for a lady. Maybe next time."

Parking in Chinatown was always a nightmare so I walked. Despite the rain the sidewalks there were jammed with people. Women rattled along with little metal carts, their heads wrapped in clear plastic bonnets, oblivious to the downpour. Vendors and soaking wet deliverymen barked at one another in Cantonese. The wind and rain had not managed to wash out the smell of rotting fruit and offal from restaurant kitchens.

The 1300 block of Grant Street was just south of Pine. I slowed my pace and searched the busy storefronts for addresses, avoiding the sidewalk invasions of plastic-draped bins full of odd vegetables and embroidered slippers. The rib of someone's umbrella jabbed me in the back of the head and a rivulet of water slid over my collar and down my back. Few of the buildings had visible addresses, but 1326 was clearly marked by black numbers, nailed against a dirty white wall, right above the doorway. Above the address were the words "Yung Hee Seafood Company," in red. I stepped inside. It was dark and cool, and quiet but for the sound of bubbling water in the acrylic tanks of live fish, which covered one wall, and stretched deep into the shop.

A man stood at the counter, flipping through receipts. "Excuse me," I said, already knowing how he'd respond. "I'm looking for the offices of *The Barbary Quarterly?*"

He squinted at me and tried to repeat what I'd said, destroying the *r*'s and the *l*.

"Yes," I said.

He shrugged.

"It's a journal," I said. "Like a magazine."

"Fish only," he said.

"Is there an office here? Upstairs, maybe? Downstairs?"

"Fish upstairs, fish downstairs, fish only," he said.

"Okay," I said. "Somewhere close by, maybe? Offices? A publisher?"

He shrugged and gestured toward the wall of tanks, as if to provide the visual equivalent of his "fish only" message. And then the voice of that strange violin came drifting down to me. My head jerked up and I searched the ceiling for speakers. "That music," I said. "What is it?"

He shrugged again.

"The music," I said, my voice a little louder than I'd intended. I couldn't see any speakers. "It sounds like some sort of violin. What is it? Do you have a radio on?"

He was squinting at me again. "Music?" he said. He shook his head. "No music. Just fish."

"No, the music you have playing," I said. "I don't want to buy it. What's the name of it? The name?"

"No music," he said again.

I took a deep breath and looked hard at him. He looked genuinely perplexed. Perplexed and uncomfortable. He'd stopped searching through his receipts and his hands had disappeared beneath the counter. I took a deep breath and spoke slowly. "I hear violin music," I said. "Do you?"

He craned his neck, turned his head one way and then the other, and then shook it. "No," he said. "Sorry." The look on his face was one of pity.

**

By the time I reached my block I was soaked through and chilled to the core. Through the smell of rain I caught the scent of coffee and I pushed through the door of Ike's corner store to find he'd just brewed a fresh pot. His lights were bright and he had his heater cranked up, and though most of me was buried beneath too many layers of wet clothing to feel it, the warmth broke across my face like a wave. He gave me a little nod without smiling and went back to flipping through the pages of a magazine. At his self-service coffee station I filled the largest of his cups and fixed the lid over the top. I took a sip and felt the bolt of heat fall down my throat and into my belly, where I imagined it glowing. I walked to the counter.

"Buck seventy-five," he said, needlessly, pushing the magazine aside. I extracted a pair of damp dollar bills from my wallet. Just as he tucked them into the register the power went out. Complete blackness took over the room; the compressors and fans of his refrigerators fell silent. "Ain't that a bitch," he said, his voice a growl. He chuckled. "Should have seen that coming, I suppose." I heard the small tinkle of coins and the scrape of one of them against the plastic of his till. "Hold out your hand," he said. I reached cautiously into the darkness between us. With one of his hands he found the back of mine. I could feel his calluses and cracks against my knuckles. He put a quarter in my palm, and when he felt me close my fingers over it, he let it go.

* * *

I walked back outside into darkness so complete it was palpable. I groped my way up the street, swinging an arm back and forth in front of me, hoping for a pair of headlights to sweep through and illuminate the block. Every step I took was a small panic, and I began to realize what it is about the darkness we find so terrifying. Our fears—muggers, wolves, public speaking—all remain at bay in the light, because we have our eyes to tell us they aren't there. Without sight there is only faith, which wavers easily, and when it does our imagination surrounds us with criminals and carnivores, the expectant eyes of a waiting crowd of strangers. For me the fear is falling. I know of no particular incidents or threats that should have led me to this, but as a boy I lost great amounts of sleep because of that feeling, in the first moments of sleep, when a dream, just underway, seems to lose its flooring, and drops the dreamer back into bed, his heart pounding, his eyes wide. Some nights I was knocked back and forth between dreams and my mattress four or five times, disoriented and nauseous, my pillowcase souring with sweat.

That night as I groped my way home each concrete square of sidewalk had been replaced with a deep hole, and it was only the taste of my coffee that kept me connected enough with my neighborhood to keep my feet moving forward. Somehow the holes all managed to close up just before I fell into them.

I made it to my door and felt my way up through four flights of stairs and down the hallway to my door. Inside I groped through gloom for an open spot on my bookshelf for my coffee cup. I pulled off my raincoat and headed to the kitchen, where there was a drawer with a flashlight and a couple of candles.

"So you know about the Northern Expedition?" Eva asked, from somewhere in the darkness, perhaps the couch.

I lit a candle and put it on my desk. She was indeed on the couch, a blanket pulled up to her chin. "What's that?" I asked. I sat down and went to work on the wet knots of my shoelaces. Rainwater dripped from the cuffs of my pants and pooled on the floor.

"Those soldiers. They were in the service of Chiang Kai-shek, marching north to fight the warlords. So that's why they were on the road that day, with Li-Yu and Henry and Rose," she said.

"Okay," I said. In the gloom I couldn't see enough to get my shoes untied, so I pulled out my cell phone to use its light. My sister's name was on the screen. I'd missed her call—she'd been the call that interrupted the mahjong game.

"You can look it up. It was one of the biggest military campaigns in history."

"Okay," I said. I finished one shoe and moved to the other. I wasn't in the mood to discuss irrelevant story details with Eva. I now had the phantom violin music swirling in my head along with the mahjong players and their anachronistic workshop. "But they're just extras," I said. "It doesn't matter where they're going, or why."

"It matters," she said. "It matters a lot."

"I just wanted to bring the poems into it," I said. "They could have come from a farmer, or a vendor, or Henry's teacher, or anyone else."

"But they didn't," Eva said. "They came from the soldier."

"Yes. Because the other day I saw a Chinese actor downtown dressed as a soldier."

There was a soft thump from Eva's direction; it sounded like she'd banged her leg on the coffee table. I waited for her to yelp or grunt but there was only her breathing, which seemed suddenly loud in the darkness.

"An actor?" she said. "From which play?"

"I don't know," I said. I dropped the shoes next to the raincoat and began working my arms out of my sweater.

"You didn't wonder?"

"Wonder what?"

"I'm not sure there are any plays running now that would feature Chinese soldiers."

"There is, because I saw him."

"You're sure about that?"

I ignored her question. This was getting tedious. My sweater fell to the pile and was soon followed by my socks. I headed for the hall closet, where I had two clean towels on the top shelf.

"I used to have the poem," she said.

"What poem?" I retrieved the towels, hung one in my bathroom, and stepped back into the living room, trying to mop the water out of my hair.

"The poem the soldier gave to my mom. To Rose. It was called 'Sighs of Autumn Rain.'"

"What do you mean, you had it? What does that mean?"

"The sheet. The page. The page the soldier tore out of his book for my mom on the first day she and my grandmother walked my uncle to school."

I tried to see her face, to read something sensible into her story, but the candle was behind her, illuminating only the hard thin edge of her brow and cheek. "So what happened to it, then. Where is it?"

"It's in a trunk," she said, "on the floor of my basement apartment, which is now flooded."

I wadded the wet towel and dropped it on the floor. "I don't suppose the trunk would be waterproof," I said.

"No."

I squinted again, but her silhouette was featureless, immobile.

五

That night, when her children are sleeping, Li-Yu sneaks across the room to the side of Rose's bed, finds the bundle of paper and pencils, and quietly unties the cord. She extracts a single sheet and a pencil, reties the bundle, and pads across the room to the doorway. In the hallway outside she finds just enough light to write. Holding the sheet against the wooden floor she addresses a letter to her sisters. Please help me, she writes. She tells them about Bing, about Xinhui and Mae and the house and the rice paddies and Rose and Henry and a bleak future that threatens to swallow them whole. I have nothing here, she writes. I have nothing and I hate it. Please help me. She folds the letter and hides it beneath her mattress, and in the morning before the children rise she takes it in both hands and approaches Mae's sofa with small steps and her head bowed.

"Mae," she says. "May I please have just a few coins?"

"Why? Everything you need is here in the house already."

Li-Yu holds up the sheet. "It's a letter for my sisters."

Mae holds out her hand. "Give it to me," she says.

Li-Yu hands it over, and Mae unfolds it. "Why don't you write in Chinese?" she asks.

"They do not read Chinese," Li-Yu says.

Mae snorts. "What does it say?"

"My father was ill when we left," Li-Yu says. "I am asking them how he is doing."

Mae looks over the letter. "What else?"

"I ask about them, and their husbands and their children."

Mae hands it back to Li-Yu, reaches into her robes, and produces a small silk purse. She unties the yellow threads, pulls out a coin, and drops it into Li-Yu's hand.

"This will be more than enough," she says.

Li-Yu closes her fingers over it. It is the first time she has touched money since she left California. "*Do je,*" she says, bowing. She walks back to her room, where Rose and Henry have begun stirring. Before entering, she refolds the letter and hides it in her robe so her children won't see it and ask questions, and force her to remind them of their aunts, and their grandparents, and the home they once had. She rouses them and sees them dressed, and after breakfast she takes Rose aside and leans in toward her ear.

"Rosie," she says, "I need you to stay home, just for today. I think someone has been going through our room while we've been gone, and I want you to stay home and keep an eye on things. But don't let anybody know what you're doing. Act normally, be nice to people. But keep an eye on everyone. Can you do that?" Rose furrows her brow and nods, and Li-Yu kisses her on the cheek. "You're a good girl," she says.

After taking Henry up and over the ridge and depositing him at the gate of his schoolyard, she finds her way back to a shop in the center of Jianghai where she had noticed a sign advertising postal services. She reads over the letter again, selects and carefully addresses an envelope, and then seals the letter inside. The clerk takes the letter and her coin with a smile and a bow of his head. He selects two smaller coins from a small purse, reaches out for Li-Yu's hand, and places the coins into her palm. Li-Yu hides them deep inside her clothes, in two different places so there will be no chance of them clinking together, and she hurries home. Mae calls to her when she comes through the door.

"Where is your change?" Mae asks, her hand outstretched.

"After the cost of the envelope and the postage, there wasn't any," Li-Yu says.

Mae's eyes flash. "There should have been."

"I'm sorry," Li-Yu says. "I do not know what things should cost here. I'm still learning these things."

Mae dismisses her with a wave of her hand. "Learn them faster," she says.

SIX

I remembered the stack of mazes the next day when Eliza Low approached me, her completed geography worksheet in hand, just five minutes after I'd passed it out. I'd been hoping the exercise would buy me at least twenty minutes. I was standing on my counter, taking down an alternating series of construction-paper Christmas trees and menorahs that had been hanging in a row across the tops of my rain-smeared windows. Somehow I'd gone through two weeks of school without noticing they were still up, despite the many minutes we'd all spent watching the storm through the glass.

"I'm done," she said, looking up at me. "Now what?"

I hopped down and pulled the stack of mazes out of a cabinet drawer. "Solve it in pencil first—if you can." I winked at her. "After that, go over it with something vivid, like a red marker. I'll hang it up there." I pointed to the tops of the newly cleared windows.

"Cool," she said.

On the schedule for that afternoon was our annual school-wide assembly about safety and emergency preparedness. I lined my students up at the door and led them through the breezeways, keeping toward the walls so they would be less tempted to dart into the rain or into the waterfalls that poured from the over-loaded gutters. By the time we arrived at the multipurpose room, a few hundred chattering, squirming students in damp clothes had already taken their places in the sea of folding chairs. The heat was up high and the room smelled like rainforests and mushrooms. We filed into our row and took our seats. Just as the program was beginning Annabel Nightingale appeared in the chair next to me.

"You came alone?" I asked her. "Where are your charges?"

"Kindergarten's still just a half-day," she said. "They don't schedule these with us in mind. Apparently little is expected of five-year-olds in times of emergency."

The stage curtains rustled and some poor bastard in a seal costume stepped through the opening and approached a microphone. This was Sammy the Safety Seal, who'd been making annual visits here ever since I could remember. "Are you kids ready to get excited about safety?" Sammy asked. They were indeed.

"And are you all ready to become badge-carrying members of the Sammy Seal Safety Squad?"

"*Sí, señor*," Annabel said under her breath.

"So you're here just for fun?" I said.

"I need to review," Annabel said. "I can never remember if it's duck and cover, or cover your ducks, or something else entirely."

The curtain opened to reveal the same five-foot-tall façade of a two-story house that Sammy had been hauling around for a decade. The house, which had turned from red to pink at some point, was equipped with dry ice and red lights for a fire simulation, and a vibrating motor for the earthquake demonstration. This year, a giant electric socket had joined Sammy's collection of props.

"I thought it was stop, drop, and roll," I said.

Sammy's trusty sidekick, Fireman Fred, stepped out from behind the house. He was starting to look a bit old, but he called out, "Hey there, Sammy! Who are all your friends?" with his usual gusto.

"So when were you planning to ask me out again?" Annabel said.

"These are the boys and girls of Russian Hill Elementary School," Sammy said. "Everybody say hello to Fireman Fred!" The kids said hello. Fred said hello back.

"Hopefully it will be just before you say yes," I said.

"Well, you're in luck," she said, looking at her watch. "I'm scheduled to say yes in about ten seconds."

"Do you kids know what firemen do?" Sammy asked.

Five hundred voices answered. Someone behind me said, "They drive red trucks."

"Will you have dinner with me this Saturday?" I asked Annabel. She gave me a half-smile. "Maybe," she said.

"Do they fire people?" Sammy asked. No, the students shouted. They did not. That's what bosses did.

"Ouch," I said. "Really?"

"It depends. But let's have coffee after school. Yes?"

"I'll take it," I said.

"I'll find you," she said, and stood up.

"Do they set things on fire?" Sammy asked. No, the students howled. That was absolutely crazy. It was just the opposite.

"Wait," I said to Annabel, "you're not going to know what to do if you catch fire."

"Have you been outside lately?" she asked. "Nothing is going to catch fire, ever again." She headed for the back of the room.

***

When school was over we walked down the hill to a nearby corner café, the edges of our umbrellas bumping together. We took our drinks to a corner table and shrugged off our bags. A picture window stretched across the café's front wall. Pedestrians hurried past, just a few feet away from us. Cars piled up at the light, waited, and then waded across the flooded intersection, clearing room for more to stop and wait, and wade again.

"So on what does dinner depend?" I said.

I expected I'd get one of her quick retorts, so I was surprised to see a wash of sadness fall across her face. She gave me a half-smile.

"Honestly?" she said. "It's going to sound strange, but it depends on the weather."

"The weather?"

"It's a long story," she said.

"I've got all afternoon," I said.

"It's longer than all afternoon," she said. She took a sip of her mocha. Whipped cream clung to her upper lip; she swept it off with her tongue. "Let's start with something a little lighter. We both have a story about being named for birds. You go first."

A woman led a miserable dog in a raincoat past our window. A Muni bus rumbled past, light pouring from its windows and water flying from its tires.

"About ten years before I was born, my mom had a late-term miscarriage," I said. "She was crushed, and she didn't get pregnant again for seven years. Things went well that time, and my sister was born. Nothing out of the ordinary happened. And then three years later she got pregnant with me. But this time she said she felt exactly like she'd felt the first time she'd been pregnant, when she miscarried. She said it was unmistakable." Outside the light was draining out of the sky. The intersection was thickening with commute traffic. "She figured she'd already been pregnant with me. That I hadn't been ready the first time around, so I'd wandered off."

Annabel watched me over the rim of her glass. "Hence, Peregrine," she said.

"Hence," I said. "There's more. I was born on my brother's due date."

"Wow," she said. "What's your sister's name?"

"Lucy," I said. "My dad wanted to name me Linus. My mom prevailed."

She laughed. "You two would have had a great theme song," she said. "Okay. My turn. I'm a direct descendent of Florence Nightingale. She was my great-great-great-great-great grandmother." She shrugged. "That's it. It's much less interesting than your story." She sipped her mocha and watched the rain fall. The light turned green; a taxi driver honked at the car in front of him after waiting a half-second. "Ask me about my first name, though," she said, "and I'll try to redeem myself."

"Let's hear it," I said.

"There are four of us, all girls," she said. "Annabel, Bernice, Carla, and Delilah. In that order, of course. My parents had to be very organized."

"How far apart are you?"

"Forty-two minutes, from the oldest to the youngest."

"Quadruplets?"

"Indeed," she said.

"That's amazing," I said. "I ran into a set of quadruplets earlier this week, at Pier 23. Playing mahjong. What are the chances of that?"

"Zero percent," she said.

"I know, right? But I'm sure of it—four old Chinese ladies, playing mahjong, all identical."

Annabel shook her head. "No, I mean, literally. Zero percent possibility. There are two sets of us that include San Francisco residents: the Nightingales and the Malones, who are Irish men in their forties. They grew up in the Sunset."

"Maybe they were from somewhere else?" I said.

"There are fifteen sets in the Bay Area," she went on. "We keep pretty close tabs on one another. None of them are old Chinese ladies. The closest would be the Trans, but they're Vietnamese men, and one of them died last year."

"I'm telling you they were identical. I know what I saw," I said.

She backed off a fraction of an inch. "Okay," she said. "I suppose it could have happened. How old did you say they were?"

"Maybe they just weren't registered, or whatever," I said.

"There's a set of Chinese women from Orange County," she said. "They're in their thirties. Maybe they were up here for some reason? Where did you say you saw them?"

I took a sip of my coffee. "It doesn't matter," I said. "Forget it."
She shrugged. I wanted her to stop looking at me. I pretended to be
intent on something outside the window. Connections were forming
in my head, spurious and confusing. Eva had mentioned mahjong
ladies, and then I'd seen ladies playing mahjong, and they had been
identical, and now Annabel was sitting here telling me she was a qua-
druplet. It was like watching someone else's stream of consciousness.
I wondered what would be next. A flock of nightingales, perhaps,
flying through a rain of coffee.

"Are you feeling all right?" she said.

"It's been sort of a long week," I said.

She might have pointed out that it was only Tuesday, but she
didn't and I was grateful, but still I felt like I was blowing it with her.
Here I was complaining when she knew that a large chunk of my
workweek to that point had consisted of watching someone in a seal
costume bounce around on stage.

Suddenly the rain picked up. Long streaks of it shot down the
windowpane. On the sidewalk, the few passersby began running.

"You know, Saturday night will probably be fine," she said quietly. She reached out and wiped a few droplets of spilled coffee from
the table with her napkin, and then she turned her attention to the
sky and the street. Together we stared through the window for a
minute, and then another. I wondered what she was noticing, what
she was thinking. I wondered what she thought about me. I decided
that as long as she was willing to give me her Saturday night, she
could think whatever she wanted. Maybe she could even help me
figure out what I thought of myself.

"Can you believe this rain?" she said, after a time. "It's going to
wash us all away."

***

Annabel declined my offer of a ride so I saw her onto her bus and headed home. The YMCA sat midway between the café and my apartment, and as I approached it my thoughts of Annabel and the afternoon we'd shared were eclipsed by a sense of precariousness. I thought of the pool and imagined the ground was nothing more than a thin, brittle crust, and the planet was filled with dark water, and that it was only a matter of time before this storm broke through and sent us all down into that great round chasm. My heart fluttered and heat flashed across my palms. When I reached the Y, something pulled me through the doorway.

Doris was at her usual post. "It's empty in there," she said. "Everybody else is at home, trying to stay dry."

"I'll only be a second," I mumbled. "I think I left something."

She shrugged. "Take your time," she said.

I stood beneath the awning on the pool deck, my hands jammed into my pockets, listening to the rain hammer on the canvas above me, watching it drum the pool's surface into a thick layer of opaque movement. Inside me fear and attraction arose simultaneously and jostled each other for my attention, so that I fluctuated between a desire to leave and a desire to leap. I chose neither, continuing instead to stare at the water, trying to see through the froth.

Eventually my phone buzzed. A call had gone straight through to voice mail. My sister's message was brief: "Perry, it's Lucy. Fucking call me." I hit the call button, grateful for the intercession of something familiar. It would be good to have Lucy back in town. I hadn't seen her in probably a year and a half, not since she'd moved to New York with an aspiring chef named Greg who had a pierced eyebrow. She and I didn't speak too often, not because we didn't get along, or didn't have things to say to one another, but because neither of us really put forth much of an effort. She was busy, I assumed; she probably assumed the same thing about me.

As kids we'd played together while our parents worked. Usually we acted out scenarios she invented, cast, and directed. "Okay," she'd say. "First you'll be the bank teller and I'll be the robber, and then I'll say 'switch' and then you'll be the bank robber and I'll be the undercover policeman. Got it?" And I'd nod and then we'd act it out, often running through several takes until she was satisfied. I might be a prince one day, a Dalmatian the next, and then maybe a frog. Often my role was to be frozen or paralyzed or turned to stone. Many of the games included a prolonged scene of me being dead. "No, you're still dead," she'd say, while performing some complex series of wild gestures above me. "What are you doing?" I'd whisper. "You can't talk, you're dead!" she'd say, with a look that told me I was about to ruin any chance I had of being brought back to life. When I got older she allowed me a little input, so I became a bank teller with x-ray vision, or a prince who drove race cars. Even when she became a teenager and got her driver's license she'd still spend time with me. She'd take me to movies, or on late-night runs for french fries and milkshakes. Later I realized it was our father's death as much as anything that had created this closeness—we had a bond and an understanding that neither of us could replicate among our friends. After graduating from high school she had enrolled at Berkeley, so I was still able to see a lot of her, especially after she procured a fake ID for me. Since then, though, she'd been largely migratory, and spending time with her had taken on a fleeting quality, like seeing trees bloom, like watching the Olympics.

She picked up in the middle of the second ring. "Peregrine, what the hell?" she said. "I've been trying to get a hold of you for days now."

"You have?"

"You haven't gotten my messages?"

"I got the one today."

"What about the others?"

"I don't know. Maybe one. Things have been kind of weird here. Sorry—I've been meaning to call."

"What's weird?"

"What?"

"You said things have been weird. What's weird?"

"Well, there's this storm. More hectic than weird, I guess."

"You said weird. Weird isn't the same as hectic."

"So Mom said you're coming home for a bit?"

"Christ, Peregrine, what's with you?"

"Me? What's with you? You sound like you're freaking out a little bit."

"Shit, Perry, you don't even know the half of it. Things here are weird as can be, believe me. I can't wait to get the hell out of this city."

"What happened? Mom mentioned something, but I don't . . . ."

"Perry, I got fired again! I got fucking canned! Can you believe that?"

I could indeed believe it. It wasn't the first time, or the second, or even the third. The reported reasons varied, but they all basically amounted to the same thing: apathy. Failing to show up, chronic tardiness, rudeness. And I knew she didn't care much about the job she had held for the last few months, at the front desk of a plastic surgeon's clinic in Manhattan. I couldn't understand it. She was smart, and she could have done anything she wanted to—if there was such a thing. She'd had probably twenty different jobs in the last ten years, in twenty different fields.

"You're kidding," I said. "How come?"

"I'll tell you later," she said. "It's a long and sordid tale." She sounded a little out of breath, like she was walking somewhere, fast. From around her the sounds of the city seeped through the phone line—traffic, car horns, a blaring radio. "So what's been going on in good ol' San Fran?" she asked. "Man, I can't wait to get out there. It's going to be like a vacation in the countryside after this goddamn place."

"Not much," I said. "What happened with Greg?"

"We broke up a couple of months ago," she said. "He revealed himself to be a colossal prick. So listen. Can I stay with you? Mom says she doesn't have any room."

"Sure," I said. "It might be a little crowded though."

"How's that? You got somebody else staying there?"

"Yes, as a matter of fact . . . ."

"What, like a girl?" She sounded excited.

"No. A lady."

"Oh, well ex-cuse me. A lady? What is she, a goddamn duchess or something?"

"No, she's kind of old. It's a long story."

"You got an old lady roommate?"

"It's a long story."

"An old lady fetish?"

"Yes," I said. "That's it. I guess it's not a long story after all."

"Whatever," she said. "All I need is some floor space and occasional access to a shitter. So listen, I'll be there on Thursday. This Thursday. Two days hence. Can you come get me at the airport?"

"I'm a teacher, remember?" I said. "Thursdays are usually school days."

"I'm aware of your strenuous schedule," she said. "I get in at six or seven o'clock, I don't remember exactly. I'll let you know later, I gotta run. Sleep tight now."

She made a kissing sound and hung up. I pocketed my phone, took a final look at the pool, and headed for the door.

"Did you find what you were looking for?" Doris asked me on my way out.

"No," I said.

六

Li-Yu and Henry grow accustomed to the walk to Jianghai. At first, Rose accompanies them each day, but the following week she asks to remain at home, and by the end of the next month she is a rare companion on their trips. Li-Yu misses her company but reminds herself how important it is for Rose to find ways to sustain herself. She turns her attention to the walk with Henry. The hill that once left them short of breath seems to shorten, and they devise games to play along the way. They find faces in the bark of the trees along the ridge, and give them names, and devise stories to explain why one looks upset, and another happy, another frightened. They watch tiny wildflowers emerge from the grass and they notice when leaves appear on the branches. They begin to recognize the habits and patterns of the people of Jianghai—an old man who is always walking down the same alley, a woman with three missing teeth who always watches the street through her front window. Li-Yu drops Henry off, hurries back to Xinhui for the middle of the day, and then hurries back to pick him up, snacks hidden in her pockets. They walk slowly on their return to Xinhui. Henry tells her about his day in class, and Li-Yu tells him about her day at home with Rose.

The days grow longer and warmer and the hills flush bright green with grasses, which release their fragrance as the sun's heat steams the dew away. The rice seedlings in the planting beds reach knee height and the men of the house begin to talk about the task of sowing. A new sense of purpose falls over the village of Xinhui. The men unhook their plows from the water buffaloes and replace them with logs, which they drag sideways across the fields, smoothing out the bumps and filling the depressions.

"You have no idea how your back will hurt," Mae says to Rose one afternoon. Li-Yu hears this from around the hallway corner, just as she is about to enter. "Everybody with big feet like yours has to work all day long, and then it is all you can do to make it home to bed, only to rise and do it all again the next day." Li-Yu flushes with anger, and has to take a moment to compose herself before she can continue into the room.

"Do you know why Mae said you have big feet?" Li-Yu asks her daughter that night, when they are in their room, in bed. Beyond their whispers and Henry's soft breathing, all is quiet.

"Yes," Rose says.

"So you know you don't have big feet?" Li-Yu says.

"Yes," Rose says. There is a silence, and then Rose asks, "Why does she hate me?"

"She doesn't," Li-Yu says. "Some people are just unhappy."

"Well, I hate her," Rose says.

"Enough," Li-Yu says. "Come with me to take Henry to school tomorrow."

"Why?"

"I'll tell you later, after we drop Henry off."

The next morning, when her children are eating in the kitchen, Li-Yu darts back into their room and stretches across her bed. She reaches down beneath the bed frame and back up into a small hollow in the structure, where her fingers find a piece of fabric. She listens for sounds in the house, and then pulls the sock free. The coins hidden inside it rattle together but she closes the bundle in her hand and squeezes it, and listens again. She quickly pulls two coins from the sock, and then a third, and then returns the stash to its hiding place. She hides the coins in separate places inside her clothing, tight against her waist, and returns to the kitchen.

"Okay," Rose says, once she and Li-Yu have kissed Henry and watched him walk through the school's gates. "Why did you want me to come?"

"Close your eyes," Li-Yu says, "and turn around. No peeking." Rose complies, and Li-Yu extracts the coins. "Now, keeping your eyes closed, turn back around and open your hand." Rose's eyes snap open when she feels the metal in her palm, and Li-Yu has to stifle a laugh.

"Where . . ." Rose begins, but Li-Yu holds a finger to her lips, and then she takes her daughter's hand and leads her into the center of Jianghai. All night she struggled with the question of what she should tell Rose about the coins. Back home in California she never imagined that she might have to steal, but she feels no shame about it. The growing sock beneath her bed is the result of her patience and vigilance, and she is proud of it. She would love to tell Rose the true origin of the coins—dropped by one of the men during a drunken mahjong game, perhaps, or left on the table for just a few minutes by one of the maids after a shopping trip—and she promises herself that on the day they sail from China she will announce to both her children that their escape was financed by her willingness to lie, to cheat, to steal, to do anything that might bring them back home. But Rose can't know this yet. It will give her a glimmer of hope, and a glimmer would be too much. And while Li-Yu does not allow herself to fear the possibility of failure, she understands that this endeavor might take a very long time.

She doesn't know how much the passage back to California will cost for the three of them, but she knows where the money is kept in the house. When the maids are sent out to buy things, or when they return with change, Mae presides over their transactions with a red silk purse, which ties closed with a braided gold cord. The purse she keeps locked in a heavy lacquered cabinet of open woodwork in her bedroom. Mae doesn't know how much is in the purse. Li-Yu has seen her drop handfuls of coins into it without counting, and she has seen her hand money to the maids without keeping track of how much change she is due. There must be a good amount in the purse, Li-Yu figures. When Mae shifts the purse in her hands the coins make a sound like a small rainstorm.

Mae almost never leaves the house, but one day Li-Yu returned from taking Henry to school and found Mae had gone to visit a sick cousin. The men were in the fields, the maids in town. She sent Rose out on an invented errand and walked quietly into the front room, where she sat down and listened. When she was sure the house was empty she waited another ten minutes, and then another five, and then, with her heart thudding, she slipped into the back of the house and into Mae's room. She went straight to the cabinet and stood before it. It was taller than she, its wood dark and heavy. Through the open spaces of the cabinet's woodwork she could see the red purse, in the middle of the center shelf, red and round like a heart. She tugged at the cabinet door but it barely shook in its frame, and the lock made no sound. She orbited the cabinet, testing joints with her hands, feeling for weaknesses. There were none. She leaned into it and it seemed to push back. With a running start, she figured she might be able to move it a few inches. She sat down on the floor, crossed her legs, and frowned at it for several minutes before rising and slipping from the room.

Beyond the carelessness of the men and the occasional sloppiness of the maids there are few other sources for money, so the three coins she has selected for Rose today represent much work and diligence, but it is all worth it when they stop at the first stall they find and buy sticky pork buns. It has been weeks, months, since she has had the pleasure of buying a snack for her children. It was the dockside *congee* stand in Canton, she remembers, when they first landed, before Bing died, before Mae and China ensnared them.

They wander through town, eating and talking happily, looking through shop windows and exploring back alleys. They discover a small courtyard with a pond in it and they linger there, flicking pebbles into the water and watching the ducks paddle around. When they are hungry again they venture back into the alleys and find a restaurant where they order bowls of noodles in broth with bean curd and vegetables. They are the only women in the restaurant.

Occasionally Li-Yu's mind flits back to the house and the questions she will face when she comes back that evening with Henry and Rose. Why were you gone all day? What about Rose's chores? What about yours? Isn't she hungry? What kind of mother are you, who would keep your daughter from food, all day long? They will feign concern for Rose to make her look like a bad mother. We weren't hungry, Li-Yu will say.

Rose happily slurps the dregs of her soup from the side of her spoon. Li-Yu leans forward and places a hand on her daughter's shoulder. "Rosie," she says, her voice low enough so that nobody around them will hear her. Rose leans forward to receive the secret. Li-Yu points to the table. "Nobody can know about this," she says, in English. She hasn't spoken English to either of her children in weeks. "Not even Henry."

Rose nods, her eyes wide.

"I wasn't supposed to have those coins," Li-Yu says, switching back to Chinese. "But I wanted them to be for us. For you. Do you understand?"

Rose looks unsure, but she nods. Li-Yu hopes she won't ask any more questions. Rose has always taken an interest in the affairs of the adult world, and back in California she had liked to involve herself in conversations about auto repairs, the cost of groceries, local politics.

"Where did they come from?" Rose asks, true to form.

"I found them," Li-Yu says, wincing, knowing immediately that Rose won't believe her. "Here and there." She stands abruptly, hoping that will be the end of it.

"Why do they have to be a secret then?" Rose says as she stands, her voice rising above a whisper.

Li-Yu heads for the door with Rose right on her heels. Once they are outside, Li-Yu says, "Because Mae would have wanted me to give them to her. For the food and the clothes and things they buy for you and for Henry."

"They don't buy me anything," Rose says.

"That's why I wanted it to be for you," Li-Yu says. "Now that's enough questions. We have an afternoon to spend together, and we have some money left."

They wander into the maze of a shopping district where busy food stands and little businesses spill out of the front rooms of the small houses that form the sides of narrow, twisting alleys. They wander along slowly, enjoying the smells, examining the wares. Li-Yu sees many things she knows Rose would like, and she waits for her to ask for something, but she never does. It is as if her daughter has come to understand the worthlessness of everything here to them.

Just before it is time for them to collect Henry, a final shop catches Li-Yu's eye, not so much because of its goods but because of its proprietor. He stands still as a statue among tables heaped with miscellany, staring into the alleyway. There is nobody in his shop. Nailed to his door frame is a small sign, reading, "Things bought and sold." Li-Yu cannot help but slow down, and as she drifts past his shop she runs her eye over his wares. She realizes he is watching her. There is the slightest change in his face—a hint of a smile, maybe, or just the twitch of an eye. It is there and then just as quickly it is gone.

"Let's go in here," she says to Rose. The man smiles at her and bows as they enter. There are irregular patches of white hair on his cheeks and chin. Li-Yu nods to him. He clasps his hands behind his back and looks away, the smile lingering at the corners of his mouth. Li-Yu scans the piles on his tables. There are teapots and dishes, bamboo chopsticks, shoes, knives, and threshers for rice, most of them worn, some of them at the ends of their serviceable lives.

"Are you looking for something?" the man asks her, after a time.

Li-Yu shakes her head.

"Nothing you want? Nothing you need?"

Li-Yu shakes her head again and moves on to the next table, which contains a picked-over stock of gloves and used rubber boots. The clerk watches her.

"I buy things, too," he says. "Maybe you have some things to sell. I pay good prices." He nods and Li-Yu thinks she sees a wink.

Li-Yu thanks him and pulls Rose back out into the alleyways. On her way back to the main road she memorizes the route, taking special care to pick out markers from amid the noise of the crowded alleys—a faded red awning, a noodle stand. They collect Henry and hurry back to Xinhui.

SEVEN

"What's next month?" I asked my class the next morning.

"February," they said, in loose unison.

"Right," I said. "So when will it be Feb-you-ary?"

They looked around at one another, sensing the danger.

"Next month," answered a handful of the less wary.

"No," I said. "It will never, ever be Feb-you-ary, because there is no such thing. Next month will be . . ." Here I pointed at my mouth and drew out the syllables. "Feb-ru-ary. Say it."

They said it. "Now I'm going to come around and listen to each and every one of you," I said. "Pull out your homework and look it over while you await your turn. And if I hear any 'yous' in the middle of your Februarys, there will be no recess."

"We're not going to have recess anyway," Eliza said, pointing at the rain.

"Right," I said. "So let's not make it any worse."

She ignored me. "So is today Wed-nes-day?" she asked.

"No," I said. "Today is Wendz-day."

"Why?" she asked.

"Because yesterday was Tuesday," I said.

When I was halfway through my pronunciation inspection I heard the squeak and tromp of little rain boots in the hallway and I looked up to see Annabel leading her class toward the cafeteria. I hurried to the doorway. She gave her students a signal and they all stopped in their tracks, turned to their partners, and began playing pat-a-cake. Annabel came over to my side.

"We got flooded out again," she whispered. "We're on our way back to our class away from class."

"Bummer," I said. "We're still on for Saturday, right?"

"We are," she said.

"Good," I said, "I'll come get you."

"I live in the Outer Sunset," she said. "I'll come to you."

"We're in this neighborhood all week," I said. "I could use a change of scenery. I'll come out there. We can grab something on Ocean Avenue, maybe."

"Maybe we could meet there, then."

"It's not a big deal. It will probably be raining, and there's no need for us to be looking for two parking places on a Saturday night. I'm happy to come by and pick you up."

"I'd rather we just met there," she said. "Please." She gave me an unconvincing smile and I knew I'd strayed off some course whose delineations I couldn't see.

"Okay, sure." I said. "Whatever you want to do."

"Thanks," she said. She put a hand on my arm, guiding me back on course. "I'm looking forward to it." She returned to her spot at the head of her class, issued another wordless command, and her students followed her down the hall.

I returned to my February quiz; Kevin was next on my route. "Hey, Mr. Long," he said.

"Hey, Kevin," I said.

"It's been sixteen days in a row now. Do you think it will rain until Feb-ru-ary?"

"I hope not," I said. "Good job."

***

The next night I headed for the airport to collect my sister. Because of the weather her plane was two hours late, and because I failed to check her flight's status before I left home I had to spend the time on a bench just outside the passenger-only zone, watching people emerge from their respective gates, converge in the hallway, and stream toward baggage claim. Flights arrived from

Phoenix, from Austin, from Spokane, from Tulsa and Boise and Denver, and then finally from JFK.

She came down the hallway in a long white coat, her cheeks flushed, her black hair tied up in a bun, her gait a little unsteady. Her skin was paler than I'd seen it in a long time, drained of color by a northeastern winter.

"Perry!" she said. She threw her arms around me and kissed me on the cheek. I returned her tight hug. She smelled like a gin and tonic, and her face was cold.

"Look at you," she said, letting go, grinning, looking me up and down. "You're all freakin' skinny." She shifted a heavy purse from one shoulder to the other. "So I have a ton of crap to pick up. I hope you have room in your car." She made for the escalator that led down to the baggage claim carousels. Once aboard she pulled a little mirror out of her purse and checked herself. "Jesus, planes make a girl look like hell," she said. She snapped her head up. "What's with this crazy-ass weather, anyway?" I wasn't sure if I should answer or if it was a rhetorical question.

"Yeah, it's been crazy," I said, when she didn't veer immediately to another topic. "So how long will you be here?"

"Forever," she said. She snapped her mirror shut and dropped it back into her purse. "That's how long." She fished out a stick of gum and her cell phone.

"Seriously? You're back for good?" She was jabbing at buttons on her phone and though I think she intended to drop her gum wrapper into her purse, she missed and it landed on my step. I reached down and picked it up just as the escalator deposited us on the floor. The baggage claim area was cavernous, but most of the carousels lay still and empty in darkened sections of the room, like metal dragons asleep in their caves. Lucy shut her phone and squinted up at a monitor. "Number twelve," she read. She dropped her phone back into her bag. "Sorry," she said. "What did you ask me?"

"You're going to move back?"

She held her hands out, as if presenting herself. "Not going to," she said. "Am. Right now." She pointed at carousel number twelve. "See all those pink suitcases? Those are mine. And that's not even half of it." She glanced around at the faces in the room, as if searching for something. "I mean, what do I have to go back for? Greg is an asshole. My boss was an asshole. That whole city is an asshole." She shrugged. "I never belonged out there at all. Don't get me wrong; it's an amazing city. For like two weeks. And then you just want it all to shut the fuck up." She grabbed a stray luggage cart.

"I think you have to pay for those," I said. "That must belong to somebody."

"Help me out with these suitcases, would you?"

In all we packed six sizeable suitcases onto the luggage cart. It was a precarious stack, and I had to get low and lean hard into it to get the wheels moving. "You mentioned your boss," I said. "So what happened there?"

"That's a hell of a story, Perry. What did I tell you on the phone?"

"You said you got canned."

She was walking quickly through the corridor that led to the parking garage.

It was all I could do to keep up with her. There were a number of other travelers walking our direction, including a family of four with two little girls. I imagined one of them straying from her path and getting flattened by our cart.

"Did I tell you why I got canned?" Lucy asked.

"No."

"Stealing. I got canned for stealing."

Instantly I thought of Li-Yu, and the sock full of coins hidden beneath her bed. "You're kidding me," I said. "Why did they think you were stealing?" I asked.

She laughed. "Because I was robbing those fuckers blind."

We arrived at the elevator. "Fourth floor," I said. "You're kidding. Money?"

She hit the button. "Hell no," she said. "I told you about that plastic surgeon I was working for, right? Total douchebag. He kept trying to talk me into a titty job. Said he'd do it for free. And his practice was making ridiculous money, and meanwhile, there was this little clinic around the corner from our place in Washington Heights that always had about two dozen busted-up Dominicans lined up out the door."

We boarded the elevator and began to rise.

"So I started stealing supplies from the office. Everything I could carry. And I gave it all to the clinic by my house. I got away with it for about two months, and then one day my boss calls me in and says 'I know what you're doing,' and I say, 'okay,' and he says, 'so I should probably fire you, and then prosecute you.' And then he gives me this look that makes my skin crawl, Perry, it makes my skin crawl, and you know what comes next, right?"

The door slid open and I leaned into the cart again.

"He looks at me with this sicko grin and says, 'Maybe we can work something out, though,' and I don't even want to hear him say it, so I tell him I wouldn't touch his dick or any other part of him even if it would keep me off death row and I walked right out, but get this, Perry, I swiped a stethoscope right off his desk, right in front of his stupid face. Like he even needed it—he just kept it around for an excuse to touch his clients' tits a few extra times. So he tries to make a grab for it but I snatch it and jam out of his office. He catches up with me in reception and starts saying something about calling the police but I screamed at him, screamed at him, Perry, in front of everybody else in the office, that if he did I would hit him with the biggest sexual harassment suit he'd ever heard of, and how would his titty-building career work out for him once all of Manhattan knew he was a perv. And then I swiped the tape dispenser off the reception desk and got the hell out of there."

"Wow," I said. "That's insane." It wasn't, though, not really. Not for her. She was good for a couple scenes like that each year.

"Goddamn right," she said.

We arrived at the car and somehow I managed to pack all of her suitcases into it. There was a bag wedged behind my seat and I was uncomfortably close to the steering wheel but I figured I'd manage. I paid the parking attendant and drove out into the rain, and with the wipers on high I joined the cautious procession heading into the city.

Lucy cracked open her window just enough to let in the cool air. "That smell," she said, more to herself than to me. Some of the sharpness had come out of her voice. "It's been too long since I've seen this city," she said.

"Almost two years," I said.

"Has it really been that long?" She sniffed at the air again. "I wonder why I didn't miss it more," she said. She opened her window another fraction of an inch. "I should have. Hell of a storm, though," she said.

"Seventeen days straight," I said. "One of my students is keeping track."

"You know what I would love?" she said. "Some tacos. In New York all the Hispanics want to make you sandwiches."

I guided the Corolla into the Mission District. We found a parking spot on Valencia, ducked into the nearest taquería, and placed our orders.

"So what about you?" she said, once we'd taken seats. On the table between us sat a basket of chips, a small stone dish of tomatillo salsa, bottles of beer. "The other day you said things were weird."

"I said they were hectic," I said.

"But first you said weird," she said. "You changed it to hectic because you didn't want to explain 'weird' to me. But now here I am, and I'm calling you on it. Start with our old lady roommate, why don't you?"

The food came. Lucy dove in as if she hadn't eaten in a month. "Damn, you fuckers are good," she told her tacos.

"Her name is Eva Wong, and she thinks I know where her uncle is," I said.

Lucy raised an eyebrow. My own tacos went neglected as I talked about *The Barbary Quarterly* and Eva's arrival at my door. I told her an installment had appeared in print before I'd submitted it. I told her about my futile expedition to Pier 23, and my encounter with the quadruplets. She grew more and more rapt. She stopped eating. At one point she stopped me with uncharacteristic politeness, returned to the counter, and bought two more beers. I told her about Annabel, and how I'd learned that the quadruplets could not have existed. But I couldn't bring myself to tell her about the pool at the Y, or the music of that strange violin.

When I finished she took a long swallow of beer. "You're right," she said, her voice not much more than a whisper. "That is weird." She took a bite of her last taco, chewing without interest, and dropped the rest back onto her plate.

"So I guess that's pretty much everything so far," I said. "But we're about to head back to see Eva, so who knows what might happen next."

"No," Lucy said, wiping her hands on her napkin. She drained the last of her beer and stood up. "It's not everything. I only told you half the story of why I left New York."

We walked back out into the rain. Next door there was an abandoned storefront; Lucy stopped just beneath its rotting awning. Its plate glass windows were covered in graffiti and old handbills and patched with duct tape. Deep inside the entrance, in front of the recessed door, lay a pair of sleeping lumps, stretched out on cardboard. She fumbled around inside her purse, eventually producing and lighting a cigarette.

"You smoke?" I asked. "Since when?"

She shook her head. "Almost never," she said. "Only when I need to." She took two or three long drags and then flicked it away just before climbing into the car. It hit the side of the nearest building, sparked, and died on the wet sidewalk.

"So what's the other half, then?" I said, pulling out onto Valencia.

She turned and stuffed her purse into the back seat with the rest of her luggage. "About a month ago I was on the subway," she said. "It's crowded, like usual. People are packed in everywhere, but a ways down I notice this old Chinese guy, dressed in the full Mao Tse-tung blue worker outfit, with that little hat, and he's looking at me. He gives me this big smile, and then this big wink, like he's some Asian leprechaun or something. And then he goes back to staring into space, like everybody else."

I could picture this man and his hat and his wink without effort. Maybe I was remembering an image from a picture, or maybe I was imagining him sitting in the shadows somewhere in Mae's vast house—an uncle, perhaps, silently watching Li-Yu and her children. Or perhaps his was one of the faces out on the road somewhere between Xinhui and Jianghai. I thought of the soldier's guide and his gifts of poems.

"I didn't think much of him at the time," Lucy said. "He's just a friendly old guy. Fine. Maybe I look like his granddaughter or something. No big deal. But then I see him again the next day, on the subway, in a totally different part of the city, at a totally different time. Exact same guy; I knew it because of this big mole he had on his cheek. And either he doesn't see me or he doesn't recognize me, but he makes no acknowledgement that I'm there."

I slid over to Franklin Street and stopped at a light. The raindrops on the windshield collected points of red light and held them a moment before the wipers slapped them away.

"And then, a couple of days later, I see him again. And then again. And then all of a sudden, this guy's everywhere. For the next couple of weeks, I swear to God, he was all over the place, this old Chinese guy, always wearing the same thing. On the trains, walking down the street, standing on the sidewalk. He's never with anybody, never really doing anything, just sort of staring, like he's lost. And he never sees me again."

I kept at the speed limit and made all the timed lights. The street grew steeper as we climbed Russian Hill.

"So it started to get pretty creepy, but coincidences happen, right? But then, Perry, I see him at a fucking Knicks game. Inside the goddamn Garden, Perry, by himself, just staring."

There was an open parking place on my block, just a couple of doors down from the building, and I gratefully angled the car into it. I killed the engine and the sound of the rain took over. Lucy took a deep breath. "So then I start to think that maybe this guy wasn't even real," she said. "Maybe I'm going nuts, and maybe he's not even real. Does that sound crazy?"

"You already heard my story," I said. I opened the door and plunged into the rain, pulling the first of her bags from the back seat.

"I felt like I was losing it, Perry," she called, shouting over the concussions of the rain on my car's roof. I unlocked the lobby door and we tossed her things into the entryway where they'd prop it open. We went back for more. "You've heard me mention my friend Angie, right?" she said, panting from the exertion. "Well, I told her about everything, and she decided she'd help me by getting me out of the city for the day." We finished emptying the back seat and went to work freeing her giant suitcases from the trunk. "So we took the train down to New Jersey and headed for the beach. We ended up in this little town that was all closed down for the winter. It was eerie. Nobody on the boardwalk, nobody anywhere. But it was great to be out of the city, and in the silence and clean air."

We were soaked by the time we'd herded her bags into the lobby. We dragged them to the elevator and I hit the button. The machinery rumbled to life. I wondered if it could handle us and our cargo.

"So we went for a walk along the water, and it was nice. I'd forgotten how the sea tasted and sounded. I started to feel sane again. And there was nobody, nobody at all around," Lucy said. "So Angie and I went walking up this beach, and we walked for probably a good couple of miles." The elevator door slid open and we piled her things inside. Her bags filled the floor space, so we climbed on top of them and sat. The car groaned and shuddered but lifted off and rose steadily. "So eventually I spot a guy up ahead of us, sitting on a bench by himself, wearing blue, staring at the sea," she said, "and I knew it was going to be that fucking guy, Perry. I just knew it, and I was right. I freaked out. But Angie saw him, too, so at least I knew he was real."

The elevator jolted and stopped, and when the doors slid open I remembered the image of the hat I'd seen on my reflection in that puddle the day the storm had started. As we hauled her luggage down the hallway I tried to recall the details of that image, of me looking up at myself. Had that really been me? Was there some connection between Lucy's story and mine? I thought about the genes we shared, and our parents and our upbringing. I was going to have to tell her about the pool. The pool and the violin.

Lucy was quiet while we worked, and when we'd piled everything outside the door she leaned against the wall, breathing heavily, and watched me as I fumbled for my key in the hallway's dim light.

"And you know what? That's not even the end of it," she said.

We pushed through the door, dragging the first of the suitcases. Eva had been resting on the couch, but now she stirred and arose as we came through the door. I introduced them to each other and Eva sank back into the corner of the couch, her legs curled up beneath her, watching us with half-closed eyes. We dragged the luggage through the door, leaving her suitcases wherever we could find floor space. There was barely enough room to walk when we were finished.

Lucy dug into a suitcase, searching for dry clothes, while I went to the closet for towels. "So we went back to the city," she continued, with a little waver in her voice, "and by the time I got to my apartment I had almost succeeded in calming myself down. I guess I shouldn't have bothered, because I had to freak out all over again. Somebody had been there, Perry. Somebody had broken in while I'd been gone. But listen to this—nothing was missing. Nothing at all, not one thing." She sighed and straightened up, a set of blue flannel pajamas dangling from her clenched hand. Strands of wet black hair stuck to her cheeks and jaw but she made no attempt to brush them away. "Instead, the burglar, if you want to call him that, left me things. He rearranged my fucking furniture, and he hung up mirrors," she said. "He hung up these little round mirrors all over my apartment. Eight of them, in various corners in different rooms." She pointed at another suitcase. "I brought them," she said. "I'll show them to you later." She dropped her pajamas, reached for the towel I'd tossed onto one of her suitcases, and buried her face in it. "So that was it," she said, when she emerged, her face red. "That was last week. I packed my shit up, tied up a few loose ends, and here I am."

Eva stirred on the couch. "It's *feng shui*," she said.

Lucy pulled her face from the towel. "What? What is?"

"Someone broke in to adjust your *xi* flow. Mirrors represent the water element," Eva said.

"Who the hell would do that?"

Eva shrugged. "Maybe you had a water deficiency."

As I watched this exchange a numbing warmth swept up through me. I couldn't feel my damp clothes against my skin. My hands began to feel hot. I couldn't feel the weight of the wet towel in my hands. Before she'd even had a chance to dry off, Lucy had plummeted directly into the center of our mystery here, bringing with her events from thousands of miles away. She was a meteorite filled with metal from a distant but related galaxy; around her was the cratered wreckage of suitcases and bags and backpacks. Eva seemed to be thinking the same thing. She was looking intently at us, back and forth between me and Lucy, back and forth, back and forth.

Lucy glanced at the rain-covered glass doors that led out to my small patio. She forced a smile and repeated what Eva had said about having a water deficiency. She looked pale. Pale and weary and older than I remembered.

七

Three days after discovering the old man's junk shop, Li-Yu decides on a plan. She thinks it through for another three days, rehearsing it in her mind, observing, and on the following night she lies in bed, breathless, her eyes wide. It seems to take longer than usual for the house to quiet down. Finally the servants finish their tasks and depart. She listens to their feet recede across the gravel as they cross over to their quarters. Still she waits. Somewhere in the house a roof joint emits a loud crack and she twitches atop her covers. There is a hitch in Henry's breathing and he shifts in his bed, but then he sinks back into deep sleep. She waits as long as she can bear it. Perhaps an hour elapses, perhaps two; her heightened senses distort the passing time. And then from beneath her blanket she pulls a burlap sack she found in the shed. She creeps to the kitchen, holding her breath, and without a wasted motion she makes her way to the cabinets where the dishware is kept. She opens the doors but does not immediately reach inside—instead she drops to one knee, rests her hands and the sack across her upraised thigh, and closes her eyes. She listens to the stillness of the house, and, hearing nothing but her blood in her temples, she reaches inside. She takes one plate from each of the stacks inside—four in all. They disappear into the burlap sack. She presses the bundle tightly against her chest to keep the dishes from rattling together and hurries toward the front door. She pauses there, listening again, not only to the stillness of the sleeping house, but also for any movement outside. Hearing nothing, she releases the latch and swings the door open.

The night air surprises her with its cold wetness and sends such a shudder through her that the dishes knock together in their sack. She secures the bundle again and accelerates, her feet crunching through the gravel. She can allow nobody to see her. It would be scandalous enough for her to be out late like this, and unaccompanied, even without the stolen dishes. But the roads are empty and there are no shouts of alarm, no movements as she circles the edge of the village, keeping low and hurrying. Alongside the pathway, just before it begins the climb to the ridge, there is a small thicket of waist-high bushes whose leaves, though narrow like the blades of swords, grow in dense thick clusters. She runs to the thicket's base, stoops, and slips the sack inside it. The leaves swallow it whole. Quickly she rises, panting, and turns and hurries home. The front door is unlatched, as she left it, so she is able to enter noiselessly. She eases herself onto her bed, and when her heart rate finally drops, and her breathing grows steady, she undresses, crawls under the covers, and shuts her eyes. Perhaps she drifts in and out of sleep for a time; perhaps she does not—at some point the silence changes from the thick quiet of a deep late night to the fragile calm of a house about to awaken.

Henry and Rose are breathing in unison, deeply and peacefully. Li-Yu matches her breath to theirs for a time, envying them their oblivion. She wants to rise and prod them into their day, but it is too early. Today everything must seem normal. Finally she hears stirring elsewhere in the house, so she rises and shakes the weariness and the stiffness out of her legs and arms. She rouses her children, dresses them, and follows them into the main part of the house, her heart thumping in her chest. But all is as usual. Mae is on her couch, sipping tea, and the servants are busy in the kitchen. A fire crackles in the stove. Plates have been removed from the cabinet and are scattered across the table, each of them holding piles of bite-sized bits of food. There is no indication that any of them have been missed. Li-Yu has no appetite, but she forces herself to eat and make conversation. Finally it is time to go.

Li-Yu kisses Rose on the forehead and guides Henry outside. The roads in the center of the village are busy, but once they are away the traffic thins. When they fall alongside the rice paddies, Li-Yu takes another burlap sack, shakes it out, and drapes it over her arm, making sure her son sees her movements.

"What's that for?" Henry asks.

"I might do some shopping in Jianghai," she says.

"Oh," he says. He glances at the bag again and then turns his attention to the men working in the fields.

It happens that there are few people along the stretch of pathway near the thicket where the plates are hidden, and Li-Yu's breaths begin to come a little more easily. Alongside the bushes she stops suddenly. "There's something wrong with my shoe," she says, and squats. She squints up at Henry. "Come here," she says. "Block the sun for your mother while she fixes her shoe." She takes Henry in her hands and pulls him in front of her, turning him so he is facing away.

He squints up at the sky. "But it's cloudy," he says.

"You're doing a great job," she tells him, tugging at her shoe. Henry's attention returns to the men working in the rice paddies. Li-Yu's hands dart beneath the thicket and within seconds the sack of plates is wrapped inside the second sack. She pinches the plates against her side and lets the mouth of the sack drape over her arm and hang loose, as it had been before. She stands and puts a hand on Henry's back.

"There, I fixed it," she says, and tousles his hair. "You're a good boy. Let's go." She walks the rest of the way with the dishes clamped against her side to keep them from rattling. She distracts Henry with conversation, pointing out a white crane on the edge of a paddy, a dark cloud shaped like a horse. The muscles of her arm begin to ache but she does not let herself adjust the sacks. At school she kisses him goodbye, sends him through the gate, and finally relaxes. She heads back into the center of the town and plunges into the entrance of the network of alleys. She quickly finds her way to the little shop.

The old man is in the same spot, standing behind his tables. He smiles and bows as she steps across the threshold. There is an empty spot on the table just in front of him, and without saying anything Li-Yu frees the dishes, sets them down, and takes a step back. He stares at the topmost plate for a time, and then he flashes Li-Yu a smile that makes her think he knows everything. She stops breathing, wondering if he will shout for the police, or accost her himself. He picks up the plate and holds it just an inch from his nose, exploring it with his fingertips, squinting and smiling. He flips it over and rubs its smooth back with his palm before setting it down. Without examining the rest of the plates he reaches into his pocket and pulls out a handful of coins. He counts out several and extends his arm. Li-Yu accepts them with two cupped hands, her eyes wide. It is ten times what she has amassed in her sock. She drops the coins into the burlap bag and wraps them tightly so they'll make no sound. She hides the bundle in her other sack, bows to the man, and hurries back out through the alleyway maze.

EIGHT

The next day was Friday. My classroom had begun to smell like a neglected fish tank. "Eighteen days now," Kevin had said to me that morning. "And guess what, Mr. Long? A Mini Cooper with nobody in it slid all the way down our hill last night. My dad saw it. It crashed into a light pole." He grinned and punched his palm. "I wish I'd been there. That would have been so awesome to see!"

During the rainy lunch hour they worked on my mazes, and by the end of the day a line of them, their solutions inked over in red pen, hung along the tops of the windows. At some point I suddenly remembered my progress reports would be due in another week or two. I hadn't thought about them at all, and by now I'd typically be done with half of them. Panic threatened, but I told myself that if I could get a good jump on them that night, and crank out maybe four or five of them, I'd have a good start.

I got home that afternoon and found Lucy gone and Eva standing at the window, staring at the sky. "My grandmother wasn't a thief," she said, without turning around.

"Okay," I said. "I didn't say she was, strictly speaking."

Eva turned, her lips pursed. "That's not how she did it."

"Did what?"

She crossed her arms across her chest. "I'm beginning to have some doubts about this arrangement," she said.

I adjusted my expectations for my night's work from four or five progress reports to two or three. "You didn't before?" I said.

"Have you ever had somebody disappear on you?" she asked.

"My dad died when I was little," I said.

"Everybody's dad dies," she says. "That's not what I mean."

"Then no," I said, trying to keep myself steady as the heat of impatience rose across my temples. "Why does that matter? I have a lot of work to do tonight for school."

She looked hard at me; her eyes were wide and her breath came and went through flared nostrils. I had the sense I was in trouble for something someone else had done.

"I probably shouldn't do this, but I'll show you something."

"So show me," I said.

"It isn't here," she said. "We have to drive."

"How far?"

"Not far."

"It's rush hour," I said. "Everywhere is far."

The door opened and Lucy came in. "It looks like you guys just broke up," she said. "Should I leave?"

"No," Eva said. "You can come with us."

"Where are we going?"

"We're not going anywhere," I said. "I have to work on my progress reports."

Eva turned to Lucy. "We're going to Colma."

"Colma?" Lucy said. "What's there, apart from the dead?"

Colma was just south of San Francisco and consisted of some car dealerships, a strip mall, and acre after acre of graveyards. I'm not sure if it held any neighborhoods at all for the living. Our dad was buried there. I hadn't been down to visit him in years. I'd had something of a complicated relationship with his gravesite. In the months following his death we'd gone to visit several times, and all it held for me was a sense of injustice. I searched his entire row, and the one behind it, and the one in front of it, and I couldn't find anybody else who'd died as early. The youngest of my dad's neighbors had made it to fifty-seven. And yet there he was, dead at the age of forty-three, sitting among all those seventy- and eighty-year olds. And not only had he died early, he'd known he was going to die, so the end of his life, those last few years, had been devoted not to living life, or even to lying around feeling sorry for himself, but to working, to making sure there would be something to leave me and Lucy and our mom when he was gone. I thought he should have been in a special section somewhere. He did not belong among the ordinary dead, among people who'd lived out the full length of their lives, who'd known their grandchildren. His headstone, which my mom had picked out, was even a little plainer than everyone else's. She told us that he hadn't wanted anything fancy.

I did, though. I made her take me often, and I'd buy flowers with my own money, and I'd place them not on the ground in front of the stone, like everybody else did, but on top of it, so they could be seen from all around. This went on for years. When I got older, I'd take the bus by myself. And then I started to discover other graves, in other areas of the cemetery, of men who'd died young. I found a couple of kids, including, once, on a cloudless summer day, the fresh grave of a six-year-old girl named Sarah. And then it hit me, all at once—nobody was any more or less dead than anybody else. Death was uniform. Congressmen, cab drivers—they were all the same here. It didn't matter anymore. And I was fine with that. I went back a couple more times over the following years, and then I stopped going altogether.

"I'll come, as long as we can stop and pick up some food," Lucy said. "I'm starving."

Maybe I'd get one progress report completed that night. At least that would be enough to get me started.

The traffic and rain were both worse than I'd expected. The wipers dragged across the windshield, half swiping, half smearing the water one way and then the other. It took us an hour to reach the gates of Woodlawn Cemetery. I had worked up a theory on the drive down—this would be Eva's way of establishing her identification, of proving she was who she said she was. She'd show me her husband's grave and her own empty plot next to it, with her name and date of birth, and then there would be trust between us. Her papers and belongings might have been wiped out in her flood, but her headstone would be standing, indelible, polished by the wind and rain.

I drove through the entrance and Eva guided me through a network of narrow lanes. All around us the hillsides bristled with marble and granite tombstones, and on their crests sat mausoleums, at once gaudy and somber. Splashes of color broke up the pattern in places: flowers yet to wilt, marking the recent visits of next-of-kin. Eva faltered in her navigation at one point and we had to circle back.

"Park here," she said. "It's over by that tree." She nodded toward a solitary oak standing some distance from the road. Its branches reached out and sheltered a patch of twenty or twenty-five graves. We climbed out of the car and stepped onto the wet grass. Brown water oozed up from the ground around our shoes. Eva led us toward the tree, twisting through the grave markers until we reached a salmon-colored headstone. We stopped and arranged ourselves in front of it. The headstone held an oval frame that contained a black-and-white photograph of a woman in black. The main engraving was in Chinese, but beneath that, the name "Li-Yu Long" was carved deep into the stone.

I gasped and looked to Eva, but her head was bowed, her eyes closed, her lips moving with her silent prayer. I started to feel a little dizzy. Lucy said something, but I couldn't understand what. I squatted and planted a hand on the wet earth to steady myself. When I looked up I found the photograph floating in front of my face. The plastic over the photo had fogged, rendering the woman's features indistinct, but I didn't need to see it. I knew exactly what she looked like in there.

"This isn't what I expected," I finally managed to say.

Eva was watching me closely. "Interesting," she said.

"You never told me her name was Long," I said.

She shrugged. In my mind my thoughts were colliding, merging, negating one another, disintegrating. From out of the mess one question surfaced. "What if I were to ask you where Rose is?" I said, beginning to walk along the row, reading the names on the neighboring headstones.

Eva crossed herself, turned away from the grave, and headed for the car. "Wrong neighborhood," she said. "My mom's still alive."

***

We were halfway home before I could compose a response to that. "Why wouldn't you tell me that?" I asked. "Why didn't you tell me your mom was still alive?"

"Because it doesn't matter," she said. Her mood had changed. Her words were quiet, dismissive. I glanced at her in the rearview mirror. She was looking out the window. Lucy sat beside me, staring at her fingers.

"How could it not matter?" I asked, wanting to punch something. "I thought—think—I invented her, and now you're telling me she's alive. Of course it fucking matters."

"I understand that you would think so."

It was all I could do not to swerve off the road. I took a deep breath, swallowed my first reaction, put a little space between myself and the car in front of me, let a few seconds pass. "That's incomprehensible," I said. "You're trying to persuade me that these are your stories. Why didn't you tell me? Why didn't you show me that a long time ago?"

"I'm not trying to persuade you of anything." Eva was still staring through the window. Her voice was flat, as if we were reading through a script that bored her.

"Of course you are," I said. "Why the hell did we just make this trip, then?"

"Because I need you to focus," she said. "I need to know what happened to my uncle."

"Right," I said. "And along the way, you're trying to persuade me to help you. But to do that, you need me to believe that your story is real."

"It doesn't really matter what you believe."

"That makes no sense whatsoever," I said.

"I think it could make a little sense," Lucy said.

"Thank you," Eva said.

"How?" I said.

"This is a delicate process," Eva said.

"I can see that," Lucy said.

"I have no idea what the fuck either of you are talking about," I said.

"It doesn't matter," Eva said. "I've already said too much. I just need you to keep writing."

"Can we get something to eat now?" Lucy said.

***

I spent the rest of the drive in a state of agitation, consumed by thoughts of Rose. I could sense her presence now, out in the world somewhere, and though I should have come home to start my progress reports I could think only of her exodus from my story and onto the planet. By what mechanism, what act of transformation, could this have happened? When it became too much to think about, I told myself it was a coincidence; it had to be. Of course Eva had a grandmother by the name of Li-Yu—why would she have tracked me down, otherwise? They were parallel occurrences, nothing more. But I couldn't get that to sit right. As the coincidences accumulated it became more and more difficult to adhere to commonplace explanations. Now I had to find Rose. I had to find Rose, and not only was Eva unwilling to take me to her, she was maintaining that her existence didn't matter. The more I thought about it the less sense it made, so later that evening I decided I had nothing to lose and I cornered Lucy.

"Let's go swimming," I said. The pool was open until ten. I didn't need much time; five minutes would be more than enough.

She'd been at the fridge, gulping orange juice out of the carton. She wiped her mouth with the back of her hand and looked over my shoulder toward the windows. "Is that some sort of code?" she said. "Some kind of new Bay Area lingo?"

"It's code for getting into a swimming pool," I said. "Lots of people do it."

She wiped her mouth on her arm. "Yes," she said, "and there's a place for them all this time of year, called Australia." She took another gulp, put the carton back in, and shut the door. She pointed at the piles of her luggage. "Besides, do you have any idea how long it would take me to find my suit?" she said.

"I need you to come with me," I said. "I'm going to go change." I went to my room and came back out a minute later, ready to go.

Lucy had put on her raincoat and found an umbrella. "Look, I'll come with you, just to get you to stop acting weird. But I don't need to get any wetter than I've been, water deficiency or not. I'm bringing a book."

"Fine," I said. We walked down the hallway and into the stairwell. The echoes of our footfalls clattered all around us. "So do you want to tell me what that was all about earlier?" I asked.

"What what was?"

"Your comments in the car. You sound like you're on her side."

"Her side? I didn't realize there were sides."

"You know what I mean."

"We've spent some time talking."

"Great."

"What's wrong with that?"

We pushed through the door and into the storm, and Lucy's umbrella snapped open. Someone rode past on a bike; a streetlight caught the flat fan of water spraying from its rear wheel. "Swimming?" she said. "You're crazy, you know."

"So what has she told you?"

"Various things. Mostly what you told me."

"That's it?"

"What were you hoping for?"

"Oh, I don't know. A few minor tidbits, like an explanation for why one of my characters is buried in Colma, and why another one's walking around somewhere."

"Don't get pissy with me about it," she said. "I'm just along for the ride."

"I'm not pissy," I said. "I just want to know what she told you, and what you told her."

"What I've told her about what?"

"About anything," I said, but my thoughts were turning to the pool. What was I planning for Lucy, for this exploration? She hadn't brought her suit, so I couldn't ask her to come in with me. Would I simply ask her to keep an eye on me? Was that going to sound insane? Did I just need to have the reassurance of her company?

Doris let Lucy in for free and instead of heading for the changing rooms I went directly for the pool. We stepped through the doorway and into the awning's small shelter.

"It's a fucking outdoor pool?" Lucy said. "I never for a moment considered that possibility. When did you lose your mind?"

But her words and the Y and the storm all belonged to a receding world now. The chasm beneath the pool's surface was rising and spreading, and even before I had stepped out from beneath the awning's fragile shelter I was engulfed. I had only a slight awareness of movement through rain and Lucy shouting things, about my clothes, about how I was freaking her out, and then the water was rising to meet me.

Beneath me all was blue-white, and endless. I floated down, easily, awash in a sudden surprising calm. Something in me turned—it was as if my organs had all somersaulted, and now down was up, and up down, and I was swimming upwards, toward a narrow glowing ribbon that looked like a far-off river. It took me what seemed like whole minutes to reach it. I began to see the undersides of flat-bottomed boats, their brown planks tinted with algae. High above, a wavering sun sent thick bars of light plunging into the green water. I struck for the surface, anticipating breaths of air that would taste of the countryside, and sunshine. Just as I began to feel the pressure decrease of shallow waters, everything inside me somersaulted again and the boats and sunlight disappeared, and that heavy blue-white emptiness returned. I looked up and saw, through what seemed like a hundred miles of water, the oblong, spinning lights of the pool's deck. Only then did I feel the strain in my lungs. I pushed for the pool's surface, fighting hard, and finally broke through, breathing heavily.

Cold air seized my head. I kicked for the shallow end, my clothes thick and heavy, my heart clattering in its cage, and got my feet onto the pool's floor. I would have to convince Lucy to come in with me, somehow—without her I had no way of making sense of anything. She was gone, though. The space beneath the awning was empty and the deck was clear. I climbed out of the water and headed for the door, a sense of that cartwheeling feeling still turning in my chest. I concentrated on the light streaming through the glass doors; I fought to keep my wet clothes from dragging me to the floor. And then Lucy's still-open umbrella blew across the deck and struck my leg. It caromed off, and climbed on an updraft over the wall and out into the night. I ran the last few steps to the door and found Lucy inside, sitting in the hallway as though she'd been shoved backward through the door. She had one arm wrapped around a knee and the other hand pressed against the wall behind her. Her face was white.

"Lucy! What happened?" I said. I squatted down and put a hand on her shoulder. She was trembling.

When she spoke it sounded as if her voice was coming from somewhere far beyond this hallway. "I just remembered something," she said. She was staring past me, through the glass door at the water.

"What is it?" I tried to pull her up, but she pushed my hands away, her movements clumsy and abrupt. She looked at me, and back at the pool, and then back at me, and then began to rise on unsteady trembling legs. I put a hand on her arm and readied myself to catch her if she fell again.

"We have to go see Mom," she said, "right now." And suddenly she was on the move, a burst of frantic energy barreling down the hallway. "We have to go right now."

On the drive down, dull green rivers crossed the sky, small quiet boats traversing their lengths like blimps. The bay tipped and groaned, as though it had grown weary with its horizontal repose. Lucy was silent, and I glanced over at her frequently to make sure she was still there. I held to the taillights in front of me and hoped my instincts would carry us to our mom's door.

We managed to arrive. Mom answered the door. Her joy at seeing her daughter evaporated when she saw the look on Lucy's face. "Sweetie," she said, "whatever . . . ."

Lucy took a half-dozen strides into the house and pulled her coat off. She whirled around and her eyes flashed and when she spoke her voice rolled out like thunder. "Something happened to Peregrine." She pointed a finger at my chest but her eyes continued to bore into Mom. "What was it?"

I had just closed the door and now I froze, standing just inside it. All around us the leaves of her crops trembled in the gently cycling air of her ventilation system.

"He's fine," Mom said, her voice quiet. She turned and looked me over. "Aren't you?"

"When he was little, I mean. What was it?"

Mom turned back to Lucy. "Lots of things happened to him. What's made you so angry?"

"Something about a pool," Lucy said. "We had that little kid pool and something happened."

Mom twitched at the mention of the pool. She went very still. I came a step closer. Lucy's eyes were round as planets; she seemed to be watching events unfold in the air above us. And then my mom muttered something I couldn't quite make out.

"What did you say?" I asked, stepping closer to her. "Lucy, what are you talking about?" I could picture the pool. It was one of those little blue ones with the plastic edge that always caught your toes. I could see it in the corner of our yard in Redwood City, killing a four-foot circle of crabgrass.

Mom shook her head. Her face had turned red. She sank down onto one of the kitchen stools and planted a heavy elbow on the counter. Her hands were shaking. "Who told you?" she said. "How did you find out?"

"Find out what?" I asked. Numbness reached up my legs and began to squeeze at the bottoms of my lungs.

"There was an ambulance," Lucy said.

"But you didn't—you couldn't know that," Mom said.

"Was there an ambulance or wasn't there?" Lucy yelled.

"There was," Mom said. She turned to me, a look of helplessness on her face I'd never seen before. "I'm sorry, Peregrine," she said.

"For what?" I said. "What the hell are you talking about? Lucy, what is this?"

Mom closed her eyes, shook her head again. "I'll tell you in a minute," she said, her voice thin. She turned back to Lucy. "How did you find out?"

"I just remembered," Lucy said. Her shoulders rose and fell with her heavy breaths. The anger on her face had turned to pain. "I watched Perry jump into the pool at the Y and it just suddenly came back to me."

It seemed like an hour before Mom turned back to me. Everything in the room went flat, two-dimensional. "You fell in," she said. "When you were two."

"And?" I said.

"You were playing in the back, and we had left the empty pool in a corner of the yard. At least, we thought the pool was empty. But the neighbors had been watering at night, and with a few months and the chain-link fence, a couple of inches built up in the bottom." Her eyes were wet now. "We should have checked, Peregrine. The pool should have been upside-down, or leaning against the fence. We never really went back there." She was no longer looking at my face, but downward, into my chest, as if studying my heart, my lungs. For a time she didn't speak. Hints of expressions, nearly imperceptible, flashed across her face and then vanished, as if she were watching events spool out inside me.

"Finish the story, Mom," Lucy said. Her voice was soft but urgent.

"You were playing back there, in the grass, with some of your toys," Mom said. She still wouldn't look at my face. "I had been checking on you every couple of minutes, but the gate was closed and latched, and there was no way you could get out, and not much trouble you could really get into back there." She closed her eyes. "And then I looked out and you weren't on the grass, or anywhere I could see from the doorway." She was crying now, and her face twisted with the effort of speech. She was almost unrecognizable. "I ran outside and found you in the pool, with your face in the water. I pulled you out and you weren't breathing. I had no idea how long you'd been there like that."

She went still again. We watched and waited as the memory passed through her face, as its reverberations flattened and eased. Lucy stayed where she was, her hands on her hips, her eyes riveted on Mom. I couldn't feel anything in my body. I might have been floating in lukewarm water.

"You came back, obviously," she said. "You came back in the ambulance and you were fine. But you hadn't been breathing. Your pulse had stopped and there'd been no heartbeat. You'd gone. Completely gone."

The room turned gray. I couldn't even smell the reek of her plants. My throat felt like it was full of water.

"They kept you at the hospital for a couple of nights, but then you were back, happy as ever. We never told you it happened because we didn't want you to be scared of water. We didn't even get rid of the pool." She slumped an inch. "And also, I suppose we weren't eager for you to know you had the sort of parents who could let this happen to you."

"And all this was when?" I said. Now I was picturing myself lying in the back of that ambulance, a tiny blue-gray figure on a white gurney, full of tubes.

"That's what I can't understand," Mom said. "It was when you were two. But it was summertime."

"I remember seeing him through the window," Lucy said. She closed her eyes. "I remember him lying on the grass, surrounded by paramedics. He was wearing his Spider-Man shirt and his diaper. There were three men and one woman, and one of the men was bald."

"Yes," Mom said, "that sounds about right."

"So why am I just now remembering this?"

Mom lifted her hands to her head and began massaging her temples with her fingertips. "That's what I don't understand. You weren't home. You were in Iowa, visiting your grandparents."

NINE

That night I dreamed I was alone in a room with walls made of intricate cabinetry. In each one there were hundreds, maybe thousands of drawers. Many of them were opening, slowly, of their own accord. I was terrified of their contents, but I awoke before I had to see what they held. Rain was still drumming against my bedroom window. It was almost noon.

I wasn't quite sure what I should do with myself. I wandered out into the living room. Eva was out, and Lucy had stayed back at our mom's, both of which suited me fine. I wasn't in the mood to talk to anybody. In some increasingly neglected corner of my mind there was an alert about progress reports. Though my senses were much too fogged to hope for a productive afternoon, I shouldered my laptop bag and headed out. I wandered around the neighborhood a bit, not really paying attention to where I was going, watching water run through the gutters. Everything seemed different, secretive. I had the sense that the whole planet and all its inhabitants and contents, even the smallest of things— trash, insects, dust motes—had been somewhere without me, and had come back conversing in references I would never understand. I kept imagining my little stopped heart, gray and inert. Every now and then I had to slip my hand beneath my coat and check on it. After a half-hour of arbitrary turns I found myself in a café I'd never noticed before, sipping a cup of strong black coffee, surrounded by pairs and trios of friends happily talking. They seemed like the sort of people who had been alive continuously since birth, and as such I found them all vaguely foreign. I booted up my laptop and tried to steer my thoughts toward my students and their progress, but I couldn't picture a single one of them. I ended up drifting around on the Internet, looking for stories about people who had died and come back. There were a handful of them—a man in Venezuela who'd awakened during his autopsy, someone's uncle who arose during his wake, a lady who came to in the morgue three times. She made me feel a little better. At least it wasn't a habit with me.

It wasn't until late afternoon that I remembered I was supposed to have dinner with Annabel that evening. I had the staff directory on a spreadsheet in my computer. She picked up on the third ring.

"You caught me at school, where I find myself again impressed with you, Mr. Long!" she said. "You and your most sophisticated celebration of the lunar new year."

"How's that?" I said. My sense of inhabiting someone else's experiences was growing a little too familiar.

"Chinese calligraphy is quite a step up from the usual dragons-and-firecrackers stuff," she said.

"I think you've got the wrong guy," I said.

"Room eight is your classroom, is it not?"

"Yes," I said, "but I'm not sure what you're talking about."

"Your classroom window!" she said. "Your students' penmanship is quite lovely."

"Penmanship?"

There was a brief silence on the other end of the phone, and then she asked, "This is Peregrine, right?"

"Yes," I said.

"I'm talking about the Chinese characters you have stretching across the tops of your classroom windows," she said slowly. "Did someone else put those up?"

I took a deep breath. I still had people coming back from the dead in my browser window, people I had not yet begun to contemplate. I folded the screen shut and yanked the cord out of the wall. I took another deep breath. "They're mazes," I said. "Those are the mazes you saw me photocopying the other day."

"Okay," she said, with a little laugh. "But their solutions are Chinese characters. You didn't know that?"

"No," I said.

She laughed again. "How funny. Well, where did you get them?"

"I drew them," I said, "when I was a little kid."

She stopped laughing. "You drew them?"

"Yes."

Silence.

"I'm on my way," I said.

As I walked up the hill I felt the last of the tethers that held me to the known world growing thin. I think I hardly would have registered surprise if I had risen from the sidewalk and floated through the rain to the top of the hill. An odd sense of peace came over me. I could die and recover. I was a Chinese calligrapher; I could swim through the planet. Maybe I could even find Henry.

Once on the school playground I saw immediately what Annabel had been talking about. The red ink had seeped through the back of the mazes and somehow spread and flowered into graceful brushstrokes. I got closer and realized what had happened—the seal above the upper window had failed, and the wind had driven the rain through to dampen the sheets. The rainwater had transformed the skinny, shaky ink lines into the wet strokes of calligraphers' brushes. A minute later Annabel appeared and slipped her arm through mine. We stood there for a long time, together.

"So what does it say?" I asked her.

She pointed to each character and gave its Chinese pronunciation. I closed my eyes and listened to the music of the syllables. She reached the end and paused, and when I opened my eyes she was looking at me. "Boat, desire, home, dreaming," she said. "Traveling, small, a few others." Her straight black hair clung to the sides of her cheeks like strips of lacquered wood. Beads of rain perched on her eyelashes. "You say you don't speak Chinese?"

"Right," I said.

She looked back up at the row of mazes. "I find this a little peculiar," she said.

It was a glorious, refreshing understatement, and I couldn't help but laugh. "I visited my mom's last night, down on the peninsula," I said, "and I found out that when I was two I died for a little while."

"Say that again?" she said, returning my laugh. "It sounded like you said that you died for a little while."

"Right," I said. "It happened when I was two. I drowned in a wading pool, and I was dead for a while. Nobody really knows how long. I found out last night, when my sister suddenly remembered. Only she was in Iowa the day it happened, and my parents never told either of us about it."

I wasn't sure I wanted to see Annabel's reaction to that, so I continued to stare at the red characters. Rivulets of rain ran down the sides of my nose and the back of my neck. My raincoat was saturated and leaking.

"And speaking of my sister," I continued, "it seems she is being haunted by an elderly Chinese phantom who broke into her apartment in New York, apparently just to make *feng-shui*-related adjustments. And I have a houseguest right now who claims to be a descendent of Rose, one of the characters in my story. You remember Rose—you read that first chapter. Or two."

"Three," she said.

"What?" I said.

She cleared her throat. "Three chapters. I've read three chapters," she said.

"Well, that's another item for this list," I said. "I only actually ever submitted one. I've written several, but I only sent one in. Somehow they're appearing of their own accord."

That's probably enough, I thought. Best just to leave it at that.

"And speaking of my story," I said, "I'll tell you where the idea came from." I pointed through the window to my desk. "It came from inside a teacup. On the first day of school back from break. I saw the family's reflection in the surface of my tea."

Stop talking, I told myself. You're going to scare her.

"Deep in the pool at the YMCA there's an upside-down river with boats in it. Oh, and I keep hearing strange violin music in various places, music nobody else can hear," I said.

You're an idiot, I told myself. That was way too much. Find a way to retract at least those last two. Annabel took a small step away from me and reached into her pocket. I stiffened. Would it be pepper spray? Mace? A call to 911? "I'm sorry," I began, but she shook her head. Her hand emerged from her pocket with her keys. She would have to go now. She would have to go, and there would be some reason she couldn't meet me for dinner.

"I want to show you something," she said.

"The last time somebody said that to me I was taken to the gravesite of somebody I thought I'd invented."

"No graves," she said. "Come with me." She reached down and took my hand in hers, and led me to her car. She guided the car over to Van Ness, which was knotted up with Saturday night traffic, and down to Geary, where she took a right and plunged into the city's western flank. I watched the blocks tick past, one after the other, their buildings huddling together against the fall of rain. I resisted the urge to ask Annabel where we were going. It was comforting, not knowing. As long as I could keep this small mystery alive, I knew there was at least one question to which there would be an answer. There was at least one knowable thing in the universe. I wanted the city to stretch on forever; I wanted everything to vanish but this rain, these blocks and their concrete and neon, this woman and her car and the trace of warmth her hand had left in mine, and this little pinprick of hope.

The inevitable ocean eventually rose before us, though, and Annabel turned to the south. In the last of the day's light the sea and the storm were indistinguishable. Each turbulent mass of gray reached into the other, as though competing, the border between them marked only by occasional explosions of white froth and foam. In my mind we drove in seconds down the length of Highway 1, through Pacifica and Santa Cruz, through Big Sur, to Mexico, where it was warm and dry, and things made sense. At Sloat, though, Annabel hit her blinker. She turned away from the ocean, took another left, and parked. I followed her out of the car and across the street, toward the row houses that were home to the city's oceanfront inhabitants.

An odd accumulation of items had gathered along the sidewalk, in the gutter, and in the street. There were receipts and ticket stubs, disintegrating in the rain. There were socks and toys, and a T-shirt with the name of a middle school I didn't recognize emblazoned on its front. There was a green baseball cap and a magazine. The collection grew thick—against the iron gate of one of the homes there leaned a knee-high mound of wet papers, backpacks, clothes, shoes, a tennis racket. It looked as though the door had opened and the house had vomited all its loose items into the street. It was here that Annabel stopped. She unlocked the gate and yanked it open hard, scattering the pile across the sidewalk.

"Quick," she said, "inside." I followed her over the garbage and the gate clanged shut behind us. "My home," she said, unlocking her front door. Inside it was warm, and lit by a glow that came from thick glass globes on the walls. The floor was a clean dark wood, the furnishings sparse. Her couches were midnight blue, and low, and looked comfortable and hard to get out of. On an immaculate marble coffee table sat two large books, nothing else. There was a matching pair of low bookcases. Abstract paintings, one on each wall, hung inside wooden frames. It smelled like a just-extinguished fire. She led me into the kitchen and produced a bottle of vodka and a pair of shot glasses.

"You're probably wondering about all that stuff out front," she said. She uncapped the bottle, poured the drinks, and handed me one. Her hand was shaking. I waited for her to offer a toast, but she declined. We drained our glasses; heat flashed through my bloodstream. She set hers down with a thud. "That mess is part of what I wanted you to see," she said.

"What is it?" I said.

She poured herself another shot and reached for my glass. The second shot thudded down through me and joined the first. She collected the glasses and sat them next to the bottle, and then seemed not to know what to do with her hands—first she laced her fingers together, and then she unlaced them. Eventually they came to rest on the counter in front of her, palms down, one on top of the other. She looked me in the eye.

"Things find me, Peregrine," she said. "Lost things. They find a way to get to my door, or in my path, or they get tangled up in my legs when I'm walking. I return what I can. Some things I store for a while, and then I throw them out. Even then, sometimes things come back."

"What do you mean?"

"I don't know," she said, and I saw my own uncertainty, my own hesitation mirrored in her face. In that moment, something inside me revolved and loosened. It rose up, branched, and pushed against the inside of my skin, and when it broke through, I knew I was in love with her.

"There's more," she said. She circled the counter, took me by the hand again, and pulled me out of the kitchen. She led me up a staircase, through a doorway, and up another staircase. She threw open a door and flipped a light switch.

The entire third floor was a single large room. The front wall was a solid bank of tall windows. I couldn't see the ocean through the room's opaque reflection, but I sensed its tumult before us. Along the back wall stretched a solid line of file cabinets and shelving units that reached the ceiling, and tables, which housed dozens of overflowing plastic bins. On one table sat a laptop, stacks of envelopes and flattened cardboard boxes, packaging tape, shipping labels. The rest of the room was empty but for a single tall drafting chair that sat in the middle of the floor, facing the wall of windows.

Annabel began to walk along the length of tables and shelves and cabinets. Against this wall of debris she seemed small, uncertain. It was strange to see her diminished like this; I had grown accustomed to her ease as she navigated the corridors of school, kindergarteners trailing her like a comet's tail. I followed her across the room.

She stopped in front of a file cabinet, opened a drawer, and produced from a hanging file a dirty sheet of lined paper ripped from a spiral notebook. "Someone's homework," she said. She showed it to me. A child's unsteady hand had penciled words across the sheet, with little regard to the blue lines. In the corner was the author's name: Madison B. "There isn't much to go on with this one," Annabel said, "but Madison is or was a student of a Mrs. Zabriskie, and there's mention of a two-hour car ride to Maine."

"I don't understand," I said. "How did it get here?"

"I couldn't tell you. Maybe some wind blew it onto a freight train. Maybe it got sucked up into the jet stream."

I surveyed the bins, the tables, the cabinets. There must have been thousands of items there. "Why do you go to the trouble to return them?" I asked.

"They go through so much to get here." She slid the sheet back into its file and shrugged. "It's just my duty, I figure," she said.

We continued our slow tour of the wall. There were boxes of wallets, pet collars, shoes. "What about your sisters? What were their names again?"

"Bernice, Carla, and Delilah," she said. "What about them?"

"Does this happen to them, too? Or do they have other . . . talents?"

She shook her head. "No talents," she said. "Actually, that isn't true. Carla has the talent of fake boobs." She laughed a small laugh. "You'd be amazed what she can do with those."

"What about people?" I said. "Lost people? Do they ever find you?"

"Sometimes," Annabel said. "A brother and a sister at the mall downtown. An old Japanese guy who'd been separated from his tour group, up near Fisherman's Wharf. And once, at Yosemite, a mother who'd been missing for two days. That one was in the news. You can look it up." We reached the end and she stopped and turned and started back toward the chair in the middle of the room. "To tell you the truth, it's gotten a bit overwhelming lately," she said. "Ever since this storm started. My front door didn't used to look like that. Like a junkyard. I just hope it doesn't all find me at school."

She gave the chair a spin and watched it rotate once, twice. "There's more," she said.

"More stuff?" I said. "Where?"

"No," she said. "Sit down." She patted the chair's seat.

I complied, and she turned me square to the windows. Our reflections looked back at us. Together we were dwarfed by the towering, cluttered wall of lost items behind us. She walked over to the doorway and threw the light switches.

One world vanished and another appeared. Dim black light bathed the room. A web of glowing yellow-green lines emanated from a spot beneath the chair and fanned out across the floor. They reached and climbed the opposite wall and stretched up to the bottoms of the windows. Written along the lines on the floor were tiny glowing words, the same bright color. Our reflections had vanished from the window and in their place the ocean now roiled, churning into the sand on the far side of the Great Highway, where a series of burned-out streetlights rose into the storm.

"The city used to come out and fix the lights once a month," she said, "but they gave up. I've learned to be a pretty good shot." She walked carefully out across the glowing web of lines, looking down at them. "From that seat I can see about 400 square miles of ocean. I spend hours in that chair," she said.

"What are you searching for?" I said.

"I'm not the one doing the searching," she said. "I'm the one being sought." She sat down on the floor and crossed her legs. "Come take a look," she said.

As my toe touched the glowing web a ripple of something like electricity shot up through my leg and filled the rest of me. I squatted and silently read the writing along one of the rays: HMS *Prince of Wales*, British. December 10, 1941. 3.56, 104.48. Malaysia. 10:56 P.M. August 9, 2008.

"The *Prince of Wales*," I said. "A ship?"

"Sunk by eighty-six Japanese bombers out of Saigon," she said.

"On the tenth of December," I said. "Latitude and longitude?"

"Yes."

"At 10:56 P.M. What's the second date?"

"No," she said. "10:56 on the night of August 9, 2008 was when the *Prince of Wales* found me."

"Found you?" The words beneath me went fuzzy, and then came back into focus. I sat down across from Annabel.

"Ghost ships," she said, when I was settled. The whites of her eyes jumped out of the dark purple light. She gestured toward the windows. "They appear all along the horizon and sail toward me. I identify them, and record their arrivals."

"And then what?"

"And then they disappear."

I looked down and read another entry, and then another. There had to be hundreds of rays, maybe a thousand.

"Sometimes it gets crowded out there," she said. "If I go away for a week or so and it's been stormy, I might come back to find a couple dozen ships lined up on the horizon, waiting for me."

I stood up, peered through the window, and tried to imagine one of these collections—schooners, battleships, barges, yachts—convening here, just off the coast, searching for a lone figure bathed in black light in a third-floor window. "They just disappear?" I said.

She shrugged. "They vanish," she said. "They flicker, and they become even more translucent, and then they're gone." I strained my eyes, struggling to see through the storm, but there was only darkness and rain. She joined me there at the window and stood close enough so that our shoulders were touching. "It's quiet out there tonight," she said. "Usually nights like this are busy."

I put my forehead against the window. The gutters in the street were flooded, and the surfaces of the puddles were a chaos of splashes. The sound of rain hummed in my skull. "Why?" I said. "Why do they need you?" A glint of light from the edge of a pair of passing high beams swept across us.

"And why you?" she said. She shifted her weight, and leaned into me a little more. We stood that way for a minute or two, watching the rain. "Do you like long walks on the beach?" she asked. We put on our coats and went back downstairs to her gate, where the pile of items had re-formed itself. She shoved it aside with her door and we made our way across the Great Highway and walked across the sand to the waterline. The waves rushed in, fast and angry, and the rain beat down into them. Through it all rose the familiar sound of that violin. I strained over the sound of the waves, trying to locate it. It swelled and receded, swelled and receded, although the wind was holding steady. And then the music and the waves converged and I realized: The song was in the ocean, washing in with the waves and racing back out with the current.

"Do you hear music?" I asked Annabel, raising my voice to be heard over the rain.

She shook her head. "Do you see any ships?" she asked.

I squinted, but with the rain on my face I could barely keep my eyes open. "No," I said.

Annabel said something I couldn't hear.

"What?" I said.

She took my arm and leaned in and when she spoke the warmth of her breath filled my ear. "Where do you think you went, when you died?" she said. "Something can't just disappear and be nowhere and then reappear. You must have gone somewhere."

"I don't know," I said. "I can't remember."

"Try to," she said.

"I will," I said.

"I'd like to help you," she said.

"Thanks," I said.

"You should kiss me now," she said.

***

I stayed with Annabel until midnight or so and then I drove home, climbed into bed, and lay there, wide awake, as you do after a first kiss. But this kiss had been different—it had sealed a strange exchange, an agreement I was just beginning to understand. Annabel had doubled the list of mysteries before me, but she'd also given me herself, her lips and her teeth and her tongue, her own confusion, the humidity of her words in my ear. It was a worthwhile trade—I knew this from the sense of peace and purpose that warmed over me as I lay there, staring through the ceiling, listening to the rain. I eventually fell asleep with the vague shapes of plans forming in my mind, and when I awoke after my brief sleep I went to Eva.

"Listen, I've been thinking," I said.

She'd been lying on the couch, reading something that looked like a supermarket romance novel. She let it fall to her chest but declined to sit up. "Okay," she said.

"I think we should try to be a little more methodical about finding your uncle," I said.

"I'm listening," she said.

"I don't have a specific plan. I just thought we could get a little more organized. Be a little more active."

"Great," she said. "Thanks." She picked her book back up.

"Well, what do you think we should do next? Should we go see Rose?"

"No," she said. "We aren't going to do that."

I sat down at my desk, considering responses. My newfound resolve wavered but I thought again of Annabel's words in my ear. "I'm sure you'd understand if that makes me feel like you're hiding things," I said.

"Yes," she said, sitting up now. "That's because I'm hiding things."

"I'm not sure I understand that," I said.

"That's okay," she said. "You don't have to."

It was taking an increasing effort to fend off exasperation now. "Well, maybe I'd like to," I said, trying to keep my voice even.

"I need you to be open," she said. "I probably shouldn't have even taken you to see Li-Yu's grave."

"'Open'? What does that mean? Wouldn't it be better to just tell me what you know? Why do you get to decide this on your own?"

She took a bookmark from the coffee table, slipped it into her book, and held it on her lap, her eyes down, as if studying the cover image. "If I'm not telling you enough, I can always change that. If I tell you too much, I can't go back and ask you to forget things." She looked up. "What's this sudden change in you, anyway?"

Outside the city was heavy and quiet as a tomb. Even the rain seemed somehow muffled.

"There's a girl," I said.

She grinned. "That sounds about right," she said.

"What does that mean?" I said.

"There's always a girl," she said. She held her arms out, inviting me to look her over—shoeless, graying unkempt hair, the same blackish wrinkled clothes she'd been wearing since she had appeared at my door two, or was it now three weeks ago—and laughed. "And I'm not exactly leading lady material," she said. She opened her book and lay back down. "Actually, that reminds me."

She pointed at a manila envelope sitting on the corner of the coffee table. "I found that outside the door last night."

There was nothing written on it. She'd already opened it. I upended it and a new copy of the journal slid out. On its cover was a Chinese ink painting, a monochrome landscape of mountains and rice paddies.

"You don't need my mom," Eva said.

Henry's school term comes to an end just as the men finish smoothing the paddies. They put the buffaloes back into their paddocks and on a cool spring day they open the floodgates. Li-Yu stands with her children at her side, among the rest of the villagers, and watches the diverted water race across the topmost paddies, through more gates, and into the surrounding terraces. Within a half-day the job is finished and the gates are closed again, and each of the many paddies reflects its own segment of the sky, and holds its own collection of clouds. They gurgle and moan for hours as the men check the walls and channels and gates.

The seedlings are pulled out of their beds and stacked carefully on wooden rafts, one in each paddy. Everybody in the village who can walk takes to the water. Bending at the waist, they wade backward, transplanting the seedlings in neat rows. Once Li-Yu masters the technique the hours become monotonous, their tedium broken only by variations in her discomfort. She finds herself taken over by thoughts about this new watery world, and all that could be lost beneath it: clothing cast aside and swallowed, shoes lost, personal items dropped—anything could disappear into the dark waters in a single unguarded instant, only to be carried back into the river when the paddies are finally drained. She wonders how many children have been lost to this crop. The planting takes days, and after each of them Li-Yu and her children fall into an exhausted sleep, their backs aching, their feet and fingers raw and pruned, the growing smell of mildew in the air.

The sun's daily arc climbs higher and the stalks grow and branch, matched always by their constant reflections. Tiny white flowers appear and seem sometimes to glitter. On the hottest days the sun drives the moisture into the air, creating hot vapors that drift like ghosts among the plants. It becomes so humid that she and the children spend whole afternoons trying not to move.

School resumes and Li-Yu works to relieve the house of everything that won't be missed. Dishware, chopsticks, bits of fabric, tools, and all manner of household items make the trip to Zhang's tables. She develops a regular network of pathways and schedules, lies and pretenses, and methodically she shifts things from the house to the alleyway shop, either smuggling them in her clothing or using the bush as a waypoint. She and Zhang discuss the weather or the condition of the roads as Zhang scrutinizes her wares and counts out coins. Nobody in the house seems to notice the small disappearances, and it is some time before Henry notices that she often has problems with her shoe when they pass the bush, or that the sun is often in her eyes. Occasionally one of the men or one of the maids seeks for and can't find something, but the household is a busy place, and it is hard to keep track of things anyway. Li-Yu learns to use this to her advantage and makes sure that no one has reason for suspicion. Her sock of coins threatens to outgrow its hiding place. She makes cursory searches for a new spot, but finds nothing safe enough.

At school, Henry proves to be a quick study. The speed with which he picks up the language astounds Li-Yu. He comes home from school and teaches lessons to her and to Rose, correcting their pronunciation in a voice she assumes is a mimicry of his teacher, and it makes Li-Yu laugh to herself. Some of the other boys in the village befriend him, and sometimes when Li-Yu sees him playing with them after school it is hard for her to remember what he'd been like before, playing with his toy cars in his bedroom in California, or playing board games with Rose at the kitchen table. Rose pays only half her attention to Henry's short Chinese lessons, and makes no other attempts at speaking Chinese beyond monosyllabic conversations with Li-Yu, and as a result she makes little progress with the language. She disappears for hours on end, occupying herself somewhere on the property. Li-Yu does not press her for details because her daughter has no privacy but this.

School lets out again when the days begin to shorten. The farmers drain the fields, sending the water rushing back into the river, and again the villagers spread out across the paddies, which are now bright green with the mature plants. They slog through the mud, pulling the stalks from the earth and heaping great shaggy bundles on wooden racks to dry. Once the plants have been collected they beat the bundles against woven mats, shaking the rice from their hulls. The mounds grow to waist-high and the elders of the village circulate, stroking their chins and nodding.

The days continue to shorten and cool; winter comes and the river surges. The Year of the Tiger becomes the Year of the Rabbit; the paddies take their annual inhalation and exhalation of water. The Year of the Rabbit becomes the Dragon. Rose is now as conversant in Chinese as Henry, and seems to be fully a girl of Xinhui. Only occasionally does Li-Yu detect in her daughter the weight of memory, the heaviness of the phantom life elsewhere that once promised to be their future. The children never speak English anymore; not even when they are alone together, and do not know she is listening.

Li-Yu now keeps both her money and the immigration papers hidden safely in a wooden box in Zhang's shop, where she has become a secretive partner of sorts. He knows her story well— he has heard several different versions of it now. She finds ways to bring things into his shop, and when he sells them he puts the money into the box and returns it to the same spot every time. She has become not only an expert thief but also a skilled trader—she makes withdrawals from Zhang's box on occasion and returns with more merchandise than the money should buy.

Meanwhile the rice stalks rise and fall; the fields flood and drain, flood and drain.

The Year of the Snake draws to an end among heavy rainfall. Rare snowstorms sweep across Xinhui, covering the fallow fields in flat white blankets. The villagers stay inside by their fires, drinking tea and eating *jook*, burning incense to keep disease away. On one cold day, Li-Yu returns from Zhang's shop with a small silk purse of coins pinched in her armpit. Rose has asked for more paper, so she has made a tiny withdrawal from her hoard in the shop. She is hoping to slip quickly into her room to hide the coins until she can make the purchase, but Mae calls her name as soon as she comes through the door.

"Come here," Mae says. She is sitting on her usual couch, looking tired, and suddenly older somehow. Li-Yu wonders how it is that this can come as a surprise. Perhaps it has been that long since she has taken a close look at her. Li-Yu pinches the coins against her side, wondering what explanation she might offer if the coins should jingle together.

"I have something of yours," Mae says. Though her eyes are on Li-Yu she keeps her face turned to the side, her eyelids heavy. Li-Yu waits, motionless, saying nothing. Finally Mae produces an envelope from within her robes and thrusts it toward Li-Yu.

"Read it to me," she says.

At first Li-Yu is confused. Unlike many of the women in the village, Mae knows how to read. Why should she need this help now? Li-Yu takes the envelope and turns it over, and a burst of light flashes through her body. It is addressed to her. In the envelope's top corner is a San Francisco address, and above that her sister's name, written in a beautiful hand that Li-Yu had almost forgotten. It has already been opened, and when Li-Yu pulls the letter from the envelope it is obvious that the letter has been refolded and stuffed back. She wonders how long ago the letter arrived, and what attempts Mae has made to find a translator.

"What's wrong with your arm?" Mae asks.

"I slipped and fell," Li-Yu says. "I bruised my shoulder on a rock, but it will be fine." She will not move the arm even the slightest amount.

"You should be more careful," Mae says. "We can't afford doctor bills."

Their household is one of the richest in the village; even the maids receive doctor visits when they need them. "I will," Li-Yu says. "I'm sorry." She unfolds the letter, wincing slightly from the fictional pain in her shoulder. In California, her sister's letters had always been in Chinese, but this one is in English. She skims it quickly, her eyes darting down the page, grabbing random words and phrases. They have nearly saved enough money to bring her back, they write. In just a few more months they should be able to bring all three of them home, if she can hang on for just that much longer. Li-Yu is weightless, all of her skin alive with warmth and hope. She gasps and widens her eyes, and makes her hands shake. She tries to make her shoulders droop and sink, despite their desire to rise to the ceiling.

"What?" Mae snaps. "Read it, all of it."

"It's my father," Li-Yu says. "The children's grandfather. He is dying."

Mae looks down. She adjusts the silk blanket over her lap, and then looks away. Li-Yu thanks her for the letter, sniffles, and walks back to her room, her head down, the letter in her hand, the few silent coins hidden in their silk pouch and a ball of light in her chest.

TEN

Monday the storm leaned hard against the city. The wind rushed in off the ocean and twisted through the streets, blowing raindrops like bullets against the sides of buildings. Awnings tore loose and unmanned umbrellas raced along sidewalks like tumbleweeds. I arrived at school and found that the drains on the far side of the school had clogged again and the kindergarteners were back in the cafeteria. "We're used to it," Annabel said, when I saw her in the teacher's lounge before the first bell. "The lunch ladies have been baking cookies so it smells homey." She leaned in close when she said it, and gave my hand a surreptitious squeeze before heading back to her class.

When Kevin came through the door he gave me the storm tally (twenty-one days) and the damage report on his block (a broken tree branch on a neighbor's windshield). My kids were captivated by the mazes' transformations, and a number of theories emerged about the leaking window seal. Being well-trained Californians, they decided it must have had something to do with fault lines. I could think of nothing that sounded more plausible. The seal had stopped leaking water, but the room was about ten degrees cooler than it should have been. Albert, the custodian, told me there was nothing he could do until the rain stopped. Until then, we'd have to crank the heater up.

"That's pretty cool, how the mazes look like Chinese characters," Eliza said. "I didn't notice that last week."

I wasn't about to offer further information. "Thanks," I said. "Do you speak Chinese, Eliza?"

"No," she said.

"I do," Kevin said. "It says 'bing bong ching chong chung.'"

Eliza whirled around. "That's not what it sounds like."

Kevin shrugged. "Sorry, but it does to me."

At some point that morning I remembered my progress reports. I was facing seven or eight a night for the rest of that week—hours' worth, each evening. I tried to push the thought from my mind and pressed on with my day. For the block of time just before lunch I'd planned a science exercise, an activity about mass that required a baseball and a tennis ball—neither of which I could find in my cabinets where I thought I'd stashed them.

"I'll go get them for you," Kevin volunteered.

"From where?" I said.

"The sports shed."

The shed sat against the tall fence, across the puddle-ridden playground, across forty yards of sopping wet grass and mud. We could barely discern its outline through the thick gray rain.

"I appreciate the offer," I said, "but that storm will ruin you."

"I have my raincoat," he said, "and I'm wearing these." He hiked up his pant legs to show me knee-high rubber boots. "I'll go and be back in one minute. Sixty seconds. You can time me."

I didn't have a backup activity planned, and I couldn't go knocking on the doors of other classrooms, asking for balls. "You'd better take the hall pass," I said. He snatched it from its nail and flew out the door. We watched him run across the playground, deliberately steering through the centers of the largest puddles. He ran onto the field and the storm erased his details, reducing him to a bouncing, shrinking patch of gray.

And then one of my students, a girl named Violet, let out a cry. "The shed!" she shouted. "It's moving!"

She was right: The outlines of the shed were shifting. The corners rounded and sank down and the roofline sagged. There was an awful second of electric silence, and then the shed simply vanished. I was out the door, down the hallway, and across the playground within seconds, my arm up to shield my eyes from the rain, my heart frantic. The field was more water than dirt, and after two steps I was soaked up to my knees. I churned across, fighting to pull my feet out of the muck.

Where there should have been a shed, earth, and a retaining wall, there was now a gaping hole. The ground began to slope; I could feel myself sliding toward the opening. Through it I could see nothing—empty space and beyond it parked cars lined up far below along the sidewalk. I turned and scrambled back up to level ground and bolted for the school's driveway. Panic ripped through me; it felt as though my heart were pumping sand through my veins. Images of Kevin's little body, broken and ruined, shoved their way into my head. I reached the edge of the grass and turned and ran down the sidewalk, mud flying from my shoes, my feet slipping on the concrete, everything inside me screaming.

The shed's wreckage lay in the middle of the street, a mass of bent corrugated metal and broken wood, half-buried in mud. The handles of hockey sticks and baseball bats jutted out of a tangled soccer net. A steady stream of brown water was falling through the gap in the broken retaining wall, bringing with it gobs of mud that splattered against the rubble and burst on the street like wet bombs. A few brightly colored rubber balls dotted the mud mound like toppings on a sundae. There was no sign of Kevin.

I continued to run, searching the street and sidewalk. I reached the edge of the wreckage and leapt into it, kicking chunks of concrete aside, slicing my fingers as I pulled at crumpled sections of metal, looking for a protruding arm, a leg, any hint of clothing. I could hear myself roaring, yelling Kevin's name as I searched. I was breathing in such great sawing drafts that I was pulling rain into my lungs. I launched into a spasm of coughing. My vision began to darken; the colored balls around me began to lose their color.

"Hey Mr. Long," a voice said. I whirled and found Kevin standing a short way up the road. In one hand he held a baseball, in the other a tennis ball. The hall pass stuck out from his pocket. "You ran right past me!" he said. He looked up at the hole in the wall. "Am I in trouble?" he asked.

***

When I arrived home that afternoon I found Lucy sitting on the top step of my building, beneath the awning, smoking a cigarette. The smoke mixed with the smell of the rain and made me feel for a second like I was somewhere far away. I ducked under the awning and dropped back the hood of my raincoat. Lucy looked down at the burning cigarette and then she looked at me. "I know," she said. "I shouldn't be doing this."

"I've heard people say it's not good for you," I said. "How'd you make it back? I was expecting I'd come down to pick you up."

"Trains and taxis," she said. "Jesus Christ! What happened to you?"

She was looking at my hands, each of which was wrapped with multiple Band-Aids. They were still raw and stung like hell, but none of the cuts had required stitches. The blue-gray smoke of her cigarette tinted the air between us as I told her about the shed. Albert, the custodian, had found a pair of pants in his truck for me, too large but clean and dry. My socks were in the school dumpster. I had hosed off my shoes and attempted to dry them over my room's heaters. Inside them my feet felt like cold bread dough.

Franklin Nash had helped me deal with the aftermath. He suggested I put on a movie and while I stayed with my kids he ran through my class's phone list, summoning parents who were available, offering reassurances to those who weren't, leaving detailed messages when he couldn't get through. As their rides arrived he called my kids to his office and had them collected there. I told him I wanted to talk to parents myself but he said I'd have the chance later. He said I should focus on my class, or what remained of it, until the final bell.

Kevin had handled the rest of the day well enough for an eight-year-old who'd just sidestepped oblivion. He returned to the classroom to an uproarious reception, dripping rainwater, still holding the balls like trophies. He absorbed the attention and questions with his usual humor and energy, but once we'd dried off and eaten and settled and the adrenaline was gone and the movie was rolling he grew very still. I took a seat nearby and watched him, descending along with him into reimaginings of the morning's incident, into the full realization of what a shift of a few seconds would have meant. By the movie's halfway point my confidence as a teacher was badly rattled.

"My God," Lucy said, when I was finished. "You must have been freaking out. Are you going to get in trouble? Because you shouldn't."

"I don't know," I said.

"Still, though, if I were that kid's mom I'd go bananas. Not at you. Bananas in general. But listen, I did some meditating up at Mom's."

"Meditating? I didn't know you were into that sort of thing."

"Some people might describe it as 'eating pot brownies and staring at redwoods,' but it doesn't really matter what you want to call it," she said. "Anyway, I figured some shit out, about how you drowned and how I knew about it and about that guy I kept seeing in New York. What's your theory on that, by the way?"

"On what?"

"Your dying, or my remembering. Both. Either."

I shrugged. "Some other things came up," I said. "I didn't get much of a chance to think about it," I said.

"Other things came up? What the fuck, Peregrine?" she said. She jabbed at the air with her cigarette. A spray of ash leapt from its tip and fell to the steps. "You were dead. You were *dead*. That's *crazy*. What the hell else was more important than that? You put that on the back burner because you ran out of milk or some shit?"

"Mystery calligraphy and ghost ships," I said. "Oh, and there's a girl."

She jumped and let out a yelp, and threw her arms around me. "Oh my God! It's about time!"

"Thanks a lot."

"But you can tell me about her later. And that other crap. So that guy I was seeing in New York? The Chinese guy?"

"Yeah?"

"So at first I lumped him in with the city. I thought of him as just another of the many reasons I had to get out of there. But I don't think that's right. I think he wants me to be here. I think I'm supposed to be here." She sucked on her cigarette and blew another plume into the rain. "Now don't start thinking that I'm pulling some kind of everything-happens-for-a-reason bullshit, because I'm not. I don't believe that crap for one second. This is a world where toddlers step on land mines and if you can look at that and say there's a reason for it, then you're not thinking very hard." She swiped her cigarette through the air as if to underline her words. "When you jumped into the pool the other night, it was as if those images were just suddenly in my mind, like someone kicked open a hole in my head and threw them in. So where did they come from? I wouldn't have remembered all that if I hadn't been there with you at the pool. And this guy, and your story, and Eva's. This has all got to be related, because otherwise there's just too much crazy shit going on all at once."

A taxi trudged up the hill, rain falling through the cones of its headlights. The barren trees on the sidewalk in front of the building turned from black to white to taillight-red and back to black again.

"But anyway," she said, "I think I'm supposed to be here. You need my help. Or I need yours. I've got to find that guy."

"You're going back to New York?"

"No. He's here. He led me here. And don't say I'm paranoid— it's not paranoia if I *want* to find him. Besides, I think he's on our side. I'm going to find him. We're going to find him."

"And then what?" I asked.

"Hell if I know," she said. She took a final drag of her cigarette and flicked it into the rain. The butt flashed and vanished.

I wanted to ask her a dozen other questions, but she didn't know the answers to those either, any more than I did. But I could feel the weight beneath her words, the weight and the momentum. It had always been like that with her. When I'd faltered, she'd acted. When I'd sought information, she'd sought movement. She was right; I did need her. She might not have known where to take the search, but she would see to it that once a direction arose, we'd follow it to the end of wherever it led, obstacles falling along the way beneath her onslaught of profanity and pepper spray.

I went upstairs and took a hot shower and pulled on pajamas and a bathrobe. I sat down at my desk with my laptop and found I couldn't type, so I peeled the Band-Aids off my fingers and left them in a little beige pile alongside the keyboard. I launched into my progress reports, forcing all else from my mind. I made it through one, and then another, and I was halfway through a third when the fatigue of the day's stresses overwhelmed me. My eyes clamped shut involuntarily; my head felt as though it weighed a thousand pounds. I pushed my computer back, folded my arms on my desk, let my head sink, and fell directly into a dream. In it I was sitting alone and cross-legged in the middle of a hot field of dead, flattened straw, directly beneath a piercing sun. The air tasted of dirt and heat. From my pores seeped not beads of sweat, but tiny red flowers.

An ache in my bent neck woke me up. The typing, perhaps, had opened up one of the cuts on my fingers, and now I saw that there were small spots of blood on my keyboard.

九

The days grow longer and the snow turns to rain, and then it stops. The village comes to life, as though it had been hibernating. Voices grow louder and more cheerful and the children run through town on legs that have been cold and idle for months, searching in the shade for clumps of snow that have yet to melt. The men hitch their plows to the water buffalo and drive them back into the fields, where they sink their tines into the mud and begin their slow treks. When the last terrace is ready they open the floodgates. As it has each year for generations, the community turns out in full strength and before long the planting is finished. The water's surface settles and the sun migrates across a reflected sky through fields of transplanted seedlings.

One morning later that summer Li-Yu awakens to find the village humming. She learns that one of the oldest farmers, a man named Peng-tze, who prides himself on being the earliest into the paddies, has discovered a peculiarity in this year's crop. She rushes into the paddies along with the rest of the village, where they pull the young plants close to their eyes, using their fingertips to turn them this way and that, studying the new panicles, counting the little buds that will become rice grains. There are nearly twice as many as usual. The townspeople wade through the fields, moving as quickly as the mud and water will let them, examining plant after plant. As the reports come back from farther and farther out, the excitement builds. Every plant in every paddy looks as though it will produce nearly twice its normal number of grains.

The farmers rush to take the news to the elders, the *feng shui* masters who synchronize the village's activities with the energies and movements of the universe and the ancestors. Their chief is Hui, a short man with a deeply lined face and eyes that are barely glints. The news does not make him smile. "Such a fortune was not foreseen," he says. "Perhaps the grains will be half as large."

But the excitement is more powerful than Hui's pronouncement, particularly among the younger farmers, especially when stories begin to spread about a similar occurrence in a village in Guangxi, or maybe it was Hunan, where the grains doubled not only in number but also in size, and the village became the richest in the province. These stories circulate until they become truth, and the village erupts in revelry. An impromptu feast is planned in celebration, and within an hour two pigs and forty chickens have been slaughtered and are roasting on spits. The festivities go on for days. The farmers come out of the paddies each evening, singing. They buy liquor on credit and stay up late, toasting the crop and their farming skills, and then fall asleep at one another's homes, bottles dropping from their hands.

And then Peng-tze ventures out into the fields early one windy summer dawn and makes another discovery. Every rice plant ever raised in these fields has borne white flowers, but now he finds tiny red flowers emerging from between the growing grains. He examines another plant, and then another, and finds all the flowers have turned red. He rushes back to the village to report his findings, and again the other farmers fly into the paddies to examine their plants and word begins to come in from one field after another—there isn't a single white flower anywhere to be found.

It is one of Peng-tze's grandchildren, a small girl with sharp eyes, who looks out over the fields and says, "Look, everything is pink," and she is right—the low sun is making the fields blush, their flowers pulsating like warm capillaries beneath a layer of skin. Before there can be any consternation an explanation quickly emerges, irresistible in its simplicity and cheer: What better to herald this bountiful crop than flowers of red, the color of wealth and celebration? Misgivings are further quieted when men arrive all the way from the university in Canton two weeks later. They offer giant sums in exchange for several days' lodging, access to the fields, and a few plants, which they take back with them in carefully packaged bundles, wet cloth strips wrapped around the fragile roots.

For Li-Yu, the promise of the crop is a windfall. Mae sends the maids out for new furniture, new fabrics, new dishes for the kitchen. Suddenly there are piles of displaced, forgotten things around the house, with nowhere to go. Li-Yu steals as much of it as she can. She transports sack after sack to Zhang's shop. She has done this now for so many years without attracting suspicion that she has grown careless, and now among this glut of riches, and with the assurance of her sisters' promise, she grows almost reckless. Several times she leaves money out in plain sight, in her room. She creates flimsy pretenses to head to Jianghai—there is even talk among the maids that she has taken a lover there. She still does not know what the passage back to America will cost, but she writes a letter to her sisters—I have a little money, she tells them. Maybe we won't have to wait as long. Maybe now, maybe this could be the time.

Her children still know nothing of Zhang, or the money, or their aunts' efforts, or her own steady determination, and now they have been here so many years she has to wonder how they'll receive the news of the move back to California. The two of them have become fully Chinese over the years, especially Henry. At some point she realizes he has spent more of his life in China than in America. In public, he is indistinguishable from the other boys. He walks to school and back with them, speaking Cantonese as easily as he'd once spoken English, laughing loudly. And he is the heir of a grand household, with its wings and its outbuildings and its servants. They are only rice farmers, but he is a prince among them, the only son of an oldest son. When the time comes, Li-Yu will be asking him to leave much behind.

Rose's assimilation has been slow and painful, but she has managed to find a place to survive. She has made friends in the village, and her Cantonese is beautiful—lyrical and rounded, its angularity tempered by the English of her first years. Now she is nearing the age where in America, at least, it would not have been unusual for her to start spending time with boys. The truth is, Li-Yu doesn't know much about her daughter anymore. The truth is, she realizes, she has let her children slip away from her. She began with the best of intentions: the refusal to doom them to the lives of outsiders, as foreigners, and the determination to give them the best lives they could possibly have amid these cruel circumstances. With Henry it had been easy. He had been young, and everyone had embraced him. But with Rose—with Rose she had no choice but to reel her out, to turn away from her so this girl would not be reliant on a mother who could do so little for her. Now, even though they sleep in the same room, they sometimes go for a full day or two without speaking, like strangers. It is the best thing for her, Li-Yu tells herself, on her strong days. Rose has learned to survive; she is filled with a quiet strength all her own. In Li-Yu's worst moments, though, she wonders if perhaps she turned her back on Rose simply because she could not bear the sadness of it. Or, perhaps, it is her own monumental failure to protect her children that she can't bear to face.

And now maybe it has taken too long; perhaps it is too late. What does Henry even remember of California? What could have survived in his memory when she forbade him to speak of it, or to long for it? Rose has her memories, she knows, but how has she transformed them, what ramparts has she built between them and herself, out of self-preservation? Li-Yu remembers forcing them to speak Chinese upon their arrival, all those years ago, and now she wishes she'd let them cling to their English. At least at night, in their room, away from everyone else they might have been allowed to remember. She wants badly to tell them her plan, especially Rose. Do you ever think about home, she might simply ask. But it would betray too much, and she can't take the risks—either the risk of discovery, or the risk of what might happen if she fails. It will have to wait, she knows. It will have to wait until the very hour it is time to leave.

Meanwhile the plants continue to grow and though their stalks push toward the sun, their grain-laden heads grow heavy and begin to droop, as though they are too tired to stand. A steady wind blows into autumn, and the plants rattle and knock and sound like a thousand voices conspiring.

ELEVEN

That night I dreamed Kevin hadn't made it out of the shed in time.

***

By the next morning, San Francisco was a tangle of public works projects: a broken water main in the Haight, stopped-up sewers in Hunter's Point, a sinkhole in the Outer Richmond, flooding in China Basin. The city would not be listing our retaining wall high among its priorities. The extent of governmental involvement thus far had been to ship out some intern from their engineering office who declared the hillside stable. A single strand of thin yellow tape now stretched between the tetherball poles at the edge of the asphalt, forming a childproof barrier and guaranteeing everyone's safety.

I didn't know what Franklin had said to the parents yesterday, but few of them came to my door during the drop-off, and those who did were polite, deferential. Kevin was a celebrity in the hallways. Even after he'd made his way to his desk I'd catch groups of kids from other classes standing in the doorway, pointing and whispering.

Eliza came to my desk and asked me what would happen if the rest of the retaining wall were to crumble.

"The city says it won't," I said.

She informed me that in 1966, a mudslide in Wales had buried a school and killed more than half of its students.

"Don't worry," I said. "That's not going to happen."

"Good," she said.

At lunch, Franklin Nash slipped into my room, just as my last kid slipped out. "Hello, Peregrine," he said. "Got a few minutes?"

179

"Sure," I said. I started to rise from my desk but he motioned for me to remain. I set down my pen.

He closed my door, sat down on one of the desks in the front row and looked me directly in the eye. The winged pickles on his tie did nothing to diminish the solemnity of his gaze. "How are you holding up?" he said.

"Okay," I said. "A little rattled, I guess."

"That's to be expected," he said. "I'd have to wonder about you if you weren't." He glanced through the window, at the spot where the shed had been. "Kevin seems to be doing well, all things considered. He's holding court out in front of the bathrooms, with about half the student body. Seems to be making the most of his newfound celebrity."

"He's a good kid," I said.

Franklin nodded. "They are resilient at that age. But these things can have consequences that reach far beyond the immediate fallout. As you know."

I nodded.

"Dr. Eliot will be working closely with him and his parents, who fortunately understand the need for such conversations in times like this. And she'll be depending on you to keep an eye on the rest of these boys and girls and to bring it to her attention the first time you have a suspicion of something amiss."

"Of course."

"Great," he said, opening his arms as if to hug me, though he was half the room away. Briefly I wondered if I was supposed to get up and go to him, but then he brought his hands back down and pushed himself back to his feet.

"Thanks for helping me out yesterday," I said.

"Anything less would have been a dereliction of duty," he said, with the smallest of smiles. When he was nearly to the door he stopped and turned back around. "Peregrine," he said, "on a similar but related note. I've been at this a long while, and I know that some teachers come to school, teach, go home, correct their students' papers, make dinner, and go to bed. Others go home and do other things. Pedagogy is a noble and crucial profession, but I do not pretend that it has to be all-consuming."

I nodded. I wasn't sure exactly what he was talking about, but I had the sense that something inexorable was bearing down on me.

"I make it a policy not to stick my nose into the private lives of my faculty," he said, "but sometimes factors outside campus can become distracting. They can become . . . ." He paused, as though searching for words. "They can become detrimental to a teacher's ability to teach at the level of his or her full potential."

I picked my pen back up and put it down. There was an itch on my neck; I resisted scratching it.

"I mentioned the assistance that will be provided to Kevin and his family. Well, the district has similar resources available for faculty. Of course, I hope my teachers will think of me as one of those resources, but I'm certainly not the extent of it," he continued.

"Okay," I said, so quietly I don't think he could have heard me.

He pulled the door open. "Don't want anybody twisting in the wind," he said over his shoulder. He reached up and knocked on the door frame, twice. "Take care now," he said.

***

I don't know what impelled me to Pier 23 when school let out the next day. Maybe it was the instinct we all have to retrace our steps when we reach dead ends. Maybe it was a sense of the unfinished—Lucy's phone call had frozen me on the threshold of that strange workshop, before I could take it all in. Perhaps there was nothing there—a storage room for some antiquated equipment, some people with no better place to meet. But there were also those quadruplets to consider, whose existence Annabel couldn't explain.

I zipped up my raincoat, pulled my hood up, and headed for the waterfront. Even in the sheltered bay the water was tumultuous.

Gray waves churned together, their tops white and foamy. Sprays of water leapt up above the pilings and beat into the wharves. Pier 23 soon came into sight. Its big door was open and the windows of the building inside were full of light. Forklifts crisscrossed the road that led down the center of the building, shuttling into and out of the cones of orange light cast by the giant hanging fixtures. There were distant shouts, the quick beep of a horn, a faint strain of music.

The office was empty. It looked more or less like I remembered it—clipboards, stacks of paperwork, calendars. I headed for the stairs, trying to decide what I'd ask the mahjong players if I found them there again. A doorway in the back of the building led into another lighted room, where a man in coveralls sat, hunched over a desk. When I reached the bottom of the stairwell he saw me and rose suddenly.

"Can I help you?" he said, in a way that made it clear he wasn't offering help. He circled his desk with surprising speed. He was Chinese. The top of his head was bald, but a sweep of shoulder-length hair hung down from the sides and back and bounced with his steps. He had a thin curving mustache and his eyes were hard and sharp.

"It's okay, I have an appointment," I said, heading up the stairs.

"No appointments," he said, quickening his pace.

"Yes, they're expecting me," I said. I started to climb two at a time. I had to see that room.

"Closed area!" he yelled at me. I expected to hear his footsteps running after me, up the stairs, but they didn't come. I made it to the top of the stairs, hurried down the hallway, and threw open that final door. There was no machinery, no table, no women. It was nothing more than a cluttered storeroom, a fraction of the workshop's size. Junk spilled out of metal shelving units. A photocopier half-blackened with dirt and toner stood against one wall. Parts of office chairs had been tossed in a heap. There were stacks of cardboard cartons in various states of deterioration, an upright vacuum cleaner with a cracked housing.

Then came the burst of footfalls and the man appeared at the top of the stairs, breathing heavily, a length of iron pipe in his hands. Something about the way he held it made me think he'd actually hit people with it before. He saw I was only staring at the garbage in his closet, so he stopped where he was. He watched me carefully over the course of three or four heavy breaths. "What the fuck you doing?" he said. It was not a rhetorical question. He was genuinely perplexed.

I pointed into the storeroom. "The other night, I thought," I said. "Maybe a different room? Four women? A workshop?"

"Time to go," he said. "Now."

"Four women," I said again. "I'm looking for four women."

He shook his head. "Wrong place," he said. "*Ware*house, not *whore*house." He allowed himself a small smile at his joke—apparently my threat levels were decreasing. "You should learn how to spell. Let's go."

"No, please," I said. "Mahjong players. I'm looking for the mahjong players in that machine shop. With the printing equipment."

He lowered the pipe a few inches but his face showed no recognition.

"Does that sound crazy?" I said. "Do I sound crazy to you?"

"Crazy or drugs," he said. "Either way, time to go."

"What about a magazine?" I said. "A journal? Is there a journal here?"

He shook his head. "No books here," he said. "It's a warehouse, not a library."

"No, its offices," I said. "The *Barbary Quarterly*. Is its office here? Do they print something here?"

He shook his head.

"Publishers?" I said. "Editors?"

"Shipping only," he said. "Nothing else."

"Do you play mahjong?" I asked him.

Impatience flashed back across his face. The pipe rose; the threat levels were rising again. He stepped away from the stairs and pointed down them with his empty hand. "We can talk more outside."

I glanced back into the storeroom and beneath a low shelf along the back wall I noticed what looked like the corner of a small white block. "Hang on," I said. I darted in, ignoring the man's shout. I picked up the block and turned it quickly over in my palm. It was cool and heavy and smooth, and it seemed very old. A Chinese character had been carved into one side, and painted blue. I slipped it into my pocket just before he rushed through the doorway. He was holding the pipe in both hands now, like a batter ready for a fastball.

I turned away from him and tried to cover my head with my arms. "I'm sorry!" I said. "I'm going, I'm going!"

He stayed in the doorway, the pipe still raised. I stole a look at him through the useless barrier of my arms. He was searching the room, perhaps trying to figure out if there was anything at all in there worth stealing. Eventually he backed up, but didn't lower the pipe. "You need help, buddy," he said.

Once outside I called Annabel. "Where are you?" I said.

"Still at school," she said, "working on my report cards. How are yours coming?"

"Don't leave," I said. "I'll be right there." I flagged down a cab and ten minutes later I was in Annabel's classroom. I dropped the tile into her hand.

"It's a mahjong piece," she said.

"I know," I said. "I found it."

She took it and turned it around and over in her hands. "It's hand-carved," she said. "Ivory. Rare. Where did you get this?"

"Pier 23."

"The bar?"

"The office in the warehouse. Remember when I asked you about the Chinese quadruplets?"

"Sure," she said.

"I went back. So what does it say?"

"*Bak.* North."

"North?"

"It's one of the wind tiles. The North Wind. *Bak Feng.*"

"Come with me," I said.

"Where?"

"To the top of the hill."

On our way out, Franklin noticed us through his office window and gave us a wave. We walked up the few blocks that led to the crest of Russian Hill and the view to the north opened up before us. The clouds seemed a little less dark than they'd been lately and though the rain was steady it had lessened a bit. The Golden Gate Bridge was mostly visible; only the tops of its towers were hidden in clouds. At the far end of the span the hills of the Marin Headlands bristled with thick scrub, all the way down to the waterline. The bay, gray and empty, stretched back and around, narrowing as it reached inland for the delta. A lone ship traversed the water, a passenger ferry circling slowly around Angel Island.

"I don't know what I'm supposed to be looking for," she said.

A trio of pelicans cruised through the rain in a loose wedge, far away and high above us.

"Neither do I," I told her.

She slipped her hand into mine and we stood there watching for a time, waiting for something to reveal itself.

***

That night a vicious surge arrived and killed five people across the Bay Area, three of them in San Francisco. Of these, two were the victims of a car crash in which a little pickup truck, going too fast down Valencia, had hydroplaned through a red light and slammed into a bread delivery truck. I watched the coverage on the little television in my room when I awoke. The graveyard-shift camera crew revealed the scene—a crumpled pickup on its side, the banged-up bread truck, and all around them loaves of bread wrapped in cellophane, pieces of metal, broken glass. The shards glinted in the cameraman's spotlight and looked like a constellation in the roadway. The third death was an elderly man who had fallen, hit his head, and drowned in his flooded backyard. The newscaster, wrapped in a shapeless black raincoat, stood out on the sidewalk, ropes of black hair whipping around her face. She squinted into the wind and rain and shouted wild speculations about sleepwalking and medication. Behind her, the paramedics wheeled a gurney through the rain, a white sheet draped over the body. A sudden gust of wind came up and pulled back a corner of the sheet, revealing a booted foot.

I arose and climbed into the shower with the image of that boot stuck in my head. I have never liked seeing dead people's shoes. I don't mean the slippers sitting on the floor next to the hospital bed, or the loafers on the guy in the casket. I mean the regular shoes of people who awaken and get dressed with no idea they will die that day. The pictures appear on the news: the jeans and worn-out tennis shoes sticking out from beneath the earthquake wreckage in some third-world backwater with no building codes; the basketball shoes and too-long shorts on the inner-city kid caught in a drive-by. I always picture these people on the morning of their deaths, in that quiet, concentrated moment as they tie their laces, or clasp their buckles. I want to go to them then and say, I'm sorry but you're going to die today—are you sure those are the shoes you want to be in when it happens? When I die I don't want to be wearing shoes. I want to have just enough notice so that I can pull them off and get comfortable. Shoes mean death snuck up on you. Shoes mean you had other plans.

In the living room Eva was asleep on the couch and Lucy had stretched out on her piece of floor behind my desk chair. She heard me in the kitchen and after some stirring and grunting she opened her eyes.

"Hey," she said when she saw me. "I need your help."

"The guy?" I asked.

"I got a job interview." She yawned and shot a dirty look at the weather.

"I think you're supposed to do those on your own," I said. "Do you want some coffee?"

"Sure," Lucy said. "I just need a ride. And maybe a reference, but not as my brother."

"What, as your landlord?" I said. I went to work grinding the beans.

"As a teacher."

"That wouldn't be too much of a stretch," I said. "What kind of job is it?"

"A nanny," she said, "in Tiburon."

"A nanny? Do you even like kids?"

"It's live-in," she said. "They have a separate cottage on their property and I'd get some meals and cash and all I'd have to do is hang out with a couple of kids. It would solve the majority of my current logistical issues."

"Boys or girls?"

"One of each."

"How old?"

"I don't remember, exactly. One of them, the boy, was kind of young, I think, and the girl was kind of in-between."

"In between what?"

"In between young and old."

"Wouldn't you need a car?"

"They want me to use one of theirs," she said. "So maybe you could say that I volunteered in your classroom, and that I'm great with kids, and whatever. You'd know what to say."

"Okay," I said. "But under two conditions. Come volunteer in my classroom, and be great with the kids."

She sat up. "Seriously?"

"Seriously. When's your interview?"

"This weekend."

"Better get your ass up," I said.

***

"It's been raining twenty-four days in a row," Kevin said to Lucy, by way of an introduction. He turned to me. "Hey Mr. Long," he said. "Did you see about that guy that drowned in his yard last night?"

"Yes," I said.

He hooked his thumbs beneath his backpack straps. "And did you know that a fish can drown?"

"I don't think so," I said.

"Well they can," he said.

"You mean if they're taken out of the water?"

"Even in the water it can happen," he said, "if there isn't enough oxygen. Isn't that weird?"

"Yes," I said. "It is."

He shook his head as though awestruck by the world's great nuances and headed to his desk for a session of multiplication drills. I invented a couple of activities for Lucy that morning to get her involved with small groups of some of my more reasonable kids, but just after lunch I had a better idea. I collected the class on the floor, planted Lucy on a stool, and handed her my worn copy of *James and the Giant Peach*. My plan was to knock out a couple of progress reports while Lucy and Roald Dahl occupied my kids for twenty minutes or so. But when I sat down at the computer I couldn't shake the image of those little red flowers.

✝

Throughout the summer the strange plants continue to grow. The grains grow at their normal rate—perhaps even a bit faster, some say—and as autumn approaches the town throws itself with zeal into planning the annual harvest festival. It will be in proportion to the crop: twice as long, twice as festive, twice as debauched.

It is within these heady days that Hui, who has spent much of the summer out of sight, emerges, and begins to voice his concerns. As bountiful as the crop is this year, he cautions, it is a bad omen. He has been studying the signs carefully, he says, and he has found nothing in the calendar that foretells this fortune. The ancestors are indifferent to this year, he says. It is great luck, yes, but it is misplaced. It is someone else's luck. He is too easy to ignore, however. There is dissent, even among the council. Hui's interpretations become even easier to disregard when he issues his recommendation—if the plants are producing twice as many grains as they should, then half of the crop ought to be destroyed. Balance will be restored. The coming debt will be averted. Those who have been ignoring him continue to do so, and those who haven't react with anger. What Hui is asking is unthinkable. Many of them have already spent much of the money they will be earning after the harvest. It is madness, they say, for him to try to erase this fortune. His age is catching up to him; the stale air and the incense in his rooms have softened his brain. But Hui is persistent. This winter will bring cold and misery, he says. Once the crop is harvested and sold, he says, the ancestors will find a way to collect their due. When the crop is harvested and sold, the villagers retort with laughter, and the winter grows cold, we will be able to burn our riches, and warm ourselves by their fires.

And then early one foggy morning Peng-tze makes his third discovery. He wades into the paddies to check on his plants and when he reaches the first row, he finds that some of the developing grains have fallen from their panicles. He bends closer and finds the empty spots are stained a dark red. A light breeze arises, and as he watches, another grain loosens and falls to the water below. In the resulting wound, a single droplet of blood appears. Peng-tze leans closer, feeling cold and ill. The droplet grows, begins to droop, and finally it lets go of the plant. It plummets to the water and spreads into a flower, with ragged petals that grow and thin, and disappear. Another grain falls, and then another. Peng-tze turns and runs back to the village, as he has done twice before. By the time the other farmers have made it into their fields, there is no need for a careful examination. The sound of rice grains splashing into the water is like a hailstorm. The farmers retreat to the fields' edges and watch the water change from brown to deep red.

The first of the sicknesses is discovered that afternoon. It is one of the farmers' sons. He lies on his bed, the color drained from his face, his mouth dry as a desert, his eyeballs shrinking in their sockets, his breath rasping in his chest like the sound of a breeze stirring up dead leaves.

The council convenes immediately, and nobody speaks as Hui declares, in quiet tones, what must be done. It is decided.

TWELVE

The bell was ringing. I looked up with surprise and more than a little disappointment to find my class watching me expectantly and Lucy sitting with *James and the Giant Peach* in her lap. This wasn't where I wanted to be. It was time for their afternoon recess, or it would have been if their playground hadn't been buried under six inches of water. Lucy had been reading for nearly an hour.

I hopped up from my desk. "Okay, bathroom break," I said, pulling myself out of my story. "Get some water. Do some jumping jacks. Come back dry." They stood and shuffled out of the room, still subdued from their extended story time.

"Sorry," I said to Lucy. "I got hung up with something."

"That's okay," she said. "I could read this book all day long. I forgot how good it is."

"They like you," I said. "I don't think I've ever been able to keep them quiet for that long." Not that I would have tried. I had to hope none of my kids would report that their teacher's sister had read to them for half the afternoon. Too many of their parents considered it their personal duty to ensure that I was properly spending California's tax money, which usually meant I was to be doing things at all times that they themselves couldn't do at home—and they could all read *James and the Giant Peach*.

After the final bell, once my kids had all stomped back out into the wet city, Annabel came through the door. I made the introductions. Lucy knew about her, but I hadn't yet had the chance to tell Annabel much about Lucy.

"I came out to help you guys," Lucy said.

"With school?" Annabel said, looking confused.

Lucy shook her head.

"I can fill you in later," I said. "It's sort of involved."

"An old Chinese phantom rearranged my furniture, led me across the country, and may or may not have had a hand in helping me remember seeing Peregrine drown, which occurred when I was halfway across the country," Lucy said. "So I'm an official member of this little team here."

Annabel looked like she was on the brink of losing composure. She looked at me and then back at Lucy. "Um, welcome aboard?" she said.

"Thanks," Lucy said, with a big smile. "Maybe we could get some shirts made or something."

"Well, since we're all here," Annabel said, recovering, "I've got an update." She pointed at the mazes and their smeared red solutions. "I have a translation. Ready?"

I nodded.

"'I think of my little boat, and long to be on my way,'" Annabel said.

Chills rippled across the skin of my arms. I watched her face for a smile, a flash in her eyes, some indication that she was putting me on. But none appeared. She was watching me as closely as I was watching her.

"So clearly something happened there," she said.

I would have liked to think I was forgetting something—some template I'd copied, or a pattern from a coloring book, some characters lifted from the back of a cookie fortune, anything—that could explain how this line had worked its way into my mazes. But I knew I wasn't. The memories of working on them on the floor beneath my mom's table were absolutely clear. I looked up at them, studied their red strokes. They made me feel very small, small and not myself. And then I realized something I probably should have noticed before: I'd hung them up facing inside. She'd read them from the outside. The solutions to my mazes were not the characters themselves, but their mirror images.

"There's more," Annabel said. She handed me another manila envelope the size and thickness of a copy of *The Barbary Quarterly.* "This was in your box." On the cover of this one was a photo of an old Chinese man sitting on an upturned bucket, a small stringed instrument perched on his knee and a bow in his hand. I couldn't remember having seen the instrument before, but somehow the crash of recognition was strong enough to push the mazes right out of my thoughts. I knew the angles of the musician's wrist and the curve of his right arm as he held the bow against its strings. I could see the way his left hand would dance and tremble up and down its neck. I could hear—had been hearing—the lilt and warble of its mournful voice for weeks now, coming out my shower, coming out of the sea.

Lucy was looking over my shoulder. She planted a finger on the musician's chest. "I know that guy," she said, excitement in her voice.

"What, personally?"

"Yeah. I made out with him at a party. No, not personally." She pointed to the photo's background. "That's Sproul Plaza," she said. "He's there all the time. At least, he was when I was at Berkeley, however many years ago that was."

I leaped out of my seat and started gathering my things.

"I'm coming," Lucy said.

"Me too," Annabel said.

It wasn't yet rush hour but traffic knotted the streets leading to the Bay Bridge's on-ramps. We learned the reason from a radio report—there had been a wreck on the span and three of its five eastbound lanes were blocked. It took us over an hour to make it onto the bridge and up to the site of the accident, where a tight circle of ambulances, police cars, and tow trucks hid the wreckage, as if shielding it from our eyes. Or perhaps it was us they were shielding, from this reminder of the fallibility of our reactions, the fragility of our cars and lives.

After another half-hour we'd found a parking spot and were making our way on foot up Telegraph Avenue, where the weather had done nothing to diminish the clamor. Silver jewelry on vendors' tables glittered darkly inside caves made of tarpaulins. In the air above the sidewalks incense smoke drifted, resisting the rain's attempts to drive it into the sidewalk. We crossed Bancroft and entered Sproul Plaza, the heart of campus. It was the top of the hour, between classes, and the plaza was busy.

We didn't have to search long. The musician sat squarely in the middle of the plaza on his upturned bucket, a dripping gray cloak draped over his rounded shoulders. He looked like an ancient boulder amid a river of collegians. He was facing us, as if he'd been waiting for us.

His instrument stood on his knee. Its body was a small round drum, and from its top rose a long neck, to which two strings were held taut. With his right hand he worked the bow; with his trembling shaking left he fingered the wet strings, whose vibrations emanated wavering notes and tiny cloudlets of mist. The song—my song, the song I'd been hearing—descended into its final measures as we approached, and came to an end just as we paused before him as though it had been composed and timed for our entrance. We clapped; he smiled and bowed his head.

"That was beautiful," Lucy said. "What's it called?"

The man shook his head but continued to smile. He laid the instrument and the bow across his knees, reached into a plastic bag that sat on the ground next to him, and pulled out a little notepad and a red marker. He scratched on the pad and showed it to us. A pair of Chinese characters stood in the middle of the sheet, already beginning to disintegrate in the rain.

"Cantonese, mute," Annabel said. "Nothing we can't handle."

"Ask him where he learned how to play," I said.

Annabel translated, and he jotted another character on his pad.

"From his father," she read.

"Where?" I said.

Again she translated, and again he scratched on the pad.

"Oakland," she said.

"Not China?"

She verified it, and told me again.

"Where was he born?"

Again the answer came back: Oakland.

"He was born here but he doesn't speak English?" I said. "How is that?"

"That's what he says," Annabel said. "What else?"

"What's your instrument called?" Lucy asked.

He wrote down a pair of characters, and Annabel had to try out a few different pronunciations before he smiled and nodded. "It's called an *erhu,*" she said.

I pulled the issue of the *Quarterly* from my jacket. "Ask him if he remembers who took this picture."

Annabel took the journal from me, showed it to the old man, and asked the question. The sight of the photograph brought a deep laugh out of him. He took it from her hands and studied it carefully, his smile broad, and then he jotted another character on the pad and tapped it.

"He doesn't remember," Annabel said.

He jotted down another string of characters and showed the pad to Annabel. "He wants it," she said.

"He can have it," I said.

Annabel gave him the news, and he clasped his hands together and gave me a deep bow. He slipped the journal into the bag.

"What was the song called?" Lucy asked.

Annabel translated the question, but his sheet was full, and it was the last page. He dropped the spent notebook into his bag and fished around and found an old postcard. On the blank side he jotted down the name and handed it to Annabel.

"River of Sorrow," she read.

"A real pick-me-upper," Lucy said.

She handed me the postcard. I took it and stared at the characters. There was nothing familiar about the name. I thought of the network of tributaries that had carried Li-Yu and her family from Canton to Xinhui, but I knew I was stretching for connections, stamping meaning onto phenomena whose echoes were probably just coincidences.

"River of Sorrow," I repeated. "Are you sure?" I handed the postcard back to Annabel.

She gave it another glance and nodded. "Yes," she said. She tapped the characters and translated them, one after the other. "Anything else you want me to ask him?" she said. She looked at Lucy. "Is this getting us anywhere?"

It didn't seem right that this path should end here, with a California native sitting by himself in the rain, playing a song that meant nothing to me, his only audience disinterested students. There had to be more, somewhere. "Yes," I said. "Ask him who he is and why he matters. Ask him why he was on that cover. Ask him who brought it to me, and ask him about that song. Ask him why I keep hearing it. Ask him why it comes out of my showerhead, and ask him why I heard it washing up on shore that night we went down to the beach. Ask him why I came here to find him, and ask him to tell us what we need to know next."

Annabel gave me a sad little smile. "Oh, Perry," she said.

"I don't know if you should ask him all that," Lucy said.

"Please. Just ask him."

"Really?"

"Please."

Annabel took a minute to compose the words in her head, and then she spoke to him for a long time. The old violinist nodded as he listened, that same little smile playing on his lips. When Annabel finished he looked at me. He nodded a few more times, as if in agreement. As if to say, Yes, those are the right questions.

And then he shrugged, and his smile grew wider. He picked the instrument up from his lap, set it on his knee, and fingered the strings. He dragged the bow across them and the opening strains of another mournful song rose and filled the rainy plaza.

***

"We found the violinist," I said to Eva when we got back home. "It was entirely anticlimactic."

"What violinist?" she said.

"What does 'River of Sorrow' mean to you?" I sat down at my desk and sent the most recent installments of the story to my printer.

"What are you talking about?"

"It's a song," I said.

"Never heard of it," Eva said.

When the last page slid out I punched a staple through the pages and tossed the stack over to her. The sheaf landed on the couch and splashed up against her leg. As she read the only sounds were those of the rain falling and Lucy in the kitchen, making instant ramen. Eva finished and tossed the papers back on to my desk.

"It is decided that what?" she asked.

十一

It is decided that the masters will voyage into the world of *yin*, the realm of ancestral spirits and hidden causes and sources. On the day the ceremony is to be performed the men of the household are still and somber. Mae sits on her couch, lost in thoughts, making only occasional demands of the maids.

"The masters," Li-Yu asks her. "How do they get to the world of *yin*?"

"On the backs of spirit horses," Mae says. "Hui will summon them and then remain here to light their way."

"How long will it take?"

Mae shrugs. "There are many levels. It depends how deeply the causes are hidden."

"And what will they find?"

"The ancestors will show them how to restore the proper circulation of *xi* through the village," she says. "They will learn how to restore order."

"And then what?"

"You can see for yourself. We will all be there. Henry must be there especially—he may have to participate in *guo-yin* someday himself." She explains that it has been two generations since the ceremony's last performance, and only the oldest of the townspeople can remember their grandfathers taking the trip, searching for the causes of floods that plagued the valley one long-ago springtime. "No more questions now," she says, rubbing her temples. "Leave me to my thoughts."

That night after sunset the villagers crowd into the public meeting hall in the center of town. They push and jostle for positions along the walls, nervous and silent. Li-Yu and her children are among the last to arrive, and they are barely able to squeeze in through the doorway. Li-Yu can just barely see over the shoulders of those standing before her. Her children lean into her waist, seeing nothing but the back of a wall of bodies.

Seven of the eight masters sit on a low bench of painted wood, shoulder to shoulder, wearing heavy blindfolds; the lower halves of their faces glow orange from the light of the lanterns that hang from the hall's support posts. Hui, the eighth, stands in front of them. He opens a small red book and begins to recite incantations. Incense smoke curls from the wooden bowls on the ground and thickens the air. The men on the bench pass a bottle back and forth a few times and then return it to Hui. Each of them picks up a cord of woven rice stalks and clutches it in his hands, like reins. Hui's incantations grow in volume and pace; his voice becomes rhythmic and driving, and the beats of it push out through the smoke and thud into the first row of the crowd. The masters' knees begin to bounce. Hui chants for several minutes and their legs bounce faster, until the floor is shaking. Rose and Henry had pushed up through the crowd to get a better view, but now they return to Li-Yu's side and draw in close. From all around them now comes a sound like the pounding of hooves against the earth. With spasmodic quickness, Hui tips up the big bottle, takes in a huge draught, and then sprays it from his mouth into the air before the men on the bench. In the smoky light the mist bursts into a great bright cloud before sinking to the ground.

The ghost horses arrive in a herd; their hooves shake the walls and rattle the roof. Their restless pacing forms appear outlined in the incense smoke, which puffs and billows under the force of their movements and exhalations. Rose and Henry press back into their mother. Even Li-Yu has to fight the urge to back toward the door. And then one of the blindfolded men half-rises from the bench, shakes, and falls back down. The men lined along the wall behind him rush forward to help. He continues to twitch and buck, but they guide him back into his seat and remain there, close by. One by one, each of the men finds his spirit mount. The hoofbeats recede and the smoke grows still again as they ride forth into the hidden world, searching. Hui continues to guide them with his incantations, pausing every few minutes to emit another great spray of water over the men. The droplets catch the light of the lanterns and glitter as they fall through the smoke. On the bench each of the horsemen rocks and leans with the motion of his mount. Behind them their helpers await, poised to catch them should they fall. Occasionally there are shouts, but because many of the blindfolds have begun to come unraveled, and fabric hangs down over some of the masters' mouths, it is hard to know who is shouting. In voices that do not sound like their own, the men holler out strings of words, only some of which Li-Yu understands. The crowd murmurs and whispers, discussing interpretations, asking for clarifications and translations. Li-Yu strains to hear what people are saying, but nothing is clear until one of the men in front of her leans over to his neighbor, and says, distinctly, "It's a woman." The listener nods. "A thief," he responds. And then he glances backward over his shoulder and catches Li-Yu's eye.

Heat bursts through Li-Yu. Instantly she finds herself sweating. Across the room are scores of faces, bathed in the lantern light. All of their eyes seem to be trained on her. She places a hand on each of her children and backs them through the doorway.

Outside the cool clean air hits them and awakens them as if from a trance. "Mom, what were those guys doing?" Rose asks, peering back over her shoulder through the doorway. "What was happening? Why did we hear horses?"

"We have to go. Right now," Li-Yu says, hurrying down the pathway, a hand on each of them.

"Why?" Rose asks again, pulling back toward the door.

"Listen to me carefully," Li-Yu says. She turns her children around and squats down. It used to be that this brought her down to the level of their heads, but now she is looking up at them. "We're going back home, to California," she says, in English. "Tonight. Right now." Rose and Henry haven't heard English from her in five years, and the sounds of her words break over them like a thunderclap. They look at one another, their breaths held, and then back at her. "Rose," Li-Yu says, continuing in English. "Henry. Listen to me. You must do everything I say, exactly as I say, right now, or there will be great trouble."

Henry's face screws up with confusion and she can see the opposing forces already working upon him. But in Rose the announcement causes an instantaneous and complete transformation. Her jaw hardens and her eyes glint. And when Henry asks about the house, and about Mae, and about his friends, she steps in front of her brother, and when she speaks her words emerge quickly and clearly. It is as if she has been secretly rehearsing, practicing for this, as if all of her being has been waiting these long years for this chance to emerge, to burst forth and explode. It is as if she has known everything all along. And Li-Yu sees immediately that nothing will keep them from getting home, not with this daughter as an ally.

"Henry, listen to me," Rose begins, her English as clear and fluent as the day they left California. "This is not the place for us. I know there are things you like about it. But there is nothing here for me, and nothing here for Mom, and though you might not remember how things were in America, I know you're old enough to see it now. I know you wouldn't want to live in a place where your mother and sister can never be anything."

Henry's wide eyes glisten in the light of the rising moon. He shakes his head. Inside the meeting hall voices rise—now many of them are shouting, and the thundering of horses' hooves grows loud again.

"You're a good man," Rose says. "We'll make new friends. And you can write letters to your friends here, and send them pictures. That will be okay, right?"

Li-Yu remains silent, speechless at Rose's command. Henry nods.

"I know it's sudden," Rose tells Henry. She bends forward and wraps her arms around him for the briefest of moments. "You're a good man," she says into his ear. And then they are flying up the path.

Right behind them, Li-Yu recovers herself. "Two minutes," she says. "Dress as warmly as you can. Bring whatever you can carry in one small bag, and in your pockets. Nothing else."

They plunge into the dark house and run to their room. Henry begins to cry, quietly, as he gathers his things together. Among his tears Li-Yu can hear him saying his friend's names, and her heart shatters. And then he begins to falter. He squats down and buries his face in his hands. Li-Yu moves toward him, but Rose gets there first. She drops to her knees, plants a hand on his back, and begins to talk into his ear.

Li-Yu catches her daughter's eye, gives her a quick, grateful nod, turns, and runs back into the main part of the house. She darts through the empty kitchen and into the back of the house, where there is almost no light. In Mae's room her hand grazes the back of a wooden chair. She seizes it, runs across the room, and swings it into the doors of Mae's cabinet, following it with all her weight. The collision is deafening in the empty stone house. She slams the chair twice more into the woodwork, concentrating her blows on the lock, and then the chair falls away, one of its legs broken, and she yanks away the remains of the doors. Her hand closes around the red bag, pulls it free, and she runs back, returning for the last time to the room where she has been imprisoned for the last five years. Rose and Henry are standing together in the darkness, ready, waiting for her.

"What were those sounds, Mom?" Rose asks.

"Not now," Li-Yu says. "You and your brother pull this mattress off of here," she says, dumping Mae's coins into her bag.

"I already got them," Rose says.

"What?"

"The money under the mattress. We already got it all. It's in your bag."

As Li-Yu shoulders her pack she wonders how she could have underestimated her daughter so completely. She vows to spend the rest of her life trying to make up for it.

Outside the roads are still empty, and they plunge back down the path. They have gone maybe fifty feet when Rose stops. "I forgot something," she says, turning.

"There's no time," Li-Yu calls after her, but Rose is gone. She heads not into the house, but around it, toward the storage sheds that huddle together near the back of the compound. "Where's she going?" Li-Yu asks Henry, but he doesn't answer. He peers into the darkness where she disappeared, his face compressed with anxiety.

Rose returns a minute later, carrying a foot-long length of bamboo as big around as her arm. "What's that?" Li-Yu asks.

"My papers," Rose says. "I'll show you later."

They stay clear of the path, sneaking through the spaces between houses, keeping low and out of sight. The sounds from the hall are louder now—even from this distance they can hear Hui's incantations over the shouts. They circle the center of the village at a distance, picking their way along the side of the hill, and just when they have retaken the main pathway they hear voices spill out of the hall's doorway and fill the night behind them. They run as fast as they can, flying past the fields of bleeding plants and up the hillside. They only stop when their hearts threaten to burst from their chests.

"Why are we going to Jianghai?" Henry says, between gasps, as he unbuttons his coat. "Isn't California the other way?"

"I have to get some things first," Li-Yu says, "and then we have to get back to Canton." Her plans end there. There is still the matter of an ocean. There will be a way, she tells herself.

"But how?" Rose says. "The ferry boats don't run at night."

"Tomorrow," Li-Yu says.

"Where will we sleep tonight?" Henry asks.

"We're going to camp," Li-Yu says.

"But we don't have a tent," Henry says.

"That's enough questions," Li-Yu says.

They make it to the outskirts of Jianghai without running into anyone along the roads. "No talking now," Li-Yu whispers. "If anybody sees us and recognizes us they will think it is strange we are here." The houses are open to the summer evening, and they spill forth the smells of cooking dinners and the sounds of easy conversation. Occasional pedestrians happen by, but nobody pays them much attention. They sneak into the heart of town and into the market's alleyways. Li-Yu lets herself into Zhang's shop with her key and the children slip in behind her, their questions silent. She leaves a note—"Goodbye, friend"—and thirty seconds later they are back on the main road. Somewhere east of Jianghai, she knows, is another river. She doesn't know exactly where it will take them, but she knows it will carry them farther away from Xinhui, and for now, that is all that matters.

"We can't go back through Xinhui," she tells her children, "so we may have to walk a long time tonight, and it will be dark," she says to them. "I need you both to be strong and brave."

Rose takes Henry's hand and wordlessly they follow her eastward. They leave the glowing lanterns of Jianghai behind and enter unfamiliar fields. A three-quarter moon lights their way from its spot in a clear sky. Li-Yu worries that they will wander off the trail in the darkness of a thick wood, or that the moon will set. But the countryside remains open, with few trees, and after they have walked for half an hour she sees the moon is climbing higher. Their eyes grow accustomed to the darkness. They begin to see details like the heads and ears of rabbits, rising and ducking in the fields

After an hour the road begins to climb. They walk up and over a ridge. Rose and Henry walk quickly, without complaining, speaking rarely. As they descend into the valley the trees grow thicker, but by now they are accustomed to seeing in the darkness. They slow their pace, and several times one of them stumbles or loses footing, but they press on. They walk along for another half an hour and then the trees above them thin, and the moonlight falls back down around them. They pass over a rise and suddenly the air cools, and then the river is beneath them, black and silent. The road bends and they follow it downriver. If only they could move as easily as the water, and the cool air that rides southward on its back, Li-Yu thinks.

The glow of lanterns comes from around a bend in front of them, and Li-Yu holds out her hands and slows her children. It would cause too much suspicion for the three of them to walk into a town at this time of night, but she sees nowhere to sleep—a steep hill rises on the other side of the path, and at its base there are only low bushes, barely big enough to hide a cat. And then Li-Yu notices a small pier made of reeds, where a gathering of fishing boats is moored. One of them looks just big enough for the three of them to crawl into and hide.

She points to the little boat. "In there," she whispers.

"We're sleeping in a boat?" Henry whispers. "Whose is it?"

She shushes him and guides them onto the dock. There is room only for the children to lie down, so Li-Yu remains sitting. It is better this way, she tells herself. This way she can keep watch. Dawn could be near—she has lost track of time. Henry falls asleep almost immediately. Rose has trouble getting comfortable, but the boat tilts and turns in the gentle current, and the rocking soothes her, and soon she follows her brother into sleep. Crickets chirp on the hillside behind them. An occasional shift in the breeze carries the hint of a human sound or smell up from the village beneath them.

Li-Yu sits and stares at the flowing water, watching leaves and pieces of branches and tiny bubbles drift downstream, envying their effortless travel. It occurs to her to simply steal the boat and float away, but she thinks of the horsemen, searching the hidden landscape for thieves. So I will purchase it, she decides, and she rips a piece of cloth from the bottom of her skirt, muffling the sound in her hands. She ties several coins into the cloth and then ties the bundled payment to the mooring rope. She carefully loosens the knot and pushes the boat away from the pier. The current cooperates and pulls them quickly into the middle of the river. She keeps herself as low as she can when they pass through the village, and when she is sure they are long past it, she cautiously returns to a sitting position. She smiles over her sleeping children, who, after all these long years, are finally hers again. When she falls asleep, she dreams that she is traveling through the canopy of a leafy forest, passed along gently by the trees' branches from one to the next.

THIRTEEN

"How do you know about *guo-yin*?" Eva asked the next morning, as soon as I emerged from my room. She was sitting at my desk, reading from my computer screen. "How do you know about rice cultivation, or any of this, for that matter?" She looked relaxed. She wasn't smiling, but she seemed like she might, somehow.

"I have a multiple-subject teaching credential," I said, "which means the state of California has certified me as an expert in multiple subjects."

"And which of those subjects covers obscure Chinese rituals, exactly?"

"I also read a lot," I said.

"No you don't," she said. "I haven't seen you read a word the whole time I've been here."

"Historically, I have been known to read a lot," I said. "Also, the Internet contains a good deal of information, in case you hadn't noticed."

"Not about *guo-yin*. I looked."

"So maybe I read about it," I said. "Or maybe I saw a show about it once. Why does it matter?"

Now she did smile. "Just try to remember. Did you read it or was it a show?"

"I don't know," I said. "Where are you going with this?"

"I just had a feeling you wouldn't remember," she said, her smile growing. "That's all."

"Well, you were right," I said, shrugging off her questions and trying to think ahead to my teaching day.

"I can see that," she said. "Have a great day at school."

Lucy had asked if she could come back to my class with me, but a schedule shift meant that my kids would be occupied that Friday morning by a visit to the science lab, so I told her to stop in around lunchtime and I headed up the hill alone. In my mailbox I found a reminder, printed on bright yellow paper, that report cards would be due on Tuesday. In my empty classroom I booted up my laptop. There was a quick thought or two I had to get down about Li-Yu and her kids, and then I'd get to work on the reports.

十二

There is a little bump and Li-Yu awakens to find the boat resting against a bank of dirt and rocks and grasses. Her children stir, but remain asleep. She turns to look behind her but instead of the opposite bank she finds herself staring back upstream, up a river that grew to ten times its previous width as she and the children slept. The riverbanks, she now sees, are no longer parallel, but run away from one another, and she whirls back around to the realization that they have come to rest against an island. She rouses her children. They collect their things and carefully climb out of the boat, stretching their arms and legs, working the stiffness out of their necks. At the top of the bank they discover a pathway that leads up the back of a treeless hill, and when they arrive at the summit they find the rest of a crescent-shaped island curling away from them, back toward the northern shore. There is a single village on the island, a few minutes' walk before them. Beyond it, there is only open ocean. Li-Yu turns to look at the little boat, parked on shore, and at the river's mouth behind it. How easy it would have been— how far more likely it would have been—for the current to have carried them past the island and out to sea. She offers a silent thank you, to the island and the current, to the boat and the river and to the nameless fisherman who unknowingly sold her this charmed vessel, and then she leads her children into the village. They arrive at a small stand along the pathway where a woman is at work, stirring a steaming pot of *jook* and frying dough. The woman makes no effort to hide her incredulity at their approach.

"Good morning," Li-Yu calls. "What is this place?"

The woman does not answer right away, but looks behind them, up the pathway, as if into their pasts. She looks back at Li-Yu and the children, squints, shakes her head, squints again.

"This is Jiaobei Island," she says, when she finally accepts they are real. "How did you get here?"

"Our boat brought us," Li-Yu says. "That *jook* smells delicious."

She buys three large bowls of the rice porridge, three boiled salted duck eggs, and a plateful of fried *yau ja gwai*. The woman lets them eat in peace, though Li-Yu can see the questions in her head. By the time their bellies are full, the sun is warm on their faces and the food is heating them from within.

"We are trying to reach Canton," Li-Yu says.

"The ferry comes once a week, at noon," the woman says. She smiles, and again looks back up the pathway. "I don't know your story, but your travels are blessed. Today is the day."

"Thank you," Li-Yu says. "Our little boat is resting on the bank on the other side of the hill. I would like you to have it."

The woman's eyes ignite. She reaches into her apron and returns the money Li-Yu had paid her for their breakfast. "You have made my son the happiest boy on the island," she says, and she pokes apart her cooking fire and then turns and runs into town, leaving Li-Yu alone with her children.

They spend the morning wandering through the little fishing village, looking into shops, pausing to watch a weaver mending baskets and a man making fishing poles out of a pile of cut bamboo. At noon the ferry collects them and the next morning they are in Canton.

They disembark with the rest of the passengers and step down onto the piers. Li-Yu remembers well the smell of soot and garbage and fish and the sprawling chaos of travelers streaming across the creaking wooden planks, laden with shoulder bags and suitcases. Teams of workers haul steamer trunks or drag overloaded wooden carts, whose bamboo racks threaten to break and spill their contents. Uniformed officials keep watchful eyes on the mass. Two men block Li-Yu's path momentarily; between them they carry a long pole from which several squawking chickens dangle, each in its own flimsy wooden cage. Rose and Henry stay so close to their mother that Li-Yu can barely take a step without treading on one of them. Finally she puts Henry's hand in one of Rose's hands, takes her by the other hand, and pulls them through the crowd.

The edge of the city near the piers is as she remembers it: a labyrinth of dark tortured alleys, all of them crowded. She finds an inn and steps inside to inquire about rates, but the clerk tells her it's not a place for children. She argues, so he smiles and quotes her a rate high enough for ten rooms for a month. Li-Yu turns and drags her children back into the alley. The next two inns are full, and in the one after that a pair of rats are fighting over a scrap of food on the floor just in front of the counter. After a half-hour of searching she finds a place that seems safe and clean enough for the children. It is more expensive than she had hoped, but she can't keep dragging them through this chaos. Perhaps she will find something else the next day. The clerk is tall, almost emaciated, and he has short gray hairs that cover his Adam's apple, but he smiles a lot and he shows them a room up three flights of stairs. It will be quieter, he explains, and better for the children to be away from the street. They leave their things and venture back into the alleyways to find food. There are hundreds of vendors selling food from storefronts, from carts, from stacks of tin buckets hanging from poles that seem impossible to carry through the crowds. She and the children gorge themselves on glass noodles and bean curd, fried pork with hot chilies, and *gai lan*. Even though Rose and Henry are full she buys each of them a custard pastry for dessert. They return to their room, sated and tired. Rose curls up on one of the beds and falls asleep instantly. Li-Yu imagines her daughter is dreaming of San Francisco. Henry stands near the window, staring down into the teeming alleyway.

"Do you remember being here?" Li-Yu asks him softly.

He nods.

"You do? It was many years ago, and you were only three."

"I was four," he says. "I remember."

"Do you remember America?"

He nods. "I remember Dad. I remember our house. Are we going to live there again?"

"We're going to have a new house," Li-Yu says. "Do you remember your aunts? Do you remember your *po* and *gung*?"

He nods again.

"We're going to go see them first," Li-Yu says. "They are very, very excited to see you and Rosie."

"And then?"

"And then we'll find a home of our own."

Henry is quiet. Together they watch the traffic streaming through the half-lit alleyway below. Li-Yu waits for his next questions to form.

"Is it better in California?" he asks.

"It's our home," she says.

"What was the house in Xinhui?" Henry asks. "Not a real home?"

"Someone else's home," Li-Yu says. "Mae's. Not ours."

"Are we ever going to go back there?" Henry asks. "Are we ever going to see Mae again?"

"I'm not," Li-Yu says. "You could, though. Maybe when you're all grown up, you might come back."

"She might be dead by then," he says.

"Are you going to miss her?" Li-Yu asks.

She wants him to shake his head, to say no, that all he wants is to go back to California, and reclaim the life she'd set about making for him all those years before. But his life has already been far different than hers, and this is a different journey for him. How much did he know? Did he know that he was the center of all these movements? That he had been the reason for their trip to China in the first place, and the reason they couldn't leave? That for years she and Rose had been little more than forgotten satellites, quiet in their hidden orbits as they circled him? Did he know that the love he'd felt in that house had been exclusively his? Rose had told him as much, there on the pathway outside the meeting hall, as the hoofbeats of the spirit horses thundered around them, and he hadn't seemed surprised. He'd plunged into the night alongside her.

"A little," he says. "She was nice to me."

"You used to be scared of her," Li-Yu says. "Do you remember?"

"That's when I was little."

Li-Yu nods. Henry lies down on the other bed and stares up at the ceiling, his fingers laced behind his head, his feet crossed. His socks look clean and new, even after two days of traveling. Mae must have gotten them for him in one of her recent expeditions to the market.

"I'll be back in just a little bit," Li-Yu says. "I have to send a telegraph. You two stay right here."

Henry glances over at his big sister, whose light, airy snores are floating around the room. "Okay," he says. "What's a telegraph?"

"I'll tell you when I get back," she says. Li-Yu locks the door behind her and climbs once more down to the street. The clerk gives her directions and just a few minutes later, in the next alley over, she finds herself in a small dingy shop, dictating a message. The clerk is a small bent man who hunches over a desk, writing down her words. "We're going back to California," Li-Yu tells him, smiling. The man grunts. He reads the message back to Li-Yu, and then taps it out on the machine. He hands Li-Yu a receipt, and a few minutes later she is back in her room, thinking about the electrical impulses flying toward her sisters. Henry has fallen asleep. She sets the receipt on a table, curls up next to him, and sinks into a deep and dreamless sleep.

The response comes back just three days later, sliding beneath the door, carried up, presumably, by the tall graying clerk. Li-Yu pounces on it and rips the envelope open. Taped to a thin sheet of paper is the short message: "3 tickets booked." There is a date, a week from then, and a time, and the name of the ship: the *Crystal Gypsy*. There is the name of another inn, elsewhere on the waterfront, where she and the children are to check in two days before their departure. Li-Yu reads the words a second time, and then a third time, and then a fourth. She stares at them until she can close her eyes and see each curve and angle of every letter. Warmth fills her; it radiates from her skin and fills the room.

Li-Yu floats through the next few days. She and her children explore the piers, watching the huge steamships and freighters sailing up and down the Pearl River. Canton feels like a vacation now. They eat well. She buys them things they don't need. On the appointed day they carry their things to the next inn and find themselves in a crowded lobby. Several times she picks the *Gypsy's* name out of the noisy, exuberant conversations. She hears San Francisco mentioned again and again, as though the city's name is a great new secret sweeping through the room. Rose and Henry smile and watch and listen.

On the following morning a team of doctors work their way through the crowded inn, examining each traveler and stamping their tickets. And then, in the middle of that afternoon, the *Crystal Gypsy* steams into the port. Li-Yu and her children watch it from a bench along the waterfront. She has been braiding Rose's hair, and Henry has been reading a book he brought in his pack, but now they stop and watch. As it plies up the wide Pearl River, plumes of black smoke billow from its smokestacks, merge with one another, and trail out behind it.

"That's ours," Li-Yu tells her children. They watch it dock, silently assessing its massive size, its unimaginable capabilities. Li-Yu barely sleeps that night, and the next morning they pack their things early and check out of the inn. They buy as much food as they can carry and arrive at the appointed pier well before they are scheduled to board. They watch the first-class passengers climb aboard, and then the second-class passengers, and after that, they are the first up the gangway. There is an American waiting for them at the top. He addresses them in a barely-recognizable attempt at Cantonese. Li-Yu smiles. "We're American," she says. "We're going home."

"You and me both," the man says, with a grateful smile. He checks their name against a list and directs them to a doorway. Through the door is a stairway that takes them below deck and aft to their bunkroom in the steerage quarters. The room is as large as a barn, and crowded with beds made of stretched canvas stacked in sets of three. Li-Yu selects a spot in the corner and takes the bottom bed. Rose chooses the middle, leaving Henry the top. Li-Yu settles back into her bed and watches as the room continues to fill. Above her she can hear Rose talking to Henry about California. She listens to descriptions of their old house, of the school Rose had attended and the shop Bing had owned, and the weekly radio programs they had once listened to. Li-Yu forgets the clamor around her as she listens to Rose's descriptions. Everything is there—the contents of their refrigerator, the smell of the car, their wooden toys and books, the other homes and trees and fences on the quiet block where the house stood that had once been theirs. She had driven so much of it from their conversations, from their lore and remembrances—and from her own mind—in an attempt to create a future in China for her children. But the past had been there all along, vivid and rich, thriving in her daughter's memory. It should not have been a surprise that Rose had known exactly what to do when the time had come.

Finally the idling engines roar, shaking the walls and the beds. The three of them rush outside to a small deck and find places along the crowded railing. From the deck above them, which is reserved for the higher-class passengers, a white handkerchief falls. Li-Yu watches it as it drifts, turning in the wind, and then it disappears into the darkness between the ship and the pier. The deck lurches and there are renewed shouts and great bursts of smoke, and then the pier begins to drift away. The ship performs a slow pirouette and rumbles down the wide river. Buildings line the banks for miles. Rose and Henry point to things they spot on the riverfront streets: a pair of stray dogs, a man carrying a giant basket, an occasional automobile. The river widens and then its banks turn away, running in either direction, away from the ship, and the ocean takes them in. Li-Yu stays at the railing until China slips completely beneath a liquid horizon, finally relinquishing its hold on her family.

FOURTEEN

When Lucy arrived later that day my students were delighted to see her, so I wrote a recommendation extolling her natural abilities and her extensive experience with kids, and the next morning we climbed into my car and headed north to her interview. A newscast came over the radio: Sometime the previous night there had been a mudslide at the south end of China Beach and two of the backyards of the homes along Sea Cliff had collapsed onto the sand below. The reporter described the scene—a mass of grass and mud and smashed gazebo pieces atop the storm-littered beach. There were other items amid the wreckage—an oak wine barrel, several shoes, the door of a car—but it was unclear whether they were part of the mudslide or if the sea had contributed them.

We drove up and over the crest of Russian Hill and dropped down toward Lombard Street, which we found to be full of cars, their progress hampered by rain and red lights, and by the big green-and-white Golden Gate Transit buses that doddered along, swerving in and out of the right lane. We made it through the long series of stoplights and the road swung to the right and climbed and narrowed, its lanes merging and merging again as they approached the bridge's narrow toll plaza. Drivers competed with one another for spaces that were too small for their cars; sprays of water pounced on our windshield again and again. I took it slow and held my ground and it was mostly manageable until a bus moving a bit too slowly tried to muscle into a small space just in front of me. I slammed on the brakes, expecting to hydroplane into the back of it, but my tires held. To reinforce its vehicular superiority the bus assaulted us with a steady spray from its tires, which continued until I'd dropped well behind it.

"Asshole," Lucy said. "You'd think people would have figured out how to drive in the rain by now." The final words of her sentence sounded strangled though, and she reached out and clutched at my sleeve. Her face was white; her eyes were wide and still, her mouth agape. She looked the same way she'd looked when she collapsed in the hallway by the side of the pool.

"What?" I said. "Lucy, what?"

"That's him," she said.

"Who?"

She let go of me and pointed through the windshield. Through the bus's rear window we could see the back of a man's head and shoulders. He was sitting by himself, wearing a dark coat and a dark cap. "How can you tell?" I said. "That could be anybody."

"It's him," she said. "We have to follow him."

"But how do you know?" I said. "What about your interview?"

And then he slowly and deliberately turned, looked right at us, and smiled. Lucy leaned forward and stared up at him, her forehead inches from the windshield. The muscles of her jaw stood out through the drawn skin of her cheeks. Her eyes were narrow and her brow thick with furrows. The windshield wipers pushed patches of shadow back and forth across her face. She stared at him like that all the way across the bridge and up through the tunnel, as though everything we were searching for might be revealed in a single small gesture of his. Traffic was moving more easily here, and we stayed on the bus's tail, just beyond the spray of its tires, as it lumbered back down the hill. We arrived at an exit in Sausalito and the bus slowed and, without signaling, pulled into a freeway-side bus stop. A pair of signs, one on each side of the road, told us not to enter. Buses only, they said. Lucy lifted a hand as if she was about to yank on the steering wheel.

"Stay on him," she said. The hand inched closer.

"Okay, okay," I said. "Relax. I'm on it."

We eased in behind the bus. Lucy unbuckled her seat belt and reached for the door handle, ready to jump out if the man moved. He didn't. We followed the bus back onto the freeway and continued north. The sequence was repeated in Marin City, and then again at Tiburon Boulevard. This time, though, the bus didn't pull back onto the freeway. It took a right turn and headed east toward downtown Tiburon.

"There you go," Lucy said. "Maybe we can figure this out and still make it to my interview," she said. She chuckled. "Maybe he's interviewing, too."

The road curved back and forth and eventually settled along the shoreline. The bus pulled in and out of a few stops along the way, and each time we followed, but the man's head and shoulders remained immobile, framed by the rear window. The road straightened and the homes gave way to restaurants and shops. We were reaching the end of the peninsula now, and Angel Island appeared in front of us across a narrow strait. The gray sides of Mount Livermore rose from the water, their details washed out by the rain. The commercial stretch of Tiburon Boulevard ended in a roundabout next to the marina, among the last block of shops. The bus slowed and eased into its final stop. The man rose. Lucy was out of the car before I'd even stopped it. I yanked on the emergency brake, flicked on the hazards, and followed her into the rain.

I caught up to Lucy at the bus's door. She stood with her arms folded across her chest, leaving barely enough room for the passengers to disembark. There were only a handful of them—an old woman in a clear plastic raincoat with grocery bags, a pair of weekend commuters in business attire who gave her dirty looks as they stepped around her. The man didn't appear. We waited for long seconds, staring up the empty stairs. "What the fuck?" she said, to nobody. She sprang up the steps, turned the corner, and peered into the darkness of the bus. She turned back to me. "It's fucking empty, Peregrine!" she said, and darted out of sight.

The bus driver was a wiry man with a thin neat mustache and the air of a bridge-guarding troll. "Hey, I need your fare, lady!" he yelled, twisting in his seat.

I stepped onto the bottom step. "We're just looking for someone," I said. "It will just be a second, if that's okay."

"You can't just run onto somebody's bus like that," he said to me, jabbing his finger at the floor, dispelling any questions about whose bus was under discussion. "It costs two dollars."

"She's not riding," I said. "We're just looking for something."

"Well, it's not here. Can't lose something on a bus you ain't ridden. I need two dollars, and I need it real quick."

"There's nobody!" Lucy yelled, from the middle of the bus. "There's nothing!"

"I guess you better look somewhere else," the driver yelled at her. He turned back to me. "You see that line right there?" He pointed to a yellow stripe at the front of the aisle.

"Yes," I said.

"Hey, what happened to the Chinese guy?" Lucy yelled. "The guy that was sitting right there, in the back?"

"Crossing that line and I don't have two dollars is fare dodging, which is not welcome to occur on this bus. Not when I'm driving it, anyway." He reached down and started fumbling through a bag. I had heard that lots of taxi drivers carried guns, but a bus driver on the Tiburon route? Over two dollars? I tightened my grip on the railing that led up the steps.

"She's getting right off," I said. "Please, just give us a couple of seconds."

"Where are you?" Lucy yelled into the emptiness of the bus.

The driver paused and glanced at her in the big mirror that stretched across the top of the windshield. Wipers the size of hockey sticks thumped back and forth across the glass. "Nope," he said, shaking his little head. "Doesn't look like she's getting right off at all. Looks like she's messing around in the back of my bus. Messing around on my bus definitely costs two dollars."

I sighed and reached for my wallet. I couldn't see what Lucy was doing, and I didn't want to climb the stairs and put myself within the driver's reach. Besides, it had become well worth two dollars to put an end to this conversation. I only had a five. I handed it over.

"I don't have change," he said.

"Um, Peregrine?" Lucy called. "Come take a look at this."

"Be my guest," he said, nodding toward the back. "You're covered, too." He waved my five. "Thanks for choosing Golden Gate Transit. I'll be heading back out in about five minutes, so feel free to get comfortable."

I hurried past him and down the aisle. Lucy was standing still, looking down at the seat where the man had been sitting. On it was a small red book, bound in worn red cloth. Traces of gold clung to the cover where Chinese characters had been stamped. A red ribbon protruded from the top. When I slipped it into the inside pocket of my coat it curled perfectly over the contour of my chest as if it had spent hours there.

I turned and headed back for the door with Lucy right behind me. The driver was watching us in his mirror. "That's not yours," he said, rising to block our exit.

Lucy shoved me aside and bore down on him, her arm upraised and something in her hand. "Here's how this is going to work," she said. "You give me back that five dollars right fucking now, or you first get a face full of pepper spray, and then you get a sexual assault case that will leave you unemployable and subsequently homeless, and then you get to spend the rest of your life wondering how you could have been so colossally stupid as to fuck everything up over five dollars."

The driver froze, his face white.

"I can see you're confused," Lucy said, "so I'll make it real clear. You just stole money from me and then groped my ass. Didn't he, Steven?"

"That's my baby sister you pervert," I said, completely unconvincingly.

Lucy continued. "And now you have a one-time opportunity to avert your ruined future for the low price of just five dollars. But the offer expires in two seconds. It's fate knocking on your door, Rick, a fucking fork in the road. Which path are you going to take?"

"My name's not Rick," the driver managed to say, his voice squeaking.

"I don't give a shit. You have one second left." She flicked the safety off on the pepper spray. The driver dug into his pocket and produced the bill as quickly as he could. "Thanks very much," Lucy said to him with a smile, descending the steps. "You've been a terrific help." We climbed into my car, whirled around the roundabout, and sped back up along the peninsula. "Fuck that interview," she said. "I don't think I'm ready to be in a position of goddamn influence over a couple of impressionable kids. Give me that book."

I was so dazzled by her performance that I'd forgotten about it. I pulled it from my coat and tossed it onto her lap. "Tell me what you find," I said.

She thumbed through it for five or six seconds. "It's old, and it's Chinese," she said. "That's about all I can say so far."

"What about that bookmark?" I said. "What's on that page?"

"More oldness, more Chineseness."

I punched Annabel's number up on my phone.

"Hi there!" she said. "I was just talking about you."

"Please tell me you're home," I said.

"Sorry," she said.

"Where are you? I just need you for about ten minutes."

"I'm in Sacramento, visiting my sisters. Why? What's going on?"

"Shit," I said. "Hold on a sec." I'd missed a merge sign somehow and now the lane in front of me was blocked off with an echelon of traffic cones. The lane next to me was congested and I had little time to slide over.

"What's going on?" Annabel asked.

"These people are right on my ass," I said. "Hold on." I forced my way into the lane, provoking an extended honk. "Where the hell else am I supposed to go?" I yelled at the driver in the car behind me.

"Seriously," Lucy added.

"What?" Annabel asked.

"Are you coming back tonight?" I asked her.

"That's the plan. What's going on over there?"

"Call me when you get in," I said. "Actually, would you please just come over?"

"Can I 'just' come over? What does that mean?"

"We found something," I said. "A book."

"Okay," she said.

"It's in Chinese," I said.

"Oh," she said. "Where did you find it?"

"On a bus," I said. "Shit. Hold on." The car ahead of me had stopped for no reason and I had to hit the brakes.

"I think we should talk later," she said. "You sound pretty distracted."

"No, it's just this traffic. People in Marin don't know how to drive. So we've got this book."

"You told me."

"So what time are you coming back?"

"It might be late," she said. "I don't get out here too much."

"Like how late?" I said.

"I really don't know," she said.

"Well, can you call me when you're on your way back?"

"I should be able to manage that," she said.

"No idea at all? Ten? Eleven?"

"I'll call you, Peregrine."

We said our goodbyes and I hung up the phone.

"Shit," I said to Lucy. "She's not around. You don't know any-one who can read Chinese, do you?"

"I don't know anyone in this city at all," she said.

***

The look on Eva's face gave everything away when she opened the book to examine its pages. "You know that book," I said.

"No," she said.

"Bullshit. Tell me."

"I don't know."

"We chased a man across two counties, broke I don't know how many traffic laws, almost got in about three wrecks, and threatened to destroy a bus driver's life to get that book," I said. "You need to talk."

"He was an asshole," Lucy said. "He deserved it."

"True," I said. "But that doesn't mean we enjoyed it."

"Speak for yourself," Lucy said.

"Let me think for a minute," Eva said.

"I'll make it easy," I said. "You tell me what you know, or you're not reading any more of my work. You have an hour."

十三

Each day the seas are calm and the skies are cloudless and the days merge with one another and those who do not keep tallies lose track. Rose appoints herself the recorder for her family and marks a sheet of paper every morning when she awakens. Three times a day they are given tea, rice, and a portion of stir-fried meat. There are vegetables for the first week. A few beds away there is an older man, traveling by himself, who reminds Li-Yu of the father she hasn't seen in years. In the second week he begins to cough. He coughs for two days, and then he is taken to a different part of the ship, and they do not see him again.

Li-Yu thinks often of her parents and herself, a not-quite-born baby girl, who followed this same route thirty years earlier, enacting a story she would come to hear so many times the scenes would take on the clarity and vitality of memories. Now as the *Gypsy* returns her to California she becomes aware that the sum of her life's efforts has been to circle back around to that same point. Everything—her parents' efforts, her upbringing, meeting and marrying Bing, the move to China, the stolen and secreted coins and their flight—has simply returned her to the start. As momentous as it had all seemed to her, it amounted to precisely nothing.

But then the voices of Henry and Rose carry to her from across the bunkroom or their snores sink down from the beds above her and she remembers that they are the difference, the two of them. She exults to hear them speaking English. It comes back easily to Henry now, and though he sometimes fumbles for words, he has no accent. His vocabulary will only be that of someone half his age but she knows he'll learn quickly, especially with the help of Rose, who continues to astound Li-Yu. Sometime in the third week there had been a discrepancy over how many days they have been at sea. Rose's tally had stood at twenty-four, but a man with a long beard insisted that his count, twenty-three, was accurate, and another, a tall bald man, declared it to be twenty-five. She informed the first that he'd missed a day, and then informed the other that he'd counted a day twice, and then she'd smiled and run off with Henry to play. They had gone by her count since. Watching her children sometimes leaves Li-Yu breathless now. It is stunning, after five years in Xinhui, after their father's death and her own helplessness, to find them intact and happy, roaming the ship's deck with ease.

The *Gypsy* continues to push through the waves. It is always hot inside their quarters but the sea breeze keeps the deck cool. Occasionally they see another ship in the distance, and one time they come close enough to a freighter to wave to the crew. Finally, on the thirty-eighth day, they approach a few tiny, rocky islands, covered in sea birds. Li-Yu cannot remember their name, but she knows they signal California's approach. "Your aunts and your *po* and *gung* are just there, on the other side of that line," she tells her children, pointing to the horizon. When the mainland rises into view the engines slow and drop to a shaking rumble, and after several weeks of their steady groan the sudden quiet is vast and startling, as if they have stepped off a busy city street and into an empty cathedral.

The ship continues to slow until it is drifting, and then the Coast Guard ship comes into view. On the trip over she has heard dozens of accounts of how this encounter could go for passengers, but being an American, with American children and American papers, she knows she has little reason for concern. The passengers grow quiet as the patrol ship pulls alongside the *Crystal Gypsy* and suddenly there are crewmen everywhere, shouting at one another and tossing ropes back and forth. Within minutes the two ships are bound together.

A while later several officials enter the bunkroom. Some of them are in uniforms, and some are not. Li-Yu sits quietly with her children, one pressed against either side of her, and watches the team sweep through the room. Doctors listen to heartbeats and examine eyes and ears. Customs agents dig through bags and suitcases. Others inspect papers and ask questions through translators. Each person is given a marked form and then the men move along. They arrive at Li-Yu's bed, and the translator greets them in Cantonese. "We speak English," Li-Yu says, with a smile. "We're Americans."

"Papers, please," says an officer. He reads them over while the doctors examine first the children, and then Li-Yu.

"What are you bringing in?" another man asks.

"Just some clothes," Li-Yu says. She indicates their little bags, on the floor beside the bed. One of the uniformed men pokes through them. "What's this?" he asks, holding up a thick piece of bamboo.

"That's mine," Rose says, and then Li-Yu remembers her daughter's last-minute dash to the shed, just before they fled Xinhui. The man turns the tube and looks into its core, and then with his thumb and first finger he reaches inside and pulls out a thick stack of rolled paper. There are hundreds of sheets, all covered in tiny pencil script.

"You're a writer," he says to Rose, with a smile.

Rose nods.

"Good," he said. "So is my daughter." He flips through the first few sheets and then looks up at the officer. "It's all in English," he says. The officer nods, makes a mark on their tickets, hands them back, and then he and his men move on to the next stack of beds.

"You had that in the shed?" Li-Yu asks her daughter.

Rose nods.

"What do they say? What are they?"

"Just stories," she says.

"Stories about what?"

She shrugs. "Lots of things."

There are hundreds of hours of work there, Li-Yu can see, hundreds of hours her daughter spent in hiding, bent over this manuscript, when Li-Yu thought she was working somewhere on the property, or roaming the village. Could she really have lost track of so much of her daughter's life? And what else might there be? What other secrets had the emptiness of the last five years pulled into being?

After several hours the officials return to the Coast Guard ship. The crewmen untie the thick ropes and wrestle them back into neat coils. The engines roar back to life and the ship pushes toward the shoreline again. She thinks again of her parents, standing at a railing like this one, waiting for this same shoreline to rise into view. But that had been before the immigration station on Angel Island had been built. This part of the story would be her own.

* * *

"Your time's up," I said to Eva. "That must have been at least an hour." After the glow of my laptop screen she and Lucy were little more than dark shapes on the couch, illuminated faintly by the glow of the television. I might have continued writing but my computer was misbehaving in protest over the demands I was putting on it. I'd been reading about steamships and steerage quarters, about immigration to California. I'd also been scrolling through some public television documentaries on a website about Angel Island. Like most people I knew, I tended to think of the island as a nice place for a summertime day trip. There were some old forts and battlements out there, left over from long ago. Until recently, I'd only had a vague awareness of the role the island had played. I wondered if the immigration station there had even been a waypoint in my mom's family history. The more I learned the more likely it seemed.

"Actually it's been closer to three hours," Lucy said.

"Good. So?"

Eva sat forward. "Can I read what you wrote first?"

"No," I said. "It isn't going to change. The book. You need to tell me something."

She shifted on the couch and seemed about to say something, but then hesitated. She reached out and took the book from the coffee table. "It's a book of poems."

"Okay," I said. "So what?"

"It's the guide's book. The soldiers' guide who walked with them on the way to Henry's first day of school."

"That's nonsense," I said.

She opened the pages and held the book up and showed me where one page had been ripped out, and then another. "I told you I had one of the poems, until the flood. I recognize the paper, the print, everything. It's the same book."

"You could have ripped those out, just now," I said.

"It's been sitting here in front of your sister this whole time."

"That just can't be," I said, quietly. "How can that possibly be true?"

"You tell me," she said. "Now can I read what you wrote?"

I stood and began pacing, trying to think. She handed me the book as she passed me on the way to my desk. I stood there while she read, staring at it, feeling its heat against my palms. After a few minutes she rose. "Then what?" she asked.

I could see the coast rising into view. I could see it more clearly than I could see the storm-smudged outlines of my own city.

***

The headlands of Marin rise in the north, and San Francisco's peninsula rises to the south, and the *Crystal Gypsy* sails through the narrow gap between the two and into the bay's embrace. All the passengers gather on deck, pointing things out to one another, talking excitedly. Alcatraz lies directly ahead of them, crouching menacingly in the bay. Orderly streets and homes reach over San Francisco's northernmost ridge, where the sights of moving cars and pedestrians seem like alien life after weeks of ocean.

The *Gypsy* veers away from the city, passes Alcatraz, and circles the southern edge of Angel Island, heading for its leeward corner. There is the shouting of the crewmen again, the throwing of ropes, and then the engines drop again into a low hum. Li-Yu and her children shoulder their bags and join the crowd, which grows dense and pinches together as they reach the gangway. She bangs her shins on somebody's steamer trunk. A man swings a bag from one shoulder to the other and hits Henry in the head, and he cries out in surprise. Once down the gangway they enter immediately into a series of fenced walkways. In the open space stand several uniformed agents, guns on their waists. The pathway diverges, and when Li-Yu reads the signs her heart sinks. She squats down in front of Henry. "Okay, little man. You're going to have to go with the other men, for just a little while. Rosie and I have to go with the other women. They just need to see our papers, and when they realize we're Americans, they're going to put us all right back together and we'll go see your aunts and *po* and *gung*. Okay?"

Henry's forehead bunches together but he nods.

Rose comes over to him and gives him a quick hug. "See you in a little bit, Spider," she says. "You be a good kid."

They continue up the pathways. Li-Yu watches Henry go for as long as she can, and then a cold wooden building with a concrete floor swallows him up. She and Rose are shown to a bunkroom, very much like the one on the ship. "No," she says, to the official. "This isn't right. We're Americans. My sisters, my parents—they live in San Francisco. We're coming home."

The official is polite but uninterested. "It can take a little time," he says, softening his words with a smile and a friendly nod. "We just want you to be comfortable while you're waiting."

"When does the ferry leave?" she asks.

"The end of the day," he says, and slips out. He returns a minute later with another distraught woman and shows her to a nearby bunk.

She and Rose file to a dining room for lunch, and then again later, for dinner, and then they are taken out into a concrete yard. There is a fence that separates the men's side from the women's and they find Henry waiting there, searching for them. Li-Yu touches his fingers through the metal grate. "How is it?" she asks. "It's not bad," he says with a shrug, and gives her a smile that almost convinces her. "There are some other boys, and everyone's being nice to us." They hear a ferry sound its horn as it pulls into the pier, and they do not talk about their mutual realization that they will not be on it when it departs. The thought of Henry sleeping by himself among strangers keeps Li-Yu awake until morning, when an official comes for her. "Long, Li-Yu?" he calls out, standing in the doorway. She pats Rose on the knee and rises. They lead her to a large room, which is empty but for a small desk, covered with files and stacks of papers. There are two men sitting at the desk, and an armed guard standing behind them. On Li-Yu's side of the desk is an empty metal chair. She sits and finds the metal still warm from the heat of the previous occupant.

"It says here you were born in America," one of the men says.

"That's right," Li-Yu says, relaxing. "Right here in San Francisco."

"What was your father's name?"

"Hsu Bai."

"Mother's?"

"Hsu Xiaoli."

"Address where you grew up?"

"689 Grant Avenue."

"And how many windows were on the north side of your house?"

This question throws Li-Yu off; she isn't sure she has heard right. The man asks her again. She remembers the apartment where she lived—it was on the corner of Pacific, and the north side ran along Pacific. She goes through the rooms in her mind, counting, and then answers, "Four."

He goes on to ask her many more questions: What did your father do? What did your mother do? What school did you go to? What were your teachers' names? What are the names of your brothers and sisters? Your neighbors? What were the names of the shops on the ground floor? What were the names of the shopkeepers? Li-Yu tries to answer each question, but there are some things she can't remember. Finally there is a pause in the questioning and Li-Yu thinks the interrogation might be over, but then the guard knocks on a metal door and another man enters the room, his face impassive. He is wearing a black suit and his hair is oiled carefully, tightly against his head, revealing the exact shape of his skull. He replaces one of the two men at the desk. The men shuffle papers. Some of them appear to be telegrams; the men point at their messages, exchange looks, and then the new interrogator looks at Li-Yu a long time.

"Who is Henry Long," he asks. His voice does not rise into the end of the question.

"My son," Li-Yu says.

"And where is his father?"

"He is dead," she says.

"Where?" he says.

"In China. A town called Xinhui, in Guangdong."

"Where was he born?"

"Henry or his father?"

"We are discussing Henry."

"Stockton."

"Where?"

"At my home."

"Not at a hospital?"

"No, at my home."

"What day?"

"July seventeenth, 1921."

"And what was the weather like that day?"

Li-Yu is not sure she has heard correctly. "The weather?"

"The weather. Outside," the man says impatiently. When he is not talking he grits his teeth; Li-Yu can see the muscles on the side of his head pulsing through his oily shell of hair.

"It was sunny," she says.

"Aren't all days sunny in Stockton in July?" he asks.

"Yes, mostly," she says quietly, confused.

"And who is his father?"

"My husband, Bing Long," she says.

"The deceased?"

"Yes," she says, remembering him wasting away in his dirty bed.

"Where was Bing born?"

"In Xinhui."

"Did he ever have another wife?"

The air vacates her lungs; her veins feel suddenly as if they are full of lead. The man glances down at the papers in front of them. He is holding them with their tops curled back so she cannot see what is on them.

"Yes," she says, trying to control her anguish.

"And what was her name?"

"Mae," she says.

"Louder, please. First and last name."

"Mae Long," she says.

"And when did they divorce?"

"They didn't," she says.

"Speak up, please," the man says.

"They didn't divorce," she says.

"So he had two wives?"

"Yes." Even if these are formalities, Li-Yu still feels some measure of defeat. In the weeks since fleeing Xinhui she has expunged

Mae from her mind, leaving the bitter woman on her wooden couch far behind, in a land that no longer exists. But now Li-Yu can feel her presence again, as if she has entered this interrogation room, and if she turns and looks into the back corner she will see those hard black eyes, that little mound of robes and blankets.

Papers are shuffled, consulted. "You have a daughter?"

"Yes. Rose Long. Born October thirtieth, 1918, in—"

The man holds up his hand. "Just answer the questions you're asked," he says. "What is her relationship to the boy?"

"The boy?"

"Henry."

"It's fine," she says.

The sides of his head twitch. "No," he says. "How are they related?"

"They are brother and sister," she says, wondering now if she has missed something, if there is some piece of information that would make this line of questioning sensible.

"Full brother, full sister?"

"Yes, of course. Bing was their father and I am their mother."

"You're quite certain of that?"

"Am I certain of my own children?"

"Just answer, please."

"Yes. I am certain."

"And Rose would agree?"

"Yes, of course."

"You've all been together on that boat for a month now," the man says. "Certainly that would be enough time for someone to rehearse a story a few hundred times, would it not?"

Li-Yu looks from one man to the other and to the guard for an explanation, but none is forthcoming. She remembers conversations aboard the ship about the processes and interviews here, the tricks and the traps, conversations she'd ignored, thinking none of it really pertained to her as a citizen with papers. She remembers hearing of paper sons, boys and men who sought entry to the country with forged documents that proclaimed them to be the sons of Americans. Many of them had been successful but many of them had been caught, and either sent back to China or detained on the island, for weeks, months even. One passenger aboard the ship, a man perhaps ten years her senior who reminded her of Zhang, told a story about his cousin who'd been held there for almost a year. Li-Yu was sorry for him and for the others she'd heard about, who'd done nothing worse than her parents had in undertaking this voyage. But these were the problems of other people; she could not imagine they would have anything to do with her, or with Rose and Henry.

"I don't understand," Li-Yu says. "Henry is my son and Rose is my daughter, and they were both born in California and I have the papers to prove it."

There is no response but for the further shuffling of papers. The men thank her and the official escorts her back to the bunkhouse. They leave her there and immediately lead Rose away. Separated now from both her children, unease seeps into Li-Yu. It spreads through her, triggering thoughts of Mae, of Bing and his deception, of the helplessness she thought she'd finally escaped. When the guards bring Rose back to her she fights the urge to leap up and embrace her.

"What happened?" she asks.

"They asked me lots of questions," Rose says, with a shrug. "I answered them."

"What did they ask about?"

"You. Dad. A lot about Henry."

Li-Yu nods. "Me too," she says.

They continue to wait. After lunch they are shown to the yard again but she catches no glimpse of Henry. There is a man walking nearby, his hands clasped behind his back, his head down, and she calls to him to ask him about her son, but he shakes his head and says something that might be Korean or Japanese. A few hours later they call her again and ask her all the same questions, and more, and then they take Rose again and do the same. After dinner they tell her they were able to reach her sisters, and that she is free to go. The ferry will be leaving in a half-hour, they tell her, and she flushes with relief.

"And my son?" she asks.

He points to the list on his clipboard. "I only have females on here," he says, with a smile that is not unfriendly. She and Rose gather their things and hurry back down through the walkways to the pier, where they join a small group of travelers and station employees awaiting the coming ferry. The *Crystal Gypsy* is there, too, having discharged its white passengers onto the mainland, undergone an overnight cleaning, and returned, its hulking mass moored at the end of the same long dock they'd arrived on the previous day. On the other side of a fence, waiting to board, sits a group of miserable-looking passengers. Disinterested guards form a loose perimeter around them.

Li-Yu finds a place to sit and keeps one eye on Rose and the other on the door of the men's quarters. Rose splits away from her and walks over to the dividing fence. She laces her fingers through the openings and watches the other group.

The door to the men's quarters still does not open. She looks back at her daughter and sees that her attention now seems to be directed at an old man sitting by himself, at the edge of the group. He seems to be awakening from a daydream. She and Rose watch as he sits down on the ground, crosses his legs, and unsnaps a ragged leather case. He pulls out an *erhu*, places it on his knee, arranges his fingers around the handle of the bow, and begins to play. It is a slow and mournful song, and makes Li-Yu think of a funeral. It reminds her of China, a nation that is already beginning to fade in her mind. When the song is over, Rose calls out to the musician.

"Where are you going?" she asks him, in Chinese.

"Back to China," he calls, without raising his head to meet her eyes.

"Why?"

"They won't let us in," he says.

"Why not?" Rose asks.

The violinist doesn't answer. He just shakes his head and raises his bow again. He plays another song, sadder than the first. When it is over, Rose opens her bag and withdraws the tube of bamboo and its enclosed stack of papers. Li-Yu expects her to produce a pencil, and perhaps to take some notes, but instead she listens, astonished, as Rose calls one of the guards over and instructs him to deliver the package to the musician. Rose throws it over the fence and it lands neatly in the guard's hands. Still wearing his bored expression he walks over, sets the tube in the instrument case, and returns to his spot. The musician tips his head, and issues a sort of salute with his bow. Rose returns to her mother's side.

"You didn't want your stories?" Li-Yu asks.

Rose shakes her head. "I want him to have them."

"I would have liked to read some of those," Li-Yu says.

"I think they probably belong in China," Rose says. "Besides, I remember them all." She wanders off again, heading toward the water.

Li-Yu turns her attention back to the door of the men's building, which has grown maddening in its refusal to swing open. Finally it does, but three grown men emerge, heading for elsewhere. It swings shut again with a definitive clang. A few minutes later she approaches one of the nearby guards. "My son is supposed to be coming out of there," she says. "We're going on the ferry."

"I'm sure he'll be out soon," the man says, automatically.

"What's taking him so long?" she asks.

The man shrugs.

She continues to watch the doorway, a ball forming in her stomach, until she hears the ferry's horn approaching. Now she can feel panic rising into her throat. She chokes it down and approaches another guard. "My son, Henry Long," she says. "He's supposed to be here. He's supposed to be on this ferry."

This one is more sympathetic. "Okay," he says. "I'll go look." He heads up the walkway and disappears into the building. The ferry continues to approach. Li-Yu swivels her head back and forth from the doorway to the boat, watching one and then the other. Just as the ferry pulls up to the pier the guard reappears in the doorway, alone. It seems to take him forever to walk down to the pier.

"What did you say his name was?" the guard asks.

"Henry! Henry Long!" she cries. "He's only ten years old!"

"Spell that for me?"

She does, and he returns to the men's quarters. The ferry's doors rumble open, and two members of the crew wrestle a metal ramp into position. Some of the other passengers drag their luggage across it, chattering happily. "Are you coming?" one of the crewmen calls to Li-Yu and Rose.

"Yes," Li-Yu says, "we're just waiting for one more. My son."

The man nods and trots across the ramp, his footfalls reverberating loudly across the metal surface.

After a long minute the guard re-emerges, bringing with him an official, who carries a clipboard. Again it seems to take them an eternity to close the distance between the building and the docks. The guard points at Li-Yu, says something to the official, and returns to the group waiting to board the *Gypsy*. The violinist begins to play another song.

The official approaches with maddening calmness. "What seems to be the problem?" he asks.

"My son!" Li-Yu yells at him. "Where is my son? Henry Long!"

The man consults the clipboard, shaking his head. "He's not on my list."

Li-Yu screams, "He's here! We came together, just yesterday, right on that ship!" She jabs a finger toward the *Crystal Gypsy*. "We sailed from Canton! Tell them, Rose!"

"He's my brother, Henry," Rose says, her voice cracking. "He's with us."

The official looks down at his clipboard. "I don't have a position on that, ma'am," he says, disinterested. "He's just not scheduled for this ferry."

"But he's only ten! He's my son!"

He flips to another sheet on his clipboard, and then another. "There appears to be an irregularity," he says. "But we have your sister's address—we'll contact you there."

"We have to go," calls the crewman, from inside the ferry's doorway.

"Please!" Li-Yu shouts. "Just one more minute!" She turns back to the official, and when she speaks her voice seems disembodied, as if emerging from a louder and more desperate version of herself. "He's only a boy!" she shouts. "He can't stay here alone!"

"He's hardly alone, ma'am. I'm sorry. I understand your concern, but there's nothing else I can do. You should board the ferry, and you'll be contacted."

Li-Yu squats down and buries her head in her knees and wraps her arms over her head. The official is saying something about the infirmary, but all she can hear are the ferry's engines idling and the faint voice of the *erhu*. And then something bursts within her and she is up again, running toward the door of the men's quarters with an energy that seems not her own, but she has only taken a few steps when there are arms around her. A dark woolen blue falls over her eyes and shuts out the light, and then a wailing rises from somewhere far away and obliterates the engines and the song and all else.

FIFTEEN

I saved my file and shut my laptop. Rain slapped at the windows. Lucy reclined on the couch, watching a sitcom I didn't recognize, in which a couple was arguing about someone's company picnic. Eva sat next to her, her head back and crooked to the side, her mouth open, her eyes closed. I checked my phone. It was ten o'clock. Annabel hadn't called.

"I believe her," Lucy whispered, when she saw me looking up. "There's something in the front that looks like a table of contents. If we can get Annabel on the case, we might be able to figure out what's going on here."

"And then what?"

"Where's Annabel?"

"I don't know," I said.

"Let's go to Chinatown," she said. "The restaurants down there are open all night."

"It's pouring out," I said.

"You noticed?" she said.

Eva had awakened and was watching us now. "You're finished writing?" she asked me. I stood up and headed into the kitchen. She crossed the room and slid back into my desk chair. I yanked the cap off a beer and dropped into the couch spot Eva had just vacated.

"Maybe you should call her," Lucy said.

"I don't think so," I said. I gulped down beer. On TV someone fell down and canned laughter erupted. My phone rang. I dug it out of my pocket to find Annabel's name on the screen.

"Hey," I said. "Are you home yet?"

"No," she said. "I'm still here."

"But it's late," I said. "You're not going to be—"

"I'm staying overnight," she said.

"But the book . . . ."

"The roads are a mess, Peregrine," she said. "I've had a couple of glasses of wine, I'm sleepy, and it's pouring down rain. I can't very well translate anything if I end up under the wheels of a semi on I-80, can I?"

"Eva thinks it might be the book from my story," I said.

"What is that supposed to mean?"

I explained to her about the missing pages, and reminded her about the soldier's gift.

"That doesn't make any sense," she said.

"I know," I said. "That's why I really need to see you."

"You've made that clear," she said. "I'll see you tomorrow."

I hung up and dropped my phone on the couch next to me. "She isn't coming," I said.

"I gathered," Lucy said. "You must have some Chinese neighbors or something."

"It's ten at night," I said. "It's way too late to go out racial profiling."

On the screen a thin woman in a sweater stood in a clean sunny kitchen, extolling the virtues of her laundry detergent while her children played at the table behind her. At my desk Eva put her hands in her lap and said something I couldn't make out.

"Well, let's take it down to Chinatown," Lucy said. "I also happen to need some food."

"Be my guest," I said. I turned to Eva. "What did you say?" I asked. She had her face down and she might have been talking to herself.

"What happens next?" she asked. I thought I caught a tremor in her voice.

"What, you want me to walk down there?" Lucy said. "You won't drive?"

"No, I won't." I turned back to Eva. "I've been writing for hours," I said. "Can't that be enough for one night?"

"Okay, to hell with the research," Lucy said. "But I'm still hungry."

"So forget about the writing," Eva said. Her voice sounded quiet, unnatural. "Just tell me. Have a conversation."

"Sorry, but story time is over. I'm off the clock."

"I'm ordering Chinese food," Lucy said. "If someone wants something, speak now."

"I was just wondering . . ." Eva said, her face still hidden, and now I was sure of it—there was some just-contained urgency in her voice. I could tell she wanted to say more, but she let it go, and I decided I didn't give a shit what she was wondering.

We ordered pork chow mein, chicken and black mushrooms, black pepper beef. Lucy vowed to interrogate the delivery guy about the book, but he turned out to be a Mexican kid. Lucy asked him if he spoke Chinese anyway. He laughed, handed us a few soaking wet plastic bags and hurried away.

When I'd eaten and had another beer or two I took a notebook and went to my room. The window hummed with rain. Muffled indecipherable voices came through the wall. I climbed into bed, my back against the headboard, my notebook propped on my legs, but I fell asleep before I'd written a single line. I dreamed I was walking out on the streets of my neighborhood. Dirty water flooded up out of the sewer grates, surged up the hills, and rejoined puddles in the intersections and potholes. Everywhere the rain leapt up and climbed back into the sky.

***

The next morning I awoke, retrieved the notebook, uncapped my pen, and stayed there in bed, trying to find a way into the next episode. I wrote a few lines about Li-Yu being pulled onto the ferry, but her desolation seemed inauthentic, her performance melodramatic, overwrought. I tried to enter the scene through Rose, to see through her eyes the images of her hysterical mother, the island receding, and the listless deportees waiting in the *Gypsy*'s shadow, but I had no sense of how she felt, so it all felt like simulacra. I jumped forward in time, perhaps a few days, to a room at her sister's house in Chinatown with bare floors, sparse furnishings, where Li-Yu sat in a wooden chair, waiting, her panic writhing inside her. It was little more than a still image, a drawing; I couldn't get it to move or breathe. I scribbled everything out and tried to see Henry instead, but nothing came. There were no images around him, no snippets of conversation, no faces or sounds or smells or any of the other things I could use as a way into him. He had vanished, not only from his mother and sister, but from the story. I arose, got dressed, and headed for the living room, still carrying the notebook.

Eva was sitting on the couch, dressed as if she were about to leave, her bag on her lap. Lucy sat at my computer.

"What's that?" Eva asked, eyeing the notebook.

"No Annabel yet?" Lucy asked.

"It's nothing," I said. "No," I said.

"What do you mean, nothing?" Eva asked.

"Nothing," I said. "Scribbles." I held up my page of scratched-out false starts.

Eva was sitting very still, very straight. She glanced at the sheet and then looked away, as though braced for a blow. "What did those say?" she asked.

"Not much. I wrote some notes and I crossed them out."

"Is she still pissed at you?" Lucy asked.

"What did they say before you crossed them out?" Eva asked, seeming to address a spot on the couch's arm.

I shrugged, not that she was looking at me. "Here, have a look for yourself," I said. I threw the notebook toward the couch. The pages fluttered and it landed like a wounded bird next to her. I circled the counter and went about making coffee. "Who said she was pissed?" I asked Lucy.

"I was sitting right next to you when she hung up on you last night," Lucy said.

"She didn't hang up on me."

"Okay," she said, her eyes still on the computer screen. "So is she still pissed?"

"Why did you cross these out?" Eva asked.

"Because I didn't like them," I said, working to control my impatience. "You're asking a lot of questions for somebody who's continuing to withhold the star witness."

Lucy looked at me and Eva, me and Eva, and then back to the computer, and muttered something.

"What?" I said.

"You all should play nice," she said.

Eva set the notebook on the couch next to her, took a deep breath, and leaned forward, her arms crossed against her chest, and scanned the room as though seeing it for the first time. She looked as though she'd just tasted something bitter. With one palm she reached down and pushed against the edge of the coffee table, as though testing its solidity.

"What the hell is with you?" I asked her.

"I'm getting that book translated this morning, that's what's with me," Lucy said. "I didn't haul across the country to wait out your lovers' quarrel."

"It's not a quarrel, and I wasn't even talking to you," I said.

"It's a quarrel. You men are just too stupid to know when you're in the middle of one. I'm taking it to Chinatown."

"Let's just wait," I said. "I'll call Annabel in a little bit."

"I'm taking it to Chinatown. You can come with me or not."

"Would you just hold on for a fucking second?" I said. "I'll call her. Let me drink a cup of coffee first, okay?"

"Sure," she said. "Here's me holding on." She stood from the desk, collected the book from the table, flipped me off, and went out the door.

Fine, I thought. There were too many people in this apartment anyway. I watched the coffee drip into the carafe and as soon as there was enough for a half-cup I poured it into a mug. I sat down at my desk and started poking through my e-mail inbox. Eva was still on the couch, studying the lines I'd crossed out. I didn't notice her rising, but suddenly she was standing at the edge of my desk. She tapped the notebook and its scribbled-out lines. "You were trying to write last night," she said. Her voice sounded shaky, and she still wouldn't look at me. Though we were a foot apart it seemed as if she couldn't quite find me.

"This morning," I said. "Tell me where your mom is and then maybe I'll write some more."

She traced one of the crossed-out sentences with her fingertip, as though trying to feel hidden meanings in the layers of ink. "This hasn't happened before," she said.

"What hasn't?"

"False starts," she said.

"I don't get what the hell's going on here," I said. "I erased a few lines, and you're acting like it's the end of the world."

"Maybe it is," she said, quietly.

"Okay," I said. "Then maybe it is." I packed up my computer, grabbed my things, and headed out the door. I didn't know where I was going, but I knew I didn't want to be at my apartment anymore. Outside the storm had reached a ferocious pitch, and I was soaked before I'd gone a half-block. The inside of my car smelled like a swamp. A faint sheen of green sat atop the dashboard. It was probably the reflection of the traffic light on the corner but it wasn't hard to imagine that it was a layer of algae.

The engine wouldn't turn over. I tried the starter four or five times and then yanked the keys out and threw them on the dash.

I sat there a minute, listening to the rain hammer against the roof. A Muni bus, its colors and shape distorted by the sheet of water sliding down my windshield, appeared over the crest of the hill in front of me. Its headlights pushed weakly into the storm. I watched it descend a block, and then another half-block, and then on impulse I grabbed my bag and ran across the street to the corner bus stop.

I paid my fare and headed for the back corner. There was no one else aboard. The heater was on high and the windows were opaque with fog. I tucked my bag beneath my legs, smeared a hole in the foggy window, and watched my apartment building approach. Just as we passed by the lights of the lobby flickered and went out—another power outage. I thought of Eva sitting up there in the dark, with my notebook. She'd probably just go back to sleep. I took my coat off and laid it across my lap like a blanket. I didn't know exactly where the bus was headed, but it didn't matter. It would make its way downtown, eventually, weave through the empty Sunday streets of the financial district, swing through the transit terminal, and make its way back along some northern circuit. Maybe I'd get off at some point. Maybe I wouldn't.

We turned and descended to the Embarcadero without stopping. Finally, when we were just across from Pier 23, the bus pulled over and leaned down to admit a passenger. I smeared another porthole in the foggy window and saw that the warehouse's doors were closed. No light came from the windows that flanked the doorway. The bus righted itself and pulled back into the lane while the passenger, a shapeless mass of raincoats, fed coins into the box in the bus's darkened entrance. He turned and the cabin's light revealed him to be our Berkeley *erhu* player, his instrument case under his arm and rain dripping from his jacket. I should have been struck by the infinitesimal chances of his appearance here, but I was mesmerized by the way he moved. He seemed to float; under his dark layers of clothes there was no visible movement, no

stride, no sway. If he recognized me he didn't show it. He came to
the back of the bus and set his case on the floor. After removing
and folding his jacket he opened the latches, removed the instrument, sat down, and settled it on his knee. He closed his eyes and
began to play. The sound of the engine fell away, as though making room for the song. The bus's heaters had driven through my
wet clothes by then, and a uniform warmth now enveloped me.
I didn't want to move. We had taken a couple of turns and I no
longer knew where we were.

When the song was perhaps halfway over the bus stopped again
and leaned down to admit a group of passengers. At the front of the
group was a short, older man in dark blue clothes and a matching
cap—Lucy's phantom. He had Hui's face, I saw. He winked at me
and then found a seat, crossed his ankle over his knee, and closed his
eyes. Behind him were the two soldiers and their guide, their clothes
still torn, still dirty. Their rifles banged against the metal poles and
handholds as they came down the aisle. The soldiers found seats,
settled their rifle butts on the floor, and closed their eyes. Hui pulled
a small red book from his jacket and offered it to the guide, who
accepted it with a smile and a deep bow of his head. He opened it
and began to read, his lips moving slightly. Behind him were four
women, Chinese, all of them identical, wearing matching cheon-
gsams, their hands stained with black ink. They sat in a row, shoulder to shoulder, and folded their hands into their laps. The bus
began to move again. The song swelled.

Zhang boarded at the next stop. He came into the back, sat
down, and studied the musician's hands as he worked at the
strings. Mae came aboard next, walking slowly, painfully on her
bound feet, helped along by two of her maids. They were followed by Bing, who looked frail, dried out, the shell of a man.
They sat down in the first open seats, ahead of the mahjong players. Li-Yu and Rose came next, walking hand in hand. They sat
down near Zhang and joined him in listening to the music.

At the next stop my dad climbed aboard. He dropped his coins into the fare box and tottered down the aisle, leaning heavily on the bus's poles, his breathing laborious. He looked exactly as I remembered him in those final days of his life.

He took the seat next to me. The music diminished to a whisper.

"Hello, Peregrine," he said.

"Hi, Dad," I said.

"Give me a minute," he said, "and then we can talk."

"Sure," I said.

The bus continued to plunge through the city. Faint changes of light and color were all I could see through the windows. After a few blocks his breath came back to him.

"So you've been okay?" he said.

"I guess so," I said. "You?"

"I can't complain," he said. "But listen. I hear you found out about that swimming pool thing."

I nodded.

"I'm sure sorry about that," he said. He looked sad. "It won't happen again."

"It's okay," I said. "I'm all right."

He shrugged. "Maybe so. Still, though."

"It's okay," I said again.

We stopped at a light. The musician ended his song and began another, something a little faster. Dad looked up. "Crowded bus today," he said.

I nodded. Our fellow passengers all wore expressions of peace, their eyes closed or half-closed as they listened to the music, or read. In this shared state of repose they were the embodiment of patience, of contentment; it seemed as though they could abide a bus ride of ten thousand miles, so long as they had the music to listen to, and the book to pass around, and the warmth of the bus's heaters, and the purr of its engine, which seemed now to be coming across a very great distance. We drifted another block or two before my dad spoke again.

"Listen, I've been wondering something," he said. His brow rippled with thought and he was chewing on the corner of his bottom lip, a habit of his I hadn't thought of in a decade.

"Yeah?" I said.

"I've been wondering how you did it," he said.

"How I did what?"

"How you went back," he said. He scratched his head, right fingertips to left temple, another long-forgotten but instantly recognizable tic of his. "My experiences here haven't shed much light on the question."

"I don't know," I said. "I don't remember anything."

"Of course, of course," he said, almost looking embarrassed he'd asked. When it came to other people his curiosity had always been minimal. He was a man who had only posed questions to his computers, to the potential of the intellectual frontiers he'd explored. "And of course, the circumstances were entirely different. About as different as they could have been."

I nodded. The *erhu*'s song continued, slower again. Our fellow passengers were still silent, motionless; those who had their eyes open were not looking at one another but into space. My dad pointed at the fogged window, and behind it the nebulous shapes of the city filing past. "Strange," he said. "You can hardly see a thing. We could be anywhere." We rode together in silence for a few more blocks, and then he leaned forward. "This is my stop," he said.

"Okay," I said. "Thanks."

He paused. "You take care of yourself," he said, "and your sister." He worked his way back up the aisle as the bus slowed and pulled over, and then he was gone. At the next stop Li-Yu and Rose climbed down, and then Bing and Mae at the next. Zhang exited next, followed by the mahjong players and the soldiers and

Lucy's phantom. The musician finished his song, packed up his *erhu*, and climbed down at the following stop. A group of teenage girls boarded, shopping bags dangling from their arms. They took seats, chatting noisily. The engines grew loud again; knots of stiffness arose in my hips, my back. I shifted in my seat and wiped away the fog on the window. We were not far from my neighborhood, heading up Van Ness, whose shops and restaurants were lit and bright and busy despite the rain. The bus turned and climbed back up Russian Hill. A block short of my building I reached down and groped for my laptop bag. My hand closed on empty air. I shifted my legs and looked under my seat, and under the seat next to mine, and the one in front of me and the one in front of that. It was gone.

***

"Where the hell have you been?" Lucy asked. She was sitting on the couch next to Eva, holding a beer. The red book sat on the table.

"Have you been writing?" Eva asked. "You took your computer."

"On the bus," I said. "And no."

"What bus?" Lucy said. "Where did you go?"

"Muni," I said. "Nowhere."

"What do you mean, 'nowhere'? You've been gone all day."

"Why? What time is it?"

"Almost five."

"That doesn't seem right," I said.

"Okay," Lucy said, "you're right. I just made that up, because I enjoy being wrong about easily verifiable facts." She took a swallow of her beer. "What do you mean, 'nowhere'?"

"Nowhere," I said. "My car doesn't work."

"What does that have to do with it?"

"I was hoping maybe you might have been writing," Eva said.

"I'm aware of that," I said. I sat down at my desk and started rubbing my temples. The parade of characters still filled my mind; I'd never had a dream so organized, so literal. Even the bus's advertising placards had been accurate—local tax lawyers, the MOMA, Giants season tickets.

"What did you find out about that book?" I asked Lucy.

"It's a cookbook," she said.

"A cookbook?"

"Yes," she said. "Tofu recipes."

"I thought they were poems."

"They are," Eva said. "I'm sure of it."

"Tofu recipes, every page," Lucy said.

"Says who?" I said.

"Says Chinatown," she said.

"A tofu cookbook in verse?" I said.

"Maybe we still need your girlfriend," Lucy said. "Have you called her yet?"

"No," I said.

"Well, you should."

"I can't," I said. "My phone got stolen."

"You're that scared of her? She seemed pretty friendly to me."

"It really did get stolen. On the bus. Along with my computer."

"You're serious?"

"Yes." I turned to Eva. "So no, no writing."

Lucy sat forward, her eyes bright. I was reminded of her enthusiasm for theft. "You got mugged? Someone stuck you up? Gun? Knife?"

"I think I fell asleep," I said.

She sat back, clearly disappointed. "You fell asleep and someone swiped your bag? That's lame."

"Sorry," I said. "I'll try to do a better job of getting robbed next time."

"Good," she said. "You missed a great opportunity."

During our exchange, Eva had been making small movements, and now I saw that she'd been gathering her things together. She rose to her feet and pulled on her coat. And then I saw her face. She looked stricken.

"What's wrong?" I asked. "Where are you going?"

She didn't answer.

Lucy looked up and understood something in Eva's face or in her movements and with an almost audible snap her entire demeanor changed. She leapt from the couch. "Eva, wait!" she said. "It's just a coincidence! Give it some more time. You'll see!"

Eva ignored her. She buttoned up her coat, shouldered her bag, and headed toward the door.

"Eva, please!" Lucy said. "You've got to believe me!"

"What are you talking about?" I said. "She'll see what?"

"Fuck, fuck," Lucy muttered. She took a few lunging steps toward Eva, but she turned her foot on the edge of one of her suitcases, stumbled, and would have fallen had she not been able to catch herself on another stack of luggage. Eva yanked the door open, stepped through, and slammed it closed. "Eva!" Lucy yelled again. We listened to her footfalls recede, and then we listened to the machinery of the elevator carry her away.

***

In the quiet that followed her departure I came to understand that I was on the verge of completely abandoning all attempts to make sense of my life that month. I'd just been robbed and I'd just had a chat with my father, either of which should have been enough to leave me reeling. In the context of these last few weeks, though, they seemed almost mundane. Lucy had come to know things, somehow, and maybe I should have been alight with curiosity about what, and how, and why Eva had just stormed out, and maybe a half-dozen other things somebody with a more level head might have seen fit to question. But fatigue had come over me, and it filled all the spaces that curiosity and ambition might have occupied otherwise. In that thin slice of my life I once considered professional, there were other pressures mounting—all my progress reports would be due in just over forty-eight hours, and I knew I hadn't heard the end of my decision to send one of my students on an errand that had almost killed him. It was now the first of February; I was sure there were January bills still waiting to be paid.

"She's gone," Lucy said, "and she's not coming back."

"Maybe that's okay," I said. "It would be nice if things could get a little simpler around here."

"That's what you're concerned about right now?" she said. "Simplicity? Are you really that incurious?"

"No," I said. "I'm plenty curious. But I'm sort of habituated to strangeness at this point. When something normal and explicable happens, that will get my attention."

"I'm glad you think this is a good time for sarcasm. That's helpful." She reached for her coat. "Get your shit," she said. "Let's go."

"Where?"

"I need to tell you some things. But first I need to get the hell out of this apartment."

We made our way down to Polk Street and found a table at a café. She ordered a burger and a beer; I ordered an omelet and coffee.

"Bring him a beer, too," she told our waitress. She turned to me. "You're going to need it," she said. "Are you ready?"

"For what?"

"What would you say if I told you that several times Eva told me what you were going to write?"

The hair on my arms stood up. "I don't know," I said.

"Well, she did," Lucy said. "Several times. Specifics."

"Like what?"

"Like a lot of things. Like how long they would be in China, and how they got away, down the river. So tell me: How is that possible?"

I shook my head. The lights in the café seemed too bright. I closed my eyes and pressed my palms into them until I saw fireworks.

"Well, unlike you, Eva was actually trying to figure out what was going on here. She had some theories. Do you want to hear them?"

"Enlighten me," I said.

Two open bottles of beer arrived, along with a cup of coffee. I reached for the beer.

"You know the Theory of the Thieving Historian," Lucy said, grabbing her own bottle. "She gave that up after about two days and replaced it with the Theory of the Unwitting Psychic Channeler. The names are mine, by the way, thank you very much."

"Okay," I said. "I'm neither of those things."

"Unwitting," Lucy said. "It means you wouldn't know if you were."

I took a long gulp and my beer crackled and fizzed in my throat. I suppressed a cough.

"But then, because your stories matched hers so closely, she sharpened that one until it was the Theory of Henry Incarnate."

"Meaning?"

"You're Henry."

"That's crazy," I said.

"Compared to what?" she said.

Our food arrived, sending plumes of steam up into the space between us. She smacked out a blob of ketchup and plunged a bundle of fries into it. I didn't feel like eating. I sucked down more beer and watched my coffee cool.

"At the same time," she said, chewing now, "she was wondering about herself. So she developed the Alternate Theory of Amnesia and Suggestibility. In that one, she is an amnesiac who remembers nothing about her real past, and somehow she has become convinced that your story is hers, and she's letting you dictate her memories to her."

"That's crazy, too," I said.

"You can stop saying that," Lucy said. "It's all crazy. Especially that one. Because, as I told you, she knew what you were going to write before you wrote it."

"I don't know about that. So why did she leave?"

"Because your stories ended at the same time," she said.

"Who said mine ended?"

"Henry disappeared from Angel Island in the summer of 1929," she said, "and that was the last thing anybody knew about him."

"Who said mine ended?"

She chewed off a hunk of her burger. "You couldn't write last night," she said, through a full mouth, while smearing a rivulet of beef juice across her chin with the back of her wrist. "You crossed out all those things in your notebook. And then your laptop vanished."

"It didn't vanish. It got stolen."

"Doesn't matter. It's gone. And that was enough to convince her of the truth of her final theory."

"Which was?"

"The Theory of Utter Delusion." She washed down her bite with half her beer bottle. "You're a delusion. So am I. You, me, your apartment, your story, *The Barbary Quarterly*. We're all hallucinations, and she's really dead and in purgatory, or in a coma at SF General, or caught in some CIA mind-fuck experiment. So you're really an embodiment of some part of her mind, and since she doesn't know anything in the story beyond Angel Island, you can't either. Sounds crazy as everything else, but I have to admit, she had some pretty compelling arguments." She hoisted her burger again. "Still feeling habituated?" she said.

Maybe there was an explanation for Eva's predictions about my story. Either she or Lucy had the chronology wrong, and Eva wasn't foretelling the story, but repeating what she'd read, and somewhere in the process the events had been reversed. Or maybe I really wasn't inventing my story after all, but echoing something I'd heard or read too long ago to remember, something that had stayed in some deep part of me and was now resurfacing in disguise. I'd rejected this explanation the first time it came up, but now that the hidden messages in my mazes had appeared, I had to reconsider the possibility.

I finished my beer and as the alcohol worked its way through me the problem turned over in my mind. I saw it not for all its complexity but as a simple pair of options—a pair of options that would keep me up all night. Either Eva wasn't crazy, and there really was some invisible link between my story and Henry's, which would mean I had to accept the orchestrations of forces well beyond my understanding. Or perhaps she was crazy—which would mean I was so entwined in her craziness as to be inseparable from it.

SIXTEEN

It was immediately after the first bell the next morning when the endmost fifty feet of Russian Hill Elementary School's oblong concrete foundation broke clean off, with a sound like thunder, and slid down a newly created cliffside, carrying upon its back Annabel's disintegrating kindergarten classroom, which it deposited directly beneath a cataract of mud and water.

I had arrived that morning and adjusted my route to pass by the cafeteria, where I hoped to see Annabel and to find out if we were quarreling, but the folding tables and chairs that had served as her temporary classroom furnishings had all been put away and the room was its usual dark echoing space.

I didn't have time to chase her down so I headed to my classroom, settled in, and commenced my Monday.

"It's day twenty-eight now," Kevin said to me upon making his entrance that morning. "Four weeks, in other words. It's a good thing Barney is an expert scuba diver, because his doghouse is underwater now."

"No it isn't," Eliza said, "and you shouldn't joke about it. This is a real disaster with real people getting hurt."

Kevin shook his head sadly. "I don't know what you have against Barney. He's never done anything to anybody, except for when he was in the army, and that was for your freedom." He turned back to me. "Hey Mr. Long, is Atlantis real?" he said.

"No," said Eliza. "It's make-believe."

"I don't know," I said. "It's the sort of thing that's hard to disprove."

"What does that mean?" he said.

"It means you never know," I said.

"That's not what that means," Eliza said.

And then the bell rang, and then came the boom and the crack, and then a sound like we were standing atop a breaking dam, and then a sudden crash that did not end but became a long series of smaller crashes. The floor seemed somehow loose beneath my feet for a second, and then my chair separated from my desk, rolled across the floor, and bumped into the cabinets. The kids froze, their eyes wide. The overhead lights flickered twice, and then a third time, and then went out. In the distance on the far edge of the playground I could see that the hill was the wrong color, the wrong shape.

"Under your desks!" I yelled. As Californians we were all well drilled in earthquake procedures, and within a few seconds my students had disappeared beneath their makeshift shelters. I bolted for the door, shouting at my students to stay put. Chaos had risen in the darkened classrooms I ran past; several people were shouting and I could hear crying. I slammed through the doors at the hallway's end and the storm broke over me. I shielded my eyes from the water but saw nothing unusual yet. I darted through the next hallway and burst through the door that should have taken me to the end of campus and Annabel's classroom.

It was gone, and so was the earth that should have been beneath it. My vision went gray, and then red, as though blood was flooding across the surface of my eyeballs, and then just as quickly my eyes cleared and I saw everything. The foundation had snapped and like a raft going over a waterfall, it had tilted until it was almost entirely on end, and then carried her classroom some dozen feet down the hill, where both had lodged, half-buried in mud. From unseen conduits in the hillside torrents of brown water gushed, falling onto the room and plunging in through its broken windows and open doorway.

I launched myself over the edge, jumping outward to clear the tangle of bent rebar that jutted from the sheared foundation. It was not until I was sliding down a wall of mud that I realized I was heading directly toward the other ends of the severed bars, whose broken points were waiting in the mud and water to skewer me. I tried to throw myself over and past them, but I could neither push nor kick off the steep sodden slope—my limbs simply disappeared into the mud. Something jabbed me in the thigh. I flopped over, scraped down a few feet of concrete, and slammed into the base of the wall, all the feeling in my leg gone. Muddy water crashed down all around me; black spots appeared before my eyes. With what felt like a hundred pounds of mud clinging to me, I fought my way to my elbows and knees and put my head down, where I could suck in air without breathing water. I transferred my weight to my forearms and my good leg and peered down through a corner of the doorway. The room was filling up fast. The water's surface roiled with wooden furniture and the shining primary colors of children's raincoats. I took a deep breath, and then another, and then tipped over the edge. There was an explosion in my wrist as I caromed off the edge of something big and hard and then I plunged into the black depths, the mud pulling me to the bottom, my hands groping through the darkness.

A sudden warmth washed over me and I opened my eyes. The water had become still and clear and clean, illuminated by thick rays of sunlight that reached down from the distant surface. A classroom appeared beneath me, but it wasn't Annabel's. I was drifting down, into a room without a roof that stood by itself in the middle of an ocean floor as barren and sandy as a desert. The room's walls were white and sparse. An empty blackboard stretched the length of the front wall. Clean wooden desks stood in orderly rows, each of them paired with a small backless wooden stool that shifted slightly in its spot with the current. The desks were all empty but for one near the back, which held a single sheet of paper, a small shallow bowl of black ink, and a calligraphy brush. On the sheet were two Chinese characters. I swam down toward them, studying the brushstrokes as I approached. It looked as though they'd just been written—faint lines of ink arched through the water, describing the brush's recent path from the ink bowl to the paper and then to the brush's resting place alongside the sheet. The calligrapher was not in sight.

I was just about to seize the sheet of paper when I felt myself being lifted, up and out of the quiet, bright classroom. There was a sound like a waterfall and the classroom quickly receded. The water turned cold and darkness swallowed the blackboard and desks. Something heavy hit me on the back of the head. Suddenly my lungs were spinning saw blades, tearing at the inside of my chest. I reached up and swiped at my face, as if to clear the water away, and it worked—there was air now, somehow, and I was still rising, out of the water, up through the prostrate doorway of Annabel's room. I felt something solid beneath me and I clung to it, too weak to do anything but cough out water and suck in great rasping lungful of air.

Franklin Nash came into focus, squatting beside me. He was breathing heavily and his sleeve was torn and blood was running down the side of his face. "They were all in the library," he managed to say, his chest heaving mightily. "They're all okay. We have to go now. I need you to come with me."

He reached for me. I vomited a plume of mud and coffee onto his hands, and then I blacked out.

***

Vague impressions followed: movement through space, gradations in light, temperature changes, and then, much later, a blurry grid that seemed at first to be a giant flyswatter poised above me, but which then came into focus as ceiling tiles. The edges and corners of the room came into focus, followed by a clock, and then a small television fastened to the wall with a metal bracket, advertisements on its screen and the volume low. My sister's voice came next.

"Mornin', Sunshine," she said. "I brought you *dim sum*, but the nurse told me I couldn't give you any. So I'm adapting." There was a Styrofoam box on her lap and a pair of chopsticks in her hand. "How do those feel?" she said.

"Those?" I said. My voice sounded too deep, muted, as if it was coming out of an iron box hidden deep in my chest. Everything looked too soft, too pink.

"The staples. How do they feel?"

"Staples?"

"Six of them, in the back of your head." She opened the box, releasing a cloud of steam, and chopsticked a piece of *siumai* into her mouth. Through her mouthful she listed my injuries: In addition to the staples and their associated concussion I had a broken wrist, which was wrapped in a cast that reached from the base of my fingers to the middle of my forearm, and a bruise on my thigh the size, shape, and color of an eggplant. In addition to that, she said, I had an extra-large cocktail of antibiotics and painkillers running through me, which explained the pink softness. All of which, Lucy said, put me somewhere between the craziest and luckiest motherfucker ever. "Wait until you see this," she said, still chewing, gesturing toward the television, where a handsome middle-aged man was holding a football and speaking to the camera about his erections. "You're going to shit yourself. Just wait." In the next ad strands of mozzarella stretched across the screen in drug-induced slow motion. A nurse about my age leaned in through the doorway, glanced at me, and smiled.

"He's up," Lucy said. "He said he wants more drugs." She winked at me. "I've got you covered."

The ads ended and CNN's logo darted into the frame. A reporter stood in the rain in the street out in front of Russian Hill Elementary School. "For those of you just joining us, I'm in San Francisco," he said, "where a third-grade teacher is in stable condition after plunging into *this*." The scene, shot from a traffic helicopter, was obscured by a gray curtain of driving rain, but clear enough: Annabel's classroom, on its side, wedged into the muddy hillside on its broken foundation, rebar jutting out like insects' legs, and the pipes, still pouring forth their torrents of water, all of it silent, shaky. I watched myself burst through the doorway and arrive at the edge of the precipice. The camera zoomed in and out and in again, lost its focus and then regained it, and I watched myself land on the wall amid the falling water and disappear into the room. Franklin Nash emerged running from the doorway, arrived at the edge, and immediately turned back inside. The helicopter descended; the cameraman fiddled with zoom and focus until the frame held the severed ledge, the upturned face of the drowning classroom, the door into the hallway.

"They've been looping this over and over," Lucy whispered, through a full mouth. "You're bigger than the Middle East, Chechnya, everything everywhere. How does it feel?"

For a long, terrible minute nothing happened on the screen. Lying there in the bed I imagined the water enclosing me again. I thought of the classroom, the sheet of paper and the calligraphy, but this time there was no peace, no warmth—only the precariousness of Annabel's classroom, and the sense of my tiny, fragile body trapped inside of it. I was beginning to feel panic coming on when Franklin burst back through the doorway with Albert, the custodian. Together they were carrying a long ladder, which they dropped over the edge, hooking its top over some of the protruding rebar. Franklin climbed down the rungs, taking them three or four at a time, and jumped down to the wall. The falling water obscured the details here—there was movement, and limbs, and another excruciating period of nothingness, and then the top end of Annabel's classroom blew apart like a bursting water balloon. I winced and there was a throb in my thigh that pulsated outward and sent shockwaves shuddering to my toes and ears and back. The picture veered suddenly, as if the sight had caused the cameraman to jump, and when the camera regained its focus it revealed an avalanche of water and mud, dotted with colorful specks of classroom furniture, pouring down the side of the hill. Franklin clung to the bottom of the ladder with my limp body draped over his shoulders.

"Is he married?" Lucy asked, through another mouthful.

I tried to breathe, tried to settle my jumping heart as I watched Franklin carry me to the top of the ladder, where Albert helped pull me to safety. The camera tilted to the wreckage of Annabel's classroom, a pile of unrecognizable rubble at the bottom of the slope.

A near death, I figured, should be easier to understand for someone who'd already had the experience of dying, but I wasn't ready for all those considerations just yet. I wanted to think about something else. I tried to push myself up to a sitting position, but I couldn't put any pressure on my wrist. I gasped and fell back down. Lucy hit a button and the bed's motors whirred and did the job for me.

"I was in a classroom," I said.

"The whole world knows that by now," Lucy said. "But can you believe that? What are the chances? They were en route from a fender-bender on 101, right over Russian Hill when the pilot noticed your place of employment break in half." She shook her head and bit into a *char siu bao.* "This is some historical shit here. I think your fifteen minutes is going to be more like fifteen thousand."

"No," I said. "I was in a classroom in China. I swam down through the water and it cleared and I was floating in an empty classroom. There was a sheet of paper on one of the desks, with two characters on it. I memorized them." I closed my eyes and despite the pink puffballs inside my eyelids and the specter of the disintegrating classroom I was able to visualize each stroke of both characters.

"You also got a major thump on the head," Lucy said, her eyes still on the television. "I wouldn't be surprised if you saw dancing unicorns down there." She laughed and pointed at the screen, where Annabel's classroom was blowing apart over and over at various speeds. My school photograph, taken earlier that fall, had been superimposed in the corner of the screen. "Your boss used to be a Green Beret," Lucy said. "Did you know that? Do you think they'll make a movie about him?"

I was about to ask her to bring me a sheet of paper and a pencil, but the nurse swept into the room, with her smile and an armful of things. She said something warm to me, fiddled with something, and then everything went gray again.

***

"We have to find Eva," I said with a gasp. Things in the room had changed—the colors were different; angles had shifted. It was colder, and the voices coming through my door echoed as if in a wide empty hall. The television was off. My heart was drumming. "We have to find Eva," I said again. I tried to fix on the images from the dream I'd just had, but they dissipated too quickly. All that remained was the memory of Eva's departure, and a sense of peril.

A kiss fell upon my cheek, and then another on my forehead. "I'm a forgiving person," Annabel said. "I would have settled for lunch." With her fingertips she began to trace swirls and waves on my arm. The glow of her smile warmed my cheek.

"Lucy's not here?" I said.

"She went home. You've been asleep a long while. She said you weren't too impressed with your newfound celebrity."

"It doesn't seem relevant," I said.

She laughed, and the music of it drove away the last of the dream's fragments and shook me out of my lingering disorientation. Her eyes were bright and black, like glints of light on water at night. Her smile was part joy, part pride. "You're okay," I said. "You're okay, and your kids are okay?"

"Miraculously."

I took her hand. Feeling was coming back now; patches of prickly warmth migrated through my leg and I felt as if my head was resting on the pointed end of a spike. "There was a class-room," I said.

"So I hear," she said.

"There was something written on a piece of paper."

"Hold that thought," she said. "Me first." She reached into a bag on the floor and produced the red recipe book. She held it between her flattened palms, as though she was praying. "It was lost," she said. "It's been lost for a long time, trying to find me."

"It's not about tofu, is it?" I said.

She shook her head. "Eva was right. It's a book of poetry by Du Fu. Which sounds a lot like tofu, especially if you're talking to a busy waiter in a crowded restaurant and there's a serious language barrier."

"And the missing pages?"

She unfolded a stack of papers. "There were four poems, one on each side of the two missing pages. Three of them don't matter, but this one does." She handed me a sheet, a printout from a web page. The poem was called "Banquet at the Tso Family Manor." "Read the last line," she said.

"'I think of my little boat, and long to be on my way,'" I read aloud—the same line that had appeared in the mazes in my room's window. I handed it back to her, making no attempt at all to connect the phenomena. My efforts thus far had been futile, with each discovery—the violinist, the rooms at Pier 23, the Yung Hee Sea-food Company—only posing further questions. I was an ant trying to discern the shape of its colony, a man trying to see the back of his own head. Either things would be revealed, or they would not.

"Surprised?" she asked.

"Constantly."

"All right. Your turn. Tell me about the classroom, and this message," Annabel said.

"I need paper."

She dug a small notepad and a pen out of her purse. The pain in my right wrist wouldn't let me hold a pen so I had to draw the characters' strokes with my left hand. I traced them carefully, slowly, and managed to do a passable job.

"This is *han*," Annabel said, tapping the first one. "It means *very*, or *much*." She pointed at the other character. "*Li*," she said. "That means *miles*. Many miles."

"Many miles," I said. "What is that supposed to mean?"

She shrugged. "You're asking the wrong person," she said, reaching down to tousle my hair, staying well clear of the shaved spot with the staples. "It came out of this head."

"Maybe," I said.

"My turn again," she said.

"There's more?"

"One more little thing. Do you want to know about the *Crystal Gypsy*?"

"It sank?"

She nodded.

"When?" I said, but I already knew what she'd say.

"1929."

"On its way back to China," I said.

"Right."

"So has it found you yet?"

"No," she said. "Over eighty years ago, and she's still lost out there." She reached back into her bag and produced a copy of *The Barbary Quarterly*, another one I hadn't seen yet. It was tattered and dirty, and damp. On the cover was a picture of the ship's prow, a burst of sun showing just above the deck. Its name was emblazoned on its hull in clear white letters. "It washed up on my step last night," Annabel said. She put the journal on my chest and rested her hands on my arm. "Open it," she said.

I did. The pages were all blank.

"We have to find Eva," I said. "I've got to get the hell out of here, and we've got to find Eva."

* * *

I did not get the hell out of there, however. I learned sometime that evening that I'd be staying at least one night. "You went swimming in storm runoff with a cracked-open head," my doctor explained. He had white hair and wore glasses with heavy black frames that magnified his clear blue eyes. "The good news is that with all the rain, the fecal matter was probably pretty diluted. Nonetheless, I'm keeping you here until I'm confident you're not going to turn into the Swamp Thing."

I passed the time by drifting through various medicated states, taking brief limping forays through the hospital corridors, watching stories about myself on the news, trying to keep track of all the questions I had about everything. There were reports from the hospital's parking lot: Rain-lashed correspondents held their microphones and pointed toward the hospital's upper floors. Some stood outside the lobby of my apartment building, others in front of the barriers that cordoned off the now-closed campus of Russian Hill Elementary. It was comforting, in a way—though so much was changing I could lie there in my hospital bed and travel through the familiarity of all my usual locations.

I learned things about myself, too. I learned there were about fifty reporters camped out in the hospital's lobby and in vans outside. I learned that I was conscious now, and in good condition, but hadn't been released from the hospital yet. I learned that school would be out for the rest of the week, until another facility could be readied. I wondered if Eva was watching all this somewhere. I saw an interview with Franklin. He answered the reporter's questions with precision and warmth, and then asked if he could address me directly.

"Of course!" the reporter said.

He turned to the camera and cleared his throat. "Your progress reports are due, young man," he said, without a hint of a smile.

I also had time to contemplate my newfound fame and the attention that awaited me upon my discharge. Lucy returned and told me there were a hundred messages from TV producers on my machine at home. A newscaster on one broadcast speculated about what had happened "down there," and told viewers they'd have to wait until I hit the talk show circuit to find out. I imagined myself describing to perky morning news anchors the underwater classroom I'd found in 1920s China, and the discovery of a clue that might or might not help me find a boy I might or might not have made up. It would be a short-lived circuit.

Sometime that evening a nurse came into my room with a slip of paper. "We've been hanging up on all your callers," she said. "All eight thousand of them, except your family members. But this guy was insistent. Said he was your college roommate. I told him the best I could do was to pass the message to you." Leonard's name was on the slip, along with a number. She shifted the phone onto the bed next to me before turning and heading for the door.

"Those nurses are guarding you like you're the goddamn Dalai Lama," Leonard said, when he heard my voice. "What in God's name are you doing with yourself up there, anyway?"

"Yeah, it's been an eventful couple of days," I said.

"I saw them interview this Annabel Nightingale," he said. "Attractive, poised, about your age, and when the reporter mentioned your name her eyes looked like a couple bags of glitter. Not even you could fuck this one up."

I laughed, which made the gash in my head throb. "Actually, she was already my girlfriend," I said. "I think."

"Well, you're not getting rid of her anytime soon," he said.

"That works for me."

"Listen, Perry. I'm sure you're getting all the attention you need. So I actually called to talk about me. Remember my lamentations about the death of spontaneity? Well, I'm calling from Big Bear. It was an unplanned trip. After watching you take that plunge I decided to load the family up and head for the mountains. So anyway, I wanted to thank you. You're an inspiration." He laughed. "Of course, I first made reservations, checked road conditions, inflated all four tires and the spare to the proper pressure, and filled a cooler full of the kids' usual foods. I did let them get Frosted Flakes, though, instead of the usual Wheaties."

"That's a stepping-stone cereal," I said. "They'll be freebasing Twinkies next."

"I'll teach them how," he said, laughing. "Another thing. I wrote a poem, the first one in years. Are you ready to hear it?"

"I can't wait," I said.

"Roses are red, peregrines are brownish, I'm glad you're still breathing, your day could have been drownish."

"And they say poetry is a dying art," I said.

***

Well after dark my doctor came in, at a time when my medication was wearing off and everything was getting hard and sharp and uncomfortable again. He flipped through my chart and then tossed it onto the foot of my bed. "You about ready to get out of here?" he asked.

"Yes please," I said.

"You've got a choice to make." The entire lobby of the hospital, he said, and all the streets around it, were still crawling with media. I could walk out into the spotlight, or I could head down through the emergency department, where a couple of off-duty paramedics had offered to spirit me away in an ambulance. It was an easy choice.

"Good decision," he said. "It's a mob scene down there. Too many germs." He asked a nurse to feed me a final, extra-strength round of painkillers. "In case you can't get to a pharmacy until tomorrow," he said, and gave my left hand a firm shake. A young nurse took me down a service elevator and into an employee break room, where a pair of paramedics sat drinking sodas and playing paper football. One of them was about my age; the other looked a few years younger. They jumped to their feet as we approached.

"Hey Gabriela," the younger of them said to the nurse, "when are you going to let me cook you that breakfast?"

"January thirty-second," she said. She planted a kiss on my cheek and shot him a look. "It was a pleasure meeting you," she said to me. "You've got a very lucky girlfriend." She gave a little wave over her shoulder and disappeared through the door.

The paramedic turned to me with a wide smile. "So that's what I gotta do, huh?" he said. "Jump into a flooded building!" He extended his left hand and gave my own a gleeful, enthusiastic handshake. "Cracks me up when she acts like she don't want me. I'm Hector, though. That was some badass shit you pulled out there!"

"Yeah, maybe it was," I said. The medication was starting to kick in. I felt tingling in my knees and around the gash in my head. I could put my weight on my bruised leg. Warmth was spreading up my back.

The other paramedic shook my hand with equal vigor. Like Hector, he seemed accustomed to shaking left-handed. His name was Naseem. "Ready to go home?" he asked.

"Definitely," I said.

I followed them out the door, but not before they had me pose with them for a photo. We climbed inside their ambulance, with Hector at the wheel, Naseem in the passenger seat, and me in a rear-facing jump seat in the back. We pulled out onto Hyde. All along the first block news vans crouched along the curbs, waiting in the rain, weak lights glowing in their interiors. The next block was dark and quiet, as if the streetlights had all gone out, as if the rain had stopped, as if the ambulance was gliding through air, and the next thing I realized someone was shaking me by the knee and asking me something. It was Naseem.

"Hey man, you okay? You sure this is the best place for you right now?"

The ambulance had stopped and was idling alongside the curb. Through the windshield spilled the glow of the neon sign of the bar at Pier 23. Hector was watching me over his shoulder. He muttered something to Naseem about my medications.

"This isn't where I live," I said.

"You told us this is where you wanted to come," Naseem said. "You got a ride meeting you here or something?"

"I figured maybe you wanted to pour a couple of shots in there to kick-start that Percocet," Hector said, his eyes smiling. "It looks like you're already kick-started pretty good, though."

Through the windows I could see that the warehouse doors were open, and there was light coming from the office inside.

"I asked you to bring me here?" I said.

"You don't remember that?"

"This is real?" I said, continuing to watch the office windows. "I said to come here, and this is all real? This is happening?" Maybe I'd dozed off, and spoken to them in my sleep. It had happened before, on occasion—my sister used to tease me about it. She said I'd tried to order a pizza once. And with all the medications flowing through me it certainly seemed possible.

"We're really here, I promise," Naseem said. "You sure you're feeling okay?"

"You definitely aren't in need of any cocktails, my man," Hector said. "Where do you live? You got a driver's license on you? You got some parents or friends around or something?"

"Do me a favor," I said. "Wait here for just a minute, would you?"

I jumped out and ran without waiting for an answer. I saw and heard the rain but my numb body felt no cold, no moisture. *Erhu* music enveloped me as I stepped through the warehouse's doorway. It reverberated through the cavernous room, dense as the song of an orchestra a thousand strong. A trail of wet footprints, gleaming in the dim light, led from out of the black recesses of the warehouse. I followed them into the office and up the stairs.

The cluttered storeroom had disappeared. In its place now stood a darkened theater, its walls lined with heavy deep red curtains. A disorganized collection of empty tables and empty chairs, some of them on their sides, covered the floor. On a low black wooden stage an old man sat on a stool, his fingers dancing on the strings of his instrument. He was drenched; his clothes were full of holes. There was a slight greenish tint to the deep wrinkles in the skin of his face, and a piece of seaweed hung around his neck like a scarf. A smell that was at once fresh and ancient, the way a low tide might smell during a thunderstorm, filled the air.

I sat down in one of the chairs near the stage and waited for him to finish. When he had played the song's last note he laid his bow across his lap, tipped his head forward, closed his eyes, and smiled a small smile, as though acknowledging a roomful of applause. When his eyes opened again I asked him, "Who are you? Where did you come from?"

He smiled. Most of his teeth had fallen out, and those that remained were black. He gestured for me to come closer. I rose and approached. He reached into his instrument case, pulled out a thick bamboo tube, and handed it to me with a smile. Rose's onionskin manuscript was still rolled tightly inside it, the edges of its sheets uneven and ridged like the surface of a seashell. When I touched them the paper turned to water, flooded out through the bottom of the tube, and splashed apart on the edge of the stage. I dropped down to my knees and saw, suspended in the puddles, thousands of small penciled letters sliding and drifting around one another, coming unraveled. The water poured down to the wooden floor, where it found cracks between the boards and began draining through, carrying the letters with them. Far below, I thought I could hear them all dripping into the bay. The musician nodded as if to say yes, this is what happens. He began another song. I set the tube back in his case, gave him a small bow, and returned to the ambulance.

***

Annabel gasped when I appeared at her door. "Peregrine! When did they let you out?"

"Just now," I said. "Some paramedics snuck me out. My street is a news van parking lot. I would have called, but my phone . . . ."

In the street Hector and Naseem honked and rolled away. Annabel pulled me through the door, kicking a lunchbox that threatened to follow me in. She made me a mug of tea, settled me into a recliner in the living room with a blanket over me, and went out to get my prescriptions filled. The painkillers had reached their apex and I could feel my wrist and ankle tingling, almost vibrating. Heat pulsated softly from the back of my head, where the staples were holding me together. Warmth emanated from a dozen other spots where I had smaller bruises or cuts. I fell asleep and dreamed I was walking on the sea floor. All around me swayed giant trees of kelp with trunks thick as redwoods. Sparrows soared around me, their flight paths marked by trails of bubbles. When they opened their beaks to sing it wasn't music that emerged but tiny handwritten letters, which drifted through the water, twisting and fading.

When Annabel shook me awake it felt as though hours had transpired. Heavy rain continued to pound at the windows. It was dark but faint light from the kitchen limned Annabel's face, revealing her wide eyes. When she spoke there was a quaver in her voice.

"Peregrine," she said, "it's here."

I sat up. "What?" I said. "What time is it?"

"Midnight. Can you get up?"

I swung my feet to the floor. My body felt stiff and my head felt like it was full of helium.

"How's your thigh?" she asked. "Can you walk?"

I took a few test steps and was happy to learn I could put my weight on it without much discomfort. "It's better," I said.

She led me up to the darkened third floor and to the chair in the center of the room. "Can you see it?" she asked.

I tried to look through the wall of rain, but grayish spots danced in front of me, blocking out the sea. It took several seconds for my eyes to adjust, and when they did, I saw a faint glow, shining through the rain, not far off the coast. Annabel came over to me and circled her arm around my shoulders. She leaned her head against mine. "I think it wants you," she said.

We bundled ourselves up and went out her front door. We crossed the empty highway and made our way down to the shoreline. The sea slammed into the sand before us, and though the waves tossed and twisted and foamed as far out as we could see, their movements did not disturb the serene bearing of the *Crystal Gypsy*, which was steaming straight at the coast now, toward a point just south of where we stood. Her decks and smokestacks came into focus, followed by the black portholes lining her sides and the outlines of her doors. She was massive, all of her glowing, shining with a faint white-green luminescence. She turned toward us, and continued to turn until she was running almost parallel to the shoreline, looming above us. I could make out the life preservers lashed to her railings and the creases in the tarpaulins that covered her lifeboats. The paint that spelled out her name had faded and chipped, but it was still legible. She ran aground just inches in front of us, rocking and shuddering as she came to rest in the sand, her joints and surfaces creaking and protesting as she brought her weight to rest on her keel. And then it was as though something in the ship suddenly let go, as if the bonds of her constituents gave up their hold, all at once. She became a cloud of tiny white points, her shape intact but vague. The cloud hovered there for an instant before bursting apart. It fell with the rain over the two of us, into the water, into the sand. The white scintillas ran down our coats and sleeves; they fell onto the waves' surfaces, where the motion of the sea took them. They washed up onto the sand beneath our feet, millions of them, and for a time the beach looked as though it were full of stars. It took several minutes for them all to fade away.

SEVENTEEN

The next morning we awoke to an eerie silence. Annabel noticed it, too. She sat up, turning her head back and forth. "Something seems wrong," she said. We climbed out from under her thick layer of blankets and into the cold air of her room, bracing ourselves for the next surprise. My wrist ached and itched inside my cast, but my head felt better, and my eggplant-sized bruise had become a pale plum. I started dressing myself while Annabel walked over to the windows and pulled the curtains. She started to laugh.

"What is it?" I said.

"It's the sun," she said.

I joined her at the window. A clear pale blue filled the sky; not a cloud remained. Light harmless mists drifted over the ocean. Small waves rolled in at regular intervals and fell onto the beach. The chrome on a passing car gleamed in the morning sunlight. We padded downstairs. She tuned a radio to news as she made coffee. The storm had dissipated that morning, a reporter explained. A cold, dry front had come in and splintered the system, sending small weak cells out through the Central Valley and into the foothills of the Sierras, where they were shedding the last of their moisture. Radar imagery revealed nothing but clear sky to the west, as far as Japan. The entire Pacific Ocean now gleamed beneath a sun we hadn't seen in weeks, he said.

Annabel handed me a hot mug of coffee. "Let's go get some sun," she said.

The air was bracing but clean and clear. Lost items still littered the ground outside, but now instead of leaning against her gate and clamoring for ingress they lay scattered across the sidewalk, reclining in the gutter. They seemed patient now, somehow.

She kicked a tennis ball up the street; we watched it decelerate, stop, and slowly reverse itself, inching its way back to her gate. We headed across the street, aiming for the thick sunlight pouring down onto the opposite sidewalk. "How did this all come to be?" I said, looking back over my shoulder at the wallets and keys, the socks and hats and papers and sweatshirts. "What do you remember?"

We stepped out of the building's shade and the sunlight went through my clothes and skin and into my bones. It glittered in each tiny water-filled irregularity in the asphalt roads. The concrete sidewalks were a flat, even gray, as though they'd just been poured. The parked cars had all been washed and polished. We proceeded at coffee-sipping speed, our steps synchronous despite my limp.

"Memory isn't a factor," she said. "This precedes me." She slipped an arm through mine and in her touch I could feel the sudden weight of what she was about to say. "It's hereditary." She sipped her coffee, her eyes ahead. The steam embraced and then released her face. "Matrilineal primogeniture," she said. "Do you know what that means?"

"Firstborn daughters?" I said. "Isn't that unusually specific for genes?"

"It's not genetic," she said. "It's something else." Her voice trailed off a bit. She sipped again. "But maybe one mystery at a time is enough."

"I think we exceeded that limit a long time ago," I said.

She gave me a small laugh. "You're right," she said. "Besides, it won't even seem that strange in light of everything else."

"So let's hear it then," I said.

"It's a curse," she said. "Hundreds of years old. Placed on the firstborn women of my family." She looked over at me and gave me a half-smile. "And all subsequent incarnations thereof. And their daughters. And so on."

"Wow," I said. "Old Gypsy woman?"

"Hindu," she said.

"Why?"

"Some other time." She turned her face upward to catch the sun on her closed eyelids. She opened her mouth and let it into her throat, turned and let it into the folds of her ears. "You've got updates for me," she said.

I gave her the full account of Eva's departure, and Lucy's theories. She listened, nodding between sips of her coffee, murmuring small questions. When we returned to her door we found Lucy waiting for us on the sidewalk outside Annabel's house, taking inventory of the sea of migrant detritus.

"Morning," she said. "Missing the rain?"

"How did you know I was here?" I asked.

"I didn't," she said. "But I had to get away. I'm tired of answering questions about you."

"How did you get here?"

"I got your car to work. And I figured I don't need a license for a while—with you as the man of the hour, I should have diplomatic immunity as your sister." She eyed our mugs. "Got any more coffee?"

"Let's go eat," Annabel said. "I'm starving, and your brother has been on an all-narcotic diet for the last couple of days."

Annabel drove us up through the flats and found a parking place on Ocean Avenue. The streets were thronged with pedestrians, many of whom wore shorts and T-shirts despite the cold. A group of teenagers ran up the street, dodging traffic, tossing a football. We found a small warm breakfast place on a corner that smelled of bacon and maple syrup, and we took seats at a heavy wooden table near one of the windows. We asked for more coffee and ordered our food—a spinach and goat cheese omelet for Annabel, pancakes and sausages for me, a bagel sandwich for Lucy. Our waitress had just delivered our coffee in a trio of mismatched cups when Lucy banged a fist on the table.

"I almost forgot," she said. "I thought of something the other day. The *l* and *r* sounds get muddled up in Cantonese, right?"

Annabel nodded slowly.

Lucy turned to me. "And those characters you saw in the classroom—*han* and *li*, right?" She pushed her plate aside, set her purse down on the table in front of her, and began digging through it. "Well, maybe it said 'Henry.' Maybe that was the Chinese approximation of his American name." She began pulling things from her bag and setting them on the table: a glasses case, half-finished packs of gum, keys, her phone. "I think that slip you gave me is still in here somewhere," she muttered.

Annabel's face screwed up in concentration as she mouthed the syllables and made brushstrokes in the air with her finger, trying out the theory. "You could be right," she said. "Weird," she whispered.

"Maybe that was his classroom," I said, "in Jianghai."

Things continued to emerge from Lucy's purse: pens, gum, a folding knife, the postcard given to us by the *erhu* player in Berkeley, with the name of his mournful song jotted on the back. I reached out and picked it up. "I don't see it in here," Lucy said, her face now buried in her purse. "I wonder what happened to it."

"I remember them," I said. "I can write it again." I studied the characters the musician had written. What was the song's name? Something about a river?

"Hey, let me see that," Lucy said, taking the card from my hand. "I know this place," she said.

"What place?" I said.

Lucy flipped the card over and set it on the table. I'd never bothered to look at the front. The old sepia photograph, taken by somebody who'd been standing in the middle of the street, depicted rows of wooden storefronts and a water tower in the distance, just taller than the buildings. In the foreground stood a two-story building, its wooden side patched with sheets of corrugated tin. Upstairs a pair of double doors opened out onto a small second-floor balcony. Over the doors leaned a painted wooden sign with large Chinese characters on its face.

"Remember this place?" Lucy said, tapping the photo. "Remember this town?"

I shook my head. "Nope. Doesn't look familiar."

"We used to go here," she said, "when we were little." She tapped the two-story building with the Chinese sign. "We've been in there. There's a table and chairs for meetings and a little desk in the corner upstairs, and bulletin boards, and the floorboards are all uneven and they creak when you walk on them and everything smells like dust and wood baking in the sun. Maybe you were too young to remember. Mom and Dad must have known somebody there or something."

The food arrived; Lucy had to refill her purse to make room for our plates. After a day of hospital fare, each meal looked like a small miracle. Annabel and I plunged in; Lucy continued to study the card. As my pancakes warmed my stomach thoughts of Eva returned. Whatever she thought of me, of us, I was convinced she still held keys to our mysteries. But where could she have gone? With enough effort I knew we could have found her apartment, a basement apartment still full of water and ruined belongings, to which she'd probably never return. I wanted to bring her up, but neither Lucy nor Annabel could tell me much of anything. I'd eat first, and then turn my attention to our next steps.

"So when do you think someone will recognize you?" Annabel asked, with a smile. "Are you ready to hand out some autographs?"

I held up my cast. "I'm down to one hand," I said. I waved my fork. "And it's busy."

Our waitress passed by, refilling our coffee mugs before moving on. I poured another layer of syrup on my pancakes and considered calling her back to order more sausages. Lucy still hadn't touched her breakfast.

"Are you going to eat that?" I asked her. "Because I'm not leaving anything on this table."

"There's a house," Lucy continued, sitting forward suddenly, her voice louder now, more definitive. "There's a white house on a corner a couple of blocks from where this picture was taken, and somebody lived there. You really don't remember anything?" She slid the card over to me.

I stared at the photo but no memories arose. I shook my head.

"This is bothering the hell out of me," she said. She flipped the card over. "Main Street, Isleton, California," she said. "Where's that?"

"I don't know," I said. "Never heard of it."

"It sounds familiar," Annabel said, "but I'm not sure."

"Fuck this," Lucy said, grabbing her phone. "Fuck all this." She punched at the screen and then held it to her ear. For some reason she seized her knife with her free hand and balled a fist around its handle. Her eyes were looking through the table. Annabel was watching her closely now. I continued chewing, thinking more about Lucy's breakfast than her agitation. "Mom," Lucy said. "What's in Isleton? Where is it? Who lives there?" She grew very still as she listened to the response. "Are you absolutely sure?" she said. "Absolutely, completely sure of all of that?" A second or two passed, and then she stabbed the knife through the center of her bagel sandwich. It struck the plate beneath with a thunk that reverberated through the dishes and table and caught the attention of all our neighbors. "Thanks," she said. "That's all."

She dropped her phone back into her purse. "It's in the Delta," she said, "about an hour from here." She pulled a fifty-dollar bill from her wallet and put it in the middle of the table, and gave me a smile that did not touch her eyes. "And neither you, nor I, nor Mom or Dad, have ever been there." She grasped the knife handle and thrust the bagel toward me, a breakfast shish kebab. "You can eat this in the car," she said.

EIGHTEEN

Annabel drove. I sat in the passenger seat and Lucy sat in the back. We rode in silence, each of us haunted by our own sets of questions. The storm had scoured the city; all of its surfaces glowed as if the sun had just been born. The bridge was empty. White sails cut back and forth across the water's spark-filled surface. We were quiet until we touched down in Oakland and began negotiating the junctions and interchanges that took us up to the Caldecott Tunnel and through the hills that separated the bay area from the rest of the nation's expanse. We emerged on the eastern side amid steep hills, their flanks electric with new grass. Despite the coffee, the mix of Percocet and breakfast conspired to make me feel drowsy, and I sank down in my seat a couple of inches. Mount Diablo rose before us, and though the sky was a deep clear blue, the mountain's outline looked soft and indistinct. And then I must have fallen asleep, because suddenly we were pulling to a stop in front of a hardware store that looked as though it might have been a hundred years old.

"Rise and shine," Annabel said, patting me on the leg. Lucy was already standing beside the car, looking up and down the quiet roadway. I climbed out, wobbling a bit, and tried to stomp the feeling back into my legs.

"This way," Lucy said, pointing. She marched up the sidewalk; I struggled to keep up with her. In another block the building she had recognized from the postcard appeared across the street. Its faded wood and corrugated tin sheet walls leaned to the side as though they longed to collapse. The sign still hung from the façade, its paint gone but for a few shapeless patches. Lucy studied the structure as we approached but made no move to cross the street.

"I can't read the sign," Annabel said. "The paint is too faded."

"You don't want to go over there?" I asked.

"No," Lucy said. "We're heading for the next street."

Annabel and I followed her around the corner, down two blocks, and across the road, where we stopped at the sidewalk's edge, in front of a small yellow bungalow. Knee-high weeds, vibrant with all the watering, crowded one another inside a low chain-link perimeter. An open gate invited us onto a cracked concrete pathway.

"It looks different," Lucy said, "but this is it."

"Now what?" I asked.

"I'll think of something," she said, plunging through the gate. We followed her up the path and she rang the bell. Immediate heavy footfalls sounded on a wooden floor inside. The door swung open and in its place stood an immense man, his skin so dark it left the features of his face hard to distinguish. He wore an immaculate white tunic that stretched nearly the full width of the doorframe.

"Can I help you?" he asked, his smile wide, a hint of a Caribbean accent in his voice.

"We're from the county historical society," Lucy said. "Your house is of great interest to us, and we wanted to ask you some questions about it, if that's okay. Did we catch you at a good time?"

"I don't live here," he said, "and the lady of the house doesn't speak any English."

Lucy produced her most charming smile. "We are multilingual," she said. "What language does she speak?"

"Usually none at all," he said. "But when she does, it's Chinese."

"Perfect," Lucy said, glancing at me.

"Wait just a minute," he said. He closed the door and disappeared into the house. After a minute or two the door reopened, revealing the massive nurse, and in front of him, occupying no more than half of her wheelchair's capacity, a tiny and ancient woman. Thin hair emerged from her nearly translucent scalp in tufts; wrinkles creased the entire surface of her face. But her eyes were clear and bright when she smiled at us. Annabel repeated Lucy's request and the woman's smile grew. She beckoned us inside and the nurse backed her out of the doorway.

The front of the house was one big dingy room. Visible through an arched doorway in one corner was a small dark kitchen. The windows looked as though they hadn't been cleaned in decades, and the light took on a brownish cast as it filtered through them. We were shown to a low, uncomfortable sofa, which was old and green and flecked with bits of brownish-orange.

Annabel spoke to the woman in the wheelchair throughout our entry and our seating, but received only monosyllabic responses, smiles, and hand gestures in return. She signaled to her attendant once the three of us were seated and he wheeled her into the kitchen.

"What did she say?" Lucy whispered to Annabel. "What's she doing?"

"Getting tea, I think," she said.

"Do we know her name?"

"Not yet."

Lucy studied the room while we waited, and after a minute she began shaking her head. "Something's wrong," she whispered.

"What do you mean?" I whispered back.

"I don't think we caught your names," Annabel called through the kitchen doors. "We're Annabel, Peregrine, and Lucy."

"This is Mrs. Wu," said the nurse. "You can call me Luther. We'll be right with you."

Lucy seemed suddenly uneasy; she was studying the room, its walls and doors and windows, its contents, her eyes flicking quickly back and forth. "I'm not too sure about this now," she said, a little too loudly, I thought. "I think there's been a mistake." I couldn't tell if she was talking to herself, to Annabel and me, or to Luther and Mrs. Wu.

Luther leaned halfway out of the doorway and gave us a look I couldn't quite read. Threat assessment, perhaps. "What house were you looking for?" he asked.

She didn't know the name of the street we were on, nor any other street except Main Street, and neither did Annabel or I. In the silence that followed his question Luther stiffened. He grew wary. He glanced into the kitchen—perhaps checking on Mrs. Wu, or perhaps measuring the distance between himself and a heavy frying pan.

"Where did you say you were from?" he said.

"The Solano County Historical Society," Annabel said, with a smile. "We're talking to folks all over the county."

"Bit far from home, aren't you?" he asked. All traces of hospitality left his face. He disappeared into the kitchen.

Annabel turned, her eyes wide. "Is this not Solano County?" she whispered.

"I think there's been some sort of a mistake," Lucy called again.

And then came the sound of keys in the front door, and the deadbolt snapping back. The door swung open and a familiar figure entered. Eva was carrying two plastic grocery bags, one of which dropped from her hand when she saw us. A pair of oranges rolled across the carpet. Luther sprang back into the room, found us all staring at one another, and halted, uncertain. We remained that way for an awful stretch of time, the five of us, silent, encased and motionless in that dusty brown light like insects in amber. Eva's shock turned eventually to wonder and her face began to change and shift as explanations wheeled through her mind. It was all there, as if she was cycling back through all of Lucy's theories, one by one: anger, confusion, hope, fear. As for me, my eyes held to Eva but my thoughts flew into the kitchen and swarmed around Rose, who now sat in her wheelchair, at the end of a long chronology of images that spooled out behind her, backward through time: motherhood, marriage, the disappearance of her brother, a ship steaming across the

Pacific, a trip in a stolen boat up a river to a shed where she hides in a fortress of leaning bamboo tool handles, writing in a tiny hand on a thin sheet of paper held against the rough curving surface of a metal pail.

And then the room exploded with voices and motion. I jumped to my feet and headed for the kitchen, without really knowing what I'd do when I got there.

Luther slid over and blocked my way and began berating me for being a liar, for preying upon the elderly, for faking a limp. By that time Lucy and Annabel had risen and now stood flanking Eva. They were both talking to her at once. Over their noise, Eva was demanding to know how we'd found her.

I tried to circle around Luther but he sidestepped, pointed a finger at me, and shifted from accusations to threats. There was a sudden flash of black and a slap, and my eyes went blurry and the whole room suddenly shifted one foot sideways. I had to scramble to get my feet back under me. When I was upright and my eyes back in focus I saw that Luther had taken a couple of steps back and now wore an expression of surprise and delight. Eva was standing next to me, her hand upraised, staring back and forth from me to her reddened palm. Lucy was suddenly there, between us. "It's real, Eva," she said. Her voice was even, controlled. "All of it."

"All right," Eva said. "So it would seem." She headed for a stuffed chair that sat at a ninety-degree angle to the couch. The second bag of groceries had fallen to the floor at some point and as she shuffled across the carpet, her hand still in the air, she kicked a can of tomato soup. It rolled into the fireplace. She sat down heavily. "You wanted her," she said to me, waving toward the kitchen, "you got her."

Without discussion or eye contact, as though following stage directions long memorized and well rehearsed, Annabel, Lucy, and I turned from our spots and resumed our positions on the couch.

"Why can't she speak English?" I said. "Why is her name Wu, and why can't she speak English?"

"How did you find me, Peregrine?" Eva asked.

"Lucy found you," I said.

"I saw a postcard of the town and I knew something," Lucy said. "I just knew, and I came."

"You just came?" Eva said. "How am I supposed to believe that?"

"I don't know," she said, "but it's the truth. It's like I . . . like I remembered something."

In the kitchen the teapot began to whistle. There was the sound of the burner being turned off, the plummet of the whistle, and the tinkling of small thin dishes.

"Wu was her third husband," Eva said. "And she doesn't speak English anymore. She stopped years ago."

"Just stopped?"

"Sort of like you just came here."

Luther rolled Rose back into the room, a tea tray across her lap. He parked her in a spot just across the table from me and retired to the kitchen table, where he sat down and fixed a this-ought-to-be-good look on his face. Rose set the tray on the table, her movements surprisingly efficient and strong, and looked up at me with a smile.

Now that I was here, in front of her, I had nothing to say. My face was hot where Eva had hit me. I felt dizzy. Images and questions spun through my head, all of them moving so quickly I couldn't bring any into focus. I clamped my eyes shut, but the images only spun faster. There was no center to it, no solid ground for footing. Everybody was looking at me, waiting. Finally I managed the only thing I could.

"I think I can help you find Henry," I said.

Annabel translated. Rose smiled and nodded toward me, as if in gratitude, and responded in a sentence or two. Annabel, clearly confused, shot me a look I couldn't read. She seemed to ask Rose for a clarification, which brought no obvious clarity. She turned to me.

"She says thank you, but he does not need to be found."

Rose, nodding, said something more to Annabel.

"She says there are many places for him already."

"Are you beginning to see why I wasn't in a big hurry to bring you here?" Eva muttered.

Rose watched our exchange, her expression bemused, and then continued. This time Annabel did not wait for her to finish, but began relating the translation right away, murmuring beneath Rose's story. "She says she wrote a lot of stories when she was in China. She didn't have any friends there, and she couldn't go anywhere, so she wrote about people she wanted to know, and places she wanted to go."

I thought of her in her shed, writing against the uneven curve of the metal pail, sheltered by the bamboo slope of tool handles. The details were all there, but now I saw them not from my narrator's perspective but through her eyes. I could see I'd missed the hardness of the floor against her knees, the ache in her neck and wrist and shoulder after hours of writing.

"She says she wrote about herself, and her mother and Henry, and about the others in the house, and about their village and the other villages in the area. She says she made up stories, too, about her family—stories where they could fly, where they couldn't see . . . no, where they couldn't be seen, where they were invisible. Where they could turn into animals, or into wind, or into . . . into music, I think she said?"

During Rose's story Eva smirked and studied her fingernails, her body tense, seeming always on the brink of rolling her eyes, or groaning outright. I shifted and turned my head to move her more to the periphery, trying to shut out her impatience. Lucy sat rapt, eyes wide; Annabel studied Rose's face, struggling to keep up as the story continued.

"And then when they came back to America, the stories were over, and she didn't need them anymore, so she gave them to . . . to . . . ." Here for the first time Annabel held up a hand and asked for a clarification; Rose repeated a phrase, waited for Annabel to repeat it, nodded. "The sea. She gave them to the sea, and they went into the water, and that's where Henry is."

Rose looked at each of us in turn, smiling, her eyes bright and clear and deep. None of us had anything further to ask, nothing more to say. I had the sense we were all in the process of failing a test.

Eva was the one to break the silence. "Well, if you've had enough Zen riddles for today, you might want to get on back to the city," she said, "unless you want to level with me and tell me how you found us here."

Rose held up a hand for silence, and when she resumed speaking there was a new urgency in her voice. I waited for Annabel to begin the translation, but she remained silent, listening. Rose continued, her words getting faster. Annabel opened and closed her mouth, but the narrative had surged too far already, leaving us all behind. Rose's hands rose into the air and began moving with her story—she drew invisible diagrams, made shapes, moved objects from one place to the next, transformed them, moved them back. Her creations rose and fell, submerged and emerged, and then her story softened and slowed. Annabel caught my eye and gave me the smallest shake of her head. She shrugged, just slightly, and then Rose was off again, her hands flashing in the air, her movements sharp and angular. Lucy shifted, moving backward into the couch, as if to leave more room for the story. Rose's voice grew loud and took on new momentum; she flung her arms out, and then up, her hands twisting in the air, contorting more and more with each sentence that flew out of her. She seemed to be on the verge of shouting when she clapped her hands above her head and fell silent. Her hands sank slowly, gracefully into her lap, a gesture that described a dying fall of rain. She smiled and tilted her head slightly forward. Her eyes were glassy. She seemed to be looking through the couch.

Annabel looked completely perplexed. She said something brief to Rose, but Rose made no indication she'd heard. Lucy's eyes were wide. Even Eva looked startled.

Luther spoke next. "Well," he said, rising from his chair, "I'm sure glad you all had this chance to chitchat, but it's time for Mrs. Wu to get some rest now." He backed her wheelchair away from the table. Her expression remained placid, distant; she offered no gesture of farewell. Luther spun her around. "Good luck finding your way back to Solano County," he called over his shoulder. The two of them disappeared into the hallway, making no sound on the carpet.

"I didn't understand any of that," Annabel said, shaking her head, her voice quiet. "The dialect. A few words, that's all."

"Don't look at me," Eva said, when we all looked at her.

A car with a bad muffler passed by outside, paused, turned toward Main Street.

"So what now?" Lucy said.

Eva sighed. Slowly she bent down, picked up one of the stray oranges, and dug her nails into its rind. The adrenaline began to fade from my system; beneath it awaited layers of weariness and confusion, the vestiges of my last round of medications, a bit of nausea, the resurgent pain of my injuries, little else. I couldn't think—about our encounter with Rose, about her comments about Henry, about her incomprehensible story, about the very fact of her existence. I had the sense that even with a clear head and with plenty of quiet time my contemplations weren't likely to take me anywhere. Lucy and Annabel were talking with Eva now, telling her about the book of poems and the translations, but I couldn't attend much to that, either. Something in my wrist was pulsating, and suddenly I could feel each of the staples in my head. It occurred to me that Eva might have swatted me hard enough to knock one of them loose. A throb arose in my bruised thigh, and when I reached down to rub it I felt a lump of something hard and rectangular through the fabric. I reached into my pocket and my fingers closed around the mahjong tile I'd found at Pier 23. I pulled it out and squeezed it in my fist.

Annabel was watching me. "You don't look so good," she said.

I opened my hand, shifted the tile to my fingertips, and rubbed my thumb over the engraved character. I wanted to go home.

"Can I see that?" she asked.

I passed the tile to her and she studied it. "This one looks old, too," she said. "Where did it come from?"

"It's the same one," I said, "from the pier."

She shook her head. "That was *bak*," she said. "North. This is *sai*. West."

"It's the same one," I said. "I only found one."

"It's not the same. This is west. That was north. Remember, we went to the top of the hill, and looked north across the water?"

"Sure," I said.

"Well, this is west." She handed it back to me.

"You brought these pants to me when I was in the hospital," I said to Lucy.

"And I didn't catch anybody swapping mahjong tiles in and out of the pockets, if that's what you're suggesting," she said.

"So what does that mean?" asked Eva, through a mouthful of orange.

"Maybe it's telling us it's time to go home," Lucy said.

In my mind I flashed over the journey before us: the walk back to the car; the drive back along the waterways through the delta; the haul back along the highway and into the great bowl of the bay, all the time contemplating the useless miracle of Rose's existence. And then I saw it, rising like a pyramid, its chambers full of secrets, huge and looming and completely obvious. I jumped to my feet. "Angel Island," I said. I bolted for the door.

NINETEEN

Lucy took the wheel. She sped back down through the Delta as the rest of us sat in silence. In the novelty of sunlight the colors outside seem too vivid, oversaturated. The midday sun from its place deep in the southern sky poured through the windows, filling the car with light thick enough to hold. My poorly tuned engine rattled and wheezed but the road was dry and clear, and the tires stuck in the turns. We had just crossed the final bridge onto the freeway when Eva, who was sitting behind Lucy, rolled her window down, filling the car with fresh cold air. She rolled it back up, cleared her throat, and spoke.

"I don't know how we're going to find anything there," she said.

I turned and looked at her, but I couldn't read her face. She was staring through her window, squinting. "No more secrets, Eva," I said. "Did he go back on the *Gypsy*?"

"All the records burned up in a fire, long ago."

"Yes or no?"

"If the answer was yes, then why would I be wasting your time?"

"No, then."

"If the answer was yes, shouldn't they have contacted my grandmother? Shouldn't they have let her know? If they were sending her son back to China, shouldn't they have let his mother know?"

"Maybe they didn't think she was his mother," Lucy said, softly.

Everything in me was discomfort and raggedness now; I had no more patience for mysteries or riddles or games. "So the answer is no, then?" I said.

"Mae was the hobbled provincial wife of a dead, lying rice farmer," Eva said, her voice all growl and fury. "She was nobody. She had no reach, no influence."

"Tell me what you think happened, Eva," I yelled, smacking my good hand on the glove box. "It's your family—be a part of this fucking expedition."

"Easy, little brother," Lucy said. "We're all working through this together."

"Yell all you want," Eva said. "You have no idea what frustration is. I've been out to that island more than a hundred times. I've spent nights, even a week at a time camping on the island. I know every inch of it, every face of it in every season. Every time I've come back empty-handed."

"What were you looking for?" I said. "What did you expect to find?"

"I've swum the half-mile across Raccoon Strait from Point Ione to Tiburon a dozen times, in different currents, at different tides," Eva said. "I've examined all the records I could find—police, fire, everything. I talked to someone whose father had been the police chief in Tiburon in 1929. I interviewed people—old people, people whose families have owned those houses along the water for years and years. Nothing. And Census reports. 1930, 1940, in case they'd missed him in 1930; 1950, in case they'd missed him both times. Nothing, ever."

"You think he escaped? You think he got away, and swam off the island? An eight-year-old?"

A housing development swept past us, partially built and abandoned in the wake of the storm. Piles of graying lumber and plywood littered the curbs. In one driveway sat a lone, beat-up pickup truck.

"He vanished," Eva said at last. "He didn't make it to San Francisco with my mom and my grandmother, and there's no indication he went back to China. What would you think?"

"Maybe he was a stowaway," Lucy said.

"Why didn't you tell me all this earlier?" I asked.

"What would it have changed?"

"I don't know," I said. "Something."

"No," she said. "It wouldn't have made a difference. Just like meeting my mom made no difference."

"It made a big difference."

"How?"

"I don't know. Somehow."

"We found you," Annabel said. "We needed you, and we found you, and you're here now."

"Why did you come with us?" I asked Eva. "Why did you come, if you think none of this makes a difference, if you've looked everywhere already?"

She said nothing. We passed a strip mall, its stucco tinged a mildew green, its parking lot half-empty. Lucy punched through a couple of stations on the stereo and then flicked it off. She began humming—a faint song that sometimes rose just above the motor's noise, sometimes sank into it.

We approached the shoreline and merged back onto the busier interstate, sweeping around a turn and heading south, back toward the Bay Bridge. Through the undulating landscape we glimpsed flashes of the bay, glistening like mercury beneath the slanting winter sunlight.

"Besides," Eva said. "Everything's closed right now. They're renovating the immigration station, and it won't be open until summer."

"Good," Lucy said. "There won't be any tourists in our way." She played a drum fill on the steering wheel from her private song. We reached the crest of a small hill and the bay came into full view. From this distance I could only make out the outlines of the island's shape. Its steep flanks steamed in the sunlight, their details hidden under a layer of haze.

"And there's a high fence around the whole construction site," Eva said.

"Good," Lucy said again. "There won't be any deer in our way."

Annabel chuckled. Beneath us the tires continued to hum and reel in the road, reel in the road.

* * *

An hour later our ferry was backing away from the pier, the city slowly shrinking away from us. There were only a few other small groups on board, sheltering below deck. We stood above, where a cold unsteady wind pressed against us, its direction constantly shifting as if it was trying to knock us off-balance. High in the sky, translucent fragments of clouds twisted and came apart. Seagulls gathered behind us, drafting in our slipstream, watching for signs of food. A group of cormorants circled off to one side of the ferry. One of them dipped his head, tucked his wings, and plunged into the water. A tiny white splash marked his point of entry. I watched and waited, but didn't see him emerge.

The ride took only about twenty minutes. As we waited to disembark I studied a map of the island that hung near the door. The Immigration Station sat on the island's northeastern corner, about a mile's walk from the pier. It was not until I'd begun researching that portion of my story that I realized how little I'd known about it. I assumed it had been a sort of Ellis Island of the west, the gateway to America for those who'd migrated across the Pacific. But Angel Island was something far darker—an instrument of exclusion, of xenophobia. Now it stood not as a reminder of the welcome we had extended to the immigrants of the Atlantic, but as a monument to fear, to racism.

I'd learned also about the 1940 fire in the administration building, and the destruction of all its records, and the chaos that ensued. I knew all the remaining documentation had been moved to a federal facility somewhere on the peninsula. But I wasn't looking for documents. I was looking for another teacup.

The engines' sound fell away and we glided toward the dock and moored with a bump. We disembarked and climbed a short, steep hill to the perimeter road, which was littered with eucalyptus bark, pine needles, and pinecones. In patches the asphalt showed through, polished to an obsidian shine by the month-long rains. We walked along in silence, seeing nobody, hearing only the sound of the wind in the eucalyptus trees and the occasional cry of a faraway gull.

"You asked me why I came with you," Eva said, when we'd been walking several minutes. "Well, it's because I know there's something here. There's something here, and I can't find it. So I came, hoping that one of you would." From somewhere out on the bay came the melancholy groan of a cargo ship's horn. "You've just met all that's left of my family," she said. "There's no one else. No one but me. And I can't do it. I've tried—I told you how I tried. So that leaves the three of you. Your help is more than I ever hoped for, but if you can't find it, nobody ever will."

With that I saw we were in complete possession of this quest. I caught the eyes of Lucy and Annabel, who were walking on either side of me, and saw they were thinking the same thing. I considered the two of them, and the infinity of our possible futures—decades, works, voyages, children yet to be born, the children of those children. I thought of Eva's—a mother, ancient in her wheelchair, a flooded basement apartment. And I knew that I would do whatever I could to find Henry. I felt without looking an equal resolve in the women at my side; we accelerated, as of one mind.

"You're right about something being here," Lucy said. "The man on the bus we chased? This is where he was bringing us. The only other ferry station that services the island is there in Tiburon—right at the bus stop where we found the book. The book was only a signpost. We turned back too early."

We came out of a wide turn and caught the first glimpses of the station's whitewashed buildings, which stood on the upper slopes of a shallow draw among thick groves of eucalyptus. A minute or two later the bottom of the draw came into view. It had been cleared of trees and paved over, and on the asphalt sat several large blue tarps, shielding piles of gear from the storm. Parked among them was heavy equipment—a couple of small cranes, bulldozers, a backhoe. I studied the topography and the layout of the buildings, matching them to the photographs I'd seen and the images I had held in my mind when I wrote the scenes that took place here. Nothing stood out. We continued walking.

The road veered inland and brought us alongside a high chain-link fence. It was covered in decades of rust, but it was tall and straight and unbroken as far as we could see, and its weave was too tight to provide footholds, even if we could have found a breach in the barbed wire running across its top.

"Those are the barracks," Eva said, pointing through the fence to a three- or four-story building on the near side of the draw. "That's where they were held."

"Then that's where we start," Lucy said.

"The gate is just up ahead," Eva said, "but I'm sure it will be closed and locked."

She was right. A newer section of chain-link fencing stretched across the road, the gates held together with a heavy chain and a padlock. A Do Not Enter sign hung from one of the gates with wire, and a handwritten message in a plastic sleeve offered the explanation: "Closed for Renovation." But it was a gate meant only to repel curious tourists, not the truly determined, and it was carelessly assembled. One of the sections of fence listed away, creating a triangular gap just big enough for us. Without a word to one another we plunged through it.

Inside the fence the road split into three—the central path was wide and paved, and headed straight down toward the bottom of the draw. The other two paths were narrower and made of gravel, and headed along either rim. We took the leftmost path, which took us back in the direction we'd come from. It wound through the trees and then fell away from the fence, taking us toward the barracks. Beneath our feet, the gravel crunched noisily.

We'd gone about fifty yards when a sudden loud snarl burst from the clearing and filled the draw with its vibrations. We stopped, crouching instinctively. A pair of loud coughs followed, and when they subsided we recognized the growl of a diesel engine. We waited and watched through the trees. On the far side of the draw a backhoe appeared, crossed a small clearing, and then disappeared again. Somewhere else, closer this time, another diesel engine awoke.

"Shit," I said.

"So we aren't alone," Annabel said.

"No, this is good," Lucy said, rising and continuing down the path. "They won't be able to hear us over those engines."

We walked along, more vigilant now. The trees thinned out, revealing a small muddy clearing on the hillside below us, criss-crossed with strips of eucalyptus bark and branches and leaves the storm had knocked down. We hid behind the last row of tree trunks and surveyed the area. Immediately across the clearing leaned a small wooden building with big holes in its wood-shingled roof. It was missing half its siding. Just beyond it was the barracks.

"See anybody?" I whispered.

Nobody did. I led the way down across the clearing, the ground soft and squishing beneath my feet. We might have sunk up to our ankles but for the thick layer of bark and leaves. Once across the clearing we hugged the crumbling wall and tiptoed to the small building's corner. I peeked around it and saw only the blue tarpaulin-covered mounds. The workers must have been on the far side of the draw.

It was only about twenty feet from our hiding place to the nearest wall of the barracks, where a door stood atop a concrete landing, with a short staircase leading up to it. I took another glance into the clearing and, still seeing nobody, I shot into the muddy gap. My bruised leg protested loudly—it had been content to cooperate so long as I'd been walking slowly on flat hard ground, but now with mud clinging to my shoes there were extra muscles being pulled into service, and they weren't happy about it. I grimaced and tried to shift more weight to my good leg. Once up the stairs I found the door locked. I looked across the clearing and saw the backhoes making their way up toward some of the buildings on the far rim. In the distance stood a half-dozen men in hardhats in a semi-circle, their backs to me, looking at something on the ground. I ran back to the hiding place, my leg growing hot as it fought through the mud.

"Men," I whispered. I was breathing hard now. I could feel my heartbeat throbbing in the cut on my head. Dizziness threatened, but I closed my eyes and it passed. "They didn't see me."

"Where?" Lucy asked.

"On the far side," I said. "Facing the other way." I squatted, steadying myself with a hand on the wall, and looked for options. The barracks sat on a steep muddy slope. With the door locked, two choices remained: head down toward the front of the building, which would take me out of the mud and onto the concrete, but leave me without cover; or I could scramble up the hillside and around the rear of the building, above a small walled courtyard that had been carved deep into the earth. And then I noticed a makeshift catwalk, made of lumber and scaffolding, stretching from the top of the rearmost wall over the courtyard to the barracks' rooftop. If I could scramble up the muddy slope and make my way along the top of the wall I might be able to reach it. "I'm going to try up there," I said, pointing. "There might be a way in from the roof. If I can get in, I'll come and try to open that door."

"Be careful," Annabel said, giving my arm a squeeze.

And then I was back out in the open, struggling up the slope, fighting the mud. A chain-link fence ran along the top of the steeply sloping wall; I shoved the fingers of my good hand into its openings to help keep me upright, but the rough rusted wires scraped and clawed at my skin. It wasn't more than thirty or forty feet, but I was out of breath by the time I reached the top. I paused at the top of the wall and studied the rest of my route. I was high on the slope now, level with the catwalk, and though it was only about twenty feet away, there was no easy way to get to it. The top of the wall was narrow and the storm had covered much of it with a slippery-looking layer of dirt and leaves. A misstep could send me over the edge to the concrete twenty feet below, where I'd not only acquire more injuries but also find myself trapped. I took a deep breath, steeled myself, and started walking, kicking the edges of my shoes into the hillside, trying to create footholds, ready to sprawl onto the mud if my footing gave way. It didn't, and I wrapped my hand around the catwalk's railing with a warm flush of relief. The catwalk had weathered the storm well, and though my muddy shoes slipped on the slick wood, the walkway was firm. The barracks' roofline loomed and blocked out the anxious faces of Annabel, Lucy, and Eva. The roof was a disaster of ripped-up shingles, warped plywood, and tarps blown out of place. I crept up the slope and lifted my head over the peak. The center of the clearing held the footprint where the administration building had stood before it burned. Beyond it and up the far slope stood the hospital, as big as the barracks, where the day's construction was underway. At its base the backhoes toiled, clumsy and buzzing like oversized bumblebees. I could see more men now, perhaps a dozen, all of them distant. I ducked my head, returned to the back edge of the roof, and looked over the edge into the courtyard. Near the rear corner of the building, a covered stairway emerged from the top floor and ran down along the wall to the ground, passing beneath several windows along the way. I scurried toward it, keeping myself low, stepping carefully among the debris. I scraped as much mud from my shoes as I could and then I sat down on the roof's edge. I inched down, keeping my body twisted to the side to keep the weight off my broken wrist, and carefully transferred my weight onto the stairway's rooftop. It was badly rusted, which helped my feet stick. The first two windows I tried were locked, but the third slid open. The sill was about chest high. I tested my footing, kicked off, and somersaulted through the opening, tucking my broken wrist against my stomach to protect it. The room spun around me and my bruised leg cried out but I managed to roll onto my back and hip without incurring any real damage.

I lay there, catching my breath and listening for sounds of alarm before I climbed back to my feet. The room was large and bright, its floor covered with pieces of plywood, piles of boards, boxes of tools, spools of wire, and metal wire housing. An orange ladder rested on its side. The air smelled of sawdust. By some miracle I'd managed not to land on one of the many screws or nails that littered the floor. I slipped out of my muddy shoes, found the stairway, and padded downstairs in my socks, holding my breath. The building was silent but for the distant sound of the backhoes, their roars reduced to faint hums. The side door was held closed by a simple deadbolt, and seconds later the three women were standing inside.

"Shoes," I whispered to them, pointing at my own feet.

They stooped and went to work.

"This way," Eva whispered, once there were three pairs of muddy shoes lying on the floor. She led us back up to the top of the building. "This was the Chinese and Japanese floor," she said. "Let's spread out." Keeping away from the windows, we each took a direction and walked carefully on our unprotected feet among the piles of building materials, the tools and bits of scrap metal. We weaved in and out of the rooms, making our way down the length of the building. I didn't know what I was hoping to find. I didn't even know how to look for it. Everything up to that point had come to me on its own—the image in my teacup, Eva and Lucy and Annabel, the mazes and the book and the worlds in the bottom of the swimming pool, Rose. So I just walked, trying to keep my mind empty, picking my way among the extension cords, discarded tool belts, plywood scraps. None of it murmured familiarity.

"Shit!" Lucy hissed from a nearby room. "Come look!"

I went through the door to find her crouching at one of the front windows. The backhoes were rumbling back into the clearing, flanked by seven or eight workers on foot. Eva came in behind me, followed by Annabel.

"There's no reason to think they'll come up here," I said.

"But let's hurry," Annabel said. "We can hold still and wait them out if we have to."

We crawled back into the hallway, stood, and padded toward the final set of doorways. Unlike the rest of the rooms on the floor, the last one in the back was untouched. The wooden floorboards were empty and clean. The wall's horizontal slats had been painted yellow decades ago, but now the paint was chipped and deteriorating, and freckled with exposed brown. There was a different smell to it, too—not of sawdust, but of people, of lives. Annabel stepped right up to the wall, reached out and ran her finger over something on the wood. "Look," she said. "Poems."

I'd read about these. I walked over to Annabel and stood so that my shoulder was just touching hers and watched her trace strokes over the wood with her fingertip. From out of the disorder of the scratched and chipped paint a single character formed, like a constellation in a sky of scattered stars. It stood alone, clear and shining, and then another appeared below it, and then another below that, and then, now that I knew how to see them, the entire wall began to vibrate with the echoes of a thousand different voices.

Outside one of the diesel engines shuddered and fell silent, and then the other did, too. Now we could hear voices in the clearing. Lucy slipped back into the hallway and then returned a few seconds later.

"They're coming this way," she said. "If there's something here, somebody better find it fast."

I walked slowly around the room's perimeter, scanning the walls. Some of the characters stood alone; others were grouped in long columns. Some were thick and deep, as though they'd been rubbed into the wood with the edges of coins. Others had only been scratched into the paint, as with the tips of nails. Most of them were Chinese, but there were Japanese characters, too, and characters in scripts I didn't recognize at all.

Annabel's fingertips danced across the wall's surface, tracing strokes, connecting characters. Her lips were moving.

"What do they say?" I asked her.

The workmen's voices were right outside now.

She began to mutter, first individual words—"ocean," "loneliness"—and then whole sentences—"There are tens of thousands of poems on these walls; they are all cries of suffering and sadness."

"Great," Lucy muttered. "I don't suppose that guy put together an index somewhere, did he?"

Downstairs a heavy door was yanked out of a winter-shrunken frame, rocking the whole building.

"Shit," Lucy said. "What should we do?"

"Keep reading," I said to Annabel.

Annabel continued, her fingertips flying across the wall, the words spilling from her mouth in a soft torrent. She spoke of oceans and islands, of America and injustice, of faraway villages. She scanned the wall from top to bottom, moving slowly sideways, feeling her way along. She reached the end of one wall and turned and moved on to the next.

There was a burst of excited voices from downstairs.

"Our shoes!" Lucy said.

A dozen feet in work boots tramped up the stairs.

"I'll go head them off," Lucy said. "Wish me luck." She took a deep breath, put on a cinematic flirtatious smile, and headed out into the hallway. The worker's footfalls echoed through the whole floor. Floorboards creaked and groaned; loose nails rattled.

Eva said something about the room's brightness; Annabel continued, but nothing she read held any resonance. The prisoners had written of swirling fog, chirping insects, forests, the sea. One poet reminded his readers that they would endure, that Napoleon had been imprisoned on an island, too.

Someone was yelling at Lucy now. She launched into some explanation—I couldn't hear her words, but her tone was pleading. There was a beep and the crackle of a radio-borne voice. The footsteps resumed and the pitch of Lucy's voice rose markedly. "Please," I heard her say. "She doesn't have much time left." She backed into the room, followed by a half-dozen men in hard hats. Most of them looked at least slightly bemused, but their leader was furious.

"What the hell is this?" he bellowed. His voice slapped against the walls and ricocheted back at us. He wore stained jeans and his T-shirted belly protruded through an open flannel shirt. "Get your fucking hands off that wall."

Annabel dropped her hands to her sides but kept reading. Her voice was barely above a whisper now and her words seemed almost to overlap one another, as though each of the lost voices was trying to move through her at once. I was all but leaning on her as I strained to hear.

"That's your dying grandmother?" another of the men said. "She looks pretty healthy to me."

"Hey, Grandma, good news," Lucy said. "This guy says your cancer is in remission. Isn't that wonderful?"

"I'm feeling a bit dizzy," Eva said. She leaned against the wall and brought her hands to her temples.

"Don't you touch that goddamn wall," the leader said. "Don't even fall on it."

"Maybe you should sit down," Lucy said to Eva. Their act wasn't too bad, I thought. How much time would it buy us?

"You're out here jumping fences with your dying grandmother?" another of the men asked. "Are those doctor's orders?"

"The gate was wide open," Lucy said. "We just walked in."

"Bullshit," the leader said. "I locked it myself. Everybody out, right now."

"Someone must have opened it after you came through," Lucy said. "Besides, we aren't hurting anything."

"So how'd you get in the building?" someone asked. "Are you going to tell me that door down there was open, too?"

Their leader held up a hand to silence his men. "Who gives a shit what she tells anyone?" he said. "In case I haven't made myself clear, you're trespassing. Get out, now, or we get you out."

"We're only going to be a few more minutes," Lucy said, her voice still calm. She pointed at Eva. "We're trying to find out what happened to her uncle, and she's going to be in her grave before you guys get this place open. Tell me what harm we're doing."

"Christ Almighty," another of the men said. "That's a hell of a way to talk about your grandmother."

Annabel was no longer reading aloud—she had stepped back from the wall, and her eyes had lost their focus, as if she were seeing through the wood and paint to something far away. Lucy and the men argued on, but Annabel seemed not to hear any of it. I had a sudden vision of her sitting in her chair in the room on the third floor of her house, her face empty, waiting on the edge of the sea for all those lost ships, shining like a beacon through the darkness.

A radio hissed to life. "Truck's on its way," said a crackling voice.

"Time to go, sweetheart," the leader said. "Everybody out." He took a menacing step toward Lucy.

She stepped toward him and pointed a finger at his face. "You lay a hand on anybody in this room and you will be carving your own fucking poetry into your own cell wall somewhere," she snarled. "I'm pretty sure your construction job doesn't give you the authority to use physical force."

There was a snort from somewhere behind him. A couple of the men were smiling, stifling laughter.

"Contractor," the leader said. "I'm a contractor."

"So contract something," Lucy said.

"That's not what it means," he said.

"What are you guys looking for, anyway?" another of the men asked, genuine interest in his voice.

"Shut up, Paul," the leader said.

"I don't work for you, Lars," Paul said. "Or did you forget again?" He smiled at Lucy. "You were saying?"

"We're looking for evidence about what happened to my great-uncle," Lucy said, turning to her new benefactor. "He's missing."

"She's looking for a pair of handcuffs," Lars said, glowering, "and she's going to find them."

"The room seems sort of dark, all of a sudden," Eva said.

"Is she okay?" Paul said. "Does she need something?"

Annabel was looking over a column of characters, murmuring again. She seemed to be reading and rereading it, her words unintelligible. I leaned in closer. "What? What are you saying?" I asked. She didn't respond.

"We realize it's a long shot," Lucy explained to Paul, with a sad smile and a tilt of her head, "but we've tried everything else we could think of."

Outside a truck pulled up. The door opened and closed and another set of footsteps began up the stairway. The radio crackled again.

Annabel clapped her hands. "'I think of my little boat, and long to be on my way!'" she cried, pointing at the wall. "The poem, the mazes, the book!"

I stood alongside her, studying the characters. I recognized them now, all of them—the same ones that were hanging along the top windows of my now-abandoned classroom. I thought again of my young self, sitting beneath my mother's table with my papers and pens. Who was that boy? Who was I now? The footsteps were nearly upon us.

"That must be it," Eva said, making her voice sound paper-thin. "That's what we were looking for."

A tired-looking park ranger walked into the room, talking into the radio fixed to his shoulder. He looked at the workmen, and then at us. "Eva!" he said. "What are you up to this time? Jesus, you look terrible!"

"It's nice to see you, Pete," she said.

He ran across the room, arriving at her side just in time to catch her as she collapsed.

TWENTY

A bottle of water and half of the turkey sandwich Pete had packed for dinner helped Eva recover from the stresses of the day and her drop in blood sugar, and by the time we reached park headquarters, back at the ferry dock, she was invigorated.

"Different tactics this time around, hmm?" Pete asked her as he parked his truck, trying to sound reproachful but unable to hide his fondness for her.

"You know how it goes, Pete," she said.

He nodded. "I have to ask you to come in with me to do a little bit of paperwork," he said, as we climbed out of the car. "I'll try not to hold you up too long."

His small, cluttered desk sat in the middle of a small, cluttered office where nothing looked newer than twenty-five years old. There was just enough room for our four chairs, and even then my knees pressed into the corner of his gray metal desk. He moved a dirty beige keyboard aside, laid out some papers, and began asking Eva questions.

As she spoke, I listened to the line of poetry looping over and over through my mind: little boat, on my way; little boat, on my way. What was it about this sentence, this poem? It had permeated our whole search—had preceded it, even, in those mazes. On my way where? Home? Somewhere else? Mentally I parsed the line, rewrote it with synonyms, wondered about the translation, the etymologies, even recited it backward. I replayed what I remembered of the rest of the poem—something about a poetry contest, wine, wits growing sharp as swords. There had been a moon involved, too, maybe.

Then it was my turn. The ranger produced a fresh set of forms and looked over my driver's license. "Peregrine Long," he said. "I know that name." He tapped his pen on the desk. His mustache twitched. He snapped his fingers. "You're that guy from the news, who jumped into the flooded classroom!"

"That's me," I said.

He pointed to a dust-covered television set. "Every reporter in the Bay Area is going berserk trying to find you."

I shrugged. "I've been a little hard to track down the last few days."

"And here you are."

I nodded. "At your mercy," I said.

"That was my classroom," Annabel said, putting a hand on my arm.

He looked at her and then back at me, and then set his pen down. "You know, my supervisor has better things to do than read my sloppy handwriting," he said. He glanced at a clock on the wall. "I wouldn't want you to miss the last ferry back."

***

We stood at the railing and watched the blue-green water churn beneath us. The fan of our wake spread out behind us, flattening as it widened. The rumble of the ferry's engines carried up through our leg bones and into our skulls. The island shrunk and rotated as we curled around its northern edge, heading for the mouth of the strait and the open bay. Pieces of the mystery shifted and jostled in my head, trying to fit themselves together. Images, faces, fragments of conversation, realizations, and memories all collided, in turns receding and advancing, sliding over one another like a tangle of snakes.

I was leaning against the railing and felt the mahjong tile again pressing into my thigh. I pulled it out, held it in my closed fist, and thought about its message. West. Where was west? To a Californian—a San Franciscan, especially—the word had little meaning. It was something out of the past: saloons and deserts, plains and buffalo. It was Dodge City, fifteen hundred miles to the east. And what lay to the actual west? Only more east—the

Far East. We lived on a precipice, along a coastline that marked not only the boundary of a nation and a continent, but also the endpoint of the modern migratory experience. It was the edge of the map, that point in the loop just before the course turns in on itself and begins again. From here there was nowhere left to go but the sky, or back into the sea.

In front of us the island turned. Trees swallowed the barracks; the room and its poem were dutifully taking their places among that now-vast company of unresolved questions that threatened to haunt the rest of my days. Furthermore, our trail of clues had gone cold. We'd found Eva and Rose, and the violinist, and Lucy's phantom. We'd found the book, translated the poems. The *Gypsy* had returned; the *Barbary*'s pages were blank. There was nowhere else for us to go. We were at the end of our own map, with nothing before us but sky and sea.

Unless there was something else here, something we'd missed. There had to be—too many signposts had brought us to this island, at this moment, and if we let the ferry get too far away it would all be gone. I started pacing the length of the railing, searching the shoreline and the flanks of the island, trying to think. The ferry's engines rose, their vibrations reaching new strength. I ran to the opposite deck where Tiburon was sliding past, saw nothing, ran back.

"What is it?" Annabel asked.

"I don't know," I said. I looked back down into the water and heard its music, saw the schools of penciled letters that migrated through its currents. And then something seized me. It took over as it had that day alongside the pool at the Y and I grabbed the railing, planted one foot, another foot, and then I was arcing away from the boat. The beginning of a scream followed me down, and then the water reached up and pulled me in, blocking out the sky, the island, all else. The cold pierced clean through me. I kept my hands clapped over my face, struggling to hold on to that last bit of warmth. My momentum carried me downward, downward, and then let go of me. I surrendered my face to the cold water, bent forward, and struck lower still, fighting through my heavy clothes.

The water grew warm. I opened my eyes. Far beneath me flowed a river, lined with waving green trees whose leaves turned and flashed in the sun, revealing the passage of a lazy breeze. Flooded rice paddies stretched from either bank to the ridged horizons, a blue and empty sky reflected in their surfaces. I took a deep breath that tasted like earth and springtime. As I sank the feeling drained out of my limbs, and then out of my torso and my face until I felt I was a part of the sea. I continued downward, softly, pulled as if by a gentle current, toward the river's surface where a little brown square was drifting easily downstream.

Henry was by himself on the raft, lying on his back, gazing up at the sky as though waiting for me. A sense of familiarity flooded through me, a recognition so strong that by the time I took my seat next to him I felt I'd been there, with him, for years.

"You found me," he said, sitting up. He was about nine years old, with smiling eyes and an easy look on his face.

I nodded. "It wasn't easy."

He laughed. "You were going to find your way here, one way or another," he said.

The river was noiseless, the raft's motion soothing and effortless. I was tempted to shut my eyes and lie down, but I knew my time was short. "Did you drown, Henry?" I asked him. "Did you die in the water?"

He nodded—not in response to my question, but to himself, as if he'd known I'd ask. "Didn't you?" he said to me.

"That's what I'm told," I said.

He clapped, once. His face was bright, his eyes full of light. "So we're the same, then!"

We drifted nearer to the riverbank, where willow branches reached down to the water. Their tips left tiny wakes in the river's moving surface.

"Is that how I know about you? Is that how your story found me?" I asked him.

Henry smiled, but didn't answer. He leaned down onto one elbow, lowered a hand into the river, and traced serpentine paths across its surface, weaving among the hanging branches whose wet tips left shining strips across his bare arm. "People are made mostly of water," he said. "Did you know that?"

"Yes," I said.

"And salt," he said. "Your blood has the same amount of salt in it as seawater," he said. "Did you know that?"

"No," I said.

We emerged from the willow's canopy and drifted back out into open fields.

"Do you like it here?" he asked.

"It's beautiful," I said. "Is it China?"

"No, it's not China," he said. He pulled his hand from the water and sat back up. "It's a sort of in-between place, I think."

"What is it between?"

He shrugged. "Where you've been and where you're going, I guess," he said.

A flock of small birds, starlings, perhaps, swooped overhead, changed direction, changed again, darted away. I would have to follow them now. He seemed to guess what I was thinking, and he climbed to his feet. "Thank you for coming," he said.

A sense of loss came over me, surprising in its strength. I saw how I would miss him. He reached out for my hand, the color already draining from his face, from the raft, from the river and paddies and the trees. By the time I closed his little hand in mine he had become a million points of phosphorescent light. The points held together for an instant and then the sea rushed in, washing them out of my grasp, scattering them. Sensation flashed back through me; cold water seized me. I fought for the surface with fires burning in my lungs, my face numb, explosions bursting on the insides of my clenched eyelids.

Just when I was about to inhale seawater I broke through the surface and took a great gasp of cold air. My eyes were open but the explosions continued to flower against the sky. My pulse hammered in my ears as I gulped in breath after breath. Over its sound came the deep shake of the ferry's engines. My vision began to clear and I saw the shape of the boat, churning backward, coming back to me, perhaps a hundred yards out still. I battled my heavy clothes to stay on the surface, and just when they were about to pull me back under, a life preserver splashed down next to me.

I was hauled on board by three stoic crewmen, two of whom left to find me clothes and blankets. The third, a burly guy with a thin mustache and a black-watch cap and pale blue eyes, stayed with me—perhaps to monitor my breathing as I lay gasping on my back, perhaps to make sure I didn't try to jump off again. I looked around for my companions.

"We're in a restricted area," he said, and though he nearly had to shout to be heard over the sound of the engines, which were just beneath us, his voice was calm, even warm. "The guys will let them know you're okay, and when we get you dry and bundled up we'll take you to them." He sat down next to me and put a hand on my chest. "Just rest now," he said. For a moment I lost track of which world he belonged to.

"I can see why she's missed him," I said, and though I don't think my voice could have been heard over the engines, he nodded. I wasn't sure how this could make sense—Eva had never known Henry; decades had transpired between his disappearance and her birth—but it seemed right, somehow. He was everywhere, having managed to project so much of himself into my stories, my family, into the very architecture of our rain-beaten city.

My breathing was returning to normal now, and the color was coming back into my vision, but I had no desire to rise, not yet—the weight of my soaking clothes held me to the deck, and there was heat emanating from the crewman's hand, which still rested on my chest.

"Tell me your name, friend," he said.

"I'm Peregrine," I said.

"I've heard of you," he said. His face did not change. "You've got a thing for swimming with your clothes on."

"I think I'm done with that," I said.

"Good," he said. "Things can get tricky for us down here."

He helped me to my feet. The other men returned with a dry T-shirt and two sweatshirts from the souvenir stand, a pair of rubber rain pants and some wool blankets. As I dried off and changed I thought of the things Henry had said, and of Lucy's theories. Even the most extreme suggestion—that he had somehow been reborn in me—did not account for enough. There were too many other echoes, other resonances between his life and mine: sets of quadruplets, violin music, manuscripts, crops, the strength of our older sisters, fathers who'd left us when we were still children. Each discovery along the way had gone into the construction of a pair of galaxies which now spun in unison, exactly alongside one another, in maddening proximity, their centers pierced through by Rose's miraculous, fluctuating existence.

It was too much for me to hold in my mind all at once and when I tried, it all ran through and away like the wash of water that had flooded this whole search: reflecting in my teacup, running through the gutters, sitting in rice paddies, beating down all around us, and even now, holding us afloat. I thought of the *erhu* player and his music, sinking into the Pacific with Rose's manuscript in his bag, the sea pushing its way into that bamboo tube, pulling her little penciled letters into itself, and swallowing them. I thought of myself as a child, lying facedown in that wading pool, the water pressing into my lungs, my eyes and ears, my cells, carrying its contents into places it was not supposed to be.

The crewmen bagged my wet clothes and led me out of the aft compartments and into the main body of the ship, where Eva, Lucy, and Annabel met me with solemn greetings and consternation. They wanted to keep me in the cabin, where it was warm, but I insisted on heading back to the top deck. In my makeshift outfit, and with the blankets wrapped around me, we made for the stairs. As I climbed, my whole body tingling with the temperature change, I could feel the finality of this unfolding moment. I would have to say something to Eva, and she would hear my words, take them away, and carry them with her forever, the concluding material of this lifelong search.

We took seats on benches. None of the women spoke. Eva was sitting very still, her hands folded in her lap, not breathing. I turned to her, searching for words.

"He was there," I said. "He spoke to me."

And that was all it took. I don't know if it was a tone in my voice, or a change in my face, but something inside Eva released, and her tension fell away and vanished, almost the same way that the *Crystal Gypsy*, and Henry himself, had loosened, and dissipated. She didn't ask me what he'd said.

"He went down on that ship, didn't he?" she said, looking down. She shook her head, the movement barely perceptible, and muttered something that sounded like Mae's name.

"I don't know for certain," I said. "He was a little cryptic." I glanced at Annabel. "And then he disappeared."

Eva nodded. Her eyes lost their focus; she seemed to be staring through the ship, through the water below, to a spot somewhere far beneath all this. "Thank you," she said, her voice quiet. Annabel reached out and put a hand on her arm.

We were out in the open bay now, with Alcatraz passing on our port side, dark and imperious, and farther out to our starboard side, the Golden Gate Bridge, drained of its color in the fading sunlight, standing like a battlement between us and the vast wild strangeness of the Pacific beyond it. Eva rose and walked slowly to the railing, where she stood, looking westward.

One by one we walked over and joined her. San Francisco was fast approaching. We watched it grow, its gray hills and towers rising into the silver winter sky.

ACKNOWLEDGMENTS

Despite the lone name on the cover of this book, the work in these pages is the result of a great many ongoing collaborations.

Many thanks to Ben LeRoy and Ashley Myers at Tyrus Books—Ben, whose determined advocacy made this publication possible, and Ashley, whose sensitive readings helped guide it to its final form.

Many thanks to Robyn Russell, whose faith, support, and direction have been integral to this pursuit over the last decade.

Many thanks to Tavia Stewart-Streit and LJ Moore, who first brought Peregrine and Annabel to the public, as part of Invisible City Audio Tour's production *The Armada of Golden Dreams*. A sort of far-distant epilogue to this story is available as part of the tour, which uses music, poetry, and fiction to guide listeners through a series of gold-rush-era ships buried beneath San Francisco's financial district.

Many thanks to my parents, David and Jadyne, who taught me the power and scope of language; to my wife, Rachel McGraw, who taught me the reasons to wield it; and to my son, Hawthorn, for creating a home where imagination and creativity are in constant supply. Many thanks to my sister Jennifer and my brother John for their feedback on early drafts, their support, and their respective examples of dedication, sacrifice, and excellence.

Many thanks to the teachers, staff, and my fellow students in the creative writing MFA program at the University of San Francisco—in particular to Lewis Buzbee, whose lessons, energy, and humor continue to ring in my head every time I flip the laptop open. I can't imagine what any of this would look like without those sublime years.

Many thanks to UC Berkeley's Professor Robert Eric Barde, whose book *Immigration at the Golden Gate: Passenger Ships, Exclusion, and Angel Island* (Praeger, 2008) contains some rare and crucial research on the Pacific immigration experience during the years of the Asian Exclusion Act; and to Amy Tan and photographer Lynn Johnson, whose article "Village on the Edge of Time" in the May 2008 edition of *National Geographic* provided me with indispensable insight into the customs and life of rural southern China, in particular the *guo-yin* ceremony.

Many thanks to Jennifer Reimer, Joe Cervelin, and John Ritter—your encouragement and camaraderie and your own efforts and determination are indispensable pieces of this community.

Photo credit: David Buchholz

JASON BUCHHOLZ is an editor, writer, and artist. His poetry and short fiction have appeared in *Gobbledegook* and *Switchback*. He holds a BA in psychology from UC Berkeley and an MFA in creative writing from the University of San Francisco. He lives in El Cerrito with his wife and son.